MW00414686

# I Know She Was There

# I Know She Was There

## JENNIFER SADERA

CamCat
Books

CamCat Publishing, LLC
Fort Collins, Colorado 80524
camcatpublishing.com

Hardcover ISBN 9780744310955
Paperback ISBN 9780744310993
Large-Print Paperback ISBN 9780744311020
eBook ISBN 9780744311013
Audiobook ISBN 9780744311037

Library of Congress Control Number: 2024932812

Book and cover design by Maryann Appel
Interior artwork by CSA-Archive, George Peters

5   3   1   2   4

*To my mom, Lynne,*
*who instilled in me a lifelong love of reading;*
*to the memory of my dad, James,*
*my first writing teacher, editor, and ardent supporter.*

*And to my husband, CJ,*
*for absolutely everything else.*

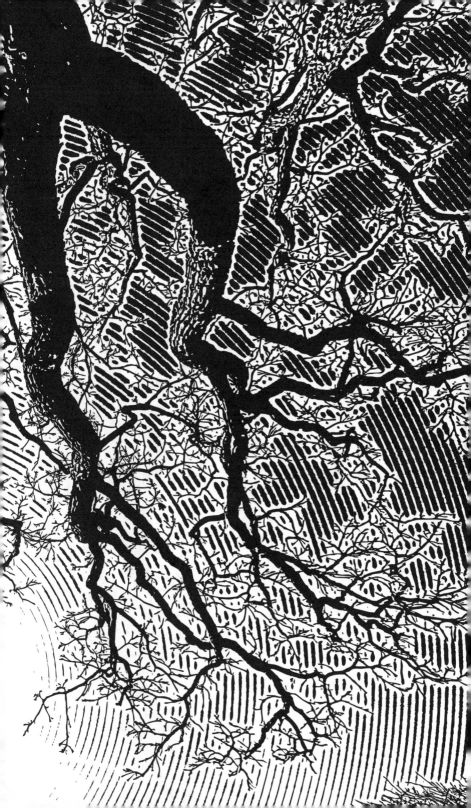

PART

1

# CHAPTER ONE

*Friday, August 11*

JANE BROCKTON WAS going to get caught.

My heart raced when Jane emerged from the side door of her home; what she and I were *both* doing was risky, but it was too late for regrets. I wondered if she thought so too. Probably. Her behavior was becoming alarmingly brazen. I pulled Emmy's stroller closer and pushed aside boxwood branches, widening the portal I peered through. Although Jane's across-the-street neighbors' hedge was directly in front of her farmhouse-style McMansion, it was too dark this late at night for me to be seen.

*Go back inside if you know what's good for you.* I pressed my fingers to my lips as the man emerged from the house next to hers. Even if I'd yelled a warning, Jane Brockton wouldn't heed it. Who the hell was I? Certainly not someone her neighbors on Woodmint Lane knew.

If Jane observed my late-night excursions through the streets of her stylish suburban New York neighborhood, her first instinct wouldn't be to worry about *her* behavior.

I was prepared. If confronted by any resident of the exclusive enclave, I'd explain I walked the streets late at night to lull my colicky baby to sleep.

I couldn't admit my ulterior motive—worming my way back onto Primrose Way and into my former best friend's good graces. And there was no need to share how, lately, the lives of this neighborhood's inhabitants had been luring me like a potent drug—or how Jane Brockton was fast becoming the kingpin of my needy addiction. Jane stood out, even in this community of excess: gourmet dinner deliveries, drive-up dog grooming, same-day laundry service, and monthly Botox parties.

Her meetings with the mystery man were far from innocent. The first tryst I'd witnessed was late the previous Friday night—exactly a week earlier. I'd strolled around the corner of Woodmint Lane just as the pair had emerged from their side-by-side houses and taken to the dark street like prowlers casing the block. I followed their skulking forms up Woodmint, being careful to stay a few dozen yards behind, until all I could discern was their silhouettes, too close to each other for friendly companionship. They'd eventually crossed Primrose Way and veered into the woods where the bike trails and picnic areas offered secluded spaces. When they didn't emerge from the wooded area, I backed Emmy's stroller up silently and reversed my route, heading away, my pulse still throbbing in my temples.

It was impossible to deny what was going on, as I watched similar scenes unfold three nights that week: Jane slipping soundlessly from her mudroom door like a specter, the flash of the screen door in the faint moonlight an apparent signal.

This night, as they hooked hands in the driveway between the houses, I slicked my tongue over my dry lips. She risked losing everything. I knew how that felt. Tim had left me before I'd even changed out his worn bachelor-pad sofa for the sectional I'd been eying at Ethan Allen. I watched them cross through the shadows, barely able to see them step inside the shed at the far end of Jane's yard.

And all under the nose of her poor devoted husband, Rod. He couldn't be as gullible as he appeared, could he?

A voice called out, shattering the stillness of the night. I flinched, convinced I'd been discovered. I scanned the immediate shadows, placing a hand over my chest to still my galloping heart.

"Jane?" It was Rod's voice. I recognized the timbre by now.

*Settle down, Caroline.*

My eyes darted to the custom home's open front door. Rod had noticed his wife's abandonment earlier than usual. Warm interior light spilled across the porch floorboards and outlined Rod's robed form in the doorframe.

"Are you out here? Jane?"

The worry in his voice made me hate Jane Brockton. I flirted with the idea of stepping away from the hedge and announcing I'd witnessed her heading to the shed with the neighbor. Of course, that would be ridiculous. I was a stranger. My name, Caroline Case, would mean nothing to him.

Rod closed the door and my gaze traveled to the glowing upstairs window on the far left of his house. The light had blinked off half an hour earlier, like a giant eyelid closing over the dormered master bedroom casement. I knew exactly where their bedroom was because I'd studied the Deer Crossing home models on the builder's website. I knew the layout of all three house styles so well, I could escort potential buyers through them. I'd briefly considered it. Becoming a real estate agent would give me access inside, where I could discover what life behind the movie-set facades was really like. Pristine marble floors, granite countertops, and crystal vases on every conceivable surface? Or gravy-laden dishes in sinks and mud-caked shoes arrayed haphazardly just inside the eye-catching front doors?

I suspected the latter was true for almost every house except for my former best friend Muzzy Owen's place on Primrose Way. Muzzy could put Martha Stewart to shame.

I wedged myself and Emmy's stroller farther into the hedge. Becoming a real estate agent wouldn't connect me as intimately to Jane and Rod Brockton (information gleaned by rifling through the contents of their mailbox) as I was at this moment. Trepidation—and yes, anticipation—

laced my bloodstream and turned my breathing shallow as I waited for Rod to come outside and start his nightly search for his wife. Some may consider my interest, my excitement, twisted, but I didn't plan to *use* my stealthily gathered information against anyone. It was enough to reassure myself that nobody's life was perfect, no matter how it appeared to an outsider.

A faint click echoed through the still night. I squinted through the hedge leaves, my eyes laser pointers on the side door Jane had emerged from only moments before. Rod appeared.

As he stepped into the dusky side yard, I thought about the people unknown to me until a week earlier: the latest neighborhood couple to pique my interest. Even though they were *technically* still strangers, I'd had an entire week to learn about the Brocktons. A few passes in my car last Saturday morning revealed a tracksuit-clad Gen Xer, her wavy hair the reddish-brown color of autumn oak leaves, and a gray-haired, bespectacled boomer in crisp dark jeans and a golf shirt standing on the sage-and-cream farmhouse's front porch. Steaming mugs in hand, their calls drifted through my open car window, cautioning their little golden designer dog when it strayed too close to the street, their voices overly indulgent, as if correcting a beloved but errant child. The very picture of domestic bliss.

I studied the Colonial to the Brocktons' right. On the front porch steps, two tremendous Boston ferns in oversized urns stretched outward like dozens of welcoming arms. The only testament to human activity. Someone obviously cared for the vigorous plants, but a midnight peek inside that house's mailbox revealed only empty space. It made me uncomfortable not knowing who Jane's mystery man was.

And did Rod usually wake when his wife slipped between the silk sheets (they had to be silk) after her extracurriculars? He obviously questioned her increasingly regular late-night abandonment. He wouldn't be roaming the dark in his nightwear if he hadn't noticed.

Perhaps Jane said she couldn't sleep. She needed to move—walk the neighborhood—to tire herself. Hearing that, he'd frown, warning her not to wander around in the middle of the night. Rod was the type—I was sure just by the way he coddled his dog—to worry about his lovely wife walking the dark streets, even the magical byways of Deer Crossing. Hence, the need for new places to rendezvous each night. But the shed on their very own property! Even though this night's tryst was later than usual, it was dangerously daring to stay on-site. Maybe Jane wanted to get caught.

A scratching sound echoed through the quiet night. I looked at the side door Rod had just emerged from, saw his silhouette turn back and open it. The little dog circled him, barking sharply. The urgent yipping cut clearly through the still air, skittering my pulse. I quickly glanced at Emmy soundly sleeping in her stroller. If the dog didn't stop barking, I'd have to get away— fast. Emmy could wake and start her colicky wailing, which would rouse the Brocktons' neighbors whose hedge I'd appropriated. One flick of their front porch light would reveal me in all my lurking glory.

As if to answer my concerns, the dog ceased barking and scampered toward the shed. I rubbed at the sudden chill sliding across my upper arms. That little canine nose was sniffing out Jane's trail.

Rod stepped tentatively forward. It was too dark to see what he was wearing beneath the robe, but I pictured him in L.L.Bean slippers with those heavy rubberized soles and cotton print pajamas, like Daddy used to wear. Daddy's had line drawings of old-fashioned cars dotted across the white cotton background. Model Ts and Studebakers. I felt angry with Jane all over again. *How dare she . . .*

"Sorry, darling," Jane called, striding from the shadows, stopping a few feet in front of him. "I was potting those plants earlier and thought I left my cell phone in the shed." Her voice was soft, relaxed. She was a pro.

"I saw it on the bookshelf in the study earlier this evening," Rod said, bending to calm the little dog, who was bouncing between them like a child with ADHD.

"Oh geez, I'm losing it," she said, laughing.

*Not yet, you're not*, I thought. *Not yet.*

# CHAPTER TWO

*Saturday, August 12*

T HE BABY'S CRY jarred me out of sleep.

I fought with the down comforter, kicking free and swinging my heels over the edge of the bed before I realized there was no longer any sound coming from the adjacent room or the baby monitor. Was that good or bad? Was Emmy lying face down on the crib mattress, a victim of SIDS? Were the cries she'd managed to wake me with the last she'd ever make? I raced across the room, falling into the bedroom door, my left wrist taking the brunt of my weight. I clumsily straightened and yanked the door open with my right hand and ran from the room like a fugitive, breath coming in halting gasps.

She lay in the crib on her back. The gently slumbering infant of diaper commercials: wispy nutmeg curls, cheeks glowing through the night-light gloom like shiny copper pennies. Her chubby limbs and tiny Buddha belly enveloped in warm flannel footed pajamas with no blanket. No toys or stuffed animals crowded the enclosure; the firm, UL GREENGUARD GOLD-

and CertiPUR-US certified mattress was hemmed by the Babyletto Premium crib's perfectly proportioned slats, too close together to trap a small child's head. I'd done my research. I took a deep breath, arms and legs shaking as the adrenaline coursing through my bloodstream dissipated. Normalcy returning in syncopated tremors. It was going to be a challenge, this day. Like all the others before it. Massaging my left wrist, I felt a sting in my smallest fingertip. Looking at the hand cradled in my other palm, I noticed the gleam of blood seeping into the ridge around my nail bed, the nail tip partially severed. Served me right. I couldn't remember the last time I'd filed and clipped my nails, much less gotten a proper manicure.

Truth was I couldn't recall exactly what I'd been doing during the months since Tim left, except worrying he'd take Emmy away. Now I had to endure another day. Close to fourteen hours until twilight would usher in soothing darkness. That's when I'd gently lift Emmy from her crib or ease her out of the ever-present infant carrier strapped to my chest. I'd transfer her to the state-of-the-art BABYZEN buggy, complete with bassinet top. Tim had scoffed when I bought it because it had cost half a week's salary, but it was well worth the money, encasing my precious girl in cozy warmth as the soundless wheels rolled smoothly over the paved streets.

I'd always found it soothing to explore the area. Tim and I used to take post-dinner summertime strolls when we first moved into the neighborhood, years earlier. Back when we enjoyed doing things together.

He'd quickly tired of those walks. Despite how I'd forced the issue when I became pregnant—recalling my mother's adamant advice against letting the baby, once born, come between us—Tim stopped accompanying me. I kept at it, wandering familiar streets and discovering new routes. Keeping myself fit even before I had Emmy, yet something new sprouted in my mind. Realizations and suspicions growing like the child in my womb: Why was I spending so much time alone? Where was Tim most evenings when I returned from my strolls to our stark, empty house?

Emmy was born in January, a dangerous time to take a newborn outside in Upstate New York, but it was an unseasonably warm winter, and by late March I was once again crisscrossing the streets of our development, this time with Emmy for company.

Our walks quickly became a nightly ritual, each foray into the dusky suburban streets calming us more than the previous stroll. Before long, I was walking for hours each evening, widening our horizons and building my stamina. I'd occasionally head out during daylight hours, even though there wasn't much outdoor activity during cold winter afternoons. I preferred the anonymity of my nighttime strolls.

That was when things started to fall apart at home—or maybe it was a continuation of the downward spiral that had begun with Emmy's refusal to nurse, my baby blues, and Tim's inability to keep us or himself happy. I thought about his after-hour stints at the firm. He'd claimed to be over-whelmed by a new project, but he'd never had to work through the dinner hour in the early years of our marriage.

The night I found a matchbook from a local bar in Tim's jacket pocket, I shoved Emmy in the stroller and beelined it through the front door, anger sparking my movements, spurring me through the dark streets and farther from home. That was the evening I discovered Deer Crossing, just a mile from my house. It changed everything, sparking an odyssey into a realm previously unknown to me. I'd dutifully returned from the exclusive enclave that night and all the others that followed, but I never really made it back to the place Tim and I had been before.

It was to be expected, of course. How could I settle for the dreary hap-penings around my house when others were living such charmed lives? These people were like my own neighbors, but younger, fitter. Happier. Especially the couple I'd been stalking lately: Barbie and Ken look-alikes I'd named Matt and Melanie at 21 Pine Hill Road. Just like the couples I'd noticed through their unguarded windows that very first night who'd laughed together and cuddled on sofas in front of large-screen televisions and flickering fireplaces, the positioning of Matt and Melanie's trim, athletic bodies struck me upon first glimpse, weeks earlier: the way their entwined forms rocked in rhythm to the strains of a song I couldn't hear, their beauty highlighted by the warm wash of incandescent light overhead. Framed by the living-room window, their faces were a blur, but I was transfixed by how her long dark hair spilled against his cheek and mingled with his blond waves. A pang sliced at my throat, making swallowing painful. The pair was maybe a few years older than Tim and me; I couldn't recall the last time Tim and I danced together. Perhaps our wedding reception? Why didn't we focus on each other the way the dreamy couple in front of my greedy eyes did? I squeezed my lids shut, trying to recall my husband's touch on my skin, but I couldn't arouse the sensation.

I felt nothing.

～～～～～～

I SPIED ON them all.

Every neighbor too careless or too foolish to keep their shades drawn. Hundreds of houses on display, their interiors glowing with life and bleeding it out into the night. A hemorrhage of strangers gathered around dinner tables, texting on phones while gearing up Netflix, doing yoga. The activities were as varied as the people performing them. And that's what it seemed like: a show, with the homes' inhabitants cast as theatrical versions of themselves.

I needed this—the feeling of being a part of something without the responsibility of involvement. Oddly, I felt a connection to these blurry-faced strangers—a connection I hadn't been able to maintain with Tim since before Emmy was born.

He blamed me for the divide. I knew he did. His seemingly innocent remarks rankled. Like his comment after my mom's fatal accident when I'd been three months pregnant: *Maybe you'd feel less devastated if you and your mother had gotten along better.*

I stared blankly at him. "My mom was my best friend," I'd said, amazed that her death seemed to be tearing us apart rather than bonding us in grief—especially since he hadn't been overly fond of her.

And then there was his advice after the postpartum depression that had set in a week after I'd given birth: *If you force yourself to get out of bed and tend to Emmy, the mother-daughter bonding will help you overcome your depression.*

I snorted just thinking of his self-righteous remarks. What the hell did *he* know, anyway? After Dr. Ellison explained that stress, hormonal changes, and sleep deprivation had combined to create a textbook case of the baby blues, Tim grudgingly attended to Emmy amid my crying jags and unending desire for sleep.

He was always willing to do pharmacy runs. I suspected he just wanted to get out of the house, away from Emmy's endless crying and my incessant requests for help. Hours after departing for the drugstore he'd reappear with excuses of long lines, drug shortages, pharmacist consultations. Anything to make the extended absences seem believable.

I couldn't pronounce the name of the script Dr. Ellison had prescribed for postpartum depression, but I'd eagerly anticipate the Xanax the doctor told me to take only in emergencies. The medication calmed me far better than my husband did. Tim, watching me pop the pills like a halitosis sufferer scarfing down breath mints, scoffed at what he called my *weakness.*

"You can't be hoovering those pills while you're taking care of Emmy," he'd complain.

"That's why you're here," I'd point out. "Until I can get myself back on track."

He'd roll his eyes and sigh. Often, he'd storm out of the house, slamming the door behind him, not returning until my frantic texts begged him to soothe our wailing child.

The postpartum meds hadn't worked, and I wasn't able to sleep without Xanax. Claiming to worry about the potential for drug dependence, Tim began monitoring and restricting my intake, leading to endless nights without more than an hour or two of rest, giving my waking hours a surreal, nightmarish quality. Every sound became oddly amplified, as though my ears had reverberating speakers tucked inside; morning light scorched my retinas, sending shards of throbbing brightness straight into my brain, settling into a baseline headache that no amount of ibuprofen could touch. That was the *weakness* Tim so readily diagnosed. I suppressed my resentment, convincing myself he was only looking out for my health.

Exercise helped. In the soothing dark and silence of my nightly strolls, I could function normally. My stiff legs relaxed into an easy, elongated ramble, and my lungs unclenched, turning my shallow breaths into deep, full inhalations. The later my strolls stretched into the night, the more I felt like myself.

That's when I realized how much I needed the residents of Deer Crossing. Muzzy Owen and her tribe were the first to catch my eye, and her reciprocal attention bolstered my confidence. I didn't live in the development, but I had every right to stroll the storied streets. Lately, I'd even taken to waving at Matt as I passed him. He'd wave back if he wasn't preoccupied by a strenuous yard task, like raking out the flower beds or mowing the lawn.

This August evening the temperature hovered around seventy degrees in low humidity. Emmy cooed like a chickadee content in its nest as I increased my speed up an incline, my arms laboring under the increased weight of the carriage. Gritting my teeth against the pain slicing through my left wrist—a reminder of my morning's sleep-deprived plunge into my bedroom door—I focused on the exertion. It felt cleansing, just like Dr. Ellison said it would. Now that Tim no longer lived with me, I could walk the streets at any time of the day or night. I didn't have to get back from my evening strolls before he came home. Didn't have to figure out where he'd been while I was walking off my resentment.

Even so, Emmy needed a mother *and* a father, no matter our difficulties. I texted Tim every day about important child-related topics. Asking his opinion about starting Emmy on rice gruel, sharing a milestone she'd reached or a worry over a minor health issue. Even though he seldom answered me, I was determined to keep him involved in our child's life, and eventually get him back home. I knew only too well how impossible it was to endure a childhood without a dad.

I scooted across the three-lane thoroughfare separating Highland Knolls, my neighborhood of modest ranches and bilevels, to Deer Crossing. Consisting of a few hundred dwellings, the upscale development had two parallel main roads leading off Route 55 and into the neighborhood: Pine Hill Road on the west side, and Woodmint Lane on the east. Connecting them at the northernmost end of each road was Primrose Way, which stretched from the bike trails at Woodmint to the pond on Lakeside, just beyond Primrose and north of Pine Hill. Each of these roads had multiple connecting paths and cul-de-sacs with winding streets and expertly landscaped lots. As I started up Woodmint, I wondered if the neighbors had banded together to create a cohesive planting plan. Even in the muted glow of the HPS streetlights, the perennials peeking around stately birches shut out the memory of the ragged, yellowing hostas lining my house's walkway. This night I meandered, noting how the light layered over the smooth expanse of lawn extending from house to house like an unending carpet. I could discern no weeds in the seamless stretches of grass.

This should have been my life, my neighborhood. As a mechanical engineer, Tim made a decent buck, and my home-based medical-billing job helped cover the extras. My virtual position meant no childcare expenses, which was fortunate. With my parents gone and Tim's entire family across the country in Seattle, my salary would have been swallowed by day-care costs had I been forced to commute to an office each day.

I'd wanted the big, impressive house, and we could have swung it. Our other expenses were minimal. We preferred our television to movie theaters, takeout to dining out, comfortable clothes to designer labels. And we'd been saving for the future. I'd talked about a big family, like the four-sibling clan Tim had been raised in, not the sad little twosome that had comprised most of my childhood. But my husband decided for us both that prudence was called for. We'd start in a house we could afford rather than live in a "monstrosity" we'd struggle to make payments on.

I'd reluctantly agreed to our simple two-bedroom ranch on Tim's assurance that as our salaries and family grew, we'd expand to a bigger place.

Seemed like a good plan, until my mother died, and my world began to unravel. Now the modest house felt like a condemnation. I needed a home like the one we'd envisioned ourselves eventually living in, a validation of sorts. No chance I'd ever have it unless I could get Tim back.

At the end of Woodmint, I'd eventually turn left onto Primrose Way and pass Muzzy's house at the other end of that street, near Pine Hill. With any luck she'd be outside, maybe sitting on her front porch. It was early enough—much earlier than most of my treks into the neighborhood. I walked faster, my gaze lasered once again on the Brocktons' sage farmhouse as I neared it. One low light was on in the living room. I glanced at the completely dark Colonial next door, which I recalled was the tawny tone of a caramel chewy in daylight.

"Good evening," came a female voice from somewhere in the shadows. Jane Brockton.

I jumped, heart slamming into breastbone. A dark figure stood like a sentinel at the end of the driveway, next to the mailbox. "Oh, uh, hello."

"I didn't mean to frighten you," she said, stepping forward. Her tone suggested otherwise.

"No, that's okay, I'm just . . ." I trailed off, my pounding heart making breathing and speaking at the same time impossible.

"You spend an awful lot of time on this street, don't you?"

*She's noticed my snooping.* My mind clicked into survival mode, sending desperate messages to my mouth.

"Well, you know how it is with colicky babies." I looked down at the carriage and back at her advancing form. "Whatever it takes to get them to sleep."

"No, I don't know. I don't have children." Jane's tone sounded oddly challenging. "What's the baby's name?"

"Emmy," I said, my quivering voice hinting at my reluctance to tell her anything about myself.

She stopped a few feet in front of me and raised her hand, which held an iPhone. She turned on the built-in flashlight, creating a harsh halo of light around her stunning figure. I'd clearly not been able to properly appreciate her attractiveness from a distance. "May I take a peek?"

*Seriously? She wants to shine a high-intensity beam into my infant's face? Good thing she doesn't have children.* I raised the bassinet hood, an urgency to get away from her overwhelming me. "I just got her to sleep; she's hypersensitive to light."

"Oh." She sounded disappointed. Perhaps she wanted a child and Rod was unwilling or unable to provide any for her. He was, after all, a good bit older than she was. She stepped back, giving me the impression of a balloon deflating slightly. "You'll have to stroll by in the daytime when the baby's awake." She accented the word *daytime.*

"I'll do that," I promised, pressing on the carriage handle.

"I'm Jane, by the way."

"Alice," I lied. "Nice to meet you," I called over my shoulder as I started to walk away.

"You look like that woman who used to go to Muzzy Owen's house." Her voice had a hard edge that sent a shiver down my spine. "But her name wasn't Alice."

I froze. "You know Muzzy?" I tried to suppress the surprise in my voice.

"I know everyone in this neighborhood. But I don't know you."

"Well, I don't actually live here."

"I know that. I can follow people too. Your name is Caroline, so why would you tell me it's Alice?"

My throat went dry. I turned toward her, my legs shaking. "Look, I don't want any trouble."

"Then don't lie to me."

"I don't even know you." I held my hand up. "I never tell strangers my name."

"You're the stranger here, and I'd prefer you keep it that way. Stick to your own neighborhood. Keep your stroller, your car, and yourself off these streets. You don't belong here."

Her petty threat burst my fear like a soap bubble.

Who the hell was *she* to tell me where I could stroll my child? I lowered my chin until my gaze was level with hers. "I can walk wherever I please. If you have a problem with that, too bad."

"You need to mind your own business. Keep your nose out of—"

"Out of what?" I sighed, impatience warring with the good manners my mother instilled in me. "Your *business* looks like a lot more fun than mine."

Jane's mouth dropped and I could see her face redden in the ambient light from her cell phone, now glowing beside her thigh where she'd dropped her hand. Before she could sputter out a reply, I turned on my heel and headed down the street, vigorously pushing the stroller ahead of me.

*Was that a good idea?* asked a voice. The voice that sounded like my mother's.

"Probably not," I muttered. But it felt fantastic to tell her off.

I couldn't properly catch my breath until I was in front of Muzzy's dark house. So, Jane had followed me home one evening? So much for my stealth. Gazing at the shadowy box that was Muzzy's house, I wondered if my former BFF had filled Jane in on my story. Sadness encircled me like a heavy woolen cape, weighing me down and notching my body temperature up a good ten degrees. I didn't care. Even if my one-time friend had gossiped all over the neighborhood about me, I deserved it. And it would be a small price to pay to get Muzzy Owen back in my life.

My gaze lingering on the dark house, I walked on. Ignoring the trickle of the fountain in the loathsome pond to my right, I turned left onto Pine Hill Road and approached Matt and Melanie's house on the corner. A porch light flicked on, illuminating the *21* over the front door, which was open to reveal the profiles of two people. Melanie, her long tresses recently chopped to her shoulders, thrust her arms around the shoulders of a tall, dark-haired man and pressed herself intimately against him.

"I don't care," she declared. "Let him find out about us. Let them *all* find out!"

I paused, staring. The man in Melanie's arms was not the fair-haired Matt.

"Don't say that, it's dangerous," warned the man, not returning her embrace. He shot a furtive glance toward the street, his eyes catching mine. Alarm crossed his features, followed by anger. With one hand he reached out and caught the edge of the door in his grasp, slamming it firmly shut.

I startled, but I wasn't sure whether it was surprise or my own anger that made me flinch.

*How dare she do that to Matt! She has everything! Good God, she's no better than slimy Jane Brockton!*

# CHAPTER THREE

*Sunday, August 13*

I STAGGERED INTO THE kitchen, squinting against the sunrise lighting up the window over the sink. My clumsy paws spilled coffee grounds all over the counter. I tidied, tried again, my mind cycling through the thoughts that had prevented rest this night and all the others: thoughts of my husband. Quite possibly my soon-to-be ex-husband.

I closed my eyes tightly, trying to squeeze out the image of our first meeting, years before, but Tim appeared in torturous detail on the backs of my eyelids.

I met him in the produce section of the Stop & Shop. I was sizing up the Roma tomatoes, squeezing one, when he angled his shopping cart next to me, nearly knocking over a cardboard fixture of avocados.

"You swing like a hammock," he said, leaning casually against the cart, offering me no choice but to meet his gaze or appear rude.

"Excuse me?"

"Your walk, it swings back and forth like a hammock."

I felt my face flush with embarrassment and a bit of pleasure. I frowned and looked at his cart, inches from the avocado display. "And you steer that thing like a drunk."

He laughed and angled the end of the cart toward me. "I used to have a hammock slung between two maple trees in my yard. Loved that thing. I'd swing for hours under those leaves. I liked the way the sun flickered through them, hitting me in flashes. Nature's strobe light."

"That's an oddly specific thing to share with a total stranger," I said, but I noticed he had nice brown eyes. His flannel shirt looked pressed.

He grinned; his gaze locked with mine. "The swaying is so enticing."

I blushed again, my face certainly as red as the tomato I held. "That's weird," I said, unable to think of anything to add. I'd never been good at flirting.

"Would you give this weirdo your phone number?" His voice was as intimate as a cat's purr.

"Probably not."

But he walked out of the store with my number digitally tucked into his iPhone. I'd watched him add my name, Caroline Messier, to his contact list, wedging it between "Erika Merchant" and "Myer's Meat Market."

A few years later, just after we'd married, I looked for the hammock in the items he was moving from his storage unit into our new garage. When I asked him where the hammock was, he didn't even pause as he explained he'd tossed the thing years earlier.

"I thought you loved it."

He shrugged. "I did until I brought it on a camping trip and spent an entire night in it. Felt like a butterfly caught in a net. My joints haven't been the same since."

I'd watched him shove boxes across the garage's concrete floor, realizing for the first time how casually Tim could discard something he'd claimed to love.

I looked toward the blazing kitchen window as if staring at the searing brightness could blast the memory from my mind. The sad truth was, I'd

become inconvenient. Maybe Emmy was too. We made his life more difficult. Uncomfortable. Maybe he felt like that trapped butterfly. Trapped in
our small house with no escape from the baby's cries. Or from me.

The doorbell cut through my musing.

"Good morning, dolly." Mary Whitton, my ancient next-door neighbor, stood on the front stoop, her ample frame swaddled in an oatmeal-col-
ored sweater over navy polyester pants despite the morning warmth. "Have
you got a cup of refreshment for a weary traveler?"

Swallowing a sigh, I recited my well-worn lines: "Those three dozen
steps between our houses can challenge even a marathon runner."

Mary seemed to draw energy from the stale exchange. As usual. Stepping over the threshold, running a hand through her already tousled gray
flyaways, she beamed. "I can smell the coffee brewing." She stretched her
hand out with a flourish. "After you, fearless leader."

I led her through the living room and nodded toward the tiny table
near my galley kitchen, though I needn't have bothered. Mary knew the
drill. She sat down heavily as I hooked my hand around the coffeepot handle and grabbed a mug from the cabinet above the steaming machine.

When I placed Tim's "#1 Tennis Player" mug in front of her, she pulled
out a mini of Bailey's from her sweater pocket, twisted it open, and dumped
the contents into the mug. "I like a strong cup of coffee. Good for what
ails you."

"What ails you today? Arthritis acting up?"

"Always." She heaved a dramatic sigh, her breath emanating in briny
waves thanks to her two-pack-a-day habit and daily gargling with salt water. She claimed it was good for her throat, though I suspected it was an
attempt to neutralize the ever-present alcohol vapors. I could hardly judge.
I'd been known to nip during daylight hours myself. Still, the stench of her
breath, reminiscent of bilge water in the hull of a dilapidated boat, churned
my stomach.

"You want some ibuprofen?"

"No, dolly. I'll . . ."

"Manage without it?" I had to do that a lot, finish her sentences, that is. She seemed to forget what she was saying *as* she was saying it.

She nodded, staring down at her steaming mug.

I filled my own cup and leaned against the counter, watching her lift her mug to her puckered lips with one hand while digging into her sweater pocket with the other, deftly fishing out a pack of Newports. She'd barely gotten the mug back onto the tabletop when she pulled out the matches stuffed between the pack and its outer cellophane wrapper.

"Mary, I've asked you not to smoke in the house. It's bad for the baby."

"I don't see no baby around here."

"Well of course not. She's sleeping."

Mary shook her head. "That poor child."

I frowned. "Goodness, Mary. It's not as if Emmy's an orphan. I'm here, and Tim is still her father, even if we aren't living together right now. You make it sound as though he's dead."

"Just like my Bill. Dead."

I sighed and opened the kitchen door. Mary was in a melancholy mood this morning. Probably still hungover. "Let's go out on the deck."

"Good idea, dolly. It's so . . ."

"Nice outside?"

She followed me to the two faux wicker chairs I'd set up in the corner. Mary settled, crossed her legs, and gulped her drink, letting her unlit cigarette rest between her yellowed index and middle fingers. "Not that Bill couldn't be a perfect bastard when he wanted to. But the baby, she didn't . . ."

"Deserve this?" I looked at Mary's quivering lower lip. "No, she didn't."

As Mary placed her mug on the rickety glass-and-steel table between us and lit up, I thought none of us got what we deserved in this life. I didn't deserve to have my father die when I was only six. I didn't deserve to have my mother taken from me just when I needed her most. I thought of all the motherly advice she'd never give me.

Mary's voice broke into my thoughts, "Caroline, things are going to be okay."

I noticed the reddish wood stain was beginning to peel at the edges of the deck boards. "Do you really think so?"

"With time." She took a long drag and held it in her lungs.

"I don't know. Tim talks like he has no intention of coming back to me. Ever."

Mary exhaled. "You need to give it . . . time . . ."

"It's been months. How long do I hold out?" I looked at her, saw the Baileys kick in as she focused her glassy stare on the weed-filled grass of my backyard. It was futile to believe she'd be capable of giving me sound advice now. "Do you have any more of that stuff?"

She looked at me for a second as if she'd forgotten I was sitting in front of her. But then she smiled and patted her pocket with her free hand. She pulled out another nip, her expression bordering on surprise, as though someone else had tucked it into her sweater pocket. But of course no one had. She lived alone. When Tim and I moved in, she'd explained her husband, Bill, had left her and then died, years before. Did Mary deserve that?

No wonder the poor woman drank. She'd been unable to hold on to her man and then was robbed of the chance for a do-over when death snatched him permanently away. Would that happen to me too? I pictured Tim twenty pounds lighter, disease carving haggard hollows beneath his eyes and a ragged cough turning his voice ominously husky. *I've only got weeks left*, he'd say, and I'd reach out to him, my hand poised to caress his cheek. Offering him the comfort he'd so heartlessly denied me.

I rubbed my lips with my pointer finger, thinking that may just be the ending *he* deserved. But as Mary held the nip toward me, regret lodged in my throat. Of course Tim didn't deserve a painful death. He was the father of my child, no matter how much I resented him these days. Jane Brockton's bitchiness must be getting to me. I seemed to be thinking just like her.

# CHAPTER FOUR

*Monday, August 14*

NEARING TWILIGHT AT eight in the evening, the temperature was still stifling but had cooled enough to head outside.

I'd have to steer clear of Woodmint Lane that evening. Another encounter with Jane Brockton could be downright dangerous. If it came to blows, I wasn't sure I could beat her back. Even though she was about ten years older than I was, she was in fantastic shape. I, on the other hand, was sporting a saggy pouch of post-baby pudge around my middle.

As I made my way out of Highland Knolls, my body laboring in the oppressive humidity, I peered into the lives of my immediate neighbors. There was Mary, blinds open, watching a retro game show as she slugged back something in a clear rounded bottle that usually held the hard stuff: gin or vodka.

Beyond Mary, Dolf Green's ranch was dark, as usual, except for his lighted office on the far left, the top of his bald head motionless in the eerie bluish glow of a computer screen. Across from him, the Washingtons' dining-room light was on, but the room was empty. I walked on. I pushed the BABYZEN up the hill through the moist, tepid air, listening to Emmy's happy babble.

"Exercise is vital," I told her as we passed bilevels and ranches, exertion turning my tone breathy. She didn't understand, but her melodious prattle told me she recognized my voice.

I thought of my own mother's voice, which came to me often but never imparted the child-rearing advice I needed. The one weary message she usually sent—*It wasn't your fault*—was tedious. But I did appreciate her tone, which was kinder than when she'd been alive.

During my childhood, the stress of single parenting often tried Mom's patience. It wasn't until I became a mother that I understood why she'd often tuck me into bed before the sun went down. Parenting was exhausting. I remembered her unending diligence: unplugging the television after discovering I hadn't finished my homework; arguing at the dinner table over my feeble consumption of lima beans, broccoli, or brussels sprouts. I smiled, recalling how she'd had to get creative to get me to eat the vegetables when I was quite young.

"A half for you and a half for me," she'd chirp, shoveling the hated morsels first into my mouth, and then into hers.

My smile faded. Nearly a year since the head-on car collision that had taken her life. It didn't seem possible that so much time had passed. She'd been both mother and father since I was six, and she'd never remarried. We might have been happier if she had.

*Must think of other things, pleasant things.*

I exhaled, unable to dredge up anything positive. Except for Emmy. One shining example of a successful life. Wrangling her colic had been a major achievement. Things could only get better, especially if Tim and I could work out our differences. Become a proper family again. Muzzy was key to making that happen.

If Tim knew my former friend and I had settled our differences, he might realize there was hope for our marriage too. I wasn't as unpredictable

as Tim had so often suggested. I paused, dabbing at the perspiration drib-
bling from scalp to forehead before pushing on.

As I neared Route 55, a meaty hound raced through the shadowy light
cast from the lone streetlamp on the block. He pressed his nose against the
chain-link fence and howled. I slowed, calculating the beast's ability to leap
the five feet it would take to clear the thing, even as a large dog of uncertain
origin to my left growled and barked in response. Ironic that only tiny pure-
breds seemed to dot Deer Crossing's expansive acreage, but massive mutts
were penned into my immediate neighbors' minuscule yards.

"Settle down," I snapped at the dogs as I resumed my trek through
the wet air, trying to ignore the clinging stickiness of 90 percent humidity
on my skin. Taking a labored breath, lungs heavy as a soggy loaf of bread,
legs sluggish, I moved even slower. Pushing the baby carriage felt more like
shoving a pile of bricks through a tight doorway.

I paused at the edge of Route 55 to look both ways. The day had been
sweltering, ringing Emmy and me in sweat no matter how many times
I changed our garments. After we'd bought our ranch, Tim had been too
cheap to install central air conditioning, overriding my complaints, explaining it was only unbearably hot in Upstate New York for two months a year.
But now the stifling humidity of August was here. And he wasn't. And the
apartment he'd moved into had the central air I craved.

I veered left and rolled onto Pine Hill Road, the entrance opposite
Woodmint Lane. If I stayed within the web of intersecting streets on the
west side of the development, I could steer clear of Jane's house as I made
my way to Muzzy Owen on Primrose Way. If only Muzzy was relaxing on
her front porch. I'd wave as I passed by. Perhaps she'd return the gesture.
Maybe she'd even invite us up for a visit. After all, it was past her children's
bedtime. They'd all be tucked into their beds for the night. And Muzzy
loved cuddling Emmy.

Pine Hill Road was flat and winding. Perfect for a leisurely stroll. If I
was lucky, I'd catch a glimpse of Matt on the corner of Pine Hill and Lakeside, just before turning onto Primrose. A picture of him came to mind:

fair-haired and tall, his toned body enhanced by a faded red polo shirt and khaki shorts, like the last time I saw him doing lawn chores. I was always struck by how much he resembled the actor Matthew McConaughey.

I thought again about how utterly enchanted I'd been watching him dance with . . .

Melanie.

The name that had come to me the first time I'd glimpsed her, watching her float through the air, her arms lifting like gossamer wings. A tune—a waltz—filtered through my mind, accompanying them as they'd shifted seamlessly left, then right. He twirled her around and around, setting her dark hair into motion; her slim body, in tank top and leggings, revolved like a ballet dancer on pointe.

A return to their place the following night after the eleven o'clock news revealed a completely dark house and a mailbox devoid of personal information. I'd shuffled through half a dozen flyers addressed to Occupant, discovering nothing new about them. I wondered if they paid all their bills online like most of us millennials do nowadays.

I hadn't seen the couple again for a week, when a mechanical whir up ahead made me step quicker through the twilight of a hot August evening. Soon, I was directly in front of Matt's house, the homeowner himself in the front yard in the day's dying light.

Approaching the hedge he stood beside, I again thought he was probably in his mid- to late thirties. His sandy hair nearly reached the tattered collar of his T-shirt, and a well-defined bicep extended over the privet hedge, his hand clutching the electric clipper like a cavalry sword. He slashed horizontally in sharp, quick motions, like a fencer trying to finesse the offending shrub into submission.

His striking light eyes, even in the waning light, caused me to stare. I smiled as I passed, but he was focused on his task. It made me feel dismissed. He was too busy to be friendly.

A window had opened in the top left dormer of the custom Cape Cod behind him. A flash of dark hair through the glass, and a rich, sensual female voice cut through the evening air. "When you're finished there, wipe down the windows in the shed."

He grunted, but with acknowledgment or displeasure, I couldn't tell. I recalled how little success I'd had with Tim whenever I nagged or demanded. He'd often grunted at me.

On this particular night, I stared at the custom Cape, recalling Melanie in the foyer with her arms slung around another man a few weeks earlier. Anger shot upward from my suddenly tight chest until it clouded my vision, fleetingly blotting out the front porch. I blinked, reminding myself that Melanie's choices were not my business. But poor Matt! Just like Rod Brockton, he was being played.

I took a few deep breaths, counseling myself to calm down. I looked ahead at the small, too-perfect-to-be-natural pond with a large, garishly lit center fountain spewing water heavenward. I shivered; I hated ponds. Especially that one.

I let my gaze wander to the right—the Owen family home at 12 Primrose Way, the first house after the pond. Tim had forbidden me to have anything to do with them after what he'd called *the incident*. Yet Tim wasn't around anymore. I could go where I pleased. I could go to Muzzy's, climb her porch steps, and knock on her door. But I wouldn't.

I swallowed. Would I ever have the courage to confront Muzzy and restore our friendship? It was a shame, it really was. Muzzy and I were just becoming close when everything happened. When I began my field trips to Deer Crossing last March—and that's how I'd thought of them: fun outings rife with educational moments—I'd study the families on each block. The Owen family was the first to capture my attention. A research project of sorts.

Each time I'd pass by their house, the dazzle of children perpetually running and squealing within their picketed perimeter enthralled me. Tiny mittened hands erected feeble snow creatures out of the late-winter slush stubbornly clinging to the warming earth; delighted squeals emanated from what appeared to be animated winter wear, jumping on the trampoline, white puffs projecting off its bouncing surface inside the netted space. A real-life snow globe. And Muzzy, bless her, always in the middle of her four-kid tribe, no matter the temperature outdoors. Her gloved hands distributing cookies or trail-mix packets.

When the thermometer climbed to the midsixties in early April, she helped the children set up a lemonade stand at the end of their driveway. I purchased their watery concoction, pressing a Dixie cup of lemon-yellow fluid against my lips and chatting with Muzzy, discovering her real name was Helene. Yet her kids' nickname suited both her generous proportions and capable demeanor: soft but as substantial as a weighted blanket.

Soon I was strolling past her house every afternoon. It was only a matter of weeks until she invited me into the yard. Accepting her bite-sized cheesecake tarts and scooting after toddling eighteen-month-old Brandon, trying to look as though I enjoyed pressing his squirming body and sour, sweat-soaked scalp close. Pretending for Muzzy, who adored cuddling Emmy. She'd reach for my wailing infant as soon as I clicked her front gate behind me.

"I do so love a baby," she'd exclaim every time we came over, regardless of Emmy's screeching. "I want another one."

"Brandon's still a baby," I said during the first visit, my eyes growing wide as Emmy settled and quieted in Muzzy's expert embrace.

"Are you kidding?" She laughed. "Brandon's big and bad already. Mimicking the monsters." She angled her head to indicate three-year-old Amber, five-year-old Alexander, and Christopher, nearly seven, intent upon chasing his siblings around the swing set. Her voice held such fondness I wondered whether Muzzy's desire for another child was altruistic or addled. Subsequent visits ensured she was neither. She simply loved children. Especially babies. Yet, she'd relayed with a frown, her husband, Johnny, had decided for them both that four children was enough.

I shared my cell phone number with Muzzy, but she never called me. When I'd stop by, she'd always lament the fact she hadn't a spare moment to phone, but she invariably invited me into her yard.

"I keep the little buggers outside as much as possible," she confided one afternoon as she shepherded Alex and Christopher off the school bus and through her front gate, holding it wide for me to stroll Emmy through. "In the yard, I can keep my eye on them. Inside, they hide in closets and under furniture." She laughed uproariously as though she'd made a hilarious joke. "I swear, they do it just to drive me crazy. They gang up."

I marveled at Muzzy's demeanor. No matter what she claimed, she never seemed outnumbered or overwhelmed. One afternoon, as we sat on the picnic bench bouncing the babies on our knees, I asked Muzzy if I could use her bathroom. I didn't have to go, but I could no longer contain my curiosity about her house.

What was it like inside? I'd often pictured toys scattered around the floors, half-empty juice boxes gracing the dining table, and children's clothes strewn across the living-room sofa.

What greeted me when I stepped inside made my jaw drop. Muzzy's rooms had the continuity, decor, and forced neatness of the featured houses in *Better Homes and Gardens* spreads. Coats hung from largest to smallest on pegs in the mudroom. Beneath them, shoes were lined up—also by size—in copper trays.

I took a few steps forward, hovering near the guest bathroom, my gaze taking in the kitchen in front of me and a great room beyond. The granite countertops looked like polished coal. I reached forward and pulled open the nearest drawer. Flatware gleamed within the confines of a built-in compartment. Every utensil was perfectly aligned. I closed the drawer, my fingers itching to open another drawer. To open all of them. Taking a resolute breath, I stepped back, dropping my hands to my sides.

The smell of bleach crept into my nose as I gazed at glistening white cabinetry and stainless-steel appliances, searching for fingerprints. There were none, not even on the lower cabinets, the fridge, or around the dishwasher handle. How was that possible with all those kids? Maybe that was why Muzzy kept them perpetually outside. I looked at the perfectly plumped pillows on the oversized sofa in the great room, my eyes searching for stray stuffed animals or a dropped toy. To no avail. The space was show-room perfect.

Seeing my dazed expression when I rejoined her at the picnic table, Muzzy didn't wait for me to speak.

"I know what you're thinking," she said, a red hue suffusing her face. "I like to keep things tidy. I really have no choice. With Johnny gone so much, it's just me holding down the fort, and I can't let the little beasts get ahead of me." She grinned. "I *do* have Edith, who comes in for deep cleaning twice a week."

"Of course." I nodded, recalling Muzzy telling me her husband was an airline pilot. She'd have plenty of money to hire cleaning help. But even so . . .

"I can't help it." She looked away from me, as though she couldn't quite meet my eyes. "I don't want Johnny to come home to chaos . . . and I like things orderly."

"Don't apologize," I said quickly, thinking of my house's messy, disorganized rooms. "I just don't know how you manage it."

"They're all in bed by seven thirty. Gives me three hours to clean. I flip on *The Bachelor* or some other inane show and go to town with Clorox." She looked at me then. "And when I'm done, I'll go just as hard with an entire pint of Ben and Jerry's. Doesn't matter what flavor, I love them all. If only I could train myself to drop that last little routine, I'd be twenty pounds lighter." She sighed. "Guess we all have our vices."

"I suppose so."

She tilted her head, her eyes scanning the length of me.

"What's yours?"

"What?" I felt my own face redden.

"What's your guilty pleasure?"

I pressed my lips together. *Spying on people like you.* Couldn't say that.

"Don't tell me you don't have one?"

"I do, but it's . . ." I let my voice trail off as my mind searched for appropriate possibilities.

"Look, you don't have to share if you're not comfortable." Muzzy shifted Brandon from one knee to the other. "I got Emmy to sleep while you were inside. She looks darling in her carriage—"

"No, I want to share. It's embarrassing, is all. So few people do it these days."

Muzzy stilled the toddler on her lap.

"I'm terribly addicted to cigarettes. Foolish, I know. The health hazards . . ." I paused when Muzzy's features scrunched into a confused expression. "What's wrong?"

"Both my parents smoked. You could smell them approaching five minutes before they arrived, but you don't carry even the slightest hint of cigarette odor." Her expression shifted slightly, looking guarded. Her narrowed eyes told me more than her words.

"That's the most embarrassing part," I jumped in, my mind working overtime to compensate for my blunder. "It got so bad, I switched to vaping." I hung my head, a blush spread from my chest to neck, a tell that I was lying, but Muzzy didn't know that. Looking at her through the fringe of my lashes, I glimpsed her rounded eyes and slightly parted lips. "Honestly, how can I cling to such a bad habit? I mean, I only vape outdoors, away from Emmy, but still." Muzzy's eyes softened.

My heartfelt revelation had worked. Our friendship notched up and clicked into place.

Fortunately, Muzzy had no desire to visit me at my house, which I'd described vaguely as being on the outskirts of Deer Crossing. She was happy to spend free time with me in her yard, and eventually, we set up a specific time for playdates: 3:00 p.m. on Mondays and Wednesdays. It was a perfect arrangement.

Until the past reared up and ruined everything.

The unfairness of it filled me with sudden, overwhelming fury. It radiated painfully through my chest, like heartburn or a muscle tear. My head shook back and forth in tiny little movements, my limbic system trying to cast off memories. I wouldn't—couldn't—think of that day. What was done was done. Suddenly fatigued, I felt like an old woman. The effort I had to expend to get air into my lungs was enormous.

The rumble of a car engine in the distance pierced the evening, getting closer, but I couldn't stop looking at the custom Cape in front of me, a multitude of images swirling in my brain: Matt's handsome face hovering over the metal hedge clippers; Melanie's shadow in the upstairs window, her sultry voice calling out; Melanie embracing a dark-haired man in the doorway of her home.

The thud of a car door closing pulled me away from my preoccupation with the couple at 21 Pine Hill Road. I glanced over my shoulder to see a dark sedan parked halfway between the pond and Muzzy's house, but it was too dim to see anything else. Beyond the car, Muzzy's living-room light popped on.

I wheeled Emmy's carriage around until I was facing away from Matt and Melanie's and began walking toward the Owen house. Unease niggled at the back of my mind. I blinked at the shadows swooping around me, darkened silhouettes popping into my peripheral vision but vaporizing when I snapped my head in their direction for a better look. Sweat broke out along my hairline and on my upper lip as I approached the car. A black Impala, just like Tim's. I studied the dented driver's-side corner of the back bumper, which I'd dinged in the supermarket lot a few months back. Of course, it was still there. Tim was too cheap to fix it.

Why would my husband be here? Recalling how he and Muzzy had connected after the incident, I stared at the car as if my intense gaze could pry an answer from it; I reached into my pocket and pulled out the mini flashlight I always carried when I walked Emmy after dark. I flicked it on, directed the powerful beam inside. As usual, Tim's neatness prevailed. Not so much as a speck of dust marred its Simonized vinyl surfaces. The only other person I'd ever known to take such precise care of belongings was . . . *Muzzy.*

I looked at her house, cozy and inviting with the glowing light diffused in the veiled windows. Was Tim inside right now? Surely, he wouldn't have been attracted to Muzzy in the aftermath of the incident, discovered kinship in mutual obsessive cleaning habits and their shared disdain for me. It was ridiculous.

*But why is he here?* I recalled how often her husband, Johnny, was away, and my heart twisted in my chest, making breathing difficult. It was well after 7:30 p.m., the time Muzzy put her kids to bed. She had hours alone to fill. Something told me if the two of them were holed up in her house, they weren't cleaning. I glanced up the street, hoping to see Tim's familiar form loping through the shadows—from the other direction. The area was quiet, empty. I looked back at Muzzy's.

Her yard had an air of disuse I couldn't put my finger on, but I sensed my former friend wasn't spending much time outdoors anymore. Was she hiding from me? I angled my head, ears alert for sound, and squinted at the pond, searching for any movement in the shadows. The patter of the distant fountain mocked me.

I stumbled backward, pulling the carriage with me. What was going on in this neighborhood? Jane cheating on her older husband was bad enough, but the others . . . perfect Melanie stepping out on Matt, and Tim . . . with Muzzy? No, it just wasn't possible.

I had to get out of Deer Crossing. I turned Emmy's carriage around and rushed across Primrose, but my hammering heart and the thick, sludgy air made proper breathing impossible. Halting again in front of Matt and Melanie's place, I gulped like a doomed fish caught on a line. The lack of oxygen made me dizzy, so I sat down on the curb beside the carriage, concentrating on breathing instead of the image of the neighborhood lovers hugging, kissing, dancing. I pressed my palms tightly against my temples to block out my building rage, focusing on the vital task of getting air into my lungs. How long I sat there, I didn't know.

When I eventually tilted my chin up to elongate my neck and unblock my passageways, I was once again standing, facing the house. Surprised, I scanned the façade of 21 Pine Hill, wondering when I'd risen, and how long I'd been standing there.

That's when I saw her.

The ghostly lines of a woman materializing in the upstairs bedroom window, pressing her forehead up against the pane with such force I feared it would crack. My body jumped, as though given a jolt from a live wire. Her absurdly open eyes were dark and searching as if scanning the street for something she desperately needed to find. When they locked onto me, her mouth popped open into what could have been a call, or even a scream, but I couldn't hear anything through the closed window. The only sound filling my ears was the pounding of my own heart, battering my ribs and attempting to beat its way out of my chest.

It was then that I noticed her hands, wrapped like a scarf around her own neck, a neon-orange thumbnail—its strangely festive hue at odds with her expression—visible just below her chin, as she beseeched me with an unflinching stare. *What does she need from me?* The hands slid away from her neck as a gush of dark liquid covered the light column of skin.

I gasped. *Blood.* I stood frozen, watching her neck turn a different hue, thinking absurdly of a child's crayon coloring the white space between black lines. But this was no children's activity. I looked at the empty driveway, my heart sliding into my stomach. It didn't appear that anyone else was there.

My legs moved as if of their own accord. And then I was running toward the house, pulling the BABYZEN behind me and hoping I didn't trip and lose control of the carriage, toppling Emmy. But I couldn't slow down. Melanie needed my help. I looked frantically around the yard, seeing a blur of grass and trees that became nothing but obstacles blocking a clear path to the front door.

Leaving Emmy on the brick path in front of the porch, I stumbled up the steps and pounded on the door.

"Jesus, Caroline, now's not the time for manners," I muttered, turning the knob, which gave way surprisingly easily, shooting me off balance. I nearly fell into a heap on the foyer floor. Instinctively, I regained my balance and looked around the gray murk, my gaze connecting with a wooden staircase a few yards in front of me. An overwhelming smell of metal and mugginess assaulted my nose. Sticky fingers clawed at my chest and throat as I ran toward the stairs.

*You've killed him,* screamed a voice. My mother's. I halted abruptly, and looked up the staircase, even though I knew I wouldn't see her there.

*How could you?* Another voice: my husband's. That was a new one.

I snapped my head from right to left, seeing nothing but shadows in the empty foyer. "Tim? Are you here?"

*How could you?* he repeated, his voice urgent. Accusing.

"This woman, she needs me," I screamed into the dusky air. "I saw her fall into the window, I saw the blood. I must get to her . . . I must . . ." I pushed my legs toward the staircase, as much to escape the voices as to help her, but a painful explosion in the back of my head stopped me where I stood. My mother's voice again, behind me. *You shouldn't be here.*

My knees gave way, and I was falling, tumbling into the vast, endless reaches of darkness.

# CHAPTER FIVE

*Tuesday, August 15*

I T WAS THE cold that woke me. Glacial numbness overwhelmed every cell of my body. I could see nothing. *I must be dead.*

But no, I was moving, my arms and legs flailing in terrifying slow motion, my eyes and lungs stinging. I gulped for air and my mouth filled with arctic liquid, freezing my gums and teeth as air heaved involuntarily out of me. *Water.* I was submerged in it. Panic reared up inside of me, my brain swinging between the wildly unthinking reactions of survival and one petrifying thought.

*Where is Emmy?*

I thrust my head instinctively upward, pain slicing through my skull as my mouth breached the water's surface and I swallowed a huge lungful of air. My insides seized as my toes found footing, followed immediately by a coughing fit that made me lose purchase, dipping my chin once more into the inky liquid. Treading water as I tried frantically to right myself, I held my breath and felt my feet once more scrape solid earth. I pushed off with all my might, feeling my soggy sneakers resisting even as I shot upward. Impossible underwater images from years earlier collided with my current predicament, legs kicking and hands grasping, disorienting me. I called out to my father for help, my voice terror-stricken.

But Daddy was dead.

*Get a grip, Caroline. You're no longer a child. You have a child of your own.* My mother's admonishing tone.

Emmy. Where was she? I hauled myself out of the water, squinting through darkness as thick as fur as I crawled onto the loamy grass. My drenched clothes clung to me like weights, making movement clumsy and sluggish, yet my heart was racing like I'd just completed a fifty-yard dash.

A mechanical hum assaulted the quiet as halogen lights cut through the night, spotlighting me. My hands shot up to shield my eyes as the car engine abruptly cut off. A door clicked open, and a figure emerged. Fear battled relief as I decided it must be Tim on his way to me. I had a vague memory of his car being parked nearby. I peered through my fingers to see a man's tall, fit frame silhouetted against the car's lights as he ran toward me, but the halogens timed out before he reached me, casting us both into utter darkness.

"Are you okay?" he asked, his voice breathy from exertion after closing the distance between us in seconds. Before I could answer, he was pulling me to my feet. "Jesus, you're soaked. Did you fall in?"

I blinked at the voice that was not Tim's, unable to speak.

"I saw the carriage beside the road, which made me slow down. It was so odd to see a baby carriage all by itself—"

"Where is it?" I looked from his shadowy face to the surrounding darkness.

"Over there." He reached out, pointing to a spot in the direction he had just come from.

I ran, my stiff, heavy clothes turning my gait into a novelty, an action I'd not fully mastered, but I didn't care. I pushed my leaden legs forward faster. When the BABYZEN materialized out of the shadows, the taste of vomit filled my mouth. Ignoring the dizzying spin that threatened to topple me,

I rushed toward the carriage, grasping the handle and peering under the bassinet hood. The baby was shadowy. I blinked water out of my eyes and waited a few seconds for my pupils to adjust to the lack of light. I could just make out Emmy's face and tiny body; her eyes were closed in sleep, but her limbs moved restlessly. She looked perfectly healthy.

I started to smile, but the effort hurt my head so badly that it felt split open. Worrying my skull was crushed, I straightened and gingerly touched the source of pain at the back of my head, a few inches above the nape, fingers probing a tangle of hair and a substantial bump.

"What happened?" came the man's voice from beside my right ear. I jumped at his nearness. In my panic, I'd momentarily forgotten about him.

"I . . . I don't—" I began. Trying to focus my thoughts, I continued, but the sounds making it out of my mouth made no sense. I babbled like Emmy. Nonsensical words, as the man before me morphed into my dad. I stared through the shadows, unable to process my father's sudden appearance. He was dressed in the same white T-shirt and blue jeans he'd worn the last time we were together. *Where have you been all this time?* I reached out to him, overjoyed to be reunited. I'd missed him so much, for so long . . . but the hands meeting mine were Tim's. Clawing fingers digging into the tender flesh of my palms. I screamed, pushing him away.

"What's your name?" he asked, his voice urgent. "How did this happen?"

I stared at the man, wondering if he was real. Maybe I was dreaming. Caught with shapeshifters in a nightmare. My gut gurgled painfully, and I swallowed hard, the image of a neck running with blood invading my brain . . . oh God. My armpits broke out in sweat despite the icy dampness clinging to me. The pain, the instant blackness. And now I was here, with a stranger. Wide eyes, a dark staircase, and bright orange fingernails spun like a kaleidoscope of colors in my mind, hitting me with patterns my brain was unable to sort through. I started to shake.

"We need to dry you off," the man said. "I have a blanket in my trunk." He turned and ran to the dark box of his car, barely discernible against the night sky.

The sound of gushing water spewed in time to my throbbing head. I whipped my chin to my right and glanced over my shoulder, instantly regretting it. Not only did pain arrow through my brain, but the hated pond between Muzzy's house and the street bordering Matt and Melanie's lot came into view, its center fountain surging. The pond I just climbed out of. Breathing erratically as nausea reared up inside me, my stomach heaved. I dropped onto all fours, vomiting violently onto the black earth beneath me.

Warm softness engulfed me, and the man's voice was beside me once again, murmuring reassurances and helping me gently to my feet.

"This blanket will warm you. Do you want me to bring you to the hospital?"

"No," I barked. I had nobody to tend to Emmy. "I'm fine." I said the second part much softer.

"I'll bring you home. We can put the carriage in the trunk of my Jeep. Does it fold up?"

"Yes," I said, my mind clearing with the need to get Emmy back to her nursery. "Let me just wrap up the baby so I don't get her wet. The latch is below." I pointed to a spot at the apex of the metal legs, above the wheels and just under the carriage bed, while plucking the baby's blanket out of the storage bin under the handle.

As the man kneeled and peered at the latch, I scooped up Emmy and swaddled her.

"My name's Jeffrey," he said, looking up and around the carriage like he was hiding underneath it. I heard a click and watched him stand.

"I'm Caroline. Caroline Case." I stepped back as the carriage collapsed between our feet. "I can't thank you enough for your help." I wrapped the blanket over Emmy's face to keep my wet hair from dripping into her eyes and waking her.

"Climb into the front seat and I'll get this thing in my trunk," said Jeffrey.

As we drove along the extended stretch of darkened streets between Deer Crossing and my house, Jeffrey glanced at me clutching Emmy. "How did you end up outside in the middle of the night with your baby?"

"She's colicky. Walking settles her." I looked down at my arms. "This swaddling should keep her from screaming her head off."

"My little sister had colic as a baby," said Jeffrey. "My parents used to drive her around town in our car. The steady motion soothed her."

I nodded. "It does, especially since she doesn't sleep well. I don't either."

"I see," he said, his voice turning hesitant. "But aren't you kinda far from home?"

I studied his profile in the glow emanating from the Jeep's dashboard. He sounded just like Tim. Another clueless man adept at judging. I looked forward and squeezed my eyes shut against the blinding pain shooting from nape to forehead.

"As I said, I have a hard time sleeping," I said tightly. "The more we walk, the easier it eventually becomes to fall asleep." I opened my eyes and studied the road. "Take a right up ahead."

"But you don't know how you ended up in the pond?" He rotated the steering wheel toward me, taking the corner smoothly.

Something unbidden fluttered in my chest. *Focus, Caroline.* Picturing myself in the pond turned my mouth dry. "I was in the neighborhood, walking, and I saw something . . ." I croaked from a suddenly tight throat.

"Was it in the pond?"

"No, I'm not sure . . ." I tried to picture it, but the image was just out of reach. "My driveway's there, on the left."

"Okay." Jeffrey pulled in and turned the engine off. "So, what was it that you saw?"

I stared at the dashboard, a flash of something sparking in my brain: my flashlight beam revealing the tidy interior of a car.

Tim's car.

*Tim's car parked by the pond, next to Muzzy's house.*

"Oh God," I mumbled. "Her lights turned on and I ran." I looked at Jeffrey.

"Who? Whose lights?"

"I stopped at the corner of Pine Hill, and I saw . . ." *What did I see?* "I couldn't remember with all the water around me—so much water—but now I . . . I need to concentrate."

Jeffrey's brows furrowed over his narrowed eyes in the ambient light from his radio display. "You ran from lights, and you saw something?"

Memories flashed in my mind: a bright fingernail, wide eyes, blood. *Melanie.*

"The woman in the house, the upstairs window. She was bleeding." I patted my pockets. Where was my cell phone? I must have left it at home. "We have to call the police."

"What?" Jeffrey's voice boomed in the confined space.

"Do you have a cell phone?" When he produced it from his pocket, I added, "Call 911."

His hand shook. "What am I telling them?"

"There's a woman, she's hurt."

"By the pond? Where exactly—"

"I don't have time to explain. Just do it."

He nodded and pressed the phone's surface, connecting immediately to a woman's voice warbling through the speaker.

"911, what's your emergency?"

Jeffrey told her his name and identified himself as a resident of Wood-mint Lane in Deer Crossing. He explained he worked at the local newspaper and had just gotten off shift when he noticed me and my baby outside in the dark.

When he stopped to check on me, he discovered I'd witnessed something disturbing. A bleeding woman. I listened to him patiently answer the dispatcher's questions, my panic mounting.

"She needs to send out the police quickly," I said. "The address is . . ." I closed my eyes, trying to recall the number of the house, but desperation turned my mind into an endless array of floating Post-it notes full of useless messages. "It's on the corner of Pine Hill and Lakeside. Maybe number twenty-one? The house with a slim, dark-haired woman."

Jeffrey relayed my information. He sounded scared. As he clicked off and looked at me, his features etched with worry. "They're on their way."

"What time is it?"

"Just after two."

I gaped at him. I'd been unconscious for hours. "They're too late."

"What do you mean, too late?" Panic crossed his features.

"We need to go over there, now."

"I'll go and meet the police," he said, his voice shaking. "I'll send them here afterward."

"Okay," I said, realizing I had to tend to Emmy. I released my seat belt and held the baby close as I opened the door and stepped out, every inch of me aching. "Thanks again for your help."

I was already walking toward my house as Jeffrey removed the carriage from his trunk. I was dying to get inside and find my painkiller from months earlier—the Percocet I should have tossed after my C-section. "Just leave the carriage by the front door, please," I said. "You can keep it folded up." I decided I'd take Xanax too.

After Jeffrey had pulled away and I'd gotten Emmy settled in her crib, I went directly to the bathroom medicine cabinet. Unlike the postpartum depression pill I took every day, I only took Xanax when needed. If the day's events didn't justify a hefty dose, I didn't know what did. The leftover Percocet would be a last resort. Clutching all the prescription bottles with one hand, I turned on the tap with the other. In one swift move, I removed a water glass, also residing in the cabinet, and angled it under the water stream.

I settled on the couch, letting the medication flow through my bloodstream, dulling the aches and softening my thoughts to a dreamlike state even as I sat, fully awake.

I didn't know how long I sat in my self-induced trance, thankful to focus my thoughts on anything but the woman in the window on Pine Hill Road. Sharp rapping on my front door startled me, making me sit forward and look around. Outside, the new day was dawning, turning the dusky sky pink and orange. Strobe lights streaked down my street, too uniform and jarring to be sunlight. I struggled to my feet and, leaning over the sofa, peered out. A police car with flashing lights was parked at the end of the driveway. As promised, Jeffrey had given the cops my address. Good. I could share with them everything I saw. But my chest tightened, my pulse jumping. What if the woman had died? I paused, biting the inside of my cheek.

The banging resumed, more insistent than before. I walked on shaky legs, reached out, and opened the door just enough to peer into the gloom.

"Hello, ma'am," said one of the two tall, blue-uniformed police officers standing on the stoop. The thin one on the left. I nodded and the other one, stocky, introduced them. Their names made no impact. I couldn't hear more than a murmur above the sound of blood rushing through my ears. I opened the door wider, and the two officers stepped inside.

We stood awkwardly in the tiny vestibule. I looked at the skinny officer, then the chubby one.

"What's your name, ma'am?" asked Skinny.

"Caroline Case."

"Do you live alone?"

"Well, I have the baby, but my husband isn't here." I looked down, feeling shame wash through me, causing my face to flush. Then I remembered I had nothing to be ashamed of. I raised my head, looked the officer in the eye. "He left me."

He nodded, my declaration not appearing to have an impact on him. "Ms. Case, did you go into a house on Pine Hill Road this evening?"

"Yes, I had to, you see—"

"And did you ask a . . ." Skinny took out a notepad and leafed through it. "Jeffrey Trembly to call in a murder at the house?"

"I wasn't sure if it was a . . ." I couldn't say the word *murder*. "It could have been a suicide attempt."

"Why don't you tell us about it," said Chubby, placing his hands on his hips.

I relayed the story, leaving out the part about hearing voices. No reason for them to know that.

"Is that everything, Ms. Case?" asked Skinny after I'd finished. His voice bounced loudly around the room.

I nodded. "Did you find Mel—the woman I saw in the upstairs window?" I stifled the urge to drag my top teeth across my lower lip.

The officers exchanged a look that fell somewhere between wary and disbelieving, then both looked back at me.

"The house was empty, ma'am," said Chubby.

"Then she must have been taken to the hospital." I sighed. "Thank God."

"No one was in the house because nobody lives there," said one of them. I didn't know which one. I was too focused on the words floating in the air between us. "We searched through our database and discovered the couple who resided at 21 Pine Hill Road recently sold the property."

I thought about the interior of the place. I didn't recall seeing furniture. But then why was someone in an empty house . . .? I shook my head. "I don't understand."

"Neither do we," said Skinny, moving nearer to my left elbow. "The place was dark and tightly locked. We had to use special tools to get inside. There was nothing in any of the rooms—no furniture or personal effects. In fact, the place looked as clean and empty as a newly constructed house."

Chubby puffed up his chest, stared me down. "We have some questions for you."

I nodded. "Yes, of course."

"Have you ever filed a false police report, Ms. Case?"

"Filed a . . . what?" I studied the officer's features, but they blurred before my eyes. "Surely you saw the blood. It was trailing down her neck. Some must have dripped—"

"We saw no blood, and it's a crime to file a false report," he said, his face looming in front of mine but blurrier than before.

I shook my head. "I didn't. I wouldn't."

"Mr. Trembly reported a crime at your behest, Ms. Case. A crime that did not occur."

"I didn't say it was a crime, just that I saw her. She was in the room in the upper—"

"We walked through the entire house, Ms. Case. No evidence of a fatal accident, a murder, or anyone residing there."

"It can't be. I'm telling you; I know she was there."

"There is no evidence of that," said Chubby. He stepped closer, as if his nearness would help him make his point. "If you ever file a false report with our office again, we will arrest you. Do you understand what I'm saying to you, Ms. Case?"

I shrank back, horrified, too afraid to speak.

Skinny looked around my shadowy living room, his gaze resting on the prescription bottles on my coffee table.

"Whose medication is that, ma'am?"

"Mine." My voice was barely above a whisper. "My name is on the bottles."

He walked closer to the coffee table. "May I look?" When I nodded, he lifted one bottle, read, then examined the label on the second before putting both where he found them, next to the third bottle he didn't bother to pick up. "These are potent drugs, Ms. Case. Have you taken any of these pills this evening?"

"Only after I was hit on the head." I turned and pointed at the back of my skull. "Someone clubbed me in that house. Knocked me out. I woke up in the p-pond with this big knot on my head and—"

"Ms. Case," he interrupted. "We have no way of verifying this information."

"B-but it happened," I sputtered.

"I suggest you come to the police department later, after the effects of the drugs wear off. You can tell us about your injury and anything else you recall about your night."

I nodded, too shocked to say anything else. *They don't believe me.* I watched them turn and walk out my front door. I had no intention of going to police headquarters. It was my word against theirs—cops in the department convinced I was some sort of lunatic who wandered the streets at night and concocted stories about what I saw inside the houses I passed.

*Only a crazy person would* . . . I caught my breath. I *did* walk the streets at night, nearly every night. And I peered into people's houses. I was everything I appeared to be, wasn't I? Had I imagined the woman in the window? The postpartum pills were strong, and I took them every morning. Were they messing with my brain? Making me imagine things that weren't there?

I thought of the woman I called Melanie. Her eyes, large and dark, searching mine frantically. She was real, I knew she was. And whether they found her or not, now I suspected something else about her: she was certainly dead.

# CHAPTER SIX

*Wednesday, August 16*

I HAD TO CONVINCE someone of my story. I saw her. Melanie. More important, I could *feel* her. But detectives didn't launch investigations based on feelings. Only proof. And the way to get it was to go back to that house.

I'd wasted hours obsessing over what I'd seen. I had to *do* something. I stared at the phone balanced in my palm. Who could I tell besides the police? Would anyone believe me? The more incredulous thought seemed to be why anyone *wouldn't* believe me. After all, I had nothing to gain by making up such a story.

Tim would disagree. How many times had he told me my efforts to reconnect us were just pathetic attempts to gain attention? Every time I'd reached out to him, he'd responded with suspicion. In fairness, I could understand his skepticism. Since we'd separated, I used many tactics to get him to reconcile our relationship. He'd be wary of this latest attempt, or what he would surely see as my ploy to once again be the center of his universe. Just last month he'd given me a tongue-lashing when I'd called him, frantic because Emmy felt warm. He'd just seen her, he reminded me. She had no fever. I was to stop calling him with nonsense.

No, telling Tim about what I'd witnessed was out of the question.

I could tell Mary. She'd believe my story. Once she was into her cups—which was almost always—she'd lap up my words like a squirrel I'd once seen slurping up every drop of water from a birdbath. Where would that get me?

A thought struck me: what about Jeffrey? What was his last name? I closed my eyes, trying to recall what the officer had told me. Turner? Talbot? Trem . . . Trembly. That was it. Jeffrey Trembly.

I didn't have his phone number, but I recalled him telling the 911 dispatcher he lived on Woodmint Lane. He was on the late shift, had to be if he arrived home from work at two in the morning. I looked at my watch. Just after six in the morning. He'd certainly be asleep now. Realizing I'd have to wait until he awoke, I paced around the coffee table, mind and body jangling with nervous energy. I eventually tried to lie down, but the heavy pain in the back of my head made it throb; racing thoughts prevented my mind from stilling, despite my self-medication. As I fed Emmy breakfast and sponged her down, I kept glancing at my watch. At half past eleven I figured Jeffrey would be up and starting his day. I scooped my handbag and car keys off the kitchen table and bundled Emmy into her car seat. I'd find Jeffrey Trembly and somehow convince him of the validity of my story. As a reporter—and a resident of Deer Crossing—he'd certainly want to know more about an accident in the neighborhood.

As I drove toward Woodmint Lane, I thought about the frantic woman with the wide, dark eyes and the gaping wound at the base of her neck. Whenever I'd read accounts of people cutting themselves in suicide attempts, it was usually the wrists they sliced, wasn't it? *Then why was her neck split open?*

I crossed over Route 55 and entered Deer Crossing, taking the entrance on the right, Woodmint Lane. I drove slowly, refusing to even glance at the Brocktons' house, lest Jane see me and think I was spying on her. At the second-to-last house on the right, the name Trembly was spelled out in black capital letters across the gray metal mailbox at the curb, just to the left of a gray Colonial's driveway. I parked next to it.

The house was much more basic than its neighbors. No shutters, which gave the façade a barren appearance. Like looking into the face of someone who'd shaved off their eyebrows.

Only a few scrubby shrubs graced either side of a plain concrete stoop with wrought-iron railings. I supposed a guy living on a newspaper reporter's salary couldn't afford the amenities other residents had. If Tim and I had lived here, our house would probably have looked very much like Jeffrey's. I stepped out of my car and, checking that I'd cracked the windows for Emmy, locked the doors before walking up the asphalt driveway.

After I knocked on the wood-paneled front door, I listened for the sounds of life: rustling inside or maybe a dog barking. I heard nothing. I walked back to my car, glancing around the yard. The front lawn was yellowing. I squinted, looking for the tiny sprinkler heads that graced all the other properties, but there didn't appear to be any. I noticed a coiled hose up against the house, behind one of the scraggly shrubs. I wondered if Jeffrey was embarrassed by his property or if he was too busy chasing news stories to care.

Glancing in my back seat as I got in the car, I noticed Emmy staring into the space around her. She didn't look content, exactly, but she wasn't wailing. A good sign. I slid behind the wheel and started the car. It wouldn't do any harm to veer onto Pine Hill Road, passing Melanie and Matt's house on my way out of the neighborhood.

The sun filtered through tattered clouds, coating everything in a lemony glow. I looked at Muzzy's place as I drove by, once again feeling oddly dismayed at not seeing her in the yard she'd once spent so much time in. Counseling myself to not dwell on my former friend's preferences, I passed the pond, breathing deeply to steady my upticking heart, and turned onto Pine Hill, pausing in front of the cherry-red corner house. No furniture or garden decor graced the front porch. It certainly looked as though the residents had moved on. A flash of color to the left caught my attention. A navy Jeep was parked on the brick pavers, just beyond the hedge. The same Jeep I rode in last night? My brows rose. A man was just getting out of the car.

I pulled into the driveway behind him, causing him to startle and look at me. I had the weird sense I'd seen him before last night.

"Hey," I called, stepping from my Honda. "Jeffrey Trembly, right?"

"Yeah." He eyed me warily. "Caroline?" He didn't look or sound happy to see me.

I nodded. "Yeah. Thanks for helping me."

He shrugged. "Well, I don't know how much I helped anyone. The police told me no one lives here."

I grimaced. "They told me the same."

"Then why are you here?" His gaze, meeting mine, was intense.

Straightening my shoulders, I walked toward him, not stopping until I reached the back bumper of his car. "I know what I saw."

He swallowed as he took in my resolute expression. "The cops said you were wrong. Seeing something that wasn't there."

"Really?" My face reddened. "If you believe that, why are *you* here?"

His eyes shifted to the ground. "I don't know. You seemed so certain." He glanced up at the house. "Thought I should look around for myself. Guess it's the reporter in me."

I followed his gaze, taking in the deceptively cheery house. "Looking at this place now, I almost don't believe what I saw."

"Do you think maybe you *could* have imagined—"

"I didn't imagine the bump on my head." My hand went instinctively to the lump at the back of my skull. "Someone knocked me out."

He sighed, rubbing the back of his own head in an unconscious display of sympathy pain. "We shouldn't even be here."

"True." I studied him. Tried to gauge his next move. He stood awkwardly, as if unsure about what to do. "We're here now, though. Might as well look around."

As if taking my comment as permission, he nodded. Closed his car door and walked around the front of the Jeep.

"Hold on," I said, turning and sprinting to my car. I opened the driver's-side door and glanced into the back seat to ensure Emmy was okay. Her head had tilted forward, the lower half of her face beneath an enveloping blanket. I could see only the top of her fuzzy head and her tiny row of eyelashes resting above pillowy cheeks. I reached over the seat and plucked at the light blanket, exposing her tiny form in a simple pink onesie. Her undefined arms and legs, like little rolls of fresh, unbaked dough, looked too still, too serene, to be real. But even the slightest discomfort would shoot those tiny limbs into motion and disrupt her peaceful visage. I cracked open the windows a little more to ensure her comfort and snagged the keys out of the ignition, then quietly closed the door, locking it with the remote. Emmy would be okay for just a few minutes. It was cool. I recalled my car thermostat displaying a temperature of sixty-seven degrees.

Looking up, I saw Jeffrey step onto the front porch and knock on the door. I crossed the yard and halted on the brick path in front of the house, noticing the wooden door Jeffrey continued to knock against was beautifully carved in an intricate floral pattern. It struck me then, the impossibility of an atrocity occurring behind such an exquisite door. I wondered if Jeffrey's suggestion might be true. Perhaps I'd only *thought* I'd seen Melanie in deadly distress. Maybe I'd fallen backward and bumped my own head.

"Nobody home." Jeffrey turned toward me with an expression that confirmed what the police had said.

I looked up at the window where I'd seen the woman, remembered her eyes, huge with horror. Beseeching. Pleading. She was real. She had to be.

"Let's go around back."

Jeffrey followed close behind. As we walked, an impression swirled in the back of my brain like a persistent fly. As we rounded the house, I tried to isolate the sensation. Pinpoint what was bothering me. But, like trying to catch that pesky insect, my mind couldn't close around the thought. Couldn't grasp the feeling.

Jeffrey's voice was in my left ear. "Why don't you check the shed out back?"

"Why?" I stopped and looked at him.

He shrugged. "Just being thorough."

"Okay." But I didn't know what he expected me to find. Disturbed dirt in the shed floor revealing a shallow grave? I'd seen a movie when I was around ten where that had been the case.

Zombie hands clawed up through the disrupted soil on my thirteen-inch television screen. Scared the shit out of me and earned me a scolding from my mom about watching inappropriate shows when I should have been sleeping.

I crossed the backyard, looking over my shoulder. Jeffrey was trying the back slider, which didn't appear to budge. I stepped into the shed, glancing at the row of gardening tools hanging on one wall. It was surprising that the previous residents hadn't taken any of the implements with them to their new place, but maybe they'd moved into a condo. *Or the murdering husband is booking a flight to Mexico.* I looked at the pegged implements—rakes, brooms, lopping shears, a shovel—all glinting in the early afternoon light like shiny new offerings in a hardware store. I noticed the shed floor was a spotless concrete slab.

When I stepped out of the small structure, Jeffrey was nowhere to be seen. I crossed the weedless grass and stepped onto the back deck. "Jeffrey?"

No answer.

I walked to the slider and pulled the handle. The door slid open with a swish. I stared at it as if it were enchanted. Jeffrey was in the empty dining room beyond the doors.

I stepped over the threshold. "How did you get this door open? I saw you tugging on it."

"Oh, that." He ran a hand through his dark hair. "Credit card." He grinned, looking charmingly handsome. "Oldest trick in the book."

I tilted my head, considering. "I thought that was one of those things you only saw in movies."

He didn't answer, just kept looking around the empty space as if trying to imagine what it might have looked like with furniture.

The thought came to me instantly—the niggling in the far recesses of my brain: *Check the vestibule.* That's where I'd been the night before—where I'd lunged inside and had my head bashed in. I stepped into the foyer and looked around the empty space.

The white Carrara marble entryway floor revealed no footprints or debris from outside—no errant blade of grass or a stray leaf marring its surface. Odd. With no doormat to wipe one's feet, how did the area remain pristine? Surely I'd brought something in on my shoes the night before? A chill ran up my spine. Someone had cleaned up.

I turned back toward the living room, looking around. Once more, Jeffrey wasn't there. I retraced my steps, entering the dining area and heading left through the expansive kitchen, all white cabinetry, granite surfaces, and stainless steel appliances—even a state-of-the-art blender like the one featured in *Top Chef*, my favorite television cooking show. A kitchen I could only dream of cooking in. Today I rushed through it, for once uninterested in the layout of the place. Next came a bathroom, stripped of its shower curtain, soap dish, and towels, and two bedrooms. Both empty as scoured bowls. I circled back to the staircase in the center of the house. Taking two steps at a time, I made it to the upstairs landing, looking to my right where Jeffrey was exiting a room.

"There you are." I huffed, unsure whether the quick shot of physical exertion or the fear of nearing the place where I'd seen the doomed woman seized my lungs, making me gulp for air.

"Another empty room," was all he said, passing me and heading to my left, down the hallway.

My heart rate accelerated as I followed him into the far room, the master bedroom with attached bath. Like the rest of the house, the empty space looked like it had just been cleaned. No dust, windows sparkling in the midday sunshine. I instinctively felt my eyes roaming over the cream-colored walls for any specks of—what? Dirt? Blood?

Jeffrey stepped into the master bath and disappeared. Only his footsteps belied his presence. I glanced at the expanse of louvered closet doors against the far wall. They looked so much like the ones in my house when I was growing up. I recalled games of hide-and-seek with my dad, peeking through the angled slats to watch his feet roaming around, "searching" for me. My eyes took in the wide plank floorboards, pine or light oak. The floor looked clean enough to serve a meal on.

"Nothing here," said Jeffrey, stepping back into the bedroom.

"Guess not."

"Looks like all the other rooms upstairs and down. Empty."

I sighed. "I just don't get it."

"Are you sure you saw . . ." He let his voice trail off.

I placed the backs of my hands over my eyes and rubbed them, feeling exhausted. "I'm not sure of anything right now." I dropped my hands and looked at him. "Could you give me a minute?"

He nodded. "Okay."

As Jeffrey walked out of the room, I crossed over and half sat on the oversized window ledge, the spot where I'd seen Melanie. I stared at the nearby birch leaves shimmering in the breezy early afternoon light just beyond the glass. The tree looked like it was covered in suncatchers. This may have been the last view Melanie had of this life. The birch tree, the street, the hedge. Me, looking up at her.

But how could violence have occurred in this room? In this house? It was literally dust-free, not to mention blood-free. I tried to recall the night I'd seen Melanie and Matt dancing, weeks earlier. Had there been furniture in the living room? Wall art? I couldn't remember. All I could recall was being captivated by Melanie's graceful movements.

Was I losing my mind? I thought about my activities of the past few days and realized I should go back to therapy. Things in my world were clearly spinning out of control. I was having a hard time holding my marriage together and dealing with the impending anniversary of my mom's death. Was it stress that prompted me to recall incidents that may not have even happened? Was I making things up? The back of my head throbbed. A subtle reminder of my most recent injury.

I shifted, facing the empty room, and let myself slide down the wall until I was sitting on the cool, wide-planked floor. I placed my palms on either side of me for support and recoiled as a sharp pain pierced the skin of my right thumb joint.

Lifting my right hand and holding it in front of my face, I saw a tiny hole in my palm filled with a minuscule amount of blood. No more significant than a paper cut. I looked back at the floor, noticing something wedged between the floorboards. I plucked it out and studied the oddly shaped object. It was less than a quarter inch long. It looked like a tiny, concave piece of plastic, rounded at one end, and jagged to a point at the other. I turned it over and my breath snagged in my throat. I was holding the remnants of a fake fingernail. A neon-orange fingernail. I remembered the woman from the night before, holding her neck. The red oozing from her throat and the bright orange thumbnail clearly visible in the twilight. I felt dizzy.

I looked back at the floor where my hand had been, at the groove between the wide floor planks. Just deep enough for a broken nail to wedge into without being noticed. My body began to shake.

Jeffrey appeared in the doorway. "We really should get out of here," he said. "We've trespassed enough for one day."

I closed my left hand around the nail shard. I wanted to reveal my finding to him, to prove I wasn't crazy, but I needed time to process everything. Nothing made sense. Why would the broken nail be here but nothing else, not even one tiny drop of blood?

Again, I thought somebody had cleaned up everything else.

I stood on shaky legs. "You're right. We need to go. Now."

My mind was spinning like a centrifuge, I followed Jeffrey down the stairs and out the back door. We were just rounding the back of the house when Jeffrey said he'd left his credit card on the kitchen counter. I didn't recall seeing it there, but then I'd been distracted when passing through the room. He turned back.

"See you around," I said.

"Yeah, see ya," he called over his shoulder. He'd already forgotten me.

Anger stirred in my chest as I rounded the house. How dare he dismiss me. How dare everyone dismiss me. I'd found something important, something that would prove I'd witnessed violence. Possibly even a woman's death. I opened my left hand and looked at the nail remnant nestled in the center of my palm. I'd show him, and everyone else. I turned and walked back around the corner just in time to see Jeffrey in profile, his body bent slightly over the sliding door handle as he twisted a shiny silver key in the lock. My mouth dropped open.

I stepped back as he reached into his jeans pocket, pulled out a tissue, and wiped down the door handle. Without making a sound, I rounded the corner of the house and ran, thoughts colliding like bumper cars through my mind: Jeffrey didn't break into the house with his credit card. He had a key, which meant he knew the people who'd lived there. Had to. He was a news reporter, not a real-estate agent. He'd have no professional reason for possessing a key to the empty house. And why would he erase evidence of his presence unless that same evidence was incriminating? I reached my car, heart thumping heavily as I thought of something else, the most frightening thought so far: Jeffrey Trembly knew who I was, what I had seen. And he knew where I lived.

# CHAPTER SEVEN

THE DOORBELL RANG, surprising me.

I opened the door, seeing Tasha Turner on the front stoop. A vision in a bright pink sundress, the luxurious drape of the garment hugging her jutting hips and accenting her tiny waist.

I self-consciously placed my hands against the stubborn post-baby pudge clinging to my waistline and blinked, taking a second to translate her into my world.

"Are you going to let me in?" she said, smiling. I realized with a start that I hadn't even opened the door all the way.

"Oh, yes." I stepped back, swinging the door wide. I had few friends. Tasha's weekly visit after work each Thursday was something I looked forward to. Of course, she had no idea how upside down my world had become. "Is it four already? I've lost track of time."

"As long as one of us remembers, it's fine."

Her teeth were dazzling.

"Oh, I remembered." I mimicked her smile. Recalling how much Muzzy had appreciated specific meeting times, I strained to keep my lips upturned. "I just got caught up in chores."

*Chores, really, Caroline?* Mother's voice was disapproving.

Tasha crossed the living room in front of me, not glancing to the left where a talk-show host doled out advice from the dusty television screen, or to the right where the sticky-looking, red-rimmed wineglass resided on the end table. Fortunately, she didn't look back at my reddened face either. The place was a mess.

Pausing before my tiny kitchen table, Tasha flowed like water into a mismatched chair that sat alongside it, its empty seat the only free space amid the clutter of baby items and knickknacks on every other surface. She placed her hands on the tabletop, and I noticed her oval-tipped nails were the shape and shade of lush red grapes.

"Can I get you a drink?" My gaze shot to the empty wineglass on the end table before focusing back on her cabernet-colored fingertips. I wondered if the chosen shade was a subliminal advertisement for her sommelier husband. "I have wine."

"Oh no." She laughed. "If I drink now, I'll fall asleep cooking dinner."

I nearly snorted. *As if Tasha made dinner.* She likely had some sort of food service. Or a personal chef. But I couldn't let my manners slip. I needed Tasha. More than she knew.

"How are the twins?" I asked. "Any recent photos?"

"Sure." She whipped out her cell phone and pulled up a picture of the adorable toddlers—a boy and a girl, of course—on an intricate wooden playset next to a gated inground pool in the Turners' massive backyard. Both kids were mini replicas of their Tyra Banks look-alike mom: hazel eyes slanted like a cat's, tawny skin.

I thought of the day we'd met, when she'd opened her wallet to remove something, and I'd glimpsed a small wedding photo that looked like a shot from the pages of *Vogue*: Tasha's model-thin frame strategically filling out a wispy blush wedding gown in all the right places. Her beaming groom, Nelson, in a dove-gray tuxedo, his dark hair and skin gleaming in the tropical-looking sunlight.

"They're such beautiful children."

"Thanks, Caroline." She placed the phone on the table and gestured to the chair across the table. "Let's talk."

I toyed with the idea of telling her about what I'd seen on Pine Hill Road.

But if she didn't believe me, I risked her abandoning me like Tim had. Most people avoided crazy.

"You don't know how much it means to have you help me hash out this marriage stuff," I said, sliding into the chair. "Tim still refuses to talk to me. Not even on the phone. And I don't know why."

She lowered her brows, slicing a vertical line into the skin of her forehead, just above her nose. She'd have to Botox that trouble spot. I was surprised she hadn't already.

"I think you do, Caroline. You just don't want to talk about it—or even think about it."

I placed my elbows on the table and clasped my hands together in front of me. "Well, would you? If Nelson walked out?"

She nodded slowly. "That would hurt me, no doubt, but I think Tim's hurting too. Things like this take time—"

I rolled my eyes. "Now you sound like my neighbor, Mary. She keeps telling me to give us more time. And time may be a luxury we don't have."

"Why do you say that?" Tasha's tone turned wary. "You're both young."

"That doesn't mean anything. My parents were young when my dad died. Neither of them had even hit thirty when he drowned." I suddenly realized they'd been the exact same age I was now.

The thought sent a quiver through my hands. I quickly placed them on my lap, out of sight.

"Your mother never remarried." It was a statement rather than a question.

"I guess she didn't want another man raising her only kid."

"Hmm, you'd think she'd welcome someone new to share not only the work of child-rearing but the fun too." Her eyes met mine, her gaze speculative. "Maybe your mom had decided that no man could measure up."

I shook my head. "I don't know. I think she was so traumatized by the way Daddy died . . ." I closed my eyes to the memory of sunlight blazing on the pond's surface, thousands of dazzling silver sequins.

"The accident," she said.

I opened my eyes; felt a sharp pain in my neck. Reaching up and kneading the area with my fingertips, I remembered our family, so close together. "As you know, we were in a rowboat on a small lake. On vacation, I think. It's hard to remember, I was so young. I'm sure I've mentioned to you, I stood up, causing the boat to capsize." A shiver raced up my arms as though I'd plunged anew into icy water. I placed my hands on the tabletop to steady them. "My father drowned saving us."

"I'm so sorry you had to go through that." Tasha covered my hands with hers. "A horrible memory."

I fought the urge to pull my hands away. "That's just it: I don't remember it at all." I gazed up, my eyes locking with hers. "I recall sitting in the boat together, and that's it."

Tasha nodded. "That makes sense though, right? That you would block out the traumatic event?"

Emmy began wailing from her bedroom. I shot out of my chair. "Hold on, I'll be right back." I ran to the nursery, swinging Emmy's door wide and peering into the crib for the cause of her sudden, violent cry. She lay in the center of the mattress, her legs raised up to her tummy and her face an angry red. I bent down and expertly scooped her up, recalling what my pediatrician's nurse had said during our first postnatal visit: *"That's the loudest cry I've ever heard out of a baby!"*

I bobbed Emmy gently up and down, rubbing her back in soothing circular motions, trying to ease the gassy spasms slicing through her, but her cries only grew louder. I bounced faster and whispered, "It's okay," over and over into her ear. Eventually, her cries died down to pathetic little mewls. I donned the baby carrier and tucked her in, angling her so her ear would be against my heart.

I swayed back and forth, knowing it was the motion Emmy liked best. As her whimpers transitioned into hiccups, I marveled at what a reliable friend Tasha had become, even before Tim left. In the beginning, I'd had my doubts. Gun-shy after Muzzy, I wasn't seeking friends, but Tasha had barreled her way into my life, intent, it seemed, to stay.

When Tim first mentioned the woman named Tasha who worked in the same office complex as he did, doing what he called "personal growth consulting," I envisioned her job as a mix of beauty advisor and career counselor. When he'd invited her to our home one Monday evening after a particularly trying weekend full of arguing and infant wailing, I'd looked at her sharply; her smooth greeting and direct gaze felt disconcertingly authoritative. *A woman in charge,* I'd thought, suspicious of what—or whom—she planned to manage.

"You need a friend," Tim had explained after she left. "We don't know the neighbors all that well."

"There's Mary . . ."

"Mary is more than fifty years older than you." He'd looked at me pointedly, his eyebrows raised. "Among other things."

"Tasha doesn't live around here though." I crossed my arms over my chest. "She's over in Glenwood Estates. Each backyard in that development is bigger than our entire neighborhood."

"She lives a few miles down Route 22, Caroline," he said, impatience ribboning through his words, as usual. "Close enough."

*But worlds away,* I thought.

As if summoned by my musing, Tasha peeked her head around Emmy's door.

"Everything okay, Caroline?"

"Yes, I'm just putting Emmy down. I'll be out in a few minutes."

"I'm sorry, I've gotta run. I have to get my kids from their enrichment program."

"But you just got here."

Tasha looked at the carrier strapped across my chest, the set of her mouth—lips thinned, the corners turned slightly downward—suggesting disapproval. "I got here forty minutes ago."

I glanced at the digital clock on Emmy's dresser. I couldn't believe how long I'd been soothing her. "Oh geez, I'm so sorry to have left you sitting in my kitchen all this time. I had to—"

"It's okay." She held up one hand. "I'll drop by next week."

"All right." I followed her as she hurried toward the front door and let herself out. "Next week," I repeated to the closed door. Would the day come when Tasha would no longer find value in our friendship? Would she realize she was getting nothing out of her visits with me? I thought of her pristine manicures and hurried into the bathroom in search of a nail file. Spotting a worn emery board on the top shelf of the medicine cabinet, I snagged it and crossed back to the living room, settling on the couch. Reaching around a now-sleeping Emmy bundled against my heart, I shaped the uneven tips.

*The pretty girls stick together.* My mother's words. How often had she told me that during my childhood? Every time I didn't get invited to a birthday party or play date.

*The advice paid off,* said Mother now. *You were popular in high school.*

I laughed at the thought. My *popularity* had more to do with my expanding bra size the summer between seventh and eighth grades than any personality advantage. I blossomed from a 32A cup to a 34C in three months. And I let the captain of the football team feel me up.

Now I must pay more attention to my grooming habits. As my mother had often chimed, friendship had standards. Motherhood did too. Scratching Emmy's tender skin with one of my untended claws would be unforgivable. I sawed away at the jagged nail edges.

"You'll get invited to everything," I nuzzled Emmy's downy head with my lips and angled the emery board with purpose. "I'll make sure of it."

# CHAPTER EIGHT

*Friday, August 18*

TIM WAS GOING to take Emmy away. I knew he was. My husband's refusal to even talk to me spoke volumes more than his previous threats. Was he avoiding me because he'd discovered I couldn't stay away from Deer Crossing, even after what had happened with Muzzy? How would he even know? I gnawed at the inside of my cheek, my teeth scraping painfully against the tender skin. He always knew what I was up to. I wasn't sure how.

Of course, Muzzy could have told him about my numerous lingering strolls in front of her house. If only she'd emerge from her front door. Engage, even if it was just to yell obscenities at me. Any interaction might help us get past the incident. I closed my eyes against the memory, counted slowly backward from ten, but it didn't work. My mind lingered on that day.

I was to blame for what happened; I was. I never should have agreed to picnic at the pond beside Muzzy's house that warm May afternoon. She couldn't have known my fear of being so close to the water—of course she couldn't. I hadn't told her about the accident that killed my father. I hadn't wanted to drag down our budding friendship with my myriad burdens. Muzzy's only emotional crutches seemed to be a socially acceptable compulsion to scrub all surfaces with Clorox, and a nightly addiction to the thousands of creamy, cold calories Ben and Jerry provided in convenient pint-sized servings. I blinked, staring at a bare wall in my living room but seeing Muzzy. When I arrived at her house that fateful Monday, I'd paused outside the gate, watching my friend line up picnic baskets on her outdoor table, the children hovering around her in an excited flurry of bright T-shirts and wildly swinging limbs.

"Are you moving outside permanently?" I joked, causing Muzzy to look up and break into one of her wide smiles.

"No, just fulfilling an annual family tradition." She stuffed a sippy cup into one of the baskets and shoved the wicker top down over the cup's protruding nub. "On the first really warm spring day, we duck next door and have our lunch pondside. I even let the boys dip their toes in the water." When she said this, Alex and Christopher jumped up and down in excitement, calling out their approval. Muzzy laughed at their antics, adding, "This year you get to join us!"

"Oh." My voice faltered. A yawning darkness opened inside me and spread outward, threatening to overtake all five senses at once. "Fun."

"Are you okay?" Muzzy's voice sounded far away. A wall of gauzy haze appeared between us; my brain wavered like heat waves emanating from scorched pavement.

"I'm fine. Just a little light-headed," I managed. "I might be coming down with the flu, so maybe I should just head home—"

"The flu in May?" She balanced her hands on her substantial hips. "You're probably just hungry—at least I hope you are. I fried up a chicken and made my famous potato salad. Can you handle the small basket?"

Before I knew it, we were mere yards from the bubbling pond. Chicken leg in hand, I looked warily at the center fountain spouting torrents high into the air. Taunting me. I shivered as Muzzy rattled on about how

Johnny loved to come home to an orderly house, how her cleaning compulsion eased the stresses on her overburdened husband. In the midst of her soliloquy, she noticed my trembling, tossed me a sweater she'd brought for herself, and continued speaking, only ceasing her running commentary to chew and swallow. Her words barely registered amid the pounding in my ears. I sat beside Emmy's dozing form in the carriage, nodding glumly.

The gag of retching made me look up, and catch Muzzy bending little Amber over the grass, both their arms covered in vomit. When the child straightened and faced me, her entire front, from chest to toes, was covered in regurgitated food.

"Oh, goodness," exclaimed Muzzy, standing and scooping up her child. "Looks like that's the end of our picnic." She began walking toward her house, shooting a glance over her shoulder. "I'll be back as soon as I get us changed. Just watch the boys and we'll pack up once I return."

Relieved, I took a deep breath. I could do this. I started gathering paper plates, telling the kids to pick up the plastic utensils.

"After we put our feet in the water," said Christopher, scrambling off the picnic blanket. "Mommy said Alex and me could."

"No!" The word came out sharper than I'd intended, but the boys were already crossing the half-dozen yards to the rippling water. I screamed again, my terror-filled tone halting them in their tracks right next to the pond's edge. "Wait until your mother gets here!"

Alex looked toward his big brother for guidance and Christopher wavered on his little toothpick legs, unsure about my authority over him.

"Get away from that pond," I yelled. My command seemed to hold them in check, but my words had no effect on Brandon, who, intent upon following his siblings, was too young to understand the order or the looming danger. Delighted with the newfound speed in his little legs, he quickly toddled over to his big brothers and before any of us could move, he plopped headfirst into the water.

Terrified, I tried to step forward, but my feet felt bolted to the ground. I scanned the portion of the pond Brandon had breached, squinting against the surface's metallic glint, glaring as a shiny layer of aluminum under the sun's blazing rays, obscuring shadows.

"Help!" I screamed, my throat stinging with the effort to amplify. "Muzzy, help!" My arms shot out as if I were close enough to reach the toddler.

Within seconds, my friend appeared from behind the stand of arborvitae shrubs edging her property, still covered in vomit and carrying Amber.

"Brandon's in the pond!" I gasped as all my senses assaulted me: the sunstruck water hurting my eyes, the children's screams reverberating in my ears, and the smell—a sudden, overwhelming whiff of rotted vegetation, like dead flowers too long in their vase. My head swam and my vision blurred.

Muzzy dumped Amber onto the grass and took off for the pond, a blur of motion. She jumped in without hesitation and, seconds later, scooped the toddler from the water. I stood watching her like a spectator at a macabre sporting event, still unable to move except for my convulsive shaking. She spread him flat on the grass and pressed her fingers against his protruding belly. Glancing up frantically, her eyes locked onto mine.

"Jesus, Caroline, call 911!" When I blinked at her, unmoving, she added, "What the hell is wrong with you? I need an ambulance!"

Her desperate tone spurred me out of my trance. I reached into my pocket, pulled out my phone, and did as she commanded.

Muzzy never spoke to me again. Not after Brandon spouted water and wailed to life, or as the ambulance came and stuffed the entire family inside and whirred away. Not in the days that followed either. No distraught or accusing phone calls, and no surprise visit on my doorstep.

But a few days after the incident, Muzzy visited Tim at his workplace. Recalling my bragging about his important job at Kinney and McKean Engineering, she'd found their office and my husband in it. Tim never told me what Muzzy said, just that he worried the Owen family would sue us.

"That's ridiculous," I scoffed. "She would have no reason—"

"She'd have every reason, Caroline," he'd shouted. "You watched her child struggling to stay afloat and you did nothing to help. What kind of monster does that?"

# CHAPTER NINE

*Saturday, August 19*

I HAD TO CONVINCE Tim we belonged together. It may not be the best thing for us as a couple, but I must keep the family intact, for Emmy's sake. I'd have to make inroads on that goal now before he discovered what I'd witnessed on Pine Hill Road and used it against me. I needed to buy time—time to prove to him I had remorse over the incident with Muzzy. Once again I decided that if Muzzy and I could rekindle our friendship, it might also strengthen his opinion of me. Emmy needed both parents continuously in her life, and I needed Emmy. Every day. I couldn't risk the part-time parenting of holidays and weekends. I reached for my cell phone next to the cup of cold, untouched morning coffee.

His line rang three times and went to voice mail. I disconnected and tried again. This time the call went directly to his prerecorded message.

Thinking about Matt's distracted wave when I'd pass by his house, I pressed Tim's name in my contact list again. "*You* don't have the luxury of ignoring me."

This time he picked up. "What do you want?"

"I want to talk to you, of course. About us, and Emmy."

"Keep Emmy out of this, Caroline."

I took a deep breath to control the hot rage that filled my entire torso like someone had opened a door in my chest and dumped a load of burning coals around my heart.

He was acting even more callous than usual.

"Fine, I'll focus on us. I thought we could discuss when you want to come home. Your apartment must be expensive, and we don't have the money to pay for—"

"How much do you need?"

"How much?" I sputtered. "This isn't about *money*. I'm calling about our family."

Tim said nothing for a beat. When he finally spoke his voice was quiet, controlled. "We aren't a family anymore, Caroline. You know that."

"We're only separated, not divorced. Remember you said we'd try it and if being apart didn't work for us—"

"It works for me."

"But not me. Or Emmy. How can you do this to us? To her?"

"That's low, even for you," he said, the anger in his voice notching up. "We've been over this a hundred times, Caroline. I'm not going to rehash it again."

"I'm sorry. Is that what you want to hear?"

"No, it's not. We're beyond that now, and you know it."

"Please, let's just meet somewhere. Talk." I cursed my wobbly voice.

"Talk about what?" he snapped. "Your emotions? How *you* are handling things?"

I paused in the face of his sudden anger. "We can talk about you. How you are doing . . ."

He laughed, a humorless grating sound. "That's rich, Caroline. When has anything in our marriage ever been about me?"

"That's not fair!"

"If I'm treating you unfairly, feel free to stop calling me. And don't drive by my apartment either."

"I only did that a few times, so you could see—"

"Stop it right now," he interrupted. "This is getting out of control, okay? I refuse to be responsible for everything you're feeling."

"I know, I know," I said quickly. "But it's hard, Tim. It's so hard and it seems so easy for you."

He sighed. "It's not. I've suffered. But our time together is done, and you know it. Too much has happened."

"We could rebuild things, Tim. If we started slowly."

"No, Caroline. You need to know something—something important."

"Tell me, please. Tell me anything."

"I'm seeing someone else."

My body went cold as my brain tried to compute this new information. "No, we're only separated—"

"My lawyer drew up the divorce papers this week. They're on their way to you. I suggest you sign them. If you refuse, I'll have no choice but to cut back on the money I send you. I don't have to give you as much as I do."

"You're so cold," I said, feeling my body shiver as if in agreement with my words, despite the day's heat and humidity. "You weren't always this way."

"We've both changed a lot. Either way, it doesn't matter anymore. I'll still hold up my end, Caroline. You'll get your money."

"But Emmy," I wailed into the phone even as it slipped from my suddenly stiff, cramped fingers. I reached down and snatched it up, hearing his words warble through the phone line.

". . . so, you know I can see Emmy anytime I want to."

My face flushed as my emotions surged upward from my chest. "I'd never keep her from you," I snapped, but my voice echoed into dead air space. Tim had already disconnected.

I threw the phone onto the couch and huffed. Why had I married the most obstinate man on the planet?

*But you won't be married much longer.*

I slunk onto the sofa as the truth hit me. He was cutting me loose and tossing me away, just like that overused hammock from all those years ago. The comfort and enjoyment worn away as he eagerly anticipated new experiences.

≈≈≈≈≈

I STEWED OVER Tim's indifference all day, worried it would turn into wariness—maybe even distrust—if he discovered what I'd witnessed at Pine Hill Road. Worse still, he'd have reason to be skeptical of my story. One call to the police would blast apart my tale and make me seem delusional. Not an ideal quality in the mother of his child.

Taking panicked breaths that left me unable to get enough oxygen in my lungs, I tried to remember the events of that awful night at Melanie and Matt's house, but my mind refused to release any more hints. Panting through my chores, mixing together the nighttime formula, feeding Emmy, and giving her a sponge bath, my anxiety mounted. Needing release, I strapped on my running shoes, settled Emmy in the BABYZEN, and headed toward Deer Crossing in the waning light.

Maybe the Pine Hill house held answers to my many questions about that night. Answers that would become evident to me once I was standing before it.

I entered the neighborhood and made a quick pass up Pine Hill, glancing into the many homes that had blinds up and occupants on display. The only passingly interesting activity was in an oversized Colonial. Its spacious living room was the scene of a strenuous mat Pilates class. Women in form-fitting tanks and leggings holding the impossible poses I'd seen on exercise segments of *Good Morning America*. I suppressed a sigh and pushed on, pausing at Matt and Melanie's house. It was completely dark inside. Were they really gone for good? If they'd indeed moved out, why had I seen Melanie that fateful night? Shaking my head, I stood there for a long time, staring at the dark building. It revealed nothing other than the suspicion I was truly losing my mind. Eventually, I looked away and turned toward Muzzy's house.

Reaching in my pocket to clutch the small canister of mace Tim had given me a few years earlier and I'd decided to carry every evening, I studied Muzzy's place.

Only one light on in its center. I scanned left, my reluctant gaze settling on the pond, twenty yards ahead. My nemesis. I had to ignore the damned hole in the ground, and all the misery it encapsulated. My mind flashed back to the other night, and how I'd ended up in the water. My breathing turned shaky, and my body trembled.

I backed up. I couldn't take even one step in that direction. I glanced back at the Pine Hill house—and saw a flickering light in the upstairs bedroom. I blinked, convincing myself what I was witnessing wasn't real. The light flashed again, almost like a signal. I whipped my head around, scrutinizing the shadows surrounding an enormous split-level across the street. That house also had a light on somewhere deep within its center, but no outside lantern. I could discern no movement in the yard, yet I had the eerie feeling someone was watching me. Keeping Matt and Melanie's place to my left and the split-level on my right, I began backing up the road.

*Don't be ridiculous. There's nothing to see here.*

I stood tall. There was absolutely no reason to cower. I couldn't let my overactive imagination fool me into feeling vulnerable. I pivoted until I was once again facing 21 Pine Hill. I settled my gaze on the window I'd seen Melanie fall against, my eyes unwavering.

No light greeted me this time, but a rustling behind me made me flinch. I whipped my head once more to the shadowy behemoth of a house facing Matt and Melanie's. Silence. But when I turned away, I heard it: a voice as soft as the stirring of leaves, but the message not so benign. *Go away, go away.*

I turned on my heel and shoved Emmy's carriage forward, running up the street as fast as I could, but a quick exit was impossible. Each time I veered off an outcrop of Pine Hill looking for a shortcut, I'd dead-end in the center of a cul-de-sac. Feeling like a mouse in a maze, I pushed back onto Pine Hill and ran straight down the road, the baby carriage in front of me, breath coming in uneven gasps. Emmy began to howl.

I raced across Route 55 and into my neighborhood. As I passed the ever-present dogs who never seemed to get inside their owners' houses, their piercing barks joined Emmy's wails in a horrid chorus of misery that made me want to scream. *Tell the world to shut the hell up.*

I reached my ranch as the baby worked herself into a frenzy, her little limbs pumping like pistons, her tiny mouth emitting a baleful yowl that echoed my agony every time I thought of a bloody Melanie pressed against the window on Pine Hill Road.

*No! Mustn't think of that now!*

Instead, I thought of Muzzy, and how things might be different if our friendship had been allowed to develop. Had she created an alliance with Tim? Against me? I grimaced. Perhaps *alliance* wasn't the right word for the kind of intimacy between them. Tim's voice from earlier in the day boomeranged in my head, telling me he was seeing someone else.

As soon as I made it into the house, I shoved Emmy into the chest carrier I found cast across the back of the sofa. Corralling her flailing legs until her little body was pressed snugly against mine, I crossed from room to room in a crazy-eight pattern. From coffee table to kitchen, then back. Losing track of how many times I'd paced the same area, I focused on calming Emmy.

I couldn't *think* when she was screaming. I had to get her to stop. Taking deep breaths to still my jangling nerves, I slowed my pace, and Emmy, always adept at tapping into my moods, eventually quieted.

I stopped in the center of the room and began rocking back and forth, feeling guilty for exposing Emmy to my anxiety. It was difficult enough that she was going to be raised by a single mom, just like I had been. I dimmed the lights and pulled the curtains closed, making sure nobody could peer in. Prying eyes could judge. Who knew that better than I?

I hummed the tune Daddy often sang to me when I was little, a Led Zeppelin song about love transcending all odds—even tumbling mountains and a world without sunshine. It still made me tear up. And it always soothed Emmy into sleep. Eventually, her fuzzy head nestled against my chest, and the deep, even breaths of her slumber signaled the opportunity to transport her, ever so gently, to her crib.

As I was tiptoeing out of her room, the baby suddenly wailed. I whipped around in the doorway, watching her limbs jerking like tiny ghosts, popping in and out of the shadows. I rushed back to the crib, gently rubbed her belly and legs until they eventually stilled. I backed out of the room, afraid to breathe.

Emmy's sleep was often riddled with wakeful moments, as though she never wanted to fully surrender to slumber. I, on the other hand, had always eagerly anticipated a languorous reprieve.

Lounging in bed watching a movie and dozing off, no matter what time of day it was. I'd been a voracious sleeper before we had Emmy, except for the first months after Tim and I met. I squeezed my eyes shut, not wanting to recall how much time we'd spent in bed *not* sleeping. I remembered one night: we'd made love three times in the span of two hours and wanted to keep going, despite our fatigue.

"Just lie on top of me," I'd whispered, not wanting to sever the sensual bonds securing us to one another. "We'll just doze a bit."

"Five minutes," Tim whispered back, settling himself so we were both comfortable, skin on skin, breath mingling.

We'd awoken the next morning in the same position. I'd felt dull aching around my knees and elbows. After I'd gently dislodged him (we were so tender with each other in those days!) I sat up, noticing the darkening bruises on my lower thighs, just above my knees where his kneecaps had lodged all night. I studied the unintentional injuries in wonder before inspecting the same blossoming discolorations above each elbow.

I swallowed the lump in my throat at the memory. It had taken two weeks for the bruises to fade. Oh, how I'd enjoyed the affliction. How I'd reveled in his marks on me, fool that I was. Had I known anything even remotely wise about human nature then, I'd have realized it was the constant pressure of love and longing that ensnared us. The weight of expectation—outwardly expressed or even hidden in our minds. Expanding exponentially. It burst the very stuff we were made of. How we wandered through life bruised and broken. Waiting for the wounds to heal, even as we cherished them.

# CHAPTER TEN

*Thursday, August 24*

C OMING BACK FROM the supermarket during a deluge, I drove along Main Street into the bustling business section of the village, careful to avoid pedestrians dodging across streets in vain efforts to stay dry. Slowing at a light, I noticed a young woman with wet, limp hair entering Catherine's Hair Designs just as an old lady exited Budget Beverages next door. I squinted, realizing it was Mary making her way heavily through the door, hugging a cardboard box. Instinct made me grip the steering wheel and look away, but guilt got the better of me. Mary was old, and it was pouring rain. I pressed the button on the driver's-side door to lower my car window and realized with a start the window was open. They were all still open. Emmy was probably drenched. I'd get her right home, but I should probably bring Mary to her house too.

"Mary!"

She heaved her load upward, muttering something as she attempted to get a better grip on the box. I tried again: "Mary?"

This time she heard me. She jerked her head up, looked around. When her gaze landed on my face, the corners of her lips rose, revealing a gnarly-toothed smile. "Hello, neighbor."

"Get in my car. You're getting soaked."

"I'm just over in the lot . . ."

"I'll drive you over."

Nodding, she hurried to the back seat driver's-side door and fumbled for the handle while balancing her box.

I leaned across the front passenger seat and opened that door from the inside. "Come around." As she circled my hood like a vague star in a hazy gray orbit, I wondered if she'd started drinking earlier than usual.

"You're a real lifesaver, a true gem, you know that?" she said, her words melding into a slurry stew of adjectives and nouns that answered my unspoken question about morning drinking. I thought about her *strong coffee*. She landed with a thud in the front passenger seat and heaved the large box onto her lap but couldn't get the door shut.

The top flaps of the box were missing, revealing half a dozen alcohol bottles of assorted shapes, colors, and sizes. I grabbed the top edge nearest me and pulled the box away from her door.

"Hey, watcha doing? You're gonna break—"

"I'm not going to break anything," I assured her. "Close the door, Mary."

She nodded, reached for the inside handle. After she awkwardly pulled the door shut, I toyed with the idea of instructing her to buckle her seat belt but quickly gave up on the idea. The box took up too much room on her lap.

"Look, Mary, it's so awful outside, I think I should just drive you home. We'll come back to the lot and pick up your car later. What do you think?"

"I think tha' sounds like a . . ."

"Good idea?"

"It's really wet in here," she said. "Is your car leaking?"

"Maybe." I pressed the buttons on my door to close all the car windows.

I drove down Main, squinting through the rain pelting my windshield and trying to ignore the annoying dinging sound alerting us to Mary's unbuckled seat belt. I risked a quick glance at her. She looked straight ahead, her gaze on the road in front of us as though she were the one driving. "Bill used to take me around," she said. "He took me shopping."

"That was nice of him." I clicked my wipers to a higher setting and glanced at her.

"He was nice." She paused, reaching up to rub the chapped slash of red under her nose that passed for lips. "Except when he wasn't."

I looked back at the lined pavement spread ahead of us and rolled my eyes. Things were getting bad for Mary.

"That's why I killed him."

My whole body jerked, my toe tapping against the brake, shooting both of us forward. Fortunately, my seat belt held me tight, and the box on her lap prevented Mary's head from hitting the dashboard.

"Watch it, sister," she warned, looking at me sideways.

"What do you mean you *killed him*?" I gripped the steering wheel tighter to keep the car centered in my lane. After checking that there were no other cars around, I looked once more at her.

"He left me. Said I drank too much." Mary looked indignant, her face infused with a rosy hue. "Can you believe it? Me, drink too much? Just because I like to . . ."

Yes, she most certainly drank too much.

I took a breath, smelling the effervescence of booze and cigarettes, suspecting Mary's sudden confession reflected not facts but imaginings fermented from the booze.

"So, you . . . what? Pushed him down the stairs? Poisoned him?" I envisioned Mary tripping an elderly man already unsteady on his feet, visualized her mixing something white and powdery into his tea.

"I showed up at Bill's apartment with his hunting knife in my hand. He'd forgotten to take it, you see, and I thought I'd give him a bit of a scare. I raised the knife right after I shoved my way in. Poor Bill. He had a heart . . ."

The metronomic sweep of the wipers on the windshield punctuated her statement.

"God, Mary." A shiver ran through me. Her words were too clear now, the details so real. I stared at the road, intent on keeping us on it, my eyes away from the neighbor I'd apparently never really known. "He had a heart attack?"

"Mmmm. I would have called for an ambulance if I hadn't been so angry."

"So, you did nothing?" A flash of little Brandon's still form in the pond seared my brain. "You watched him die?" I side-eyed her.

She shook her head. "Of course not. I wasn't sticking around to witness that. Too painful. I left." She sighed dramatically. "But you know I still miss him?"

I looked back at the road, not knowing what to say. Everyone had secrets. I never spoke about how I'd passively watched my friend's baby nearly drown. And there was Jane and the affair she was hiding from her husband. A sin Muzzy and Tim might also be guilty of. I swallowed, thinking of Melanie with her arms around a man who probably wasn't her husband. Had Matt made her pay for her transgression with her life? It couldn't be . . .

"I knew you'd understand," Mary said, interrupting my musing. "Being alone is the hardest part of life, isn't it?" I turned the car into our development, not trusting my voice.

"Yes, Mary," I eventually said, pressing my foot on the accelerator. I had to get the drunken nutjob out of my car and away from my baby. I took the corner of our street too quickly, angling both of us sharply to the left. Mary's arm collided with my right elbow.

"Jesus, Caroline," she slurred. "Don't take this the wrong way, but you're a terrible driver."

⁂

AFTER DROPPING MARY home, I fed and changed Emmy and settled her into the crib, shaking my head at the story my neighbor had shared.

*Can't be true.*

Besides being a heavy drinker, Mary might have some form of dementia. God only knew what visions plagued the plaque-encrusted brain of an octogenarian. Not a generous thought, but the truth wasn't always kind and understanding. I'd faced a lot of callous truths myself. Empathy had seldom prevailed when I'd asked my mother to tell me about my dead dad. Where were they married? Were they happy together? Did they love their child . . . love me?

She usually reminded me that badgering people was not polite. Every now and then she'd smile tightly and nod or shake an answer. Eventually, I decided that the mere mention of the man we'd loved and lost was too painful for her to talk about.

*Think about pleasant things.*

*Easier said than done,* I thought as I flipped on the television and went around the channels. None of the daytime talkies appealed. The hosts jabbered on about upcoming fall fashions, staycations, parenting rebellious teens. I headed for the kitchen and found an unopened bottle of merlot in the cabinet below the sink, mixed in with cleaning supplies. The bottle had been too tall to fit in my other cabinets. Reaching into the utensil drawer, I snatched the corkscrew. I'd have just a glass or two. Unlike Mary, I knew when to quit. I brought the bottle and a wineglass into the living room and settled onto the couch. A glass of alcohol made me think clearly. Maybe it temporarily swelled my nerve cells, shortening the gap between them so messages could flow more quickly across the synapses. That didn't seem right, but I didn't care.

A sharp rap on the front door startled me. I stood gingerly. *Why am I dizzy?* Making my way to the source of the knocking, I had trouble twisting the doorknob. *Curious.* After eventually getting the door open, I paused and stared. Tasha Turner graced the stoop. Looking professional in a navy suit, she smiled at me.

"Hello, Caroline. You look surprised to see me."

"Well, I . . . what time is it?"

Her brows lowered over her eyes. I'd confused her. "It's four, of course."

"Oh, silly me. The day's just flown." *How long have I been drinking?* "Please come in."

She laughed. "You don't know how often I lose track of time. In my job I'm always running around, trying to get it all done."

She was being kind, of course. Giving me an out.

I led her through the living room, certain she'd notice the half-empty bottle of merlot and burgundy-stained wineglass on the end table. I could almost hear the calculations clicking in her mind, the judgments being formed as I did with Mary.

"How have you been?" she asked, pulling out her usual chair from its place tucked under my tiny kitchen table.

"Oh, well, you know." I sighed. "New day, same old shit."

She frowned ever so slightly, making me feel crass. "If life was always exciting, we'd become bored and look for drama just to fill the time."

I looked at her, a vision of Muzzy filling her boring evenings by screwing my husband. "You think so?"

She lifted one shoulder in a semi shrug. "It's human nature."

"Yeah, I guess." I hadn't ever thought of life in those terms. I'd been too busy dodging the fears and worries my mind manufactured. "Maybe that's what I'm doing: creating all my problems in my head. Anticipating the worst so I'm not surprised when it happens." I crossed the kitchen in three steps and reached for the dish-cabinet knob as I looked over my shoulder at her. "You want coffee?"

"I prefer tea."

Of course she did. She never drank coffee. I knew that.

"That's right. You like ginger turmeric, right?"

She nodded. "With lemon, please. And you may be right about the problems circulating in your mind, but you've had so much to deal with—"

"Well, we both know I'm not the first woman whose husband left her." I dragged out two teacups and set them on the counter, my movements jerky.

"Yeah, but I'm thinking about *all* the things you've told me, beginning with Everett . . ."

*This again?* Tasha seemed as obsessed with my father as she'd once claimed she was with his unique name. "People die every day." I pivoted toward the fridge handle, a tremor running through me as I glanced at her.

"Hmm, I suppose you're right." She tilted her head in that superior way Jane Brockton had when we'd first met. I wondered if, like Jane, Tasha thought herself—her life—just a bit worthier than mine. I wouldn't blame her if she did. I weaved on my feet, placing a hand against the fridge to steady myself. I paused for a beat, breathing deeply before continuing the task of tea making.

I filled the kettle with warm water, set it on a burner, and turned the stovetop knob to high, then glanced at her, knowing why I didn't like telling people about my father's accident. They always wanted to ask questions, not understanding how painful it was for me to think about. I pressed my lips together. Was she trying to create a little drama at my expense? Was she one of those people obsessed with death, and the ways people died? Tasha met my gaze, no hint of malice in hers. Only a look of regret, as though it pained her to mention my father.

"What's done is done. No way to go back." I reached into the cabinet and rooted around the bottom shelf for the tea bags.

"Do you really feel that way?"

"Of course." I looked at her. Tasha wasn't afraid to make eye contact. And she never shied away from what I revealed to her. I looked at the tea bags in my hands, removed the paper wrappers, and set about slicing the lemon I'd snatched off my kitchen windowsill. I should be thankful for her attention.

"What if you *do* remember what happened in the boat that day, but your mind is blocking it out like—"

The teakettle's harsh shriek drowned out the rest of her sentence. Even though I was expecting it, the noise startled me. I set the teacups on the table and crossed to the stove, grabbing the teakettle handle. Heat infused my skin as I walked back to Tasha, so warm I worried I might drop the damn thing. I switched hands and poured water in our cups, concentrating on keeping my extended arm steady. "I recall being in the boat, but I don't remember capsizing. One minute we were sitting together, and the next minute we weren't."

Tasha reached for her steaming cup. Her nails were sparkly lavender today. "That must have been horrible. Did you know how to swim?"

"I'm not sure. I think so." I paused, the steaming kettle still in my hand. So close to her beautiful face. My arm quivered. "I have this sense that my dad taught me, but still . . . when I think of that day, I feel so tense. My body tightens up, preparing me for danger."

Tasha lifted her cup and blew on the surface, her eyes never leaving mine. "It would be dangerous if—"

That's when Emmy's wail drowned out the rest of her words. "Excuse me, that's my girl," I said, crossing back to the stove and replacing the teakettle on the cooling burner. I pivoted and hurried through the kitchen, approaching the table where Tasha sat. She stood swiftly, blocking my way.

"Hold up."

"But she's crying."

"You know, doctors now say it's healthy to let a baby cry for a bit. Teaches them to self-soothe."

"Oh, I couldn't do that. She's just a baby, and I'd be remiss . . ." I tried to walk around her, but she bent forward, invading my personal space.

"Think about this, Caroline: by running to Emmy's rescue at the first sign of distress, you may be doing more harm than good." Her voice was firm. "Robbing her of her problems."

"Robbing her of . . . she's a *baby*, for God's sake." I pushed forward, nudging her. "She needs me."

"And you're a good mother," she said, leaning close.

"Yes, I am."

"Then let her cry."

I leaned back, silently cursing Tasha and annoyed once again with Tim. If he'd only allowed us to buy a bigger house, with normal-sized rooms. I'd not be caught in the narrow space between the kitchen table and the wall with my misguided friend using her body as a barrier between me and my crying child. "I'm asking you to step aside, Tasha. I need to tend to Emmy."

"I can't stay all afternoon, remember," she called after me as I rushed down the hall to Emmy's room. I didn't bother to answer. I should have guessed she was still cross with me for losing track of time when she last visited.

By the time I reached Emmy, she'd worked herself into a fit, her legs pressed upward against her belly and her face a disturbing shade between purple and red. Realizing it would take a long time to settle her, I reached into the crib. Her little body stiffened and thrashed against my hands.

I rocked Emmy for endless minutes, eventually calming her enough to change her diaper, strap on the baby carrier, and tuck her fidgeting body in. When I padded back to the kitchen to prepare a bottle, Tasha was no longer there. I felt a ripple of disappointment mix with my resentment. Although Tasha's friendship was important to me, making me choose between lavishing my attention on a self-sufficient woman with children of her own and a helpless infant . . .

I paused, resting a hand on the refrigerator door. My mother had few friends. Perhaps she'd had to make the same tough choices. Or maybe she just hadn't had the opportunity to bond with other women. She'd worked full-time at Dr. Gleason's office since graduating from nursing school. Between her responsibilities at the office and her single-parenting duties, she'd had little time for socializing.

I opened the fridge door and peered inside, searching for the baby formula on the top shelf. When it came down to a competition between friends and family, there was no choice to be made. Emmy had to come first. I may not have made the best parenting decisions when I was in the grip of postpartum depression. Tim had to step up then. Tend to our child while I battled my way back to stability. But Tim wasn't here now. It was just Emmy and me. Like my own mom, I had to be both mother and father to our child.

# CHAPTER ELEVEN

*Sunday, August 27*

I THOUGHT ABOUT MARY dozens of times over the next week. Had she been telling the truth about how Bill died, or had I merely witnessed the ravings of a drunk? There was no way to know for sure unless I asked her when she was sober. I didn't intend to do that. Mary was off-limits. Tasha was too. I had no desire to see her anytime soon. I texted her I'd be busy this coming Thursday, so she'd need not drop by after work.

Thinking about Tasha, my body stiffened. How would she react if I tried to stop her from soothing her little ones? I imagined her composure might slip, giving me a glimpse of the fierce resentment that could turn her beautiful face ugly. I mean, honestly, the basis of our friendship was our shared motherhood, wasn't it? It was really the only thing we had in common.

But without Mary or Tasha I was alone. I'd lived in town less than a year and was now freshly separated. The only other woman I'd befriended was Muzzy Owen, who probably wouldn't let me step onto her property, much less invite me in for coffee. I sighed and stretched my neck to the left and right to ease the sudden tension in my shoulders. I must discover whether Tim felt he needed Muzzy as much as I did. And if that need was reciprocated.

*Time to go back*, said Mother.

"Go back," I repeated out loud.

*To the place you always go.*

᠅᠅᠅

I SCOOTED FROM Woodmint onto Primrose, after studiously ignoring Jane's house as I passed it. That bitch couldn't keep me out of her neighborhood. Her street had become the only way to reach Muzzy's house. Since being spooked on Pine Hill, I avoided that road altogether. Just thinking about Melanie on that fateful evening made my stomach cramp. I was no closer to solving the mystery of what had happened that night, so I tried to put it out of my mind for a while. If I was going to teach Emmy society's rules for fitting in, I had to curb my obsessive tendencies.

I paused in front of Muzzy's house, bending over the BABYZEN, pretending to minister to Emmy. Hoping my former friend would emerge from her front door with her welcoming smile and a plate of home-baked sugar cookies. We'd hug, and I'd apologize for what I'd done months earlier. She'd graciously accept and explain how she and Tim had become friends, how he'd listened to her troubles with sympathy. Tim, I knew, could be a very good listener when he wanted to be. I stared at her windows, unable to see past the sun's rays bouncing off the glass.

Muzzy never came out of the house, and I was afraid to knock on her front door, having predetermined the reunion would be more successful if we appeared to meet by chance. The more often I passed by her place, the better my odds of catching her coming or going.

I straightened and looked around the street, noticing no cars in front of Muzzy's. I glanced at my former friend's yard, my gaze taking in the still swing set and the trampoline, one side of it sunk lower than the other. I sighed. Muzzy used to spend every day outdoors, weather permitting. Had I ruined that for her? Was that my lot in life? To devastate everything and everyone I came into contact with?

I risked a glance up ahead, gritting my teeth. The small pond's fountain spewed effusively, as if putting on a great show. Vying for my notice. I forced myself to look at the gushing water pumping with the enthusiasm of an attention-seeking child. *Look at me! Look at me!*

I shivered, gazing at the gentle ripples ruffling the pond's surface, my lips pressing into a hard line. Blinking rapidly, I tried to displace the image of little Brandon's body floating motionless in the vast expanse of water, and my own flailing form, also stretched out on the water's surface. I wouldn't allow myself to look away.

Hearing the rhythmic lapping against the muddy bank, a tangy, unpleasant taste, like bile, traveled up my windpipe, stinging my throat and settling on my tongue.

I knew the mesmerizing motion of the water concealed the pond's inherent dangers, so why hadn't I tried to rescue the toddler the day of Muzzy's picnic? And how the hell had I, myself, ended up in the damned thing less than two weeks earlier?

I looked down, knowing why I'd always preferred the honest pounding of ocean surf. The relentlessly smashing waves warned of hazards that still pond water cleverly veiled.

An image of Tim at the beach invaded my brain. We'd honeymooned in an oceanfront condo in Key West, but I'd never gone near the water. Two years later, just before I'd gotten pregnant, Tim had taken me to the Jersey Shore for a few days, claiming he was sick of my nagging for a vacation. Once again, I parked myself in the sand as Tim—with exaggerated eye rolling—filled a toy bucket with ocean water for me to drizzle onto my sun-heated skin. He'd had no patience for yet another weakness. *Why take beach vacations if you hate the beach?*

What he hadn't considered was that I loved the beach. Cuddling into the warm sand, enveloping as a lover's embrace.

I closed my eyes, my mind ballooning with all the thoughts colliding in my head—Tim and his eye rolls, my last day with Muzzy and her terrified face, Jane's knowing look, Mary's boozy confession, Melanie's intense stare. I snapped my eyes open.

I had to clear my head. I hurried past Muzzy's at a near run, emptying my mind of everything but the smooth pavement under my feet and the pristine lawns hemming the street—endless yards of turf without the weeds that muscled out the grass in every other neighborhood.

It was no use. I thought of Matt tending his weedless yard, the rich green hue a perfect complement to the cheery red custom Cape. The image in my mind so perfectly at odds with the scene I'd witnessed in the upstairs bedroom window. The thought struck me like a blow to my head: *none* of my problems would be resolved if I couldn't figure out this one. That's what 21 Pine Hill, and the lives attached to it, had become for me. Not only a big problem, but a referendum on my life. Was I going to step up and admit what I'd seen, and possibly help the woman I thought of as Melanie, or would I cower in fear as I'd done that day at the pond, with Muzzy? The day I'd allowed my deep-seated dread to guide my actions—or, more appropriately, my complete lack of action.

⋙⋘

SLEEP ONCE AGAIN eluded me. My mind spun like a dozen pinwheels in a wind gust, but one thought emerged above all others: if I could convince one person of my story, I wouldn't be alone in this quest to discover what happened. I wouldn't be crazy. Closing my eyes, I saw Melanie on the backs of my lids, but her image shattered as Emmy's cries invaded the stillness. My eyes flew open, and I felt my way along the darkened walls to my baby's bedroom.

Tending to Emmy's needs was grounding. I was profoundly thankful for the respite—the all-consuming process of mothering—before having to focus once more on Melanie and her injuries—possibly deadly injuries.

*Possibly deadly injuries.* That was the thing, wasn't it? She might not even be dead. But how could she *not* be? I was not a medical professional, but that gash in her throat looked fatal. Yet I knew better than anyone that appearances could be deceiving.

Jeffrey Trembly's appearance at Matt and Melanie's house had certainly been convenient. I rocked Emmy back to sleep, thinking the man whom I'd looked upon as a helper could have very well been a killer. Perhaps he'd slashed Melanie's throat in the house he had a key to. Then he'd heard me enter downstairs and snuck up behind me, smashing something into my skull and knocking me out.

But it couldn't have happened like that. There was only one staircase. I would have seen him descending the steps.

Perhaps he'd climbed out a front upstairs window, dropped onto the porch roof, and shimmied down the post to enter the house from the front door behind me. I hadn't closed it, had I? Once I was out cold, he could have loaded Melanie, Emmy, and me into his Jeep, conveniently concealed in the garage. He'd dumped my unconscious body in the pond, assuming I'd drown, ditched Emmy on the side of the road, and stashed Melanie elsewhere. Or maybe he'd deposited her in the water too. The thought of struggling to swim mere feet away from Melanie's dead body turned me instantly cold. I rubbed my upper arms.

It made sense. I'd been unconscious for hours, giving Jeffrey plenty of time to clean up the mess. He'd be able to account for his whereabouts. He could say he was out on the beat, investigating a news story when all along he'd been at the Pine Hill house. Hell, when I'd seen him pull up to the pond, he might have just completed his grim cleanup.

I could go to police headquarters. Share my story. My heart lifted at the prospect but dropped just as quickly. Why would the authorities believe me now when they hadn't before? There still wasn't evidence of a crime, was there?

Other than the partial fake fingernail I'd dislodged from between the master bedroom's floorboards. They'd surely wonder when I'd found it, which would lead to the revelation that I'd been in the house *after* my visit from the police officers. Rather than being convinced a crime had occurred on the property, they could launch an investigation into *me*, discovering how I liked to take my sketchy nighttime strolls and spy on the residents of Deer Crossing.

I moved into the living room and turned on the end-table light. If I didn't reveal I had the nail fragment but simply shared my knowledge of Jeffrey's key to the Pine Hill house, police would want to know how I knew that. They'd eventually learn I'd trespassed onto the property but probably wouldn't care about him having a key to an empty house.

I ran both hands through my hair as I began pacing. If I wanted to know why Jeffrey had the key, I'd have to ask him, which would be foolish. I had Emmy to think about. I couldn't expose myself and my infant to a possible murderer. Even if I went to the police with my "evidence" and somehow convinced them to scrape DNA off the fake nail, it would turn up nothing about Jeffrey or Melanie if their DNA wasn't already in the system. I pressed my lips together tightly. As far as I knew, no woman had been reported missing. According to police the residents of the property had sold it and moved away.

The sudden knock on my front door made me flinch. Who could it possibly be? It had to be close to midnight. Fear stalled my breath in my throat, until I heard Mary's voice on the other side. When I yanked the door open, I was greeted by her crooked smile as if it were the middle of the day. I noticed again her top row of teeth looked like they'd been packed together haphazardly, as if someone had shoved them into her mouth quickly without taking the time to ensure they were properly aligned. In the dim night, the effect was creepy jack-o'-lantern rather than friendly neighbor.

"What are you doing here this late at night?"

"I saw your light pop on. Figured you couldn't sleep either."

"Now's not a good time—"

"Not too busy now, I hope. I just made that long trek from next door . . ." She tilted her head to one side and raised her brows inquiringly.

"Actually, I'm in the middle of something. Emmy's restless tonight, and it's been crazy around here lately." *And I've had my fill of potential murder suspects, thank you very much.*

"Tell me about it," she said, stepping up next to me so we both stood just inside the doorframe. "The timing's off, but I've finally carved out a few moments for you."

*For me?* I tried not to roll my eyes. How was I going to get her out of my house without physically pushing her past the threshold? I'd have to humor her for a minute or two and then plead fatigue.

"I need to check on Emmy. There's seltzer in the fridge if you'd like some." Maybe she'd scoff at my paltry drink selection and go home.

When I walked into my kitchen a few minutes later, Mary had two cabinets open and was rifling through one of them.

"You've got an awful lot of baby food, Caroline. Looks like you're creating a fallout shelter. Hundreds of jars—"

"Not hundreds." I tightened my lips into a thin line. "Dozens, maybe."

She looked skeptical. "Do you eat this stuff?"

"Sometimes. Baby food is very nutritious." I knew my tone sounded defensive, but honestly, I was just starting Emmy on the stuff. Why waste the food she didn't eat?

"That's why you've turned to skin and bones, girl." She closed the cabinets. "Living on baby food."

I looked down at the pouch in my midsection. "I'm afraid I'm still fighting off the excess pregnancy fat."

Mary rammed her hands onto her hips, her gaze scanning me from head to toe. "Have you looked at yourself in the mirror lately? You could stand to gain at least ten pounds."

I looked at the older woman's plump form, the approximate shape of a ripe lemon. I decided against a retort. After all, my mother had taught me to treat my elders respectfully.

*My mother.*

Something about my mom made me feel uncomfortable suddenly.

And then I remembered: the first anniversary of her death was approaching. "Would you like a drink, Mary?"

"What have you got?"

I opened the fridge. "Like I said, seltzer water."

"I suppose, if it's all you have." She dropped heavily into a kitchen chair and rested her elbows on the table. "I meant to ask you the other day, was that a police car in your driveway in the wee hours of the morning early last week?"

I looked at her. Mary's powers of observation were stronger than I'd given her credit for. But to notice the police cruiser just hours before dawn? Did the woman ever sleep?

"Yes, actually."

She studied my face, looking worried. "What happened? Did you hurt yourself?"

"No, I'm fine." I opened the fridge door and ducked my head inside, afraid to show her my reddened face. I was an abominable liar. Snagging the seltzer bottle, I tried to make my voice sound light, carefree. "Tim signed us up for some police fundraiser when we first moved here. They've been buzzing around here ever since. Looking for donations."

"Before sunrise? Rubbish. Why were they really here? Did it have anything to do with you and Tim and the . . ."

I twisted the bottle top off with a loud *pffft* and poured the bubbly water into the glass. I crossed over to her and held out the drink. "It's kind of crazy, really."

"Try me," she said, grasping the glass with both hands.

I supposed there was no reason for secrecy. Mary interacted with fewer people than I did. Even if she shared my story, she was unlikely to get a better reception for what surely sounded like a tall tale. Her age and incessant drinking wouldn't add to her credibility.

"Okay," I relented, sitting across the table from her. It took about five minutes to relay the events of the night at Matt and Melanie's. I left out my suspicions about Jeffrey Trembly. Instinct told me to keep that to myself.

"So, you think the woman you saw in the house was trying to kill herself or a murderer was inside too?" She replaced the glass on the table without bothering to drink from it.

I shook my head. "I have no idea, but since the police say the house has been empty . . . well, the whole thing seems ridiculous."

Mary rubbed her chin, her eyes going softly out of focus. "Very interesting. Certainly, something to consider. Where is the house?"

"Over in Deer Crossing—21 Pine Hill Road."

The way she sat forward in my chair, suddenly perky, I could tell I'd added a dimension to our relationship that would give her reason to drop by frequently. I'd shared a secret. A fact, in her mind, that bonded us. I stifled a sigh. It was going to be impossible to avoid her now. Her unannounced drop-ins, her neediness and, most of all, her loneliness. I envisioned myself in her same lemon-shaped body a few years from now. Once Emmy had grown and moved on. Here I'd sit, wishing, hoping, longing for my life to mean something to someone other than me. Knowing all along that, like Mary now, I was sadly delusional.

# CHAPTER TWELVE

*Wednesday, August 30*

DETERMINED TO ROOT out the truth, I passed 21 Pine Hill Road every evening now. It wasn't lost on me that I was obsessing over Melanie the way I'd once focused on Jane—and Muzzy before her. The difference, of course, was that now I had a reason to be here. I was on the trail of a possible killer.

*Of a possibly dead woman,* said my mother. *Or maybe not.*

I paused in front of Melanie's, squeezing my eyes tight against my mother's voice and the events that had occurred in Deer Crossing. Or had they? Perhaps *nothing* I'd witnessed had happened. After all, I'd seen the injured woman right after passing by Muzzy's house—the woman I suspected of having an affair with my husband. Had something in me snapped, prompting me to see things that weren't there?

I opened my eyes and stared straight ahead. The Pine Hill house was still empty. The grass was cut regularly, but even its well-maintained length couldn't mask the lack of life around the place. Each time I paused in front of the Cape, I'd search the dark windows and empty porch for any sign of life. I hadn't contacted the police with my suspicions about Jeffrey Trembly. They wouldn't believe me now if they hadn't before. Time would only make my story less plausible. How could he be charged with a murder that didn't appear to have been committed?

Still, I couldn't let it go. I fixated on the idea that Jeffrey Trembly had killed the woman. I was frustrated by my inability to prove it but was equally determined to avoid him. I didn't even venture near his house. The latest danger on Woodmint Lane. I stuck to the west side of Deer Crossing, fantasizing about tricking the killer into a confession but knowing full well I had no evidence.

As I stood on Pine Hill that night, exactly one year after my mother's fatal accident, another layer of melancholy drifted onto me like pollen, settling into every crevice and making me itch. My memories of her were complex. She'd been a stickler for always displaying proper manners, which was difficult, at times, for my child's mind to remember, but I'd never known her as a mother myself. I'd secretly harbored the notion that once I had Emmy, everything she'd ever said or done would automatically make sense to me. It hadn't.

My face burning with shame, even in the dark, I recalled my self-mutilating phase at age nine, when I'd cherish every tearful presentation to my undemonstrative mom of skinned knees, painful bruises, and broken bones, the more serious, the better. When my hurts were exceedingly painful, she'd soothe me with gentle words and tender touches, cementing in my mind the idea that she loved me. At least a little.

As a result, I became known as the fearless kid in our suburban neighborhood. The girl who climbed to the tippy-top branches of trees and challenged the older kids to fistfights. The girl I thought I never would have evolved into had my dad still been alive.

I never had to ask Daddy to sing silly songs to me. He just did. In falsetto. And when I placed my tiny bare feet on top of his wide, flat ones, we'd walk as one through the tall, silky summer grass. He'd take giant steps that made my little legs splay so far apart, I'd have fallen into a painful split if not for his strong, solid hands holding mine way above my head. Lifting me up and away from potential pain.

I bit down on my lip, trying to recall his voice as we climbed into the rowboat that last day, but it wouldn't come to me. I blinked rapidly, panicked. Why couldn't I remember his voice? I thought about that light-infused morning; we'd drifted out to the center of the lake. A tremor passed through me; I closed my eyes. Disjointed images bombarded my brain like dodgeballs: my mother's fearful face, the boat's edge tipping precariously, the greenish-gray world of water, around me, in me, pressing its unseen mass down on me. I opened my eyes, still living in the memory, expecting to see hazy daylight; the surge of black evening air filling my pupils made me think fleetingly of blindness. Instantly my mind recalibrated, catapulting me back to the present: 21 Pine Hill Road, bled of its bright red hue in the grainy darkness. This evening was darker than when I'd rushed inside to aid the woman. Now it was later, quieter. My mother's voice now was nothing more than a memory.

*You've killed him.*

I could hear the echo of her words even now, amid the nighttime cacophony. Piercing as the blatant call of crickets in the side yard. Her voice had confused me the other night, in the house's foyer, because it had seemed a palpable presence. I hadn't expected to hear anyone but Melanie. Moaning, or the gargling sound a slashed-open throat must make, trying to take in air and let out a scream.

But that night, I had expected my mother's words. It was an anniversary, after all. A time to not only remember but relive the events of our shared past. And that most vivid phrase, uttered to me by my shocked, desperate mother all those years earlier still clung to me as though attached by Velcro.

*You've killed him.*

I wondered if he blamed me. If my dad was in an alternate universe somewhere, watching. If so, would he judge me as lacking? As guilty?

*How could you?*

The other words. Accusing. Scathing. Not delivered by my mother but by Tim. Why would he say such a thing? I continued staring at the house, trying to puzzle it out. I was concentrating so hard I wasn't even surprised to see him materialize alongside the building. A filmy figure gaining definition as he neared.

*Why did you say that to me, Tim? Why?*

I expected his specter to pause. Think about my question, like he always did. Then answer in that thoughtful, deliberate way of his. But instead, his body startled when he saw me, like Emmy had as a newborn. An involuntary movement.

"Caroline? What are you doing here?" He walked up to me as though I'd invaded his property. "Did you follow me here?"

"What?" I reached out to touch him, reassuring myself he was real.

He jumped back instantly as if I'd menaced him with a cattle prod. "I asked what you are doing here."

I was confused. "I'm always here, I—"

"Have you been drinking?"

"Of course not!"

I looked down at Emmy's carriage, anger filtering through me. Who did he think he was, appearing *here*, of all places? Accusing me of tailing him. Of drunkenness. "I might ask you the same thing. What brings *you* here?"

He stared at me, saying nothing, his jaw rigid. He had a look I recognized. The concentration of calculating weights and measurements . . . or trying to determine if I was lying to him.

"What's wrong with you?" I nearly yelled. "Why are you lurking around an empty house in the dark?"

He squinted at me. "Why are *you* here?"

"I'm taking my nightly walk, Tim. It makes sense that I'm here, but you—"

"I talked to Mary," he interrupted. "I dropped by the house. Needed to pick up those tools in the utility closet but forgot my key. You weren't home, so I went next door to borrow Mary's spare key."

I shook my head as if to realign it, force his words to make sense. "Okay, so you were at the house. You talked to Mary. What does that have to do with you standing here, now?"

"She told me about the woman you saw here." He angled his chin upward, toward the house. "I decided I'd better swing over."

Icy cold rushed from my head to my feet. "I know what you're going to say. I'm seeing things again, just like I did after Emmy was born. Just like—"

"Stop, Caroline. You're putting words in my mouth." He rubbed his forehead, a gesture he made when he was frustrated. "I didn't know what to think, so I just came over here, okay?"

"Trying to think of ways to discredit me?" I challenged. "A way to take away..." I couldn't continue, couldn't even fathom him suing me for custody of Emmy. I swallowed a big lump in my throat.

"No, I had to make sure things were all right over here. I knew the couple who lived in this house. Ray worked with me. I met Annie a couple of times too. A few weeks ago, Ray didn't show up for work. He called in his resignation the next day, but he never came by the office to pick up his things, and never said goodbye to any of us. It was odd."

I blinked. "You know these people? What did you say their names are?"

"Ray and Annie Connolly. Do you know them?"

I shook my head. Matt's name was really Ray. And Melanie was called Annie. "I've never met them. I just saw—"

"Mary told me what you saw."

I clenched my jaw. "You don't believe me."

He held his hands up in front of him as if to ward off an attack from a rabid dog. "It doesn't matter what I think. Mary told me you mentioned the police don't believe you."

"By the time they got to the house it had been hours. Plenty of time for someone to clean up."

The wary expression on Tim's face softened. "Caroline, are you taking care of yourself?"

That got me. I swallowed the emotion bubbling up from my chest, causing my lips to tremble and my eyes to tear up. I got this way on the rare occasions Tim showed me an ounce of compassion. I suddenly remembered the line he'd repeated all the time when we were first dating: *You're my oxygen, Caroline.* How my heart would swell at his words; the sweet, romantic notion of him being unable to even breathe without me near made me feel special, cherished.

But I'd learned not to be fooled. Tim could breathe just fine on his own.

"This isn't about me, Tim. A woman in that house had a terrible accident. She may have even been murdered. You can believe me or not. It doesn't matter to me what you think."

"What I think is that you probably haven't been getting enough sleep. And Tasha called me. Said she dropped by Thursday, and you wouldn't see her. She's worried about you. I am too."

He was turning this into my problem, just like he always did. I locked my eyes with his. "Your concern for my welfare is touching. Had you not told me repeatedly to stay the hell away from you I might even believe you care about me."

"All I know is you shouldn't be involved in this disappearance."

"Aha," I crowed, my pointer finger in the air between us. "You think what's going on here is shady too!"

He shook his head. "I don't know what to think. All I know is you're still my wife, and you shouldn't be mixed up in someone else's relationship."

*Still his wife.* I didn't know how to respond to that. For months he'd been trying to distance himself physically and emotionally from me, and now he was reminding me we were still married. *After* he sent out divorce papers? I stared at him.

He looked down. "I don't know what's going on with this couple. I don't really know her, but he's a good guy."

He didn't sound so good to me. Moving away suddenly, leaving his coworkers in the lurch. Maybe even killing his wife. A thought struck me, prompting me to ask, "How do you know where they live?"

"I've been here before. I dropped him off when his car was in the shop and Annie was away."

"I don't recall you mentioning the Connollys."

"I don't recall having to report to you my every activity," he retorted, his tone dripping acid.

My face pinked, making me glad it was dark. "I only meant—"

"Doesn't matter, Caroline. Just stay away from this place, okay?"

"Why?"

He sighed. "You've got enough going on right now. Do you really need more drama in your life?"

He was right, of course. I had my hands full raising Emmy on my own. I bit my lower lip to keep my accusations to myself. Hurling nasty words at Tim only made him turn away from me.

"I never made it to the house," he said. "I'll swing by next Wednesday after work and take the tools—"

"And Emmy," I finished. He always took Emmy when he swung by.

He grunted. "Do me a favor and stay outside. Your hovering makes me claustrophobic."

"I don't understand why you never want me there, Tim. It's not as though I'm going to force you to take me with you when you leave."

He sighed. "You're doing it again, Caroline."

"I'm not, I'm just saying I can load up Emmy's things for your visit while you—"

"I don't need Emmy's things, you know that."

"Of course." His apartment was fully stocked with his own baby items. God forbid he use anything tainted by my touch. "But I can't just leave her—"

He sighed. Ran a hand over his forehead again. "I don't have the energy for this, Caroline. When you see me pull up front, go for a drive or take one of your weird walks."

"Fine, but—"

"No buts," he cut in sharply. "I can't endure these verbal battles every time we meet."

As I walked home, I thought about Tim's unceasing belligerence toward me and his unexpected appearance on Pine Hill Road. I supposed I understood why he'd lost patience. He'd never been particularly tolerant of my foibles, and when I'd slid into postpartum depression, I'd clearly challenged his limited empathy.

Was that why he'd appeared on Pine Hill Road? Was he concerned I'd run into the couple he'd known and embarrass myself—and him? Or was he, like me, concerned about what had happened to the two of them? Had anything untoward even happened to them?

One thing was certain: now that I had the name of the couple who'd lived at 21 Pine Hill, I planned on digging into Ray and Annie Connolly. Why did they move away so abruptly? Were they running away from something or someone? Or was it more sinister than that? Perhaps it was just Ray on the run, after killing his wife.

It sounded fantastical. After all, people moved out of their houses every day. Why was this any different from anyone else who initiated change in their lives? Because Ray hadn't appeared to tell anyone before leaving? He could have a plausible reason for not doing so. I didn't know his work situation. Maybe he'd had a beef with management and was sticking it to them by leaving suddenly without a forwarding address.

I shook my head. Two things about Pine Hill Road were becoming clear: *something* happened in that house, and every day I discovered new ways in which *I* was connected to it. There was no way I could stay away.

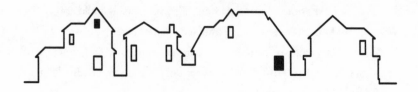

# CHAPTER THIRTEEN

*Thursday, August 31*

I SPENT AN ENTIRE day searching the internet for information on the Connollys, but the name was common, and the results were endless. Dozens of people named Ray Connolly in the US and even more hits for Annie Connolly, with multiple spellings. After hours of slogging through useless biographies of people across the country with the same or similar names, my eyes began to sting. I closed my laptop and went into the kitchen to prepare Emmy's rice cereal and pureed peas.

As I fed the baby her dinner, I decided there had to be a better way to get information on the couple. I could search the Multiple Listing Service for recent home sales, though I didn't think names were mentioned in the reported transactions.

I thought about 21 Pine Hill Road, feeling drawn to it as though both the house and I were magnetized, forever straining toward each other. As the sun set, I changed Emmy's diaper and bundled her into the BABYZEN, adding an extra blanket. It was a surprisingly cool evening for August. One of those rare nippy summer nights that offered a welcomed respite from the ever-present heat.

As I hastened down Pine Hill Road, anticipation building in my chest made my heart pump harder and my limbs move faster. I barely glanced at the houses I passed on my way to the corner of Pine Hill and Lakeside, noticing only the glow emanating from windows, halos of light piercing the gritty darkness. The minutia of the inhabitants' daily lives couldn't possibly compete with the drama I'd witnessed in the custom Cape Cod. I thought again of the woman I'd called Melanie. Annie. I once again pictured her gouged neck and intent, pleading stare. Emotions swirled in my chest, forcing me to stop dead in my tracks and take a deep breath.

There had been fear in her gaze, and desperation I understood only too well as I recalled my vain attempt to get to her. But there had been something else: shocked disbelief. Those large, dark eyes had begged me to validate the truth. She'd been attacked. Taken by surprise.

In the slew of events volleying around me since that night, I'd not been able to isolate that element of her expression, but now that I had, I was sure she did not take her own life. I began walking again, my mind turning over the idea. Of course, I'd never really considered suicide, but now I had what felt like proof.

But what good was that? Nobody believed I saw a woman bleeding out right in front of me. The police refused to acknowledge anyone had even been in the house. I stopped in front of the dark structure on the lonely corner lot, looming against the darker backdrop of trees. I thought about Tim approaching me the last time I'd stood in the same spot. He'd looked at me with hostility, openly suspicious of my motives. If the person who'd known me well and had even once loved me viewed me so warily, was *I* the problem? Had I imagined the horrible scene in the window?

I thought about an incident right after Emmy was born, when I'd been in the throes of full-blown postpartum depression. Harsh voices by unseen people rang in my ears as I looked at Emmy twisting and howling in her bassinet. Voices commanded me to stay away from the possessed infant. I recalled Tim's look of disbelief as he nudged past me and scooped up our baby, rocking her tenderly until she quieted. I'd realized then that I was the possessed one.

Was I reverting to those dark days? Reclaiming old, evil habits? I was diligent about taking my meds each morning, like I always had. The mood stabilizer rebalanced the chemicals in my brain so successfully that I still took it, months later. The meds were the reason I no longer felt the urge to shrink away from my baby, or anyone else. Hell, I even tolerated Mary, and she could try a saint's patience.

And I had proof the doomed woman was real—tangible evidence of her existence in the house. The neon-orange fingernail fragment, now tucked safely into the back of my lingerie drawer. Without that, I couldn't claim she was anything more than a specter, a figment of my unreliable imagination. A reason to get my medication adjusted.

I stared at the house. The dark obscured its charming features, rendering it a flat cardboard cutout of itself. Like a backdrop on a stage, nothing more than an enhancement to the action around it. I struggled to reconcile what I'd seen inside, my feet walking up the driveway as if of their own accord.

Pushing the baby carriage alongside the hedge, I peered in at Emmy sleeping. As a sudden breeze kicked up, I tucked the extra blanket around her and lowered the carriage hood, satisfied that she'd be amply protected from the wind.

I straightened and looked around, hearing only the *shush* of leaves in the breeze. I pushed Emmy along the driveway edge where it butted against the concrete bib of the three-car garage, not knowing what I expected, but if anyone saw me prowling around the property I'd certainly be reported for trespassing. After my recent experience with the cops, I didn't relish the idea of how they'd handle this latest transgression. Pushing the thought from my mind, I halted the carriage at the edge of the driveway where it hemmed the backyard. Circling around it, I peered into the night, black as dirty engine oil, unable to see anything. I stepped forward, Emmy now behind me, and started around the corner of the house—butting instantly against the solid build of a man.

I gasped, shrank back against the baby carriage. A hand materialized in the gloom, a large palm engulfing my mouth. My knees wobbled and my head swam. I was going to faint.

"Shhh," he commanded in a harsh whisper. "We're not supposed to be here."

He suddenly released me. I gulped air, sputtering in relief and confusion: "What the hell—"

"It's okay, it's me," he interrupted. "Keep your voice down."

I had no idea who *me* was, but the voice was vaguely familiar. I squinted through the dark, barely making out the stranger's features. Jeffrey Trembly. I stepped to the side of the carriage, trying to create space between us.

"Look, I don't know what you're doing here, but I—"

"Quiet." He lowered his brows, the shadows turning his eyes into eerie hollows. "Or are you trying to alert the neighbors to our unlawful presence?"

"No," I stage-whispered. "What are you doing here?"

"What are *you* doing here?"

*Oh God, not this again.* I was playing out the same scenario I had the night before but with a different man. A potentially dangerous man—with a key to the empty house. "You know why I'm here. I saw someone bleeding—maybe dying—in this place, but nobody will believe me." I slowly stepped back and pushed the baby carriage farther from him.

"I believe you," he said quietly.

"You do? Why?" I had to keep him talking long enough to think up an escape route.

"Because she's gone," he said, his voice hollow.

That stopped me. "Gone? Who's gone?"

"The woman who lived in this house. Annie Connolly."

I couldn't contain the gasp that escaped me. "You knew her?"

He looked down. "Don't say that—*knew* her. Makes it sound like she really *is* dead. Let's not assume that, okay?"

Thoughts flitted through my mind at breakneck speed, freezing me in place. "Okay." Who was this woman? And what did she mean to Jeffrey Trembly?

He looked up at me. "It's funny, really, that we both showed up here. I was planning on swinging by your place. I just didn't know how to do that without seeming like a stalker."

Fear spiked adrenaline through my bloodstream. "Why would you come by my house? We don't even know each other."

"I know." He ran a hand through his hair. "But you're the only link I have to her now."

"That's not true," I blurted out. "You have a key to her house." *Shouldn't have revealed that.* I took another step back.

"Yes," he admitted quietly. "I know you saw me locking the place last time we were here. I'm sorry I lied to you."

I stared at him. My eyes had adjusted to the dimness, allowing me a full view of the grief spread across his features. "You were in love with her—*are* in love with her."

He nodded, his gaze straying out to the yard beyond me. "We're in love with each other. She was initiating divorce proceedings."

I gnawed the inside of my cheek. No reason to confirm his suspicions, that maybe Ray Connolly hadn't taken kindly to the idea of his wife cheating on him. He could have flown into a rage. Killed his spouse and cleaned up after the act.

No one would be the wiser, right? They'd already sold the house. It was a foolproof plan, except for one little flaw. Me. I'd witnessed what he'd done. I thought about the handsome guy I thought of as Matt, clipping that hedge. If he was indeed Ray Connolly and I could identify him, he might be able to identify me too—even though he'd hardly ever glanced at me. Where did that leave me and Emmy? *In danger.*

"I couldn't ask this of you the other day—I was too distraught—but could you describe the woman you saw in the window?" Jeffrey's voice wobbled. "I have to be sure she's . . ."

I took a deep breath. I suddenly wanted to be anywhere but here, amid this man's grief, exposed to potential danger. Why the hell did I find it necessary to prowl the darkened streets and insert myself into strangers' lives? What was wrong with me?

"I mean," he continued, "if you could just tell me her hair color, her eyes, and build."

I sighed. "Dark. Dark hair. She was slim, hard to say more from the distance between us." I took a deep breath. "She had large, dark eyes. Probably brown. Very . . . expressive."

Jeffrey dropped his head into his hands. "That sounds like her," he said, his voice on the verge of a sob.

"I'm sorry," I whispered. "But lots of brown-haired people have dark eyes and slight builds. It may not be Annie Connolly."

He looked at me, his eyes glistening. "In her house?"

I looked away from his tearful eyes, wishing for once all the misery we were mired in was truly just in my mind. "Look, we need to get out of here."

I felt rather than saw his nod. "Yes, of course." He walked next to me. As we rounded the corner, me pushing the stroller, he looked at it. "The baby doesn't make a peep, does she?"

I snorted. "A new development, for which I'm grateful. As I told you, she's colicky. When she's in the throes of it, it's a nightmare."

"Yeah, my sister was pretty bad, back in the day. But my ex and I didn't have kids, so I never had to deal with it." He straightened. "Good thing you have her bundled up. It's cold out here."

"Yeah," I said, looking at him. "Emmy's still a bit unpredictable though. It's best if you don't just drop by my house, okay?"

"I won't," he said, his voice suddenly as cold as the breezy air. "You understand, though, I can't just let this go. If I promise not to darken your doorstep, could you give me your cell number?"

I looked down at Emmy's carriage, realizing there were all kinds of dangers I needed to protect her from. "I don't think that's a good idea. Besides, what good will it do? I told the police everything I saw, and they made it clear they will not be pursuing the matter." I backed away from him. "I know you live on Woodmint. If I can think of any way to help you, I'll stop by your place."

"Okay." His voice was bleak.

As I pushed Emmy ahead of me, I glanced over my shoulder and noticed the way he stood in the dark, looking so alone. I felt a sudden pang in my throat. I knew that feeling of loss. I'd been abandoned by the one I loved too.

But the experience had taught me something valuable: I had to cherish the one still in my life. Keep her protected at all costs. If that meant turning my back on someone I might have been able to help, so be it. I was a parent first. I had priorities to attend to.

# CHAPTER FOURTEEN

*Wednesday evening, September 6*

I SAT IN MY parked Honda in the center of the driveway as Tim gathered up his tools and Emmy and loaded his car. I gnashed my teeth, recalling how he never took my baby carriage, car seat, or even diaper bag with him when he scooped up our daughter. He had no trouble denying me the little things I'd needed, like a few self-esteem-enhancing cosmetics (too expensive) or vitamins I'd read helped diminish depression (unproven and costly), but apparently hadn't hesitated to purchase duplicates of the baby gear to avoid any lingering trace of me on them. I resented his attitude, but it was preferable to the idea of the mystery girlfriend snuggling my baby. I couldn't even think about that.

I reread the text he'd sent me just a half hour earlier. He'd be on vacation for the next week, so he was depositing my living-expense money into my account early.

I'd gladly give the cash back if he wouldn't keep my precious girl for nine whole days. I didn't know how I'd survive without her. We'd never been apart that long. I desperately hoped the girlfriend wouldn't join them on the trip.

After Tim pulled away without so much as a wave in my direction, I got out of the Honda and walked back into the little ranch where we'd once—briefly—been happy. I felt the emptiness like a gut punch as I stepped into the living room. As if to ensure Emmy was really gone, I beelined to her room and stood in the doorway staring into her empty crib. My eyes stung and my breath caught in my suddenly dry throat.

I'd need meds to get through the next week. That much was clear. Not only the usual ones, but those special pills that helped me cope in a crisis. The Percocet in the bathroom medicine cabinet.

"Half a pill for you and a half for me," I mumbled, recalling again how my mother shared everything that way, from vitamins to breath mints. I looked in the mirror over the sink. My hair appeared to have the same shade and twiggy disarray of a sparrow's nest I'd once spied on our front porch. I'd marveled at the jumble of odds and ends comprising the nest: sticks, grass, laundry lint, even a cigarette butt. I pulled a downy catkin from my bangs and looked at the greasy dark roots on my scalp. When was the last time I'd showered? I couldn't remember. Maybe Tim was right to deny me costly cosmetics. Would I even remember to use them?

I tossed and turned for hours that night, feeling a migraine coming on. I doubled up on the pills and returned to Emmy's room, snatching the blanket from her crib. Nestling it against my face as I climbed back into bed, I inhaled deeply and finally drifted into an uneasy sleep with the smell of my child surrounding me.

# CHAPTER FIFTEEN

*Thursday, September 7*

A N ALARMING CLANGING startled me awake.

Bleary-eyed and nauseated, I squinted at my bedside clock, surprised to see it was past ten in the morning. I sat up, looking around, trying to identify the source of the agitating noise. My cell phone, on the dresser.

I didn't even recall leaving it there. I lunged for the device, imagining Tim on the other end telling me all sorts of horrors that had beset our daughter: sudden fever, an accident . . .

"Hello?"

"Mrs. Case?"

I hesitated, unable to speak. *Is it the hospital calling? Telling me Emmy is in the ER?* My heart pounded, making it hard to breathe.

"Mrs. Case?"

"Yeees," I wheezed. It was hard to talk around the heartbeat pulsing in my throat.

"This is June from Dr. Ellison's office. You're past due for the six-month checkup."

I closed my eyes; my racing heart slowed even as acid reflux torched my esophagus, making my throat sting and my eyes water. "I'm sorry," I said, exhaling.

"The doctor wanted me to reach out and discuss why you've missed your last few visits. He's concerned."

"Tell him not to be, June. We're fine. Just very busy. Business has stepped up and I have a lot to juggle." My face reddened with the lie. Even before Tim left, I'd had a hard time meeting my work deadlines. Medi-Source, the medical billing company that had employed me for more than five years, temporarily suspended my assignments while I battled post-natal depression.

"Would you like to schedule a new appointment?" June asked in a mono-tone voice. "We now work on Saturdays." She didn't sound happy about that.

"Not just yet. We're fine. Healthy. No need for a checkup."

"The doctor thinks—"

"Thanks so much." I hung up on her, taking a deep breath to settle my surging stomach. Even the suggestion of Emmy in danger made my insides heave. And the meds I was swallowing like sugary treats didn't help.

Fumbling through the bathroom cabinet, I grabbed a bottle of Mylanta and drank from it like a baby hungrily devouring the contents of a nursing bottle. I sat on the closed lid of the toilet, breathing hard as I waited for the liquid to coat my windpipe and stomach. What I needed was a distraction. I shuffled to my desk in the corner of my bedroom and fired up my laptop.

As if on their own, my fingers typed in Jeffrey Trembly's name and the local newspaper he worked for. News features with his byline flashed across the screen.

I scrolled through dozens of stories from across the region. Everything from town board meetings to ribbon-cutting ceremonies, local fundraisers, and human-interest stories.

I thought about the expression on Jeffrey's face when he'd admitted his feelings for the mysterious Annie Connolly. Raw. Devastated. Would Tim look that way if I were gone? If he realized, too late, all he'd had and lost?

I rolled my eyes and called the newspaper. When an efficient-sounding woman's voice answered, I asked for Jeffrey Trembly.

⌘⌘⌘⌘⌘

I SAT ACROSS the table from Jeffrey in a local diner, Rex's Roadkill, off Route 22. I leaned my forearms on the tabletop and, noting how they stuck to the Formica surface, decided the place was aptly named. I was glad I was only having coffee. Still, meeting in a shabby eatery with dated decor was preferable to being alone in my kitchen with a man owning a key to a missing woman's house—no matter how innocuous he made the possession seem.

"I can't stop thinking about Annie," Jeffrey said, staring into his coffee cup. "I've tried to track her down, but it's as if she and that asshole she calls a husband have spontaneously combusted." He looked up. "I'm sorry, that was probably inappropriate."

I smiled. "I won't report you." God knew I spent half my days having thoughts many would deem inappropriate. "But catch me up here. When you say you've tried to track her down, what do you mean?"

"I started with the obvious: social media, online searching, and trying to follow her moves through her iPhone." He rubbed his chin, looking thoughtful. "Turned up nothing."

"And you went through her mailbox?" My favorite means of discovery.

"Obviously. I work for a newspaper, Caroline. I checked for mail about five minutes after I realized she was missing." He looked at me pointedly and my face reddened, but he seemed not to notice. He began tapping the beige Formica between our coffee cups, his long fingers strumming an agitated rhythm against the tacky surface. "I also hit up the local hospitals, coroners, and even jails. After that big zero, I accessed the NamUs system."

"What's that?"

"It's a national database. Records of missing and unidentified persons."

That surprised me but I wasn't sure why. It made sense that some agency or other would set up a digital clearinghouse for missing and potentially missing people. "Can anyone use it?"

He nodded, his gaze flicking around the diner before landing on me. "The problem is, it's no help if a disappeared person doesn't want to be found."

"So, you think maybe her husband took off with her to—"

"Or she decided to leave, either with or without him." Jeffrey's expression was bleak. "She could have felt threatened." He looked down at his suddenly stilled fingers. "Or maybe she was just done with the bullshit between us, the sneaking around. The lying."

"But you said she filed for divorce."

"That's what she told me. I can't verify she did."

I didn't say anything for a few seconds. The silence stretched between us, but the ambient restaurant noises—clashing metal utensils, other diners' murmurs, and softly filtered rock music from unseen speakers—rounded the sharp edges of our uncomfortable conversation. Finally, I asked, "Did Ray Connolly know what Annie was, um, up to . . . with you?"

He slowly raised his eyes until they met mine. "I think so. But she told me he cheated on her first. That they had sort of an open arrangement." His expression was as combative as a sullen teenager expecting a lecture on morality.

I sat back, raising my hands, palms out. "No judgment from me. I just want to know what happened—if she was the woman I saw. Do you have a photo of her?"

He reached into his pocket, pulled out his cell phone, and swept his forefinger across its surface. "I took a selfie of us a few months back. Annie was angry; made me promise I'd delete it, but I didn't." He held the phone up for me to see. "I had to have just one shot of us together . . ."

I leaned forward and squinted at the blurry shot of Jeffrey with an unsmiling dark-haired woman, her eyes half closed. It was clear he'd caught her by surprise. A portion of what looked like fingers bordered the bottom of the photo as if she'd raised her hand to block his attempt to capture their images.

"It's not the best picture of her," he added, sounding apologetic. "Annie thought it was dangerous to have tangible evidence of our . . . well, she didn't want to give Ray ammunition."

I stared at the image. If the couple had an open marriage, Ray wouldn't be angered by her actions, would he? "She has the same hair color and build as the woman I saw, but I don't know. I can't really see her eyes."

"So, you can't tell for certain that it was Annie you saw that night?" Jeffrey's voice sounded so hopeful that I found myself wanting to encourage him.

"From this photo, I can't tell if this is the woman in the window."

He sat back and sighed. "That's reassuring, I guess."

Something occurred to me. I leaned forward and propped my elbows on the sticky tabletop. "Did you ever meet Ray Connolly?"

He shook his head. "No, just saw him in the yard once."

I thought of the only man I'd ever seen on the property, the handsome sandy-haired man, Matt.

"What does Ray look like?"

Jeffrey shrugged. "A muscular guy. Annie said he was a bodybuilder, but I don't know what kind of a living he could make doing that." His voice held a note of disdain, as though increasing muscle mass through strenuous exercise was innately evil.

I rubbed my brow, recalling Tim telling me he'd worked with Ray Connolly. Should I reveal that to Jeffrey? Something told me to keep that fact to myself.

"Do you recall anything else? His hair color? Outstanding features?"

"He was wearing a ball cap the evening I saw him leaving their house."

"Hmm," I said. Of course, a man would zero in on another guy's muscle mass, while a woman noticed his overall attractiveness. I recalled Matt's trim, taut muscles. Was he muscular enough to be considered a bodybuilder?

I had no idea. I thought of something else: Matt and Melanie dancing in the living room at 21 Pine Hill Road. "Tell me, does Annie like to dance?"

"Dance?" Jeffrey's nose scrunched, making his eyes squint. When I nodded, he said, "I don't know. I never danced with her, but that means nothing. I have two left feet."

I decided Jeffrey didn't need the visual of Annie dancing with another man, husband or otherwise.

His gray eyes met mine. Tilting his head with what appeared to be curiosity, he asked, "What's your story?"

The question jolted me out of my musing. I shook my head. "You sound just like a reporter."

He smiled but said nothing more as he looked at my face. Waiting for an answer.

"I'm just a mom, recently separated from her husband,"

"Do you have any other family?"

"No, I have no siblings, my dad's been gone for years, and my mom died recently," I said, feeling suddenly shy. People so seldom asked me about my life that I was unused to revealing anything about myself. I quickly turned the focus back on him. "Are you happy in Deer Crossing? Do you live alone?"

He nodded absently. "I do. I've been divorced for just over a year. I like Deer Crossing okay, but my ex never wanted a house. She was a free spirit. Conformity didn't appeal to her. She'd take temporary jobs, save up cash, and travel. I was enchanted by her, at first. The age-old story is I thought I could settle her down, lure her into complacency with a house. My folks left me a small inheritance. I used it to buy the worst house in the nicest neighborhood, thinking I could improve it over the years. But I knew almost from the day we moved in that it wasn't going to work. Not only do I have zero ability to renovate, but my wife had even less desire to be tied to a property. Her mantra was weekends were for partying, not fixing a leaky roof. We only shared the house for nine months before she took off." He ran a hand through his nearly black hair. "I was going to sell the place. Then I met Annie at a homeowners' association meeting." He shook his head. "When I think of all the crazy twists and turns that my life has taken in the two years since I moved to this town, well . . . guess I don't make the best choices when it comes to women."

"I understand," I said. "I didn't make a sound choice either. After Tim and I had Emmy, well, our relationship changed. He moved out." I sighed. "Mine is probably a story old as time too."

"Doesn't matter. The story is new to you." His gray eyes dodged away from me. He was already losing interest in my life.

The server came with our check and Jeffrey quickly reached into his jeans pocket and pulled out a leather wallet.

"Let me pay for mine," I said, reaching for my purse handle, slung over the back of my chair.

"My treat," he said.

"But I—"

He smiled, handing the server a ten-dollar bill. "Caroline, it's a cup of coffee."

≈≈≈≈≈

I DIDN'T WANT to go back to my lonely house. I spent the next few hours driving around the area, eventually pulling into a shopping mall three towns over and hitting up the food court for dinner. Something nibbled at the back of my mind as I ate a greasy chicken sandwich. Thinking about my diner meeting with Jeffrey, it hit me: *he* had been the man I'd seen Melanie—Annie—embracing in her front foyer. Had I not been so distraught when we'd first met, I'd have likely made that connection much sooner. Lost in thought, I headed to the children's section of the department store in the center of the mall, buying Emmy a ruffled pink romper on clearance. Did knowing this about Jeffrey and Annie change anything? I supposed it did. It validated his claim of loving the mysterious woman, which probably shot my theory of him as her killer to pieces.

Toting my tiny bag, I wandered aimlessly in and out of boutique shops upstairs and on the ground floor until I noticed the sun setting beyond the oversized plate-glass window at the mall's entrance. Where had the day gone?

When I swung my car into my driveway, I cursed myself for not thinking to leave on a single light in the house. I looked at the darkened windows of my tiny ranch. Without Emmy inside, there seemed no reason for me to be there either.

I leaned back in my seat, the nape of my neck against the headrest, staring vacantly at my house. That's when I saw it: a flicker of light in the living room. I blinked, sat bolt upright. Trained my gaze on the front bay window. Sure enough, a light glimmered there for the span of a few heartbeats before going out. A giant firefly of incandescence, brief and illusionary.

Panic spiked in my chest like a syringe of adrenaline had been shot directly into my heart. Someone was sneaking around in my house.

# CHAPTER SIXTEEN

*Thursday night, September 7*

C ALL THE POLICE!

I rummaged through my handbag for my cell phone and extracted it, tapping the surface to turn it on. Out of battery! I couldn't remember the last time I'd charged it. I threw the thing on the front seat, swearing.

Should I drive to the police station and report a break-in? By the time I did that, the intruder would surely be gone. I thought of the skeptical expressions on the cops' faces when we'd discussed my witnessing the bleeding woman on Pine Hill. If the intruder escaped, would the police arrest me for submitting another "false" report?

Unsure what to do, I backed out of the driveway and parked down the street, scanning the area for parked cars that looked unfamiliar. There were none. Before I had time to talk myself out of it, I got out of the Honda, locked it, and walked back to my house. I crept along my neighbor's side of his overgrown privet hedge, for once thankful old man Schumer was such a lazy landscaper. I peeked through a hole in the hedge where he'd overzeal-ously sprayed poison ivy in a rare burst of yard tidying this past spring. As my pupils adjusted to the lack of light, I was able to see my back deck per-fectly, including the steel screen door leading into my kitchen.

The door squeaked open, and a shadow appeared on the deck. I clamped my mouth shut, breathing unsteadily. The form shuffled across the deck, appearing to be quite short. A neighborhood kid out for kicks or quick cash? It was only when the shadowy figure started down the steps that I realized who it was. The slow, jerky way she moved told me all I needed to know. Why on earth had Mary Whitton broken into my home?

As I struggled to emerge from the hedge, my blouse sleeve snagging on a twig, Mary made her way to the far side of my property and crossed through the few scraggly trees between our houses. By the time I crossed my yard and stepped into hers, she was opening her basement door.

Why was she entering her house through the basement?

Did she want to avoid being seen emerging from my house? Even in the dark, our neighbors could notice her when the headlights of passing cars spotlighted her presence on my front stoop. I heard a click that told me she'd locked her door behind her.

I rushed to the door and banged on it with all my might.

With another click her face appeared in the opening, looking innocent and confused. "Caroline, what are you doing here?"

"Don't play innocent, Mary. How dare you sneak around in my house when I'm not there." My face flushed and my breath came in uneven spurts.

"Please come in," she said, opening the door wider. "You're always wel-come in my home."

"You *are not* always welcome in mine," I said, stepping past her and into the dank basement, the smell of mildew heavy in the air. I looked around the area, a moment's hesitation making me pause, taking in the bare bulb dangling from one of the room's ceiling joists. I'd never been in Mary's cellar. Glancing around, it had the creepy closed-in vibe of all unfinished basements but looked otherwise innocuous. It was empty except for broken furniture piled in one corner, a stack of empty liquor boxes in another, and a half dozen translucent plastic trash bags stuffed with empty bottles and cans on the concrete floor between them. The walls were covered in a cheap pressed-wood rendition of paneling, the kind people thought looked good in the 1970s.

"I don't see why you're so upset, Caroline. I was looking out for your interest."

"My interest? My interest is to *not* have you or anyone else in my house when I'm not home!"

"Exactly. I noticed lights flickering in your place, but I'd seen you drive away earlier, and Tim told me he was on vacation this week. So, I went over there to find out who was in your house."

I stared at her through the dim light cast by the low-wattage bulb above us, the thick, moldy air making my nose clog. I fought the urge to sneeze. "Are you for real?"

She smiled her crooked-toothed grin. "Last time I checked."

"But I don't . . . why would . . ."

She shrugged. "I figured I had nothing to lose. I'm just a visitor, right? So, I knocked on your front . . ."

"Door?"

"Yes, yes." She nodded. "Nobody answered, but I peeked through the sidelight window and saw a shadow cross through the living room and into your kitchen."

My jaw dropped open. "What did this . . . this *shadow* look like?"

Mary shrugged. "Don't know, just a shadow, but a big one. A man's shadow, I think."

"A man?" I tried to think of what man, other than Tim, would want to be in my house. If I hadn't been with Jeffrey, I'd have suspected him, but of course I could rule that out. After our coffee, he'd gone back on shift. He'd likely assumed I'd gone straight home after our chat. My mind hovered over the idea of Jane's mystery man breaking in. After all, Jane knew my address. Ice shot up my spine.

"I was planning on telling you all of this in the morning, Caroline, but you didn't—"

"Wait," I interrupted. "How did you get in my house?"

"You gave me that spare key, but I didn't need it. The front door was unlocked."

"I never leave the house open like that," I said, wondering if locking the door was one of the many things I'd forgotten lately. Another dangerous omission in my life.

"I don't know what to tell you, Caroline." Mary sighed. "When I arrived it was unlocked, but there's nobody in there now. I checked. And I locked up behind me."

❧❧❧❧❧

AS I CROSSED back into my yard, looking constantly over my shoulder, I thought about the idea of a man in my house. I hadn't met many men in the short time I'd lived here. The postal carrier, UPS driver, and Tasha's husband, Nelson. That wasn't much of a list. Jane's mysterious neighbor, her husband, Rod, and Muzzy's husband, Johnny, were on the periphery of my life, but I'd never actually met any of them.

I entered my house through my back door, realizing as I slid the bolt and chain on it that it had probably been easier for Mary to use her basement door at night rather than pick her way through the tree roots and random stones in her side yard en route to her front entrance. I turned on every light in the house, and checked each window and door to ensure they were all intact and locked. I closed every blind and looked around the house. Things seemed different, altered. The hallway table's drawer was open. Had I merely neglected to close it? The angle of the cushions on the sofa and upholstered chair in the living room made them appear to have been pulled off and hastily replaced. I picked up a throw pillow from the floor. It was entirely possible I was responsible for the disarray. I'd been so disinterested in housekeeping lately.

Or was something more sinister at play? Had someone been searching for something to steal?

Doubtful. I owned nothing of monetary value besides my wedding rings, which were still on my left ring finger. Our electronics were modest. I glanced from the thirty-two-inch TV screen on the living-room console table to the portable stereo next to it. I was certain our other small TV and my cheap work laptop were still in my bedroom. I walked toward that room. One of two things must have happened: Mary, in a booze-infused state had imagined an intruder and used her key to enter my place—and lied to me about using it—or I'd left my doors open, inviting the world into my private spaces. An invitation someone had readily accepted.

Crossing into my bedroom, I yawned, suddenly exhausted. Looking at my desk to ensure my laptop was still there, I stripped off my clothes and opened the closet, noticing multicolored materials puddled on the floor. Had the items slipped from hangers, or had I dropped them there? I snapped my head to the right, sliding my gaze along my dresser and lingerie chest. Were the drawers open a little? I crossed the room in two strides and pulled open the top dresser drawer. The sweaters looked pawed through, didn't they? Or was that how they always looked? I opened the next drawer and plucked out a pair of pajamas. Was I imagining things, or did the sleepwear appear more rumpled than usual? I pulled on the flannel bottoms, buttoned up the top, a tremor running through me.

Items in every drawer appeared slightly dislodged, but nothing was missing. Ditto for Emmy's dresser drawers. Had Mary arrived before the intruder had a chance to take anything? Or had it been Mary herself looking for something? Perhaps her alcohol stream had run dry, and she was hoping to find a bottle in my kitchen. When she didn't, she may have suspected me of hiding it elsewhere. That would explain the state of my drawers.

Fatigue battled raw nerves. I needed rest but knew that only a pill would help me sleep on this unsettling night. I took one, washed it down with water, and tumbled into bed, waiting for the chemicals to usher in much-needed rest.

# CHAPTER SEVENTEEN

*Friday morning, September 8*

A s soon as I woke, I knew something was wrong, but my sleep-fogged brain wasn't supplying details. I sat up gingerly, like an overworked athlete knowing every muscle would be sore. The break-in and my conversation with Mary amid the moldy stench of her allergy-inducing basement finally trickled in.

As if recalling my neighbor had magically conjured her, Mary's wafer-thin voice floated through the vaporous morning air. I looked through the gravelly light, my gaze settling on the bedroom doorway. I half expected to see her walk through it.

"Caroline? Car-o-line?"

I got out of bed, blinking, following her voice like a sleepwalker obeying the dictates of a fever dream. I shuffled along the hallway and halted in my tiny foyer, spying Mary through the sidelight window on my front porch. She was tapping lightly on the glass, which made my jaw clench.

"What is it now, Mary?"

I yanked open the door, scratching the top of my snarled head with my free hand, a whimper escaping me when my fingers tangled in the knots of hair at the crown.

"Oh, dolly, I couldn't sleep knowing you were upset with me." She smiled, not looking even slightly remorseful.

I looked beyond her, to the gray light of early morning coating my across-the-street neighbor's white ranch. "What time is it?"

"Just after six."

I took a cleansing breath. I *couldn't* start my day yelling at an old lady. "If you'd waited until eight to wake me, you'd have had two extra hours to contemplate my anger. That would have really ratcheted up the drama."

"That's just it, I want to avoid extra tension," she said, her eyes going wide. My sarcasm was lost on her, but I had the sneaky suspicion it was by design. "I'll make you a cup of coffee while you shower, then we can head into town," she added. "I need to buy some things and I could use the company. I think you could too. I think it's a good . . ."

Without bothering to wait for her to finish her sentence, I turned and walked into my bathroom, hearing her shut my front door. I twisted the spigot on the shower and wiped the crust from an eye while I waited for the water to heat up. I had no energy to argue.

I stayed in the steamy bathroom for a long time, enjoying the invigorating stream of hot water on my skin and dreading an upcoming morning with Mary. When I finally emerged, wrapped in a ragged-edged towel, she was at the bathroom door with a steaming mug. I didn't know what to make of it. Nobody made coffee for me. Tim claimed to not even know how to boil water, and, growing up, my mother continually warned me of the dangers of regular caffeine ingestion. I winced thinking about what she'd make of my routine pill-popping as I took the mug from Mary.

Still annoyed with my neighbor, I shuffled to my bedroom, closed the door behind me, leaving Mary standing in my hallway. I took a sip and gagged, spitting it back into the cup. I'd not been expecting Mary's *strong coffee.*

When I finally made it to my kitchen, swathed in my detergent-blue bathrobe, Mary was shoving bread slices into my toaster. I dumped the contents of my mug and poured myself a new cup, eyeing my neighbor with a look that challenged her to protest.

She looked from me to the toaster. "The stores open at ten. I know it's not yet seven, but we need to be prepared for traffic. And with your driving challenges..."

"I don't think we'll be battling the Upstate New York hordes in this heat," I said, hearing my nasty attitude spilling into my tone. "It's not like we're lining up for the Travers Stakes in Saratoga. And my driving is just fine, thank you."

"You'd be surprised how bustling downtown gets on a Friday morning," she said, the toast popping up as if accentuating her words.

*I'm sure you'd be surprised too*, I thought. I seldom saw Mary before 10:00 a.m. It took her a while to come around after each night of hard drinking.

By ten minutes before ten, after enduring a morning viewing of *The Price is Right* with Mary—her nonstop coaching of the contestants as if she were getting paid to do it (and they could actually hear her)—I had my neighbor securely ensconced in my front passenger seat, safety belt in place. I backed out of my driveway carefully, recalling how she'd disparaged my skills behind the wheel the last time I'd driven her. After she told me she let her husband die.

I still had no idea how true that story was, just as I wasn't sure of exactly why Mary had been in my house the night before. Had she really been tailing someone?

"Why would a person break into my house, Mary?"

"Only one reason," she said instantly, as if she'd been expecting my question. "Whoever killed the woman you saw in that neighborhood wants to discover what you know about it."

I reflexively hit my brake, in the middle of the street, shooting us both forward. Again. "You think?"

"Good God, girl, remind me not to speak when you're driving," Mary griped, rubbing the skin between her clavicle and the seat belt. "You need all your faculties to focus on the task at hand."

"I'm sorry, I really am."

"Hmph," she said, refusing to say another word until we hit the main street in the downtown area, where she directed me to a parking spot.

After we stepped onto the sidewalk in front of a florist shop, she finally said, "I think it's true, you know. Someone was in your house looking for tangible evidence linking you to that bleeding woman you saw. Did you take anything from her house that night?"

I looked at Mary as if seeing her for the first time. "You sound like a cop. Do you have a background in law enforcement?" I realized as I asked that I had no idea what Mary had done for a living in the years before we'd met.

"No, but I was an insurance adjuster back in the seventies. The stories I could tell you about people. The bonkers stuff folks do to cash in on claims."

"Really?" Thinking about the nail fragment, I hoped I'd distracted Mary from her question. I hadn't taken anything from the Pine Hill house *that night*.

"You bet, especially down by the city, where we lived before moving to the Capital District. Everyone's nuts down there. Too many people, living too close together. Makes you stir crazy."

We dipped into a card store. It wasn't crowded yet; the woman behind the counter merely nodded when we walked in, a look on her face like she'd just had an unexpected sip of Mary's specialty coffee. I urged my neighbor out the door after one pass around the card racks and followed her into a pharmacy across the street. I perused the shelves while Mary stood in line for her prescriptions. As I neared the front of the store, I heard the two teen girls behind the counter gossiping, but an oversized endcap filled with beachballs prevented me from seeing them.

"Did you notice those two women who just came in . . .?" A hushed voice. I looked around, seeing only one other patron, a man at the other end of the aisle. "One of them's crazy."

"Which one?" asked the second voice.

"The one who . . ." The first voice lowered. I stepped closer to the front counter, as far as I could get without being seen. "She's a murderer. Can't believe she's allowed to walk around in public after what she's done."

Thoughts swirled in my head, making me slightly dizzy. So, Mary had been truthful when she'd told me about her part in her husband's death. And it appeared to be common knowledge among the townsfolk. But that didn't give them the right to gossip about her. How dare they disparage someone without knowing the whole story. Mary had issues, of course she did, but who among us was perfect? If she wasn't behind bars, it was because someone wiser than two wretched teens had decided she didn't belong there.

I stepped past the ball-laden endcap, into the space in front of the counter, and stared down the girls, who stopped talking as soon as they saw me.

"Well, that about does it for me," came Mary's voice from behind me. "Got my scripts filled, so we can . . ."

"Go," I finished, noticing the girls each looking at the floor, as if something engrossing was happening at their feet. "There's clearly no reason to stay."

As we walked back to my car in the escalating morning heat, Mary asked what I'd meant by my odd remark in the pharmacy.

I sighed. "Nothing, really. I overheard gossiping. God, I'm glad I'm new here. There seems to be nothing quite like having a history in a small town."

"True," Mary agreed. "People in a town like this remember everything. They'll dredge up history just to have current events to talk about." She cackled, finding her own joke amusing.

She babbled on as we crossed the blanched sidewalk and slid into the scorching interior of my Honda, not needing, it seemed, any contribution from me, but we drove home in silence. Mary must have thought I was concentrating on improving my driving while I was really seething. The shopkeepers had been unfriendly and downright rude. I was glad I got all my prescriptions refilled through the mail. I rounded the bend and pulled onto our street, slowing when I realized someone else was standing on my doorstep. I rolled my eyes. Tasha Turner was back.

# CHAPTER EIGHTEEN

*Friday noon, September 8*

TASHA TOOK A sip of the steaming mint tea I grudgingly made her, looking dainty and comfortable in the oppressive heat of my kitchen. I reached across the counter and turned on a tabletop fan, wondering how she could, quite literally, keep her cool in the tinderbox that was my house. And even drink a hot beverage!

"Why are you here on a Friday?" I asked, crossing to my fridge and pulling out a pitcher of water. I realized I didn't sound particularly friendly.

She placed the mug gently on the table, as though not wanting to risk a drop of it spilling. "I'm out in the field today. My client, Olivia, lives a couple miles from here, so I figured I'd swing by you during my lunch hour."

"That was nice of you," I said. And it was. Tasha and I might have had different ideas about parenting, but she consistently carved out time to see me. Whatever her hectic, child-filled schedule would allow.

"I was worried," she said. "Haven't seen much of you, and I suspect you've been a little down."

I rubbed the tension out of the back of my neck. *Honey, you don't know the half of it.* I should've told her about the bleeding woman I saw in the window; shared my fear about having my house broken into. But I didn't open my mouth. I couldn't.

Tasha worked in the same office complex as Tim. They were friendly. If the break-in got back to him, he'd have a reason to take Emmy away. My heart turned over, doing weird flips in my chest. If I didn't have my child, I'd be completely alone.

"I know our last chat ended badly," she began. Her voice was tentative, as though hoping I'd interrupt. "I'm sorry about that. I know a lot is going on with you. I realize you're still adjusting to your new life. There's no telling how long that will take."

I looked at her, at her smooth, shapely legs crossed casually beneath her slim skirt. She sat so confidently at my tiny kitchen table, her skin glowing, and her dark curls shining amid the shabby surroundings of my life.

"I don't want to sound crass, Tasha, but you can't relate. Your marriage is successful. You're not handling everything on your own—"

"Of course, you're right," she interrupted, reaching out to me with one hand. "I never meant to come off sounding like a know-it-all or unsympathetic. I'm trying to understand what you're going through."

"Thank you," I said tightly, realizing she couldn't possibly understand my life. I wasn't even sure why she'd want to. "Let's talk about something happier, shall we? We never talk about you. Are your twins enjoying the pool this summer?"

Her face softened. "Yes, and I'm more relaxed this year, now that they both know how to swim. Drowning is one of the top causes of death for toddlers and infants . . ." She sat back suddenly, her face taking on a grayish hue.

"What's wrong?" I took a step toward her. "Are you okay?"

She took a quick sip of tea, looking down. As she replaced the cup on the tabletop, she smiled up at me. "I'm fine."

"You don't look fine."

"It's just, you know, upsetting to think of children drowning."

"Yes." I turned away, my body trembling at the thought. Opening the glass cabinet, I added, "I hear about drownings all the time on the news. Parents need to be more attentive." I plucked a glass from the lowest shelf and poured the water into it, a strange tightness in my chest.

I turned back to Tasha. She met my gaze as if afraid to make the connection. "I suppose they do, but I'm sorry to bring it up, given your history—"

"It's okay," I said. "My dad drowned a long time ago. As I've told you before, I don't even remember it very well. It's sad, but it's in my past." I couldn't believe we had circled back to this topic *again.* Even when we weren't trying to talk about my past, there it was.

"Okay," she said, pausing, as if she wanted to say more but was unsure of how to go about it.

"I mean, I would have been one of those drowned kids, if my dad hadn't saved me that day."

"You remember that? Everett saving you?"

I shook my head. "No, as I've said before, my mom told me what happened."

"That's right."

When Tasha said no more, just looked at me as if expecting some sort of explanation, I blinked. "I was six years old. I don't recall much of anything from that time."

"Of course, you wouldn't remember," she said hastily. "The event happened more than twenty years ago, right?"

"Yeah," I said, suddenly hearing Emmy crying. I startled, took a few steps forward before I remembered she was with Tim. Strange how clear her voice had sounded. I pressed my fingers to my temples, feeling a sharp stabbing pain. Probably the remnant of the bump on my head.

"Are you all right?" asked Tasha.

"I don't think so," I said, massaging my temples with my fingertips. "I feel a migraine coming on."

"I have some ibuprofen in my bag—"

"That won't work," I interrupted. "I have prescription meds. Nothing else can touch the pain."

"Oh, no," she said, standing up. "I'd better let you get your medicine. Time is of the essence with migraines, I know. I get them too." She plucked her Louis Vuitton from its spot on the floor next to the kitchen chair. "I'll be on my way. Get some meds and some rest."

I followed her to my front door and watched her let herself out. Before she closed the door behind her, she swung back and looked at me as though she had something vital to say. Her gaze locked with mine and her expression was serious when she said, "Feel better, Caroline."

"Thanks." I mumbled, feeling as if that hadn't been what she'd wanted to say at all.

# CHAPTER NINETEEN

*Friday night, September 8*

I'D LOST THE afternoon sleeping off the migraine. No big deal. I felt better now and was happy for the dark, which usually smoothed out the daytime distractions. Or hid them. Whatever.

I got into my workout gear and running shoes and shoved the mace cannister into my sweatpants pocket. I made my way to Emmy's room for the stroller folded up and stashed in her closet when I suddenly stopped, hovering in her doorway.

I looked around the empty nursery, cursing myself for forgetting about my baby girl, even for a second. I sighed. My evening walk would feel strange without her. I calculated the days until Emmy would be returned to me: five.

I knew where I was headed: 21 Pine Hill Road. Not that I expected to see anyone there, least of all Annie Connolly. What Jeffrey had said about his and Annie's deceit struck me as I power walked across Route 55 toward Deer Crossing. Maybe Annie had left him, the neighborhood, and her husband because she was indeed tired of sneaking around and lying. He'd seemed genuinely heartbroken by her absence—and by the way she'd left.

If she'd left. Maybe she'd tried to get out but had never made it past her bedroom door. Perhaps my first suspicion of Jeffrey had been correct. He'd been obsessed with a married woman. When she told him she wouldn't run off with him he'd decided she wouldn't go anywhere. After all, he had a key to her place. But if he'd gotten rid of her, he wouldn't be hanging around her empty house, would he?

I walked up Pine Hill Road. Without the baby carriage, I felt nimble and quick, darting around the perimeters of properties, a mere specter in the wispy haze of the streetlights. This night, I wasn't a mother soothing her baby with a late-night stroll. I was a woman on a mission. I nearly laughed. What was this mission, exactly?

One of truth, I told myself as I crept through the absent light. I had to discover something—anything—about the former inhabitants of house number twenty-one. My own happiness could depend on it. Not only did I need to prove to myself that I wasn't a psycho, making up violent scenarios to please a brain spiraling into the darkest depths of human nature, but I also sensed that solving the mystery, like my intended reunion with Muzzy, would prove to Tim I wasn't crazy. I was, in fact, just the opposite of that. And not only sane but also caring and compassionate. The qualities any man desired in a wife.

Soft voices filtered into my ears, and I looked around. My eyes scanned the wide length of blacktop stretching endlessly in front of me until, far ahead, maybe the length of a football field, I saw figures walking through the particulate grayness. I couldn't tell whether they were approaching or walking away from me.

Instinct kicked in as I stepped behind a massive sycamore tree at the edge of a small, wooded lot, hoping the tree's girth would adequately conceal me. The voices grew louder and headed my way. Why not just pass them at a jog? I could be a health-conscious runner, keeping up with my fitness regimen. Recalling the mail carrier's motto, I could joke as I passed them: *Neither snow nor rain nor heat nor gloom of night keeps me from my appointed rounds.*

Except that I probably couldn't even run a quarter of a mile while keeping my breathing even. My heaving gasps for air would surely blow my cover. The voices became louder, snippets of conversation fanning out.

"He'll be home soon," said a clearly female voice. "I've got to get back before he does."

I was certain I knew that voice.

"I tell you, I don't know how things got . . ." garbled a deeper voice. I tilted my head toward his unfamiliar intonation. "There's no possible way she could know, or that she'd take off."

"I hope not," said the woman, her voice undeniable. Jane Brockton. Were the two heading back from their latest tryst? They seemed to claim the entire neighborhood as their own personal playground.

The voices paused right in front of me. I bit my lip to keep my mouth closed, concentrated on breathing through my nose, and glanced around the tree, narrowing my eyes in the murk. Sure enough, Jane's enviable figure was less than five feet in front of me, in profile, barely visible in the dark, and facing a tall, well-built man in a backward ball cap, T-shirt, and loose gym shorts. His back was to me. My pulse immediately increased. I popped back behind the tree, terrified Jane would see me.

"This is getting serious," said Jane.

"I know," he agreed.

"And now, with people asking—"

"I know," he repeated, an urgency to his voice that bordered on hysteria.

"We can't panic," warned Jane.

"Right. Give me some time to figure this out."

"Let's hope you can," she said. "Meanwhile, we can't be seen together. If we're caught in someone's headlights, there'll be hell to pay—worse for you than me. Go around the block and circle back. I'll cut through the Johnsons' yard."

"Sure thing."

I peeked around the tree trunk in time to see Jane up on tiptoes giving the man a quick peck before they parted. Once she ducked behind a fence in the yard opposite me, I slipped out of my hiding spot and looked down the road, my pounding pulse centered in my temples, threatening to reignite the migraine. As his wavering form dissolved into the deepening shadows, I turned around and ran in the opposite direction. Jane Brockton's indiscretions were none of my concern. Hadn't I bought myself enough trouble, becoming emotionally involved with the happenings on Pine Hill Road?

Still, it irked me that she could so callously cheat on poor Rod. And based on what I overheard the mystery man say in the street just now—"no way she could know"—he too was cheating on someone.

I thought, yet again, of my own marriage, of Tim's treachery, as I retraced my route along Deer Crossing's wide, empty streets and stood in front of the silent, dark house on the corner of Pine Hill and Lakeside. I heard nothing. No sounds of nocturnal animals wandering the property, no call of an owl or howls of coyotes in the distant hills. Not even crickets. The area seemed completely devoid of life.

I stared at the Cape, which appeared two-dimensional in the dark, a paper doll's house. My gaze inevitably strayed to the upper left window where I'd seen the woman. Like all the other windows strung across the house's façade, it was dark, as if mocking me. A passive-aggressive posture; telling me I was crazy. No woman had ever fallen against the window while bleeding out. Except that she had. I knew she had.

I walked home slowly, feeling unaccountably depressed. Tim wanted out of our marriage; Jane Brockton was cheating on her husband with her neighbor; the couple at 21 Pine Hill had out-and-out disappeared as a mysterious woman in that house—perhaps Annie Connolly, but maybe not— was harmed, probably dead. Why didn't anybody stay together anymore? And why were the partings so callous?

I paused at my mailbox and absently thrust my hand inside, my fingers closing around a bundle of papers. Closing the lid, I looked at the pile. On the top was a thick envelope. The return address was a local law firm.

I ripped open the letter, my breath catching, reading the words *divorce petition* under a scrap of streetlight filtering around me. Tim warned the papers were coming. Why hadn't I believed him?

There was something wrong with the way I thought. I knew that. But damn it, I still couldn't sign on the dotted line without knowing I'd tried everything I could to win him back. Our family's future depended on it.

# CHAPTER TWENTY

*Saturday morning, September 9*

I CALLED TIM. If he wanted the damned divorce papers signed, he'd have to agree to a meetup. His line rang and rang, and the mailbox in his cell was full. Rising panic battled a flare of anger, fighting for dominance in my chest.

*What a nerve!* He needed to update me on Emmy, yet even while tending *our* child he went out of his way to avoid me. I started to text him, then remembered the cell service at the cheap motel in Sandy Hook, where we'd stayed that summer and where he was probably vacationing without me, was horrible. Tim had chosen what had to be the only place at the Jersey Shore that didn't offer complimentary Wi-Fi service. He was so damned cheap. I paced around my coffee table, the forward motion soothing me even though I wasn't going anywhere. Seemed appropriate for my state of mind. I sighed and walked faster.

What if Tim had sprung for a nicer place at the beach? One with internet service. What if he was ignoring me? Maybe he was holed up in some swanky place with his girlfriend and *my* daughter, strategizing. Thinking of a way to take Emmy away from me for good. My chest felt heavy and tight.

*You're fixating!*

I halted, looking around the living room, my eyes bouncing from the worn sofa to the hated knotty pine walls. My mother's voice again, just like in the foyer at 21 Pine Hill Road. And every other damned place I went. I covered my ears with my palms. I didn't want to think of her voice or what had happened at the Pine Hill house. But I couldn't obsess over Tim either.

Suddenly everything was too bright, too loud. The sun streaming through the window was blinding, and voices chattered all around me, but just low enough that I couldn't make out what they were saying. Conspiring tones, close but far away, like indistinguishable sounds from a television in the next room.

I stumbled to the bathroom, my feet feeling like blocks, making normal walking difficult. I leaned heavily on the tiled vanity top and swung open the medicine cabinet, peering in at the prescription bottles lined up like soldiers standing at attention, ready for inspection. I slammed the mirrored door shut.

*A half a pill for you and a half for me.*

"Yes, Mom, I remember," I yelled to the still air around me. "I remember everything."

But that wasn't true, was it? I hadn't been able to recall what had happened that day on the lake when my father drowned. Why not? Why couldn't I unlock that mystery so deeply wedged in my brain?

I stared at my eyes in the mirror. These supposed "windows to the soul" were blank. My brows hunched protectively above, as if colluding with them to hide any trace of memory.

I pulled open the cabinet door again and reached for the Xanax bottle. My hands shaking, I pressed down on the lid and twisted. The top loosened, fell into the sink, two pills following it like ducklings trailing their mother. My hand swooped down like a hawk, scooping up those baby ducks and devouring them. I turned the faucet handle and bent over until my face was below the running stream, drinking greedily, water flowing over chin and cheeks.

I straightened, water dripping onto the front of my T-shirt like blood drops from an open wound. I thought again of the woman in the window.

*No, no, no.*

I walked to my bedroom, my thighs nearly too heavy to lift, as though my ankles were encased in leg cuffs. I dropped onto my bed, realizing I shouldn't have taken two pills. I seldom took two at once, right? I wasn't sure. I lay back and closed my eyes, praying that the slideshow of faces—Tim's, Jeffrey's, my mother's, Jane's, Mary's, the mystery woman's—would go away; that the monotonous stream of whispers would cease. But they drifted through my mind, even as sleep filtered in, troubled ghosts prodding and pressing. Lodging in the folds of my brain like tumors.

When I awoke, shaking my head to dislodge the unwanted visitors, they vanished. All except the woman. Why was she haunting me? There was nothing I could do to help her. Any effort I made seemed as futile as telling Rod Brockton about his cheating wife. The police didn't believe me. And why should they? I had no proof a woman had been harmed in the Pine Hill house. No proof at all.

*That's not true.*

I stood and crossed the room to my dresser, thankful my legs felt better, lighter. How long had I slept? I opened my top drawer and felt around, fingers sliding through a stream of silky panties. I paused. I usually folded my underthings. When had I abandoned that practice? Uneasy, I shoved my hand to the back of the drawer, until the tips of my pointer and middle fingers pressed against the contours of the box. I snatched it up and removed the top in one continuous movement, peering at the cotton batting inside.

Empty.

I pushed aside the plush cotton square, expecting to see the neon-orange nail tip tucked underneath, blazing like a bright coin against its cardboard canvas, but nothing was inside the small white box balanced in my left palm.

A cold sensation plunged through me like an ice bucket tipped over my head. The hairs on my suddenly shaky arms stood up. Staring into the empty box, I knew what that intruder had been looking for.

But how could anyone know I had the nail fragment? I hadn't told a soul I'd found it, and nobody had seen me take it—not even Jeffrey, who hadn't been in the room with me when I'd extracted it from between the floorboards. I'd been alone. Or had I?

I closed my eyes, picturing the layout of the master bedroom, the expanse of wood flooring, and the louvered closets against the far wall. I'd recalled my playful concealment as a child in our similar closet, watching my dad stomp exaggeratedly around the space in front of the closet, knowing I could see his feet through the downward-facing slats.

My stomach dropped. Anyone crouched in the closet could have seen me slide onto the floor, pick up the fake nail, and hold it in front of my eyes, studying it.

My mouth prickled. I dropped the box, turned, and ran to the bathroom, where I promptly vomited into the sink.

I straightened, my eyes catching the look on my face in the vanity mirror. There was fear spread across my features, and a message that pulsated through my brain.

*You're not safe!*

# CHAPTER TWENTY-ONE

*Saturday evening, September 9*

F OR THE FIRST time, I was glad Emmy was with Tim. I'd have to tell him about the nail fragment, the evidence that linked me to a murderer—and how could it not be a murder? Someone had gone to such lengths . . . breaking into my home to snatch the one item that could link us both to a crime. I hoped that once Tim heard my story, he'd let me crash on his couch for a while. He could be a real prick about things, but he'd have to see the danger of his family being so exposed.

If the criminal decided I knew too much, he could come back and kill me. I had to get away, but who could I stay with? Tim wasn't back for another four days. Staying with Tasha would be awkward. I'd only met her husband Nelson once, when Tim and I had bumped into the couple months earlier, at a pub on one of the rare nights Tim had taken me out.

Jeffrey had plenty of room in his house, but I hardly knew him. And what I *did* know—namely his possession of a key to a missing woman's house—made me wary. There was Muzzy, but she wouldn't even speak to me, or leave her house when I lingered in front of it. Much as I hated to admit it, that friendship was over. I sighed. That left Mary. She'd jump at the chance to have someone else around. A person to enjoy her strong coffee each morning, a drinking buddy throughout the day. I rubbed my chin, trying to think of anyone else who'd be willing to give me temporary shelter but couldn't produce a soul. I'd met so few locals in the short time I'd lived here. There were hotels in town, but that was costly. Tim would be livid at the expense, no matter the circumstances. Out of options, I pulled out a duffel bag and began filling it with clothes from my closet and drawers. Mary was getting a temporary roommate.

As I stuffed socks and underwear into the corners of the bag, I felt a hot stirring in my chest. *I* was the one who should be angry—with Tim and his cavalier attitude. Leaving us alone in the house without an alarm system. Too expensive, he'd said. And I resented how casual he was with Emmy when I wasn't around. He never texted to let me know how she was doing. Babies weren't toys. They had very specific needs, especially when colic was an issue. I was mindful of that—and of his all-important connection with Emmy. Apparently, he couldn't care less about my needs. I pressed down, compacting the clothes so I could get the bag zipped.

When I showed up on Mary's doorstep, she smiled.

"I knew you'd end up here." She looked at the oversized sack I still had balanced over my shoulder. "Please, drop your bag. Make yourself comfortable."

"How could you know I'd come here with a packed bag?" I asked, surprise raising my voice a notch. I swerved the duffle off my shoulder and let it slither to the floor.

"Who'd stay in a house with intruders?" she asked. "C'mon, I've got a room ready for you."

This was the same woman who walked into my empty house *after* she'd noticed a man's shadow inside. Mary was either incredibly brave or quite reckless. Or drunk. That was it. Liquid courage had likely propelled the old woman across the threshold of my house, trailing a possible murderer.

I stepped inside the small bedroom and looked from the tiny dresser to the full-sized mattress laid out on a platform, with no headboard or footboard. A floor lamp stood on the other side of the bed, and a ladderback chair resided next to the closet. Bare bones. I looked at Mary and smiled. I could do no frills.

"Thank you, Mary, you are a good neighbor." I couldn't bring myself to call her a good *friend*. "I won't stay more than four days. Tim will be back from vacation after that and, with any luck, he'll let me stay with him until we figure out the whole mess."

Mary tilted her head slightly, a ghost of a smile on her thin, chapped lips. She said nothing.

# CHAPTER TWENTY-TWO

*Saturday night, September 9*

I F MARY THOUGHT she'd have a comrade to tip cups with all evening, she was sorely mistaken. After I settled my meager belongings into her rickety dresser, I headed to the food store for provisions. She protested, saying she was fully stocked with groceries, but I insisted. Hadn't my mother instilled in me proper manners? It was bad enough she'd be disappointed with me for showing up uninvited on Mary's doorstep, duffel in hand. She'd never countenance me not pitching in for my own care and feeding.

In my car, arms stretched across the steering wheel, I took a moment to inhale deeply and hold my breath in my lungs before expelling it. After the food run, I'd park on the side street opposite and diagonal to my house, turn off the headlights, and watch my place. If anyone showed up, I'd call the cops to report the break-in.

But first, the food. I swung onto the main road that eventually swerved left, one lane splitting off into the parking lot of Great Grocer Food Store and Bee-Clean, an environmentally friendly dry-cleaning business.

Staring at the oversized line drawing of a bumblebee on the sign over the cleaners, I stepped out of my car and snagged a stray shopping cart abandoned in the center of a parking space. Once inside Great Grocer, I pushed through the wide aisles, selecting whatever items seemed appropriate for a last-minute guest to offer her host. I grabbed eggs, a carton of orange juice, a head of iceberg lettuce, comforted by the smooth glide of the cart's wheels guiding my steps. If I kept my gaze locked far ahead of me, I could pretend I was pushing Emmy through the store.

I paused at an endcap separating the produce section from the cereal aisle, watching a man bent over a display of onions. As if sensing my stare, he glanced up and our eyes met. Jeffrey. I raised my hand to wave as a look of alarm crossed his face. My hand stalled in midair when he looked down, plucked a white onion out of the bin in front of him, and turned in the opposite direction.

What was that about? Didn't he recognize me?

Abandoning my cart, I took off after him, watching his retreating back as he hurried toward the checkout section at the front of the store.

"Jeffrey," I huffed, slightly out of breath as I stepped beside him at a self-check carousel.

"Hello," he said, not looking at me.

"Hey, is something wrong?"

"No, not at all," he said, finally glancing my way, but his voice was coldly polite. "I'm just in a hurry."

"Oh, okay." I watched him bag his groceries. "Have you heard anything about Annie—"

"No, nothing." His gaze locked with mine and in his eyes was a warning. He reached into his back pocket and pulled out the same worn brown leather wallet he'd extracted at the diner. "Look, Caroline, I don't want to be rude, but I'm late for an appointment." He inserted his card into the slot on the machine in front of him.

Looking around, I wondered if someone was following him, but noticed nobody suspicious, just other shoppers ringing up their purchases all around us. No one even glanced our way. Something was wrong, of course it was. Jeffrey had been cordial enough before. What had changed? Had he found Annie?

Had she asked him not to tell anyone her whereabouts? Or, worse, had someone else gotten to him . . . and threatened him to stay away from her? Possibilities dashed through my mind even as Jeffrey scooped up his grocery bag and said goodbye.

I followed him, veering off to my own car, but keeping his retreating back in my line of vision. I started up my car as I watched him get into his. As he backed out of his parking spot, I was already rumbling along the pavement a few dozen yards behind.

Did he know I was following him? At the roundabout heading south, I let a red Kia in front of me so I could tail my quarry less conspicuously. No need to appear like the stalker I was.

He drove for miles, bypassing the turnoff for Deer Crossing, dodging onto unfamiliar streets in nearby neighborhoods. Eventually, he pulled into a convenience-store lot, quickly got out of his car, and rushed inside. I pulled up at the other end of the lot and parked, unsure what to do.

Maybe I'd buy a cup of coffee, casually approach Jeffrey and continue our conversation in the store. I grabbed my purse off the passenger seat and began rooting around, looking for loose change in the bottom of the bag, so engrossed in the task I didn't notice the man standing outside the driver's door. When he tapped my window I flinched and shot a look to my left, at Jeffrey's red face. I rolled down the window.

"What are you doing?" he demanded.

"Following you."

"Why?" He sighed the way Tim always did.

"You left our discussion so open-ended. I'm afraid I couldn't let it go."

"I didn't leave anything open-ended, Caroline. I don't know what you saw in the window at Pine Hill Road, and I have no idea where Annie is, okay?"

"But you're acting so—"

"I'm not acting," he cut in sharply. "I'm just busy. I have a life. And I can't have you trailing me all over town."

I looked into his wary eyes. "What aren't you telling me?"

He looked down and lowered his voice. "If I discover where Annie is, I'll let you know."

"Promise?" I lowered my chin, trying to get back into his line of vision.

"I promise," he said, stepping back. Not making eye contact.

He'd lied to me. Why? I watched Jeffrey fold himself into his car. After he backed out and peeled away, I sat in my driver's seat, thinking.

BY THE TIME I parked in the street opposite my house and turned off my headlights, all vestiges of twilight had vanished. I leaned forward and looked up through my windshield at the black canvas of sky above. The moonless night rendered the neighborhood a mass of blank space, a desolate landscape devoid of familiar shapes until my eyes adjusted to the lack of light. Slowly, the outline of my house materialized, like a cosmic magic trick. The front stoop's harsh lines, and the stark cut of the asphalt driveway appeared more barren in the dusky hollows of the night.

The darkness wasn't comforting. It merely cloaked the things I couldn't face—like my uncertain presence in the flimsy, unsafe little ranch, unsure of what Tim's next move would be. A choking pressure lodged in my throat as disjointed images banged into each other inside my brain, retreating as new ones edged them out: Tim's angry face, mouth moving, eyes narrowed; the empty box dropping from my hand; Jeffrey's retreating back; two teens gossiping behind the drugstore counter, their faces pressed up close, noses nearly touching; my mother's mouth puckered in disapproval; the woman at the window, her hands grasping her throat. Her eyes pleading.

"Whatcha doing?" A voice shot through the shadows and into my left ear, making me jump. I whipped my chin left, seeing Mary bent close to the driver's-side window, an inane smile across her lips.

"Jesus, Mary, you scared the shit out of me!" My breath spooled out as she laughed. "It's not funny."

"Sorry, Caroline. I saw your car's headlamps just as the last of the lights in the neighborhood were blinking off. It's extremely late, you know. I was getting worried about you."

"Why would you be worried about me?" I snapped. "I'm a grown woman."

Mary straightened, unperturbed, it seemed, by my tone. "You left for the food store nearly four hours ago."

"That's ridiculous," I said, but as I looked around me, I realized Mary was right. Why hadn't I equated the complete lack of light in the neighborhood with the late hour? "What time is it?"

"Nearly midnight."

"No, how can it be . . ." I let my voice trail. How could I have let the night slip by without even noticing? How long had I been parked in front of the convenience store?

"No need to worry, Caroline. Nobody showed up at your place tonight. I was watching."

Were my motives that transparent? Apparently.

"Come on now, we'll get you inside." Mary opened the driver's-side door.

My pulse skittered. I was losing control. "No, I'll pull into your driveway."

She frowned, looking doubtful under the yellow glow trailing from the Honda's overhead light.

I closed the door and started up the car. The headlights flashed into the shadows, illuminating my house in spotlight fashion. Without another glance at Mary, I shifted the car into drive, fighting a sudden, inexplicable urge to take off. Drive down the street and out of the neighborhood. I inhaled deeply, thought of Emmy, and turned the car toward Mary's driveway.

When I was finally sitting in her tiny kitchen, she asked about the groceries I'd gone out for. I stared at her.

Jennifer Sadera

"Oh geez, I didn't buy any."

"No worries." She smiled, looking oddly pleased. "How about a night-cap?"

I nodded. Booze would keep my mind from circling back to Jeffrey's glare and Tim's apathy.

I stared at Mary's deeply scratched tabletop, but a flash of memory obscured it as I pictured my mother's gray eyes, only inches away from mine.

*You'll get along in life if you just act nice.*

That was true, wasn't it? For her, I'd always tried, but I was not nice—hadn't been for years, if ever. But not being nice wasn't the same as being bad, right? Niceness was about nothing more than manners. Not as vital as kindness, which reflected genuine caring for others. I realized that now. Why hadn't my mother ever stressed the distinction? I shook my head. Seemed I couldn't stop thinking about Mother these days. Probably because of the dismal anniversary of her passing.

"This is just what you need," Mary said, placing a rocks glass over the table gouges, dispelling my mom's face. Bronze liquid rested in the bottom half of the glass.

My fingers encircled the cup. There was a reason Jeffrey had acted strangely, and it was connected to the terrified woman in the window. Had to be. I raised the glass and drained its contents. The sudden bitter warmth stung a trail down my throat, closing it up as if in reaction to an allergen. I coughed violently.

"You were supposed to sip that," said Mary, uselessly smacking my back.

"May I have another?" I whispered, my voice hoarse. I needed sleep. Once I was rested, I'd be able to dissect Jeffrey's apparent obfuscation. With rest would come the clarity and energy I'd need to shine the brightest light into the darkest corners of this thing and discover what had happened to the woman at 21 Pine Hill Road.

# CHAPTER TWENTY-THREE

*Sunday morning, September 10*

THE SUNLIGHT STREAMING between the slats in Mary's blinds woke me. I blinked, noticing the stripes of light stretched across her dresser. Such contrast to the dark shadow I'd seen in the corner of the room every time I'd awoken from my fitful sleep, dreaming of a woman bleeding all over me. I shivered, looking down at the thin blanket hiding my body. I tried to sit up, my head suddenly pounding and my arms unable to move. What had Mary put in the drinks last night?

I rested my head back against the hard, flat pillow and stared at the ceiling, blinking the blurriness out of my eyes. Keeping my body relaxed, I tried to raise my hands but couldn't. My heart jumped upward, and pain sliced through my head. What the . . .

"Mary!"

I listened for noise in the house beyond the closed bedroom door. Did I hear shuffling?

"Mary!" Panic elevated my voice. "Mary! Are you here?"

The door cracked open and Mary's round, wrinkled face appeared, a sliver of sunlight making her glasses glint. "Good morning, Caroline."

Her cheerfulness grated. "I can barely move. Is this your doing?"

"I'm afraid it's yours, dear."

The door creaked open slowly. Mary bounced a hip against it and the door swung wide, revealing her lemon shape, dressed in her usual navy polyester slacks and oatmeal sweater, holding a food tray in front of her.

"Why would you do such a thing?"

"What thing, dear?"

"You tell me! Why can't I move?"

She sighed, shaking her head slightly. "You had a tough night, Caroline. I'm trying to help you like you asked me to, but I'm worried about you."

I thought of the shadow I'd seen every time I stirred in my sleep. A creepy sentinel in the corner of the room, in the ladderback chair next to the closet. "Did you . . . did you *watch* me sleep?" I sputtered.

"I certainly did. How else could I ensure you'd be safe?" She smiled brightly. "I've brought you eggs for breakfast. Don't they smell delicious?"

"I'm leaving, Mary. Help me up."

Mary placed the tray on the dresser. "I couldn't allow that, not yet."

"And why not?" I demanded.

"Because you haven't had breakfast."

She shuffled to the corner of the room and pulled the chair toward the bed.

"I'm not hungry." My voice sounded petulant, obstinate as a rebellious child.

"You know the first meal of the day is the most important," she said, her voice bright as she looked down at me. "And you desperately need some food in you."

"I am perfectly fine."

"I know you think you are, but trust me, I know better."

I laughed despite my rage. An ancient lush who'd caused her husband's death was going to care for *me*. I'd have a better chance of surviving with

Dr. Kevorkian as my nursemaid. "Why would you say I'm not well? I'm perfectly healthy."

"If you're of sound mind, you'll tell me where you were all last night." She grabbed the tray and settled in the chair she'd pulled alongside the bed.

I stared at her. She had me there. Where *had* I been after my argument with Jeffrey at the convenience store and before Mary confronted me in my car? I blinked. I couldn't think of that right now. I had to get this maniac to admit she'd drugged me. "How am I supposed to feed myself when I'm like this?" I looked down at my still body.

"I'll feed you, dear," she said, digging a fork into the pile of scrambled eggs with gusto.

"Mary, you need to help me up and out of here. You know you do. It's against the law to force someone to stay in your house."

"Not if that person is a danger to herself."

"Mary, I'm warning you . . ."

She smirked and held the forkful of eggs up to my mouth. "Please try to understand that I'm feeding you only because it's what's best for you. Now let's try one little mouthful." She pressed the tines against my lips.

I jutted my chin, sending the eggs flying off the fork.

"Honestly, Caroline, look what you've done." She dropped the empty fork back onto the plate and lifted the tray as she stood. "Now you'll have to sit there, breakfast on top of you rather than in you." She sighed and left the room.

Was this really happening? Had my ditzy octogenarian neighbor managed to imprison me in her spare bedroom?

*Think, Caroline.*

I wondered what could have prompted Mary to take such drastic action against me. What could she gain by alienating me? I was her only acquaintance. No one else was ever over here. Why would she . . .

And then I understood. Mary was alone but didn't want to be. She wanted to glom on to me, ensure I was alone too.

Focusing all attention on her.

She was conspiring with Tim. Helping him prove the case against me, so I'd have no choice but to hand over custody of Emmy. Then Mary would have me all to herself.

I bit my lip. No, that couldn't be right. Tim wouldn't condone such behavior. As much as I blamed him for ruining our family, I knew he wouldn't stoop to this level to gain custody. He wouldn't have to. He made all the money. If he wanted to snatch Emmy away, he could, on the grounds that he could support her better than I.

But Mary, poor, twisted Mary, didn't realize this. She clearly figured if she could keep me here until Tim came back with Emmy, she'd convince him I was a danger to myself and unfit to care for an infant.

"Mary," I called through the closed door. "Please help me. I need coffee." It might sober me up and flush the toxins out of my system.

I waited for her to respond. She didn't. Feeling my face flush, I shouted, "You can't keep me trapped in here forever."

The bedroom door opened, and her face popped into view. "Rest assured, dear. I have no intention of doing that. As soon as you're better, you're free to go." The door slammed shut.

I let my head drop back to the mattress, searching my mind for any clue, the tiniest hint of where I had gone after I'd sat in my car at the convenience store last night. I closed my eyes, trying to visualize the scene, but only blackness gathered into the space. Why couldn't I remember?

My chest tightened, a dozen invisible hands clenching and squeezing the life out of me. I breathed through the irregular heartbeats, recalling the days just after Emmy was born, in the grips of a silent assassin who had sights set on me. I'd been able to overcome the evil last time. Ironically, it had been the darkness that had helped. The long walks in soothing blankness that had nudged me back to the light of my life. Would I be so lucky this time? I had to get myself back into the world and figure things out. It was only in the freedom of wide-open spaces I'd feel confident enough to look inside myself. And make sense of what I was to see.

# CHAPTER TWENTY-FOUR

*Sunday afternoon, September 10*

D ESPITE MY AGITATION, I dozed off. When I awoke, the room was glazed in the honeyed light of late afternoon. I'd clearly slept for hours. I stared at the ceiling, letting my thoughts gel. What had Mary told me her former occupation was? Insurance adjustor. She wouldn't have dispensed meds in that profession, would she? No, of course not. Practitioners on the other side of insurance claims did that. Still, my head throbbed with the aftereffect of more than a mere hangover. She *had* to have slipped something into my drink last night.

Could her intentions have been benign? Maybe she saw herself as a vigilante benefactor, determined to save me from myself. It was a hard visual, especially since the only way I wanted to see Mary now was dead.

My mind recoiled. That wasn't true. I just needed to get away from my demented neighbor. I lifted my arms, grateful for the wobbly mobility in them. I sat up gingerly and was just stretching when Mary walked into the room, her eyes widening, her mouth forming a little circle.

She raised her hands up as if they could halt me. "Caroline, you can't leave! You must understand—"

"I understand nothing, Mary, just get out of my way. If you don't, I'll knock you over."

After I started up my car and swung it dramatically out of Mary's driveway, I realized I had no idea where I was going. I hit the gas, suddenly not caring about the destination. I flew past my house without a glance at it.

My head pounded as I pulled into a small playground and staggered out of my car. I rubbed my temples and tried to contemplate my next move. Where was I going to sleep that night? I couldn't risk staying in my place, not with a prowler hanging around. Although I no longer believed Mary's story. She had a key to my house. She must have stolen the nail fragment. But how would she know about it? Had I mentioned it and then forgotten what I'd let slip? It was possible. I'd been forgetting so much lately.

Why would Mary want that tiny sliver of neon-orange nail? As leverage? To ensure I'd do whatever she asked of me or risk her reporting that I'd harmed someone at 21 Pine Hill Road? She wasn't that manipulative, that evil . . . was she? She was an old lady. But she was lonely. Could persistent solitude prompt such desperate actions?

I shook my head, trying to sort my thoughts. First things first. I had to change my front door lock. I'd never done it. I should call a locksmith. That wouldn't be cheap. I could hear Tim griping about that as clearly as if he were standing beside me. *Do you know how much locksmiths charge by the hour, Caroline?*

Still, I needed to be safe, and I was running out of options. Tim wasn't around to change out the lock for me. I pinched the bridge of my nose between my thumb and pointer, concentrating, and it came to me: Tim wasn't home. I could stay at his place. I reached into the car, pulled out my handbag, and rooted around for my cell phone. I'd call him and explain things. Desperate measures, and all that. He'd have to help me. Tell me where he'd hidden his spare apartment key. I'd bargain with him, promise him I'd leave before he returned if he'd allow me to stay for a few nights.

Knowing he'd ignore me if I called, I texted him a desperate message, holding my breath while I waited for it to be delivered. When it went through, I exhaled deeply and settled on a park bench to wait for his reply.

I sat for an hour, watching children scurrying from swings to slide to monkey bars as their parents stood in exclusive little circles, chatting. I suddenly yearned for the day Emmy would be big enough to play at this park, part of the tribe of kids making the rounds on the playground equipment while I made friends with other parents in the neighborhood. I imagined exchanging adorable stories with my peers about the things our progeny said and did. I smiled but felt sad as I watched them. I missed Emmy so much that I had to force the thought of her from my mind.

I massaged my forehead. I still couldn't believe Mary had drugged me. I could report her to the police.

I thought about the cop's threat when he stood in my living room a few weeks earlier. His warning I'd be charged the next time I reported an unprovable crime.

Then I thought about the bleeding woman in the window, and the empty box that had held her neon nail chip, and my heart sped up so fast it made breathing difficult.

It had all started with the mystery woman. It had to end with her too. I sensed if I couldn't figure out exactly what had happened at 21 Pine Hill Road, not only would she disappear from the world unnoticed, but so would my delicate grasp on my own life.

I DROVE TO the Dunkin' Donuts on the other side of the playground and settled at a table near a window, drinking coffee and eating an egg-white veggie wrap, waiting for Tim to respond. I'd left another text message on his cell phone just before leaving the darkening park. If he didn't text me back soon, I'd search his porch for a key. If I couldn't find one, I'd go to a hotel, Tim's carefully guarded budget be damned.

After my final gulp, I'd still not heard from Tim. I tossed the empty cup and my food wrapper in the trash bin beside the door and headed back to my car.

The drive to Tim's apartment was an easy one. I was soon ascending the hill leading to his complex entrance, aware of how cross he'd be if he knew what I was doing, but I was desperate. Still, I didn't want to park in a spot near his building in case it was one reserved for residents. Tim would holler at me endlessly for such a transgression. I pulled in beside an over-sized pickup truck at the very end of the parking area and grabbed my hand-bag. I had no overnight bag because the only clothes I'd packed at home the day before were now residing in Mary's ratty little guest dresser. I'd have to sleep in my clothes or find an old T-shirt of Tim's to bed down in. I hoped he had a spare toothbrush.

I locked the Honda and started walking toward his building, hearing voices filtering through the parking lot. One sounded like Tim's. That wasn't possible, was it? Unless he'd abandoned his vacation a few days early. Relief hit me. Tim was home and able to help me, but then I frowned . . . he'd have Wi-Fi service in that case. So why wouldn't he have texted back? Because that was Tim. Ignoring me was what he did. The blood rushed to my face as I veered toward the far end of the lot, but the urgency in the un-seen voices made me pause.

I scanned the dark, just making out human forms between two parked cars. I ducked behind a Jeep and walked around the far side of it, my ears attuned to the conversation, still too low to isolate individual words. I crept from the Jeep to a big white van just behind the pair, careful to keep my head down. The voices grew louder. It occurred to me I spent a lot of time spying on others. A habit that brought me only misery. Still, I had to know who was talking.

The voices became discernable. Tim's—definitely his—saying, "It's such a pleasure to just be normal, to be with . . . well, you know what I mean."

"Yes, it's always . . ." murmured another voice, the timbre and cadence of a woman, but I couldn't hear the rest. I scooted to the other side of the van's back bumper and peered out. Tim stood facing a woman. They were both in profile. I stared at them, waiting for my eyes to adjust to the darkness, my heart thudding.

Tim ran a hand through his hair and sighed. "I'm not sure what to do. This is getting so serious, so fast."

"Hey, it's okay. It's all going to work out." Another familiar voice. She reached out and placed her hands on his upper arms. "We're going to figure this out. Together."

"Do you think we can?"

"I know we can," she said softly, wrapping her arms around him in a tight hug. "It's not impossible, you know. No problem is so big that it can't be overcome."

My stomach clenched, acid flowing up my windpipe. Standing in the dark with her arms around my husband was Tasha Turner, the only friend I had left in this town.

She must be the woman Tim was seeing. I backed away, head pounding brutally, as I scurried behind cars until eventually reaching my own. I perched on the back bumper, hands on my knees, gulping air.

After a minute or two, a car engine started. I peered around my car as it passed, ensuring that it was, indeed, Tasha's gray Audi. The same car parked in my driveway every Thursday afternoon. My eyes stung.

Was this why Tasha showed up at my house each week? To monitor me and report her findings to Tim? Was she helping him build the case against me that would give him sole custody of our daughter? Perhaps she was planning a new life with Tim, and a new-and-improved blended family. My throat went dry.

I lost track of time as I balanced on the Honda's back bumper. Tears flowed unchecked down my cheeks and dripped onto my lap. How had everything managed to spiral out of control? I tried to swallow the sobs, wondering how I was going to navigate my life without a husband or friends. I had nothing left. No one.

That wasn't true. I had Emmy.

I turned toward Tim's building. I'd go inside and get her right now. I needed her, and she needed me.

*Really, Caroline? And where will you bring her?* My mother's voice.

I wanted to scream at my mother to shut up, but what she said was true. I couldn't take Emmy now. I was temporarily homeless. I got back in my car and sat in the dark, staring out the window at Tim's big, ugly building, my mind numb. Suddenly I realized I didn't care about Tim and his damned budget. I'd find a hotel. The pricier, the better. I shifted the car into drive.

I pulled in front of the Regency on Main and got out of the car, handing the valet my keys, ignoring his question about luggage. I casually drifted to the front desk as though I'd stayed in the luxurious hotel many times. In one smooth move I pulled out the credit card Tim had given me for emergencies and slapped it onto the marble counter.

Only after I was ensconced in the silk sheets and plush, feathery comforter of the king-sized bed did I allow myself to think about my predicament, but only for a second. Problems I had many of. Comfort and luxury were rare commodities. I pulled my prescription bottles from my purse, and popped an extra Xanax, wishing for nothing more than a deep, dreamless sleep.

# CHAPTER TWENTY-FIVE

*Monday morning, September 11*

I AWOKE THINKING ABOUT Tasha and Tim. There was no way I could stay at Tim's apartment now. I blinked away the moisture in my eyes. I would not cry over Tim. He wasn't worth it. I felt more betrayed by Tasha, but I couldn't think about her either. I needed a roof over my head. I could move back home if I had an alarm system. My brain was hazy from last night's double dose of Xanax, but I managed to get my sluggish limbs to dislodge the plush blankets and climb out of the bed. I stumbled out of the hotel room and into the elevator. Wobbling my way into the lobby, I left my key card on the front desk without even pausing, just calling over my shoulder, "Checking out of room 221. Thanks."

As the valet pulled my car in front of the hotel, I realized not only was I in the same clothes as the day before but I'd not even brushed my hair or teeth. Having no money for a tip, I smiled apologetically at the valet as he handed me my car keys. Angling the Honda off Main Street and onto Route 22, I headed south toward the nearest strip mall with a Best Buy. I'd find the most effective, easiest-to-install surveillance system on the market. The hundreds of dollars I'd already charged on Tim's "emergency" card had covered my emotional emergency.

Now I had to keep myself physically protected. I thought of the commercials I'd seen on daytime television touting the simplicity and easy setup of today's alarm systems. I wouldn't need a locksmith for the job. I could install one myself. As soon as it was properly in place, I'd drive to Tim's with the divorce papers. I'd hand them over only if he'd surrender Emmy.

I took a shaky breath. Things weren't going to work out with Tim, but maybe I could have Emmy in her room as early as this evening.

⁕⁕⁕⁕⁕

THE ALARM-SYSTEM components were spread out on the living room floor beside me as I read the assembly instructions. The doorbell buzzed, jolting the quiet room. *Has to be Mary.* I sighed. I was in no mood for a confrontation, but I knew she'd stand on the other side of that damn door all day if I didn't get rid of her. I stood, stretching my kinked neck to the left, to the right, my ears nearly touching each shoulder.

My joints snapped uncomfortably back into place as I walked to the front door, my body protesting the sudden shift from the awkward sprawl on the floor to upright, forward motion. The doorknob rattled. Someone was trying to open my door.

Mary never did that.

I paused, picturing an unknown man in dark clothes standing on my stoop. Coming for me. My heart clanged at the possibility. I looked back at the alarm system, metal and plastic pieces of all shapes and sizes scattered across the floor. A sudden, intense pounding on the front door made me jump.

"Open up, Caroline. I know you're in there."

Expelling a shaky breath of relief, I pulled the knob toward me and peered through the crack made between the door and jamb, flinching at the furious expression on Tim's face.

"What are you doing here?" I looked him up and down, noticing he wasn't holding the baby in her car seat. "Where's Emmy?"

"What have you done now, Caroline?" he thundered.

He must have discovered the latest charges on the emergency credit card.

"Look, I can explain."

"Oh, I think you've said enough for one day." He shoved the door open with his left forearm. With his other hand, he grabbed my wrist and pulled me toward him.

"Hey, what is this? What are you doing?"

"You're coming with me," he said, his voice steely.

"I'm not going anywhere with you. Not until I see Emmy."

"I'm bringing you to her now."

"Why didn't you say so?" If he'd let me have Emmy early, I'd follow wherever he led, no matter how angry he appeared.

"You beat all, you know that?" he yelled, marching me across the front yard. "Telling Nelson that Tasha and I are having an affair." He opened the front passenger door of the Impala and shoved me in, slamming the door after me.

I vaguely recalled a man's strangled voice emanating from my cell phone speaker, asking me what I was talking about. Had I phoned Nelson from the hotel after I'd taken my pills? Reported his wife's misdeeds? My face infused with red; my chest tightened as a thought—or was it a memory?—came to me: why would Tasha risk her life with her handsome, successful husband to sign on for an existence of money-grubbing and penny-pinching with Tim? He swung the driver's-side door viciously open, glaring at me as he got in.

"You *are* having an affair with Tasha Turner, I saw you," I said, the truth hitting me all over again. Like a gut punch to the solar plexus. Making breathing impossible. "And there's Muzzy, too. You were just with her—"

"Muzzy?" He settled behind the wheel and looked at me, unfiltered disgust in his eyes, reminding me of the time he'd stepped on a water bug in a pizza parlor we'd been lunching in, years earlier. He'd had the same look on his face then, wiping his sneaker against the floor to dislodge the guts. "What the hell are you talking about? Muzzy Owen moved away months ago. Her husband got transferred." He put the car in gear and pulled away from the curb with a screech.

"Moved away?" For an instant, the world went gray, and I forgot to breathe. I blinked and stared at Tim, thankful when the mist cleared, colors and shapes pixelating back into my husband. "That can't be true." But as I recalled her empty yard, the off-kilter trampoline, I knew it was. I swallowed, my throat raw. It felt as though Tim had just told me someone dear to me had died.

And, in a way, he had. My relationship with Muzzy had lived out its life cycle and now I'd never get the chance to tell her how sorry I was for helplessly looking on as Brandon floated half-dead in the pond. All my plotting to win back her trust—all my useless lingering in front of her former house—had been in vain.

"Oh, it's true, and I'm sure she couldn't wait to get out of this town, and away from you."

I stared at Tim's profile as he drove, his lips turned down in a mean frown, a rhythmic bulge along his jaw as he gnashed his teeth.

"You're awfully judgmental for a cheater," I said, my cold tone betraying a sudden hatred for the man who was my husband. "Are you going to deny it?"

He blew out a breath. "I don't know how you come up with this crap, Caroline. Do you stay up nights devising ways to torture me?"

"Stay up nights torturing *you*?" My brows shot up. "Let me tell you something, buddy, I never sleep, and you're the reason why. You left us, and now you're seeing all these women, even Tasha Turner—I heard what you said to her last night."

"Bullshit." He spared me a quick glance before looking back at the road. A part of my brain realized he was driving too fast. He could easily lose control of the car. Was that his plan? To end us in a fiery car crash now that he'd been exposed? I couldn't let that happen. We couldn't leave Emmy an orphan.

"Oh yeah, was it bullshit that the two of you were in the parking lot talking about—look out!" I closed my eyes, preparing for impact with the shaggy black dog who'd ventured onto the street, directly into our path.

Tim veered the Impala violently to the left, into the other lane, which was, thankfully, devoid of cars. As my arm smashed up against his, I popped my eyes open, noting that we'd missed the mutt by mere inches. I could feel my pulse pattering along the surface of my skin all up and down my arms.

"Not another word from you, Caroline," he growled. "I've got to focus on the road."

*You said it!*

When he pulled into the church parking lot, I stared at the sign out front: "Spots still available for Creative Kids Day Care." He'd signed Emmy up for day care without consulting me? Did he think I was unable to provide our daughter with adequate care? I opened my mouth to ask, but he was already pushing me out of the car.

"Don't manhandle me," I snapped. "And what is all this?" I pointed to the day-care sign at the front of the church.

"Just come with me," he said, pulling me along so we were walking parallel to the church on our left and a cemetery on our right.

I dug my heels in. "Where are you taking me? I want Emmy."

Tim didn't say anything, just kept dragging me along. I'd hardly ever seen him so angry. We neared the building and I tried to stop, but Tim kept walking, yanking me forward.

"I have to do this, Caroline. It's the only way," he said, conviction layering over his angry tone. "You've given me no other option."

We walked on, now only the cemetery to our right and a deeply wooded area directly in front of us. Was he taking me into the woods? To do the thing he *had* to do?

I stumbled as if my feet had instantly grown two sizes larger, preventing me from walking properly. Mary's account of a man searching through my dark house the other night cycled through my mind in a terrifying loop. What if the intruder was Tim? He could have taken the nail fragment. *The only thing he'd need. The proof of his crime.*

I froze, recalling how odd it had been to see Tim at 21 Pine Hill Road. He would have no business being there if his friend Ray Connolly no longer owned the house. It hit me: He needed to get rid of me. I'd seen too much, was making too many damning connections, like the thought that now popped into my head: what if my husband's friend on Pine Hill was never Ray?

What if his real friend—his *girlfriend*—was Annie Connolly? Maybe he'd been seeing her before Tasha. My brain spun with this new possibility. And if it were true that she had disappeared or had been killed, and Tim was behind the murder, what did that mean for me?

I looked desperately around the deserted area, at the church and administrative facility behind me. Just my luck—nobody entering or leaving either building. I looked ahead of us, at the giant oaks in full leaf and the dense shades of gray and black behind them, realizing too late that he never intended to let me say goodbye to my daughter. He probably had a shallow grave already dug way back in the forest.

"I want to see Emmy!" I dug my heels in and screamed, hoping my frantic tone would distract him or alert anyone within hearing distance to the fact I was in danger. "Please, please, just let me see my baby."

Tim suddenly halted and grasped my other forearm as well. He stood directly in front of me, very close, holding my arms so tightly I feared bruises. He looked me straight in the eyes, his own cold and dark as coal chips. "It's time, Caroline."

"Time for what?" I tried to step away, but he clung tightly to me.

"Time to see the baby."

I blinked, looking around, not understanding.

"What are you playing at?" I demanded as he pulled me down, knocking us both onto our knees. He turned his head and so did I, following his gaze. We were directly in front of one of the headstones in the small cemetery, a tiny one with an angel poised for flight atop the polished marble. I read the inscription:

*Emily "Emmy" Case*
*Aged six months, six days*
*Our Angel*

I felt a catch in my throat and a sudden pounding in my temples. The words made no sense. Another baby with our child's name had died. So sad! I read the date of her birth, the same as Emmy's. How strange. A weight pressed against my chest, overwhelming my ability to draw a breath, as I read the date of the child's death.

"Why did you bring me here, Tim? Dragging me to this, this . . . loathsome thing. The *headstone* of a child who died . . . just three days ago? Of all the warped, sick . . ."

But he ignored me, just stared at the grave. I reared back, terrified, desperate to put space between us, but unable to take my gaze off him. He was so still, his stare so intense.

As I watched this stranger whom I'd married, trying to understand what was happening, I thought about his flirty gestures the day we'd met at the food store all those years earlier. I recalled the wonder and joy in his eyes the first time he'd held newborn Emmy. A small corner of my mind registered that this was no joke, no accusation, or even vindication. A deathly cold swept through me. Oh my God. That's why he didn't answer my calls. Emmy had died while in his care. I tried to yell but my voice came out as a whisper. "You killed her. You killed our baby."

He suddenly looked at me, leaned back on his haunches until he was squatting beside me. "I didn't kill her, Caroline."

"But she's . . ." *Emmy, no! No! Please, no!* "I just left her with you and now she's . . ."

"Emmy's been gone for three years," he said, staring as though the force of his gaze could convince me. "You know this."

I looked back at the headstone, at the date. September 8. But that wasn't three years ago, it was three *days* ago. How could this be? With no funeral? How could they get a headstone carved and placed so soon? It made absolutely no sense.

"This is the wrong person, Tim, don't you see? There'd be no time . . ."

He continued to stare. His eyes looked dead. "There is no mistake, Caroline."

"No, this is wrong, all wrong!" It had to be. My Emmy, my baby was under my loving care. I always, always put her needs first. She was my reason—my only reason—for living. I stood swiftly—and just as rapidly teetered as the world spun around me and crashed, sending my body reeling to the ground, my face smashed into the grass. Emmy gone, impossibly lost . . . ?

I closed my eyes, pleading with God to stop the beating of my own heart. "Take me," I whispered. "Take me too."

# CHAPTER TWENTY-SIX

*Monday afternoon, September 11*

FLASHING RED AND blue lights carried me across town. I'd felt them echoing in my body, abusive in their power. Intrusive. God, I wanted them to stop. And they had. Replaced by one giant, round, dispassionately cold fluorescent hovering over me like a UFO. I lay across a flat surface, hoping I was dead, and this was the afterlife. I wanted to get up and explore the new realm and find my daughter. I tried to sit up.

"She's dehydrated," called a disembodied voice, bouncing around me.

A woman's head popped into my line of vision. Eyes peered at me through oversized eyeglass frames and the few sandy strands of her hair that had escaped her ponytail pointed at me like arrows. "Don't try to move," she said. "We're inserting the IV."

"I don't want—"

"It's in," called the first voice, the one without a face.

I closed my eyes, wishing they'd all just go away. Leave me to die. Please. I felt woozy and congested, as though someone had stuffed multiple layers of cotton batting in my head, covering my brain, and all my senses. Thankful for the haze, my mind drifted away.

When I awoke, the room was dimly lit, and the window blinds were closed tightly. I had no idea what time it was; only the flash and beep of machines revealed I was in a hospital. The giant round fluorescent light was no longer hovering overhead. I tried to move my arms but couldn't. Thoughts of being stuck in Mary's sparse bed elicited a child-like cry from my lips; I looked around the beige walls, my gaze eventually landing on the empty bedside chair. Why was I again tucked into a lonely place against my will? Was this to be my fate, to wallow in solitude, secured to a spot I'd be unable to escape from? I glanced at a huge, humming machine to my left, a plastic tube connecting my arm to it. The built-in screen across its face relayed what looked like a stock ticker app for tracking the Dow, but was, I realized, monitoring my bodily functions. I yanked my arm sideways, hoping to dislodge the tubing, but I didn't have enough range of motion to displace it. I couldn't, it seemed, displace any aspect of my life. Maybe that was my punishment for losing Emmy: being stuck here for eternity without her. My throat stung. I shut my eyes and again felt the undertow of sleep pull me thankfully out of the dismal room, off to a place I'd much rather be.

When I next awoke, the light around me was blinding. I squinted, watching people buzz like busy insects around me, most clad in blue scrubs or white lab coats. Some hurried through my room, connecting or disconnecting tubes or staring at the bleeping machines at the perimeter of my vision, adjusting knobs and buttons. Others lingered, looking at me as though observing something foreign and intriguing. Jotting notes on clipboards balanced in their hands before turning abruptly away. Nobody spoke to me.

I felt studied. A potentially dangerous animal secured and assessed. Separate from everyone else. Dismissed even as they focused on me.

I didn't care. Emmy was gone.

*No, no,* it couldn't be true. There had to be a reasonable explanation for her absence.

*You know what happened,* said my mother.

"Stop it," I commanded, feeling the wet trails on my cheeks.

The multitudes around me paused. For an instant, I became someone to take notice of. Someone to deal with. But as my vision blurred with tears, I saw only the movements of resumed life. The colors and shapes shifting like ever-changing patterns within a kaleidoscope. How long I existed in this alternate reality was inconsequential. I could go on like this forever if I didn't have to think about why my baby was gone.

"Oh, good, you're awake," came a man's voice to my left. I looked toward the incongruous tone. A young guy with dusky skin and even darker hair stood in the doorway. He held a clipboard in one hand, a pen in the other. "Welcome to the fourth floor. I'll tell Dr. Ellison you've woken up."

I shrugged. I didn't care what the man did.

He rubbed his nose and looked down at his clipboard. "Okay, Dr. Ellison has been in contact with Tasha Turner. She's filled him in on your most recent history."

My heart twisted. "Tasha, my friend . . ." *who is cheating on her husband with mine.*

"Tasha, your therapist. Seems she's spent a good deal of time—"

"My *what*?"

"Your therapist." The nurse stood straighter but didn't take his eyes off my face. "Have you forgotten that?"

"I wouldn't forget a thing like that." I shook my head vehemently. "She's my friend . . . *was* my friend."

"Tasha Turner is a board-certified psychologist," he said, his voice soft. "She's been assigned to your case since before you were admitted to the psychiatric ward and has continued with your care since this past January, when you were released."

What was he talking about? I narrowed my eyes, studying his face and his body language. "Psychiatric ward?"

He looked steadily back at me. "Ahh, I see."

"See what?" My pulse quickened, rushing blood throughout my system alarmingly fast. "What's going on here?"

The nurse placed both hands in front of him. His palms looked pink and soft. "Hold on. I can clear this up. I'll be right back."

I didn't want things to be clear. With clarity came pain. I had no idea what was real and what I'd imagined, and it was too daunting to figure out at this late stage. I no longer worried about the danger dancing around me. I didn't know whether it was from a malicious outside force or from my own twisted mind.

Nothing was what it seemed, and I was tired, so tired. I closed my eyes and tumbled headlong into a deep, dark rabbit hole of sleep.

When I next woke up, Dr. Ellison was standing over me, his hand gently rubbing my own. It was still dark, no light filtering through the slats in the window blinds behind him.

"What are you doing here?" I said, my voice groggy with sleep. "I don't need a pediatrician." My lower lip quivered with the realization. "I no longer have a child."

Dr. Ellison lowered himself into the bedside chair. "I'm not a pediatrician, Caroline. I'm your doctor, your psychiatrist."

"My psychiatrist," I mumbled. Maybe that was right. It seemed plausible, somehow.

"My office has been calling you lately because you haven't been keeping your appointments with me." There was no accusation in his tone, only concern, yet I felt guilty anyway.

"I told your receptionist—June, right?" Dr. Ellison nodded, and I continued: "I told June I'd be in touch with you."

"But you didn't call us back. You never set up an appointment."

I looked down. "I'm sorry."

"It's okay, Caroline. You've done me no harm. Yet you've suffered needlessly. Within the past few months, you've erased all the progress we made during almost two years at the institute." He frowned. "And now you've had to relive the horror of Emmy's passing."

My heart plunged into my stomach. *Not my Emmy.* She couldn't be gone, could she? It had to be a cruel joke.

"You'll be okay, Caroline," the doctor said, his hand on mine. "We just have to discover what caused your relapse."

"But I never knew what happened to her—"

"You did, indeed, know what happened to your child. And I'm sorry to tell you we will now have to go through everything all over again."

A shiver coursed through me.

"What do you mean by 'go through everything?'"

His hazel eyes locked on mine. "It's okay," he said softly. "You already know the worst. You may find this form of exposure therapy a relief, as you slowly recall things again."

"I don't think so."

He patted my hand. "No need to worry about that now. I'll be with you every step of the way, along with Ms. Turner, who wants to continue her involvement in your case. This will get better, Caroline, even though you doubt that at this moment. For now, get some rest."

As I watched him walk out the door, I wished I'd never have to see him, or anyone, ever again. How would I be okay without Emmy? I sighed, long and loud. The best I could do was pretend to get better. Just long enough for the doctors to trust me on my own. And then I could end it all, for good.

# CHAPTER TWENTY-SEVEN

A DIFFERENT NURSE CAME in, clutching something, just as the first rays of sun peeked through the slats in the partially open blinds. She tipped the contents of a small cup into my outstretched hand. I eagerly shoved the pills into my mouth.

The meds made me sleep.

"A half a pill for you and a half for me," I murmured, taking a swig of water from a glass I'd snatched from my bedside table.

"What was that?" asked the nurse, her large brown eyes looking into mine, reminding me of the woman at the window at . . . where was it?

"In Deer Crossing," I mumbled.

"A half a pill for you in deer crossing?" Her fingertips brushed my arm as gently as a feather touching down. "What does that mean, dear?"

"It means, well, it means a couple of things," I said, unable to form a coherent thought about the disparate topics. "The half a pill, well, that was a game my mother and I used to play. A way to get me to eat food I didn't like

or take my medicine. She'd share it with me. The woman in Deer Crossing."
I paused, thinking about her. "Annie Connolly. She was in a bad way. An
awfully bad way."

The nurse tilted her head slightly. "How so?" I watched her hand caress
my forearm, her rich, dark skin making my pale arm look stark and sickly.

"I think she died," I whispered.

Her beautiful brown eyes widened, and her brows shot up. "You do?
Why is that?"

"Because I couldn't get to her in time."

"Really?"

"Really good or really bad?" asked Dr. Ellison playfully, overhearing the
nurse's question as he entered the room. He smiled at us both and scratched
his head, sending his salt-and-pepper hair sticking up at an odd angle.

"Really bad." I wanted to reach out and smooth down his hair.

"Caroline was telling me about a woman named Annie Connolly at a
deer crossing who was in trouble—" began the nurse.

"Deer Crossing is a neighborhood," I clarified.

"Oh yes, I'm familiar with it," said Dr. Ellison, sitting in my bedside
chair. "Beautiful place. There was trouble there?"

I explained what I'd seen at 21 Pine Hill Road while they both nodded
slowly, neither taking their eyes off me. I also told them that nobody—not
even the police—believed my story, since the house was empty. Annie and
Ray Connolly had moved out.

"Is that why you were given half a pill?" asked the nurse.

"No." I shook my head.

"Half a pill?" Dr. Ellison reached for the clipboard attached to the foot
of my bed and unhooked it. Scanning the papers attached, he added, "I never prescribe half a pill. Even if a medication is too strong, I'll prescribe the
lowest dosage and advise patients to manually divide it in half. I don't recall
that being the case for you."

"No, I was telling this kind nurse that my mother used to do that: give
me half a pill."

"I see." His voice sounded concerned. I heard the pages in his hands fluttering. "And this also happened in the Deer Crossing neighborhood?"

"No, when I was a child." I shook my head. "I'm sorry, I'm getting confused."

He rubbed his chin. "So, you took half a pill more than once? Maybe even on a regular basis as a child?"

"Yeah, I think so."

"Do you recall what medication it was?"

"No." I rubbed my face. "Maybe I made it up." I didn't trust anything I said or did—or even thought—anymore.

"Okay." He placed his hand over mine. "We'll get to the bottom of this and get you well."

I doubted I'd ever be *well*. I wondered if I ever had been.

∽∾∽∾∽∾

I NAPPED A lot, thankful the drugs knocked me out. When I woke this time, the sun was slanting bronze rays through the slats in the blinds, the gilt glaze of late afternoon. My stomach rumbled and I couldn't recall if I'd eaten lunch.

"Good afternoon, Caroline. I'm glad you're finally awake."

"Tasha." I looked toward the voice to see her lounging in the bedside chair. I recalled her in Tim's arms. "Why are you here?"

She smiled, white teeth complemented by full lips glossed in a dusky burgundy. "Why wouldn't I be? You're one of my clients, Caroline. Didn't Dr. Ellison tell you we're still working together?"

I thought about that. "Yes, he mentioned you wanted to . . ." I let my voice trail.

"Good. I hope you want to continue this partnership too." She crossed her legs toward me and leaned in. She made it sound like we were job sharing, or setting off on a grand new adventure, just the two of us.

"But you and Tim . . ."

"We are not having an affair, Caroline," she said gently. "We were talking about *you* in Tim's parking lot that evening."

I looked down. "I think I told your husband—"

"Don't worry about that, Caroline. You were confused, that's all."

"You were hugging Tim." I watched her face closely.

"He was upset. It was a hug of encouragement. I've given you hugs as well, haven't I?" Her eyes met mine.

"Yeah, I . . . guess." I'd hated the forced intimacy.

"I'm a happily married woman," she said. "Nelson is a wonderful and understanding man. I think calling him was your way of reaching out to me. Your issues were becoming overwhelming, and you were looking for outlets."

"I don't recall placing that call," I said, my face pinking. I couldn't tell her about the other gaps in my memory. I'd never get out of the hospital if I admitted them.

"Instinctively you knew Nelson would tell me, right?"

"I guess so."

"Remember we talked about this, upon your release from the institute? About how problems are like potholes in your path? As they get bigger, they deepen into ruts. If you don't solve a problem, merely drag it around with you, you wear down that rut until it becomes a bottomless trench. One you can't escape from."

I shook my head. "I don't recall that conversation. I don't even remember being institutionalized." I could admit this because it had happened a long time ago. I'd already served my time for the events far back in the past.

"I believe that's a pattern you've established, Caroline, over many years. We've discussed this pattern before. It's your coping mechanism, and a form of protection. If you block something out, it can't harm you. How could it? You don't even recall what happened."

I thought of the bleeding woman pressed up against the window. My body shuddered. "But what if the bad things that occurred were only in my mind?" My voice quivered.

Tasha placed her fingers on my forearm. "Bad things happen to every-one, Caroline. Horrific things, sometimes." She paused, pressing her lips together, looking unsure for a second before continuing. "When you take away the bad, you also take away the good. Do you understand?"

I narrowed my eyes. "No, I don't follow."

"Emmy is gone now, but she was here. In your life. That was a good thing."

A sharp pain sliced through my chest, and I couldn't get air into my lungs. "I don't want to talk about Emmy," I gasped with whatever breath I had left.

"I know that, but pretending she's still with you only deepens your rut." Tasha sat back, her eyes locked on mine.

"You were complicit," I said, feeling my eyes sting. I looked away from her. "When you came to the house, and I left you alone while I tended to Emmy . . ."

"Come now, Caroline, we both know I confronted you. Remember the day I advised you to let the baby cry?"

I looked back at her. "That's quite different from telling me I'm *imag-ining* my baby—"

"Your health-care team—namely Dr. Ellison and I—felt it would be too jarring for you to confront your mental-health issues head-on without us fully knowing the root cause of your disconnect to reality. And in the nearly two years you'd been at the institute we'd been unable to unearth your underlying problems. Hypnosis was the only method we hadn't tried, and we were hesitant. Hypnotherapy is risky." Tasha nibbled on her lower lip.

"Risky? How so?"

"We aren't sure if the memories a subject dredges up under hypno-sis are real or imagined." She rubbed her hands together in front of her, as though warming them. "The patient may be manufacturing new thoughts rather than recalling events that actually occurred."

A jolt of electricity raced up my spine.

I once again pictured the bleeding woman at 21 Pine Hill Road. Had I witnessed her suffering or caused the event in my own mind?

"But we felt we were making progress," continued Tasha. "We also determined you were at minimal risk for dangerous behavior, based on our observations of you while you were in the psych unit. We thought we could speed up your recovery by continuing therapy through weekly counseling sessions at your home and quarterly reviews of your medications—"

"But I didn't play by the rules." I looked down at my hands, which had formed into tight fists in my lap. "I went back to the life I'd had before everything happened." I pictured the bleeding woman's pleading eyes. She had seemed so real, and so desperate. I thought about Jeffrey Trembly, the reporter searching desperately for her. Had I made him up too?

"I was getting worse."

"It seems that way, yes."

"Why did I do that? Go back to the way things were before?"

"Wishful thinking," said Tasha. "I think your mind was rejecting Tim's leaving. That was the catalyst for the deviation. When you got out of the hospital, you expected everything to go back to normal, but that's not what happened. After Tim left, your subconscious mind reasoned that if you still had Emmy, there was a chance of getting him back. Of course, that's just my hypothesis."

"Does Dr. Ellison agree?"

Tasha tilted her head, thinking for a few beats before answering. "Dr. Ellison hasn't seen much of you. I've kept him in the loop, but without seeing you himself, he hesitated to change medication or make a new diagnosis. We were operating under a status quo until you had your next visit. But you were digressing. Every time I tried to steer our conversations to the root of your troubles—your childhood, specifically your father's drowning—you'd hear Emmy crying. That was your mind protecting you."

I looked at her. "So, what do I do now?"

"When you want to leave one room and enter another, you walk through a doorway," said Tasha, smoothing her thick hair away from her finely chiseled face. "The only way out is to go through it. Like it or not, you are finally going to have to cross that threshold between your present and your past."

I looked back at my lap, at the white knuckles of my clasped fists. Something told me I wouldn't survive the events of my past. Not this time. But . . . that was okay. I had no desire to persevere. My fists unclenched, fingers splayed out gently on my lap.

# CHAPTER TWENTY-EIGHT

*Thursday evening, September 14*

I WAS EATING DINNER when Dr. Ellison walked into my hospital room. "My timing is perfect," he said, licking his lips in an exaggerated manner.

I pushed my plate of soggy meatloaf and lumpy potatoes toward him. "Be my guest but be warned: the contents of this tray are not fit for human consumption and may be hazardous to your health."

He smiled and crossed over to the bedside chair. "I'd better not chance it." A light shone in his hazel eyes. He didn't look away from my visual interrogation, but I glanced back at my discarded plate, awkward as a teen at her first school dance.

I looked back at him through my lashes. "And your reason for being here today . . .?"

"Is to talk about you, of course. See what I can discover."

I sat up straighter. "What do you want to learn about me that you don't already know?"

"Whatever you want to tell me."

Our exchange seemed more like a speed-dating interview than an interaction between a doctor and a patient.

"I can't think of anything interesting to share."

"Fair enough." He nodded. "Why don't you just tell me how you're feeling, physically and mentally." It was not a question.

I suppressed a sigh. "I'm groggy right now. Very sleepy." I yawned.

"Yes, that's the meds hard at work. Are you in any physical pain?"

"No, other than this IV stuck in my arm. It's getting red and raw at the injection site." I raised my hand and twisted my arm so he could see the irritated skin on the inside of my elbow.

"The IV is providing much-needed nutrients and fluids, Caroline. You were severely dehydrated and malnourished when you arrived here." He cupped his jaw with one hand. "How do you think that happened?"

"I don't know." I shrugged with one shoulder. "I guess I wasn't paying attention to my health. I was so busy tending . . ." I stopped.

*You were not caring for your child, Caroline. You no longer have a child.* My mother's admonishing voice. I opened my mouth to yell at her then; remembering she was just in my mind, I closed it.

"You were going to tell me you were so busy tending to Emmy that you had no time to eat."

"I don't want to talk about Emmy."

"Why not?" His expression remained pleasant, but I knew it was a trick. A clever way to get me to reveal the things I couldn't allow myself to even think about.

"If I talk about her, I'll cry."

He leaned back, clasped his hands, and steepled his pointer fingers. "Crying is a positive action. It's what we in the mental health field call a healthy catharsis."

"Not if I can't stop."

He placed his steepled pointers against his lips as if considering my words. "You will cry, and you may cry for a while, but you will not cry forever. Nobody does." He spoke through his fingers, which made it look as though he were shushing himself even as he was speaking.

"I don't want to cry or talk about what happened," I said impatiently. "I want to sleep."

"That's avoidance, which is not wanting to discuss what happened. I'd be willing to bet that on some level you think you deserve it. That's self-punishment."

I looked down at my hands. They were shaking. I had nothing to say, but of course I knew what had triggered my bizarre behavior. I'd killed her, my Emmy. I must have.

Dr. Ellison continued as though he were giving a lecture on the topic. "Guilt and shame block grief. They don't allow you the introspection you need to be what we refer to as the observing ego—the entity within you that objectively explores the trauma. Breaks it down and deals with it, piece by piece."

I looked at him. "I don't know what that means."

"After trauma occurs, we should step back and look at what happened, but humans aren't wired that way. There are many reasons why we have maladaptive wiring, and it has to do mainly with the fact that our species wasn't originally meant to live very long, so the initial responses to trauma sufficed—they got us through the tough times." He ran a hand through his salt-and-pepper hair. "Without getting all academic on you, I can tell you that besides punishing ourselves and trying to avoid what happened, we humans try to control the trauma. We want to make things better. That's what you did, with your daughter. You gave yourself a do-over. You recreated a life with her where you were the perfect mother."

*Perfect mother.* I flinched.

"It's a mind game we play on ourselves: solve the trauma now and we've also solved it in the past. Something that happened years ago—in childhood even—is up for grabs today."

I stared at him. "I don't understand what you mean, doctor. I'm not sure I even want to."

He smiled at me. "I really do understand your feelings, Caroline. Trauma overwhelms us. It changes the way we think. But deep down is the woman you were meant to be—the one who is desperately fighting to get out. It's our job to help her."

I wondered if he was right, or if that woman was not only resigned to hiding but longed to go even more deeply undercover. I thought of the stranger at 21 Pine Hill Road. Had my mind tricked me as I watched her bleed out? Perhaps she was a premonition, a glimpse of me in the future, the distance between us a temporary shield. A way to see my fate as an impartial observer.

"I suggest you try journaling, Caroline."

I wrinkled my nose. "I don't really like to write. I'm no good at it."

"This is a special kind of writing," he said, sitting forward in the chair. "Think of it as a cross between a diary entry and an expenditure log, where you track everything going in and out of your account. When we add this form of therapy to traditional counseling and medications, studies show it reduces anxiety and depression on not only a conscious level, but subconsciously, which retrains patients to have more realistic views."

"My child is gone, doctor. That's as realistic as it gets, isn't it?"

"It is," he said. "But journaling helps you remember the trauma. It comes out in your writing—puts everything on the record, so to speak."

I shook my head. "I don't want to remember. Why would I?"

He laid a hand on my arm. "So you can resolve the trauma. Once and for all, Caroline."

I squinted at him, not sure I understood. "So I write down my thoughts —even negative conversations I'm having with myself?"

"Exactly." He nodded. "Then you scratch out all the negative words and replace them with positive affirmations. Over time, the process becomes natural."

I rolled my eyes.

He shrugged. "It's easy to incorporate and costs nothing, so give it a shot. What have you got to lose?"

The jarring ring of my bedside phone cut into the quiet room, causing both of us to startle. Dr. Ellison stood, nodding at the jangling device.

"You answer that. I'll be back tomorrow afternoon. Meanwhile, I'll have the nurse bring you a journal."

"Hello?" I said, watching the doctor retreat.

"Caroline?" Mary's voice was tense. "I'm glad you're still at the hospital."

I swallowed my instinct to sigh. "Yes, Mary, I'm still here." My voice betrayed the fact that I still hadn't forgiven her for keeping me at her house against my will.

"That's good," she said. "You're safe."

"Of course I'm safe." I wanted to hang up on the crazy old bat. "Why wouldn't I be?"

"Because someone's in your house."

My stomach dropped into my bowels.

"What? Who?"

"I don't know. It's too dark to see from my window. Whoever it is flashed a small beam, just long enough, I think, to get inside."

"Don't go over there." I said, trying to control my shaky voice. "Just call the police."

# CHAPTER TWENTY-NINE

*Friday, September 15*

I WANT TO LEAVE *this place. I need to get out of here.*

I looked at the words I'd written in my journal and frowned. Someone had violated my home as I sat, institutionalized. I didn't even know if Mary had alerted the police. She hadn't answered her phone last night; hadn't accepted even one of my countless calls. Wasn't it just like her to call me in a panicked state, get me all worked up, then never answer her phone? A thought occurred to me: what if she was unable to? What if she took it upon herself to go to my place and snoop around, only to get herself beat up or . . . I couldn't think about it. I chewed on a thumbnail. This was going from serious to bizarre. I needed to get home; figure out what the hell was going on in my life. I crossed out the negative sentence and wrote, *I am looking forward to going home, to being in my own space, with my own things around me.*

I hoped that the latest entry—combined with the others I'd made since the day before—was positive enough to persuade Dr. Ellison to release me from the hospital this afternoon when he'd promised to swing by my room. After Mary called last night, my stomach twisted tighter with each passing hour, reminding me of an overworked rubber band on the brink of snapping. And even though I'd felt a spark of relief that the woman I'd seen at 21 Pine Hill must be real—because why would anyone be breaking into my house if not for what had happened over there?—the implication was frightening. I was still in danger.

But what could an intruder be looking for? The nail fragment had been my only evidence that a woman had been harmed on Pine Hill Road. With that gone, there was nothing tying me to the incident. I knew that, but did the intruder? Only if he or she had been the one to take it. Could there be more than one person snooping around my place?

I shivered. Why hadn't Mary called me back after she'd phoned the police? I recalled again how I'd tried her number a dozen times and got no answer. I glanced at the basic hospital-issue clock on the bare wall over the nurses' station just beyond the doorway of my room. It was just past eleven thirty in the morning. Maybe Dr. Ellison would visit me just after noon. If I could convince him to release me, I could be back home as early as midday. Meanwhile, what the hell was I supposed to do with myself until then? I decided to walk around the floor to release some pent-up energy.

I stood up and pulled one of the flimsy white woven blankets around my shoulders in lieu of a bathrobe, which I didn't have. It was too cold on the floor to be wandering around in the threadbare nightgown the hospital staff had supplied me with. I had no slippers, but the bright green socks I'd been issued by the same staff had puffy nonskid markings on the bottom, which I assumed operated on the same principle as slipper treads.

I cycled around the floor, dragging my IV with me, glancing in rooms with half-dead-looking folks hooked up to monitors and breathing machines as harried nurses buzzed around me like bees in a hive. I spotted what looked like a waiting room off to the side of one section and stepped into the only space on the entire floor devoid of people. Scanning the row of metal seats with garish neon-blue vinyl plastic seat cushions and backs,

I plopped onto one and perused the reading material on a battered coffee table plunked in front of the chairs. Passing up magazines about parenting, health, or fashion, I opted for a local newspaper with today's date.

Flipping the pages, I scanned features about inflated food prices, impending recession, and an opinion piece on the inaction of Congress. I rolled my eyes and turned the page, my gaze settling on the story of a house fire. I frowned. One person hadn't been able to escape the flames and was pronounced dead at the scene. Underneath the photo of a smoking pile of embers, a headline proclaimed a local woman missing, her prominent family searching for the interior designer named Ava Hansen. She'd not been seen for a number of weeks. Such a pretty name, I thought. Too pretty to be touched by such ugliness. Police had questioned her husband, who claimed to have no idea where she might have gone. I tossed the paper on the table, disgusted. When a woman turned up missing, it was usually her husband behind the disappearance.

But my gaze lingered on the paper. Staring at a portion of the headline's block letters, I turned the lovely name over in my mind. It touched off an odd sensation in me, something akin to déjà vu. Had I heard it on the radio or in a TV news story? I had no time to ponder. Footsteps in the hall signaled Dr. Ellison's arrival on the floor. As he walked past me, a folder in one hand, I jumped up and joined him.

"Good afternoon, Caroline. I was just on my way to your room. How are you today?"

I had to convince him to let me go. "I'm okay. Just stretching my legs."

"Good idea," he said. "Did you place an entry in your journal today?"

I nodded as he gestured for me to enter my room first. I heard his footsteps behind me. I snatched the notebook from my bedside table and held it out to him.

He circled around the bed and settled in the small chair beside it, reading. He stared at the page before saying, "I see introspection here, Caroline." He closed the book, placed it on his lap, and looked at me, now sitting on my bed. "Is this a difficult task?"

"No," I said quickly. Too quickly. I pressed my lips together and took a deep breath, adding, "Sometimes."

He nodded but didn't say anything for a few seconds. It seemed like a few minutes. I looked away from his probing gaze. Finally, he said, "I think it's time to move on."

I looked back at him, raised my brows. "No more journal?"

"Oh, I think you should incorporate journaling regularly into your life, just like you have these past two days, but there's more to do now."

I looked down at my hands, noticed how they bunched into fists. It was suddenly hard to get enough air into my lungs. "I thought I was doing everything I had to."

"You were," he said. "But now there's more." He handed me the journal. "I notice you wrote about your mother in these pages. Tell me again about her—about both of your parents."

I scraped my teeth over my lower lip. His words sparked a battle in my chest, my lungs releasing with the relief of not having to talk about Emmy, but my heart suddenly raged upward, beating too hard, too fast for my chest cavity. I took a deep breath. I had to get out of here, so I might as well play along. "What would you like to know?"

"You told me back at the institute that your father was a salesman and your mother a nurse."

"Yes. An RN." If I talked readily, he may be more likely to release me. I had to get to Mary.

"Right." Dr. Ellison tapped his temple as though tucking the information into his head.

"I told you what I could remember." I nodded, hoping he'd get to the point quickly.

"Yes, and you mentioned family activities when you were young, but you always resisted talking about the day your dad died. Why do you think that is?"

Something sharp and unbidden twisted in my chest. "I don't know. Maybe it's tied up in that pattern you all tell me I have."

A half smile crossed his lips. "Are you willing to talk about that day now?"

"Would sharing get me out of here quicker?" I tried to sound flippant, but my voice carried the hollow echo of worry.

I wondered if I should tell him about Mary's phone call but decided the news would only add another layer of information that would need to be sifted through.

"Why are you in a hurry to leave us?"

Good question. Besides ensuring Mary's safety, what was the pressing need? To install an alarm system in my house? What was I protecting?

*The truth.*

As I'd wallowed in the hospital bed, I'd had time to reflect on recent events, and the one that kept jumping out at me was what had happened at 21 Pine Hill Road. A woman was harmed there, perhaps fatally. If I didn't get out, I suspected the truth about what happened to her wouldn't either. Maybe that was my purpose—my sole purpose. My final, and maybe *only* good deed.

"I have to move on with my life, don't I?" I swallowed. "That's what you keep telling me."

"Yes, I do, Caroline. I'm glad you understand." His smile was gentle. "Tell me, do you think your parents strongly influenced you as a child—and to this very day?"

I rubbed my forehead, thinking about that. "As you know, my dad died when I was six, so I guess my mom had the most influence."

"Do you ever hear her voice in your head?"

I looked warily at him, unsure where he was going with this. "Yeah, sometimes . . ."

"Do you ever hear your father?"

I rubbed my lips together. "I don't even remember what his voice sounded like."

"That's very difficult for you, isn't it?"

I nodded, not trusting my voice.

"Is it because you feel guilty?" His tone was soft, almost tender, but I looked sharply at him, saying nothing. "Your mother told you he died because you rocked the boat the three of you were in that last day, right? You shifted the balance, which unsettled all of you."

"Kind of, but mostly she told me it wasn't my fault," I said, pushing my hands away from me. "She always told me it wasn't my fault." I sighed. "The more she said it, the less I believed her."

He said nothing, just looked at me and nodded into the silence.

"Maybe she was trying to convince herself." I glanced away; looked at my lap.

"Why did you just mime a push?"

I looked back at him. "I didn't."

"You did this with your hands as you spoke." Dr. Ellison placed his hands, palms outward, against his chest and pushed them quickly forward, as if shoving away the air in front of him.

"That's nothing," I said. "A dismissive gesture."

"Meaning you dismissed your mother when she said you were not to blame for your father's death?" His words shot forth like bullets.

I shrugged. My heart rate ramped up, and I fought the urge to duck. "I don't know what you're suggesting."

"I think you do." Dr. Ellison's voice was firm. "Did you knock your father out of the boat?"

"No!" I squeezed my eyes shut. "I don't want to talk about this anymore."

The doctor ignored me. "Were *you* pushed out of the boat?"

"No, I don't want to—"

"Someone was pushed out of the boat that day."

I snapped my eyes open and looked at him. His jaw had a determined set to it. "Why do you think that?"

"Based on your reaction right now, and what we discussed for months, Caroline, at the institute. As I said, the only thing you don't want to tell me about your parents is what happened that day. The only thing you steadfastly refuse to talk about."

"I don't remember!"

"I think you do."

"It doesn't matter if I do or I don't." I looked into his hazel eyes, usually so compassionate, now so unyielding. "It's over already."

His gaze softened. "Am I upsetting you, Caroline?"

"No," I said. But he was.

He smiled. "Let's talk about something else for a while, shall we?" I nodded.

"Do you recall all the release forms you signed in the hospital?"

"Sort of." I shrugged. "There were a lot of them."

"True. For your previous stay as well as this one."

"You mean when I was in the psych ward?"

He nodded and held up the folder. "One of the forms was to access your childhood and family health records. You and your doctor—in this case me—have the authority to review not only your files but those of your deceased parents." He placed the folder on his lap and opened it, revealing a sheath of white papers covered in notations.

"Oh, yes. Dr. Gleason's records. My mom worked for the GP for years before he retired."

"Hmm," he said, glancing at the papers he was rifling through. "There's nothing remarkable in your father's records, but did you know your mother was being treated for bipolar disorder?"

Something slippery darted through my chest, flipping my heart over in its wake. "I had no idea."

"She was on lithium citrate for years. It's a mood stabilizer commonly used to treat the disorder. The problem is, it has a couple of harsh side effects. The most severe compromises kidney function. And your mother did indeed have renal deterioration."

I took a deep breath, not sure why I suddenly felt so unsettled. I continued looking at the doctor, not knowing what to say.

"Your bloodwork suggests that you also have compromised kidneys."

"Really?" My breath left me in one shot, like a balloon deflating.

He held a hand up. "It's okay, Caroline. We can handle the kidney issue. We caught it early. Yet I wonder why you have it."

"It's probably genetic, right?" Adrenaline rushed from my chest to my limbs, as if preparing me for impending disaster.

"It could be." He nodded. "Or perhaps you were taking lithium too."

"Me?" I kneaded a brow with my pointer finger. "Did Dr. Gleason's records indicate I have bipolar disorder?" That was all I needed. Another mental-health issue.

"No."

"Then why would you think—"

"You told me your mother played a little game with you when you were young. To get you to eat your veggies or take your medicine—"

"Half a pill for you, and half for me," I said. "But my mother—"

"An adult dose of Lithium, even half an adult dose given to a young child on a regular basis, would cause a number of short-term and long-term problems." Dr. Ellison spoke softly, as though his tone could counter the harsh message.

I willed the world to stop spinning. Why would my mother give me a medication I didn't need? I asked the doctor what he thought about that.

"Extended lithium usage can cause impaired memory, poor concentration, twitching, drowsiness, blurred vision, and confusion. I believe your mother, a practicing registered nurse, knew about the side effects—relied on them even, to help you forget what happened in the boat that day."

My mouth dropped open. "Why are you telling me this now? I was at the psychiatric ward for two years."

"I just received these medical records," he said. "This is the first I'm seeing of your chart—and your mother's. We'd previously been able to dig up your father's records, as he went to a different physician." He paused before adding, "I don't know if you remember, but most of Dr. Gleason's files were destroyed in a fire at his office in the late nineties. When our office first contacted him, a new doctor was running the practice. He told us what Dr. Gleason revealed to him about the fire ruining nearly all their records before they'd had a chance to enter them in their new computer system. He also mentioned Gleason retired earlier than planned. He was suffering from Alzheimer's disease."

I pictured the jovial doctor who'd always been kind to me—sad about his dementia, which was news to me. As was the fire in his office. "If the files burned up, how did you get them?" I looked at the papers resting on the doctor's lap. "Why aren't they even charred?"

"They were hand-delivered to our office yesterday, in perfect condition."

"What?" That seemed impossible. "Who gave them to you?"

"A friend. Someone who'd prefer to tell you about it when the time is right."

"When the time is . . ." I rubbed my forehead. "Are you kidding me? Don't you have a professional obligation to—"

"I do, but the person left no name with the front desk staff."

"Then how will I track down—"

"Caroline, you're deflecting."

My eyebrows bunched. "Why do you say that?"

"It's likely your mother was drugging you—perhaps for years—but you don't seem interested in *those* details."

I felt the sudden urge to cry. Angry tears. Furious tears, just like that day in the boat.

"Was it your mother?" Dr. Ellison asked softly. "Was she pushed out of the boat that day?"

A memory flashed in my mind, mingling with my fury: my own hands, pushing outward, connecting with my mother's pale arm. I dropped my head, unable to speak. I felt my heartbeat in my ears.

"It's okay, Caroline. You can tell me what happened. You won't be in trouble. Did you push your mother out of the rowboat?"

My mouth was dry, making the next swallow painful. I willed the pounding in my ears to stop, the echoing in my head to cease.

"You're safe now," said the doctor. "You can tell me."

"She couldn't swim," I whispered, looking back at him, feeling tears washing downward, like someone had turned on a spigot in my head. I opened my mouth to say more, but the words dissolved on my tongue. Gone before I could speak.

"Did you know?"

I shook my head. *I hadn't known that she couldn't swim, had I?*

"I wanted her to stop, to just stop."

Dr. Ellison's gaze didn't waver. "What did you want your mother to stop?"

"Talking, yelling, complaining, all of it. It was endless, you see, endless..."

"What was she saying?"

I closed my eyes, picturing the harsh, angry shapes my mother's mouth was forming. "She didn't want to be there, didn't care that my dad and I had longed for the outing . . . I don't know the rest. The same stuff as always. How nothing was ever good enough."

"So you pushed her out of the rowboat."

I blinked as the tears increased. My entire face felt wet. My heart hammered so hard I could feel it in my jaw.

"It's okay, Caroline. You aren't in trouble. You don't have to protect yourself or your mother any longer. She's gone now, and she didn't look out for you as she should have. For your own sake and your father's memory, you need to tell the truth."

I just watched him, unable to speak.

He closed the file and rested his hands on the folder, clearly willing to wait me out.

Eventually, I whispered, "I . . . pushed her."

He had no reaction, said nothing for a few seconds. Then, "What happened next?"

"I . . . I lost my balance and I fell in too." I recalled the sudden shift from blinding sunlight to the murky brown beneath the pond's surface. Instant, numbing cold encased me. I saw legs flailing uselessly in front of me, her body wavering underwater, like an image in a dream. "I swam toward her, reached out . . . and she grabbed me, pushing me downward in her effort to lift herself up." I took a deep breath, remembering how my lungs tightened painfully as I sank lower. "I knew I couldn't breathe, or I'd die." I recalled the muffled explosion behind me, a cannonball into the water, and arms wrapping around me from behind. "My dad, he yanked me away from her. Pulled me outward, upward—"

"He rescued you?"

"He did. After we broke the water's surface, he made me hold on to the side of the boat while he went back into the water for my mother."

"And he saved her?" Dr. Ellison said. "Did you all get back in the boat?"

I blinked, trying to focus. "No, she was able to get back in with my dad's help." I stared at the white bedsheet covering my legs, struggling to remember climbing in behind her, but all I could recall were the noises. Her noises. My mother coughing, shrieking, sobbing, and accusing. "I was frightened. Mother was screaming that my dad left her to die. That he never cared about her as he should. How she could never mean as much to him as I did."

My throat felt like it had been burned. I looked at the water pitcher and empty glass on my bedside table.

Dr. Ellison followed my gaze, reached over, and grasped the pitcher with one hand and the glass with the other. "Did your dad drown while helping you back into the boat?"

"No, after he lifted her from the water to the boat, he began lifting me, telling her to grab me . . ."

"Did she pull you up, into the boat?" He poured the water and handed me the glass. "Do you remember?"

"I remember she was angry. She wouldn't stop yelling. But I was also pleased because I thought she was right about my dad. He loved me more, cared more about saving me."

"Did you think she'd hurt you?"

I gulped the water, recalling her reaching toward me with one hand, the other clutching the side of the boat to hold herself in place. The water from my glass tipped too quickly into my mouth and throat. I sputtered and coughed.

"Hold on," said the doctor, reaching for my glass. He took it from me and the water spilling over its rim reminded me of the way the pond water sloshed over the edge of the rowboat as my mother leaned forward.

I couldn't stop coughing. I was back in the pond, not yet back in the boat, the water splashing against my chin, overtaking my mouth, my nose . . .

"Look down," commanded Dr. Ellison, standing and pressing his fingers to the back of my head, as water trickled out of my mouth.

I reared my head up, terrified, feeling the hand at the back of my head, forcing my face downward, into the murky water. My mother's hand. I flung my head back against the pillows, putting space between me and that hand. I coughed again, panted.

"Are you okay, Caroline?"

I looked toward the voice, expecting to see my mother, relieved when the image rearranged: the doctor, and his concerned expression.

"Breathe in through your nose and slowly exhale through your mouth," he instructed. I did as I was told. After a few minutes, my heartbeat regulated, and my pulse was no longer throbbing in my temples and wrists.

"I'm all right now," I said, my voice hoarse.

"I can come back—"

"No." I had to get this over with.

"Do you recall what your father was doing during your mother's meltdown?"

"He was yelling too, and holding on to me very tightly. He threatened her, told her he would take me and leave . . ." Oh God, he *had* said that hadn't he? Then why was I picturing Tim talking? "Telling her she wasn't keeping her child safe . . ." Tim's lips moving, his face red. I closed my eyes, let my head sink deeper into the pillows.

"What happened next?"

I forced myself not to think about Tim. "The water, there was so much water. My dad had his arms around me from behind, his voice yelling up at her in the boat. I tried to talk, but the water kept washing over my face, flowing into my nose and mouth."

"Continue, Caroline," said Dr. Ellison, his voice demanding, direct.

My heart beat so fast I couldn't breathe properly. "There was something floating right in front of us." I tried to get more air into my lungs. "A thermos from our picnic. Heavy, metal, on the open lid of our floating plastic lunch cooler. We'd dumped the cooler into the water when we fell in. I saw our sandwiches stranded inside their plastic bags. They reminded me of those tiny little ships inside bottles as they bobbed on the water. My mother reached out and grabbed the thermos handle, and she . . ."

I saw the glint of sun on the rounded edge as she held it up, then leaned over us and smashed it down on my father's temple. My body was jolted by the memory.

I looked at the doctor. He gazed back, his silence an invitation to continue.

"Mother smashed Daddy's head with the thermos," I whispered. "His hold on me loosened and he started sinking. I reached for him but my hands only cupped water. I used both hands, trying to grab hold of something—his fingers or a shirttail even . . ." A tremor shook me from my shoulders down to my feet.

"What happened next, Caroline?"

"I kept reaching, reaching for him, but I couldn't even see him anymore."

My body was shaking as if still in the frigid water. I pictured my arms extended, but they were no longer those of a child.

My adult hands plunged into the bathwater, scooping up the baby's lifeless form, Tim screaming from beside me to move out of the way. I blinked, shook my head, and looked at the doctor, wondering how I could make him understand.

"I couldn't do that twice, don't you see? I'd let my dad go. I couldn't let Emmy sink to the bottom of the tub. I reached her. I pulled her out! But Tim yanked her away from me."

*How could you?* Tim's face, horror-struck.

"He took Emmy and ran out of the room, out of the house. If he'd only let me fix it, fix her. I was saving her! I wouldn't let her drift away from me like that, I wouldn't . . ."

My body shook so hard that my voice faltered.

"It's okay, Caroline. You tried to save both your dad and Emmy. You tried your hardest."

I felt the sob building from deep inside of me, like a tsunami, overwhelming everything in its path. "But I failed, I failed! How can I even . . . how can I . . . how will I go on, knowing that I can never make it right?"

# CHAPTER THIRTY

*Saturday, September 16*

"MY MOTHER KILLED my dad and was willing to risk my health to keep her secret," I said to Dr. Ellison as he signed my discharge papers.

He placed the pen next to the paper on the portable table beside my bed. "Perhaps. Only your mother knew what she was thinking, but if she was only taking half the dosage of her meds, she was still experiencing some of her bipolar symptoms. That, of course, would have impaired her judgment."

I recalled her sporadic, intense concentration on me—her voice shooting questions with the precision and timing of a staccato firearm—alternating with longer periods of reserve, where only my bleeding and broken body parts could break through the polite veneer she presented to me and the wider world.

"The meds I'd been on . . ." I began, almost too frightened to continue. I swallowed hard. "Could they have lingering effects that could have caused me to . . . I mean, Emmy . . ."

"Emmy's drowning was an accident, Caroline," said Dr. Ellison. "Plain and simple."

But there was nothing plain or simple about the incident. Whether I'd meant to or not, I'd killed my baby.

The urgency to get home fled with the image of Emmy's last day in the house. What did it matter if someone broke in? What would they take of more value than what I'd already lost? My own life? They could have it.

"Tim hasn't shown up, has he?" I'd hoped he'd give me a lift home.

Dr. Ellison rubbed his chin. "I'm afraid not."

Of course he hadn't. Tim obviously never wanted to speak to me again. He wasn't going to forgive me for Emmy's death. How could I even expect him to? His behavior suddenly made sense. All the times I'd thought he was being unfeeling, cold. He'd only been protecting himself from the reminders of Emmy's death. I was the callous one. I didn't deserve his forgiveness. I'd taken his love for our family and tossed it aside. He was right to call me a monster.

"We've called an Uber to bring you home," said the doctor.

Before I could say anything, the nurse entered the room, her rubber-soled shoes squeaking her arrival. I watched her approach with her little cup. "Doctor, you are wanted at the nurses' station," she told him, reaching for my hand.

"Thanks," said Dr. Ellison to his nurse. "I'm also late for a meeting." He reached for my hand, clasped it firmly. "Best of luck, Caroline. Please keep in touch."

I nodded, feeling strangely emotional about leaving the hospital. The doctor and his staff had given me the kind of care and compassion I'd spent a good portion of my life looking for. I didn't know how well I'd do on my own.

The nurse consulted the clipboard in her hand. "The new drug is doing a fair job of stabilizing your mood, but it's pretty effective at helping you sleep." She lowered the clipboard and looked at me. "If you have any problems, like dizziness or heart palpitations, you're to call Dr. Ellison immediately."

"Okay." I wouldn't.

"The good news is that your body seems to tolerate it well."

"Yes," I said, thinking, *too well*. "I wish there was something to make me forget."

She tilted her head to one side. "I understand why you would want to forget, but today you start fresh. You make new memories."

I smiled at her optimistic view of the world. I felt so old, so tired, and worn out. When did I first begin to fear the prospect of making new memories? Probably the instant the old ones went up in flames.

∽∽∽∽∽

THE UBER DROPPED me home at 11:00 a.m. I instinctively felt my pockets for my front-door key but realized I didn't have it. I remembered how Tim had pulled me out of my house nearly a week earlier, not allowing me to grab my handbag or lock the door behind me.

Mary may have locked it with her key. If so, she'd have to let me into my own house. She knew I was coming home. Dr. Ellison's nurse told me Mary had dropped by the hospital the day before and learned I was being discharged this morning. I pictured her standing in front of her living-room window watching the cars amble along the street, waiting for the one that would drop me in front of my house. I shivered. The irony was undeniable. I thought of all the nights I'd lurked in the shadows of Deer Crossing, spying on others. I also wondered why she wouldn't have swung by my hospital room when she'd been right there. When I was so desperate to know if she was okay, and whether or not she'd phoned the police.

I stepped out of the car and, looking at my front door, placed my hand against my breastbone, willing my heart to cease racing. Someone had invaded my home again. Watching Mary shuffle out of her house and across my yard, I once more considered it could be her.

As she chattered about neighbors helping each other out, she unlocked my front door and swung it wide. I wondered how I could get my spare key back. I didn't think I was strong enough to wrestle it away from her, which was pathetic. I was fifty years younger. Thanking her stiffly, I followed her inside, my gaze darting around the room. Everything appeared to be the same, minus the alarm parts spread across the living room carpet. I stared at the spot.

"The alarm . . ."

"Don't worry dear," she offered, beelining through my house as though she were the homeowner.

"Was someone definitely in here, Mary?"

"I told you there was." She paused halfway between the living room and kitchen and turned back to look at me. "Did you forget?"

"No, but you never called me back after I told you to alert the police."

Mary shifted her weight from one foot to the other. "Tim said not to. He told me he'd handle everything, and that the doctor requested I not bother you."

My brows gathered over my eyes. "Why? Was *he* the one in the house?"

"Not that night, no—at least I don't think so." Mary wavered on her sturdy legs, looking confused. "I called him after I got off the phone with you. I figured it's his house too. He'd want to come over and check things out. And he did, the next day. He even tidied up. He loaded a bunch of things in his car."

"Damn it, Mary, why wouldn't you just call the police?"

"I told you—"

"Someone was *in my house!*"

And then it occurred to me. Perhaps she feared the conversation I would have with the cops. Afraid I would reveal what she'd done to me. And to her husband.

"Caroline, just come over here, have a seat." She flitted around the kitchen table like a foraging butterfly. "You must be very . . ."

I spooled out the breath in my lungs. Did Mary have plans for me? Was she going to imprison me in my own house? Maybe tie me up this time? I didn't know a lot about her. Maybe her frantic call to me reporting an intruder was a ruse. A way to get me home faster. Was she somehow in cahoots with Tim? What would she have to gain? What advantage would Tim have, for that matter? I felt the pulse throb in my neck. Something wasn't right. Fear prickled the hairs at my nape, traveling up my scalp. I'd have to play it cool, try to placate the old lady until I could figure out what her angle was.

"I wouldn't betray you, you know," I said, keeping my voice calm, my tone even.

Mary's face went blank, her features appearing two-dimensional. Stuck onto her face as an afterthought. "Betray me, dear?"

"I'd never tell the police about what you did to your husband, or that you drugged me. I know you're—"

"Drugged you?" Mary leaned forward, her eyes and mouth turning to perfect O's. "I never did that!"

"You most certainly did, Mary. The night I came to stay with you, but it's okay—"

She dropped to a kitchen chair, placing her hand against her chest so abruptly I feared she was having a heart attack. "Good heavens, no!"

I narrowed my eyes as I walked toward her. "But you made me that drink before I went to bed. It was a strong drink."

"You funneled it and asked for another, but I wouldn't give it to you—not after you slugged back that handful of pills from your purse."

"Handful of . . . what?"

"I don't know," she shrugged. "You reached into your handbag and pulled out a bunch of pills. I cut you off and led you to my guestroom. When you woke up the next day you could barely move. I thought about calling 911."

"I couldn't move because you'd . . ."

Mary set her jaw. "You couldn't even lift your arms. Only your mouth was working properly, yapping on about me holding you prisoner." She let out a heavy breath. "I was just trying to help you. I even tried to get some food into you. You were too weak to feed yourself, and judging by the size of you—"

"Okay, okay." I raised my hands in front of me. "I believe you."

Mary raised her chin and sniffed. "You should. It's the truth. And what's this about my husband?"

I slunk into a chair across the table from my neighbor. "When I was driving you home that rainy day. You told me you showed up at your ex-husband's door with a knife. Scared him—literally—to death."

Mary's face was infused with a deep red hue. "Well, I could have said *that*, not that it's true, mind you. He was never my ex-husband. We lived together until the day he died." She flushed. "The truth is—and I know you know this—I drink too much. I don't always remember the crazy things I say."

I sighed, seeing the similarity in our situations. "I guess we're both guilty of telling tall tales—and even believing them."

She grinned. "I won't let it spoil our friendship if you don't."

I smiled ruefully. I'd made up the grandest story of them all: that my baby was still alive.

Mary reached across the table and rubbed my upper arm gently. "It's okay. We're both gonna be just fine, you hear?"

I nodded. Apparently, I'd imagined most of my neighbor's transgressions against me, yet she was still determined to help. I had a friendship with Mary whether I wanted it or not. Studying her wrinkled face and impish smile from across the table, I realized I could do worse. I could have no friends. We don't always choose the people who come into our lives. Sometimes they muscle their way in despite our best efforts to keep them away.

"Do you know what happened to my alarm system?"

"Yes, Tim installed it. Gave me the spare key."

*Again?* I stifled a sigh. *Might as well allow Mary to move in,* I thought wryly. I could use the rent money. "What did Tim say about the break-in?"

"He was concerned." She shrugged. "Said he was going to alert the police, but fortunately, there wasn't anything of value to take from the house."

*Only me, his wife.*

"I disagree, of course," said Mary. "I've been watching your place."

"You think someone is still interested in this house?" I placed my forearms on the tabletop.

"Maybe." She puckered her lips, considering. "Or someone is still interested in what's inside this house: you."

My stomach flipped.

"Why would you say that?"

She didn't respond, just bit her lip.

"Do you know something I don't?" I asked, sensing she did. But she shook her head. "What am I missing here? Why would anyone be interested in me?" In my mind, a row of threads dangled. I pictured myself pulling them one by one. Each one I touched dissolved as a new one took its place.

"You're right," she said in a near-whisper. "Something *is* going on, but I don't know how things fit together." Her eyes were suddenly moist. She blinked rapidly, adding, "I haven't wanted to tell you because of the . . . the baby and your delicate condition—"

"Just tell me, Mary."

"When you went away the first time, Tim moved out. He said he couldn't live here alone, without his daughter."

I nodded. I knew that.

"He asked me to keep an eye on the place." She avoided meeting my gaze. "I did, of course. I'd come over every week to make sure things were just as you'd left them. One day I noticed a file box, one of those cardboard thingies, flimsy but solid enough to hold household files. It was on your kitchen table. I'm ashamed to admit I snooped. It belonged to your mother. Contained her financial and medical records, bonds, and her marriage certificate."

I thought about the day we cleaned out my mother's house. I remembered Tim carrying a box to our car, but I didn't recall ever seeing it again. "What did you discover? Was my mom one of those secret millionaires?" I forced a lightness into my tone that I didn't feel.

"I don't know about her financial holdings, they're none of my business." Mary studied her hands, resting on the tabletop. She seemed particularly interested in her knobby joints. I knew my neighbor well enough to tell she was lying. Mary's intense interest in my life convinced me she'd likely studied every cent that had gone in and out of my mother's accounts. I pictured a spreadsheet of Mother's income and expenditures tacked to Mary's musty cellar wall. I'd tackle that issue later.

"What did you discover?"

"There were numerous medical bills from her office. Dozens—maybe even hundreds—of patients' medical procedures from the late 1990s." Her brow creased as she looked at me. "Odd items to keep. I was immediately suspicious. Remember, I made a living investigating insurance claims. I could sniff out fraud."

"Fraud?" My eyes went wide. "My mother was a by-the-book person. I don't think she . . ." I thought about the damaging pills she'd forced on me as a little girl. I pictured her hand smashing the metal thermos against my dad's temple. I began to shake. If she could kill her husband and poison her only child, she could certainly wheedle money out of insurance conglomerates.

"There are many ways to commit health-care fraud without patients knowing it," said Mary. "The most common is double-billing—"

"Yes, the doctor submits multiple insurance claims for the same service," I interrupted. "I know all about this, Mary. I was a medical biller. The other popular strategy is phantom billing—"

"Charging for services never rendered," cut in Mary, her crooked pointer finger raised in the air. "There's no way to tell whether these bills are duplicates or completely bogus, but something's not right about them. If everything was on the up and up, Lilith—your mother—would have no reason to keep them."

Something in my brain notched into place. I could almost hear the clicking. "The fire."

"What fire?"

I spoke slowly, explaining, "When my doctor's office tried to access my childhood medical files, they were told about the fire in old Doc Gleason's office. Nearly all the files were destroyed."

"How convenient." Mary grinned. "Funny how your mother knew to keep these specific files."

I sighed. It wasn't funny. Not at all. Was there no end to my own mother's deceit? "She must have kept the records so she wouldn't triple-bill the insurance companies and create a red flag. This was all before the wide-scale use of computers."

"I suspect someone was onto her, and that's why she kept the files. Maybe so she could show that Dr. Gleason had made her do it, or something," said Mary. "But what did it matter all this time later, and her dead? It didn't make much sense for Tim to keep the files, so I took them home and looked them over."

"Why would you do that?" I narrowed my eyes, searching her face.

She flushed. "I didn't plan to take action against her estate, Caroline. The statute of limitations on a fraudulent insurance claim is six years and the records were from the nineties." She raised her hands in front of her as if to ward off a physical attack. "I just wanted to discover . . ."

I looked at her reddening face, for once not finishing her sentence for her. She rubbed a hand across her lips.

"What did you hope to discover by scouring those records, Mary?" If she'd been as uninterested in my mother's financial holdings as she claimed—something I didn't believe—then her interest in the medical files was personal.

"Nothing, really." She looked down.

"That's a fib. We both know it. You were hoping to find a clue to my mother's intent—to figure out how her mind worked," I guessed. "So you could link her behavior to mine, root out the reason I killed my baby?"

"No, that's not true." She met my narrowed eyes, her own wide. "I know you accidentally killed Emmy. Tim said so."

Her words arrowed into my chest like a dagger. "Then what?" My voice was husky with the emotion I was trying to contain. "You wanted to figure out why Tim sent me away?"

When she clamped her lips together, I had my answer.

She wanted to know just how dangerous I was. If the neighbor she needed so desperately would ever harm her. I couldn't blame her, could I? Given the opportunity, I'd likely do the same thing. I thought about my mother's deviance. How much was transmitted through the genes? Was I a garden-variety criminal like my mother had appeared to be, or had nature supercharged my DNA, making me a cold-blooded baby killer? Had I even fooled Tim? Apparently, Mary had wondered about these things too.

"There's more," said Mary.

I looked at her and, once again, she didn't meet my gaze. "Lilith also had her medical files, and yours, in a small folder tucked among the phony claims."

I thought about Dr. Ellison telling me someone had dropped off our files at the hospital just two days earlier. Mary. "Why didn't you just tell me about all this?"

"How could I? When I took the files, you were institutionalized. I couldn't even tell Tim without admitting I stole them. When I went back to your house the next week to return them, the file box was gone. I had to keep them or risk him knowing I'd helped myself to your private information."

I didn't say anything for a long time, letting my eyes go out of focus as I thought about Mary's admission. Eventually, I looked at her. "Did you read our medical files?" When she nodded, I did too.

"I knew I had to give the information to your doctor, but I was afraid to be implicated. I mean, I'd stolen your medical records, Caroline. That's a felony. But when I realized how much you were suffering, I knew I had to share them. It took me a long time to do it, and I'm sorry I was such a coward."

I ran my hands through my hair. "Oh, Mary, that's the least of my problems."

"You *do* have problems," she said. "I know it makes no sense, but I can't help thinking that the files I stole are somehow linked to what you saw over on Pine Hill Road. I have no idea how, but I think these things are connected."

I pursed my lips. "Not sure how that could be."

"Me neither," she admitted, "but I can't shake the notion. I was a successful insurance adjuster because I never ignored my instincts. When my gut talks, I listen."

# CHAPTER THIRTY-ONE

*Sunday, September 17*

MARY'S WORDS ECHOED in my mind all day. How could my mother's health and financial records have anything to do with what I'd witnessed on Pine Hill Road? It made no sense. I didn't even know the couple who had lived there.

*But Tim did.*

He was the one who told me about Ray and Annie Connolly. He'd worked with Ray. Maybe Tim could tell me more about him. Or maybe not. My soon-to-be ex wasn't speaking to me.

Yet Tim was the only connection I could make between my family and the mysterious couple. I thought about my wild imaginings on the horrible day Tim took me to Emmy's grave. How I'd wondered about his connections to not only Ray, but Annie.

Had she worked at their engineering firm too? No, that didn't sound right. In fact, Ray working with Tim didn't seem correct either. I recalled Jeffrey telling me the guy was some sort of bodybuilder. Of course, that could be a hobby. I'd have to ask Jeffrey. I frowned, recalling our last encounter. Jeffrey wasn't speaking to me either.

I understood why they'd each want to avoid me. I'd killed Tim's baby, and investigative reporter Jeffrey had discovered my checkered past, realizing I was not a reliable, or particularly safe, person to hang out with. If I called Jeffrey, he'd likely hang up on me. If he'd unearthed my contact information and realized I was trying to reach him, he'd pull a Tim and ignore me.

I stood the best chance of speaking with him in person. After all, I could refuse to leave his front porch until he talked to me. He didn't seem like the type to report me to the police for trespassing. I glanced outside. The sky was darkening. Jeffrey would be on his nightly shift. I'd just begun calculating his beginning and ending work times when I remembered it was Sunday. As a full-time reporter, he'd most likely be off on weekends, wouldn't he? I grabbed my car keys. Only one way to find out.

As I cruised along the roads of my neighborhood, I was grateful to be in my car. I didn't know if I would ever resume my nightly strolls. How could I, without Emmy? A crushing weight pressed down upon my chest, causing me to pull to the side of the road and take half a dozen deep breaths until I could get my jittery body under control.

When I pulled onto Woodmint, I tried not to look at the houses, lit up like oversized lanterns, but I couldn't help but stare at the Colonial next to Jane Brockton's house as I passed. It was the only one on the street without a single light on. What was the story there, anyway? The place had an air of abandonment, yet I remembered the shadowy man emerging from the side door on multiple occasions to meet up with Jane. Was the guy living in that house or not?

It was none of my business. Driving on, I waited for my mother's voice to echo the sentiment in my brain, but she'd been surprisingly quiet since I'd remembered she'd killed my father and drugged me my whole childhood. Guess her moral high ground had disappeared. As I approached Jeffrey's place, the distinctive taillights of his Jeep were backing from his driveway onto the street. I cursed. Five minutes too late. I pulled in front of his house, watching his back lights get dimmer as he angled onto Primrose and drove away. I glanced around the neighborhood, at loose ends, and wondered if he'd return soon. I idled, listening to the song on the radio: *Gotta do it this time, if I don't, I'll die; gonna make my move, gotta prove I tried.*

Words to live by. I put the Honda in park.

I didn't have a plan as I walked back down Woodmint, just a vague idea about investigating the dark Colonial. Eying Jane's house as I crept past, I couldn't make out much through the living-room window. Gauzy curtains successfully concealed the floor-to-ceiling bookshelves I'd seen in the room countless times before. I pictured Rod splayed out in the easy chair in front of them, a book under his nose, and the fluffy dog curled on his lap.

I glanced around the yard, looking for Jane. She could be as sneaky as I was. My eyes scanned the inky void between her house and the Colonial, unable to distinguish between shadows. I ran to the far side of the dark house, slunk over the railing, and dropped onto the front porch. The street-facing windows all had coverings—blinds or curtains, I presumed. It was impossible to tell, and I didn't want to turn on my cell phone light and draw attention to myself. I tiptoed to the front door, which had some sort of stained-glass insert in the top half, making it difficult to see inside. I might have better luck at the back of the house. I scooted around the foundation on the side bordered by some sort of coniferous hedge, confident I wouldn't be observed.

I stepped gingerly onto the back deck, which ran the length of the house. It seemed gigantic, lacking the usual outdoor accouterments one would expect in a neighborhood this ritzy: high-end dining table and chairs, Weber grill, artfully arranged annuals in oversized pots. I crossed to what I believed was the kitchen window and peered in. It was too dark to see anything. Glancing around, I noted the houses on either side of this one—including Jane's—had no windows facing the Colonial. I took in the small wooded area behind the house. The dim twinkle of lights through the leaves informed me the houses on the street behind this one were too far away to see me, or what I was about to do.

I whipped out my cell phone and tapped on the flashlight icon, making sure to keep the light pressed against my chest. Pausing to ensure there was no noise coming from inside the house, I angled the beam through the window. My eyes grew wide at the barren kitchen counter, even though the major appliances were still in place. I walked along the back of the house and held my light against the French doors to reveal two empty rooms: the dining area and living room, if memory of the Deer Crossing models served. I crossed back past the kitchen and raised the phone's light to the final downstairs window. Curtains covered it, but they weren't closed all the way. I pointed the light beam in the slit between the drapes and peered in. The room was messy with backpacks against the far wall and clothing strewn around. A mattress lay flat on the floor, a mound of clothes on it.

I was trying to figure out if the garments were those of a woman or man when the clothing pile moved. Suddenly, a man sat up, looking straight into my light, which blasted the shadows from his features. I gasped. Squinting into my cell phone light was Ray Connolly, the man I knew as Matt. I turned and ran straight for the woods, shoving my hot cell phone against my belly under my shirt to douse the light. I reached the tree line as the swish of the back slider sounded. I ducked behind a tree, trying to control my panting breaths lest he hear me. I peered around the tree to see him also peeking out, the outline of his head just visible against the white grid of the French door.

I pressed myself flat against the ground, hoping he couldn't see me. After a few seconds, I raised my head slightly, seeing Matt duck back inside and silently slide the door behind him. I jumped up and ran, not caring if I made noise. He couldn't hear me from inside, where he was probably getting dressed with breakneck speed and grabbing his own light. A vision of him hunting me down crowded out other thoughts. I ran faster, tripping over tree roots and nearly landing flat on my face. When I reached the other street, I veered right and kept up my pace. Until I reached the house on the corner of Pine Hill and Lakeside. Matt's house. Would this be the first place he'd look for me, or the last? It didn't matter, I couldn't be here either way.

I started to run past the house when his mailbox, white with cherry trim, caught my attention. It looked luminous in a wash of moonlight. I moved toward it. It had been a long time since I'd checked out the contents. There just might be a clue inside revealing why the owner of this house was squatting in one around the block. I flipped open the lid and shoved my hand inside, my fingers curling around a small stack of papers. I yanked them out and kept running. With any luck, I'd make it to my car before Matt took to the neighborhood looking for me.

# CHAPTER THIRTY-TWO

*Monday, September 18*

I SAT UP IN bed, temples throbbing relentlessly. Dreams of a bleeding woman had woven through my sleep again. I'd awakened countless times during the night, my heart beating a tattoo of fear against my chest. I tumbled out of bed and shuffled toward the kitchen, thinking only of my morning coffee, but when my eyes settled on the stack of mail on the kitchen counter I paused. I'd been too frightened to even turn on a light in my place after I'd returned home the previous night. If Matt had recognized me—a big *if* since I doubted he'd been able to make out my face in the dark with my cell phone light blasting in his eyes—he might swing by my house to confront me. I was sure he knew where I lived. His lover, Jane, would have told him.

I'd sat like a sentinel on my sofa in the dark living room for hours, watching the front yard in the bright moonlight, trying to wrap my head around Jane and Matt as the illicit couple I'd been observing for weeks. Was Matt actually Ray?

Was Melanie really Annie? I wondered again how long Jane had been having a fling with another woman's husband. Had Jane and her mystery man—whatever his name was—plotted to get rid of his wife?

I thought about the strange conversation I'd overheard between them less than two weeks earlier on the dark street. Talking about a situation that was "getting serious." Something they had to "figure out." My head swam with the unanswered questions, and my stomach cramped, banishing the idea of coffee.

I snatched the mail bundle and slid into a kitchen chair. Could Matt/Ray have killed Melanie/Annie to free himself for Jane? That theory had a few holes.

First of all, I didn't know if the woman I'd seen was dead or just harmed. Second, what good would it do him to be free of a spouse if Jane still had hers? Third—and most important—Matt/Ray must realize if his wife went missing, he'd be suspect number one.

On nearly every crime show I'd ever seen it was the husband who offed his wife.

Feeling like Mary, stealing other people's documents, I leafed through the stack of flyers and other junk mail addressed to Occupant or Current Resident, seeing nothing that would clue me into the family that had lived at 21 Pine Hill Road.

Standing, I bundled the papers between my palms and deposited them in my recycling bin next to the back door. As I turned back to the table, my eye caught a small envelope resting on the white tile floor. I bent down and scooped it up, ready to toss it in with the other discards, when I noticed the addressee: Ms. S. Connolly.

The return address in the upper left corner was the local hospital, the one Dr. Ellison practiced out of. Probably a fundraising appeal, I thought as I tore open the end. Whoever addressed the envelope hadn't even gotten Annie's first initial right. I remembered the S on a keyboard was right next to the A.

I opened the letter and began reading:

*Dear Ms. Connolly,*

*I hope this letter finds you well. Please note that there is an outstanding balance due immediately on your account #44953 in the amount of $500.00 for emergency services rendered on July 18 of this year. If you have already paid this bill, please disregard this notice. If you have questions or concerns, please call 518-343-2200 and ask for the billing department.*

*Sincerely,*
*Carla Beddington*
*Billing & Payments Supervisor*

Emergency services? Annie—if that's who I saw dancing in the living room and hugging in the foyer of 21 Pine Hill—had appeared perfectly fine a few weeks after the supposed emergency service. Could this bill have been a mistake? I studied the contact number embedded in the letter, reaching for my cell phone.

The woman who answered was named Natalie something-or-other. Reading the signature at the bottom of the missive, I asked to speak with Carla Beddington.

I was put on hold for so long, I thought I'd been disconnected, but a friendly voice eventually filled the dead air space.

"Carla Beddington," she said, managing to sound both efficient and cheerful. "How may I help you?"

"Hello," I began, squaring my shoulders and pushing air from my diaphragm in a feeble attempt to sound annoyed. "My name's Annie Connolly. I just received a bill for your hospital's emergency services on July 18 of this year, and I believe there's been a mistake. I'm perfectly healthy and—"

"Hold on," Carla cut in. She also kept me stranded on hold, but this time Muzak trickled through the phone line. A Lawrence Welky version of a Rolling Stones tune, like Dr. Gleason used to subject his patients to every damn day. As a kid in his reception area waiting for my mother's shift to end, I'd hated the canned background music that distorted my favorite songs so much. I was tempted to hang up and try the hospital's billing department at a later time.

"Thanks for holding," Carla chirped. "I found records for an S. Connolly for that date. Is Annie your nickname?"

"Yes," I said, the word sounding more like a question than an affirmation.

"And what's your first name?"

"If I told you that I'd have to kill you," I joked, trying to stall. *Could Annie be short for Suzanne?* I couldn't risk it. Not knowing my own first name would raise a red flag the size of Rhode Island.

Carla didn't laugh.

I quickly backtracked, going for a phony emotional appeal. "Look, Ms. Beddington. I hate my first name. Could we just stick with the first initial?"

"I guess so. That's what you did on the eighteenth."

"Ummm, yeah, right."

There was a pause on the line. "Wait, you just said you weren't here on that date."

I tried not to sigh. Cheerful Carla wasn't a complete idiot.

"What date?" I tried for a genuinely confused tone.

"July 18."

"I wasn't."

"But you just confirmed the use of only your first initial on the eighteenth—"

"I always go by just the first initial." I gnawed on my lower lip. There was an excellent chance Carla was going to ask me my birth date next. I'd have to cut her off at the pass. "Look, I'm on my lunch hour and your office has kept me waiting on the phone so long that I won't have time to eat. Can you just tell me what I was supposedly treated for this past July 18?"

"Oh, I'm sorry." Carla's voice sounded genuine. "It looks like . . . hmm . . . would you mind if I put you on a very short hold?"

"Yes, I would. I have no more time to wait," I snapped. "Why can't you just tell me what you see in my records?"

"I see that you already paid in cash. There's a notation in the lower right corner. The data-entry person probably didn't notice it. I wanted to point this out to her."

"Feel free to do that when I'm no longer on the phone." My tone dripped nastiness. I'd have to dial it back if I wanted to get any more information out of Carla. "Meanwhile, I was treated for . . .?"

But Carla refused to detour from her sworn duty as head of the hospital's billing staff. "You can disregard the bill, with my deepest regrets for any inconven—"

"That's fine," I talked over her. "And what did I supposedly pay for?"

"I'm in billing, not treatment, Ms. Connolly."

"Yes, of course." I injected sweetness into my voice I was far from feeling. "But bills are itemized, right?"

"Well, yeah, there are codes, but I'm not at liberty to discuss—"

"I won't tell if you don't."

She laughed as though I were joking, but then her tone turned serious. "Would you like to talk with a nurse in our ER unit, Ms. Connolly?"

"About what? I don't know what my ailment is." I was thankful I wasn't standing in front of the woman. My fingers itched to reach through the phone and gouge her eyes. Counseling myself to keep my cool, I added, "Could you please just tell me what the codes indicate?"

There was a long pause. Carla was deciding how helpful she wanted to be.

"Look, from one woman to another . . ." I began, in a last-ditch effort to win her over.

"From one woman to another," she repeated, her voice low but urgent, "the records reveal contusions and lacerations. The only reason I'm telling you this is so you can get help—the same help my sister needed and didn't get." Her voice was so low I could barely hear her. "She's in a wheelchair now."

Contusions and lacerations? That was a helluva lot of bruises and cuts if it landed Annie in the ER. Perhaps she'd had a car accident. But what did Carla mean when she mentioned her sister and advised Annie get help? I said nothing, hoping she would elaborate. She did.

"There was also a concussion, and all your injuries are consistent with" —she lowered her voice—"domestic abuse. Are you sure you don't need to speak with someone on the emergency staff?"

My mouth dropped open. Someone had beaten the shit out of Annie Connolly.

⁂

MY PHONE CONVERSATION only reaffirmed my determination to help the mystery woman I now suspected was Annie Connolly. I knew where to start: Woodmint Lane. Jeffrey Trembly ignored me before, but this recent information changed everything. I needed to talk with him about it. If he arrived home from work in the early morning hours, he wouldn't go back on shift until four or five in the afternoon. I drove to Deer Crossing just after three.

Making my way down Woodmint Lane, my gaze was riveted on Jane Brockton and her little dog on their front lawn as I passed her house. She was bent over, patting the adorable fluffy head, a dog bone in her other hand. As I passed by, both she and the dog looked up and watched. I gave a quick wave and noticed her frown before I looked back at the road in front of me. Bitch.

Someone needed to inform her she lived on a public street, not a private road. But Jane Brockton probably knew all about me. Seems like everyone else in town did. Guess I'd frown too, if I saw a monster pass by. I felt my insides sag, and a tightening in my shoulders as though I'd been yoked, like an ox, to a heavy load.

Losing sight of the Brocktons' house in my rearview mirror as I pulled into Jeffrey's driveway, I steadied my breathing. I had to convince Jeffrey

I wanted to help him find Annie Connolly—that even though my mental state was compromised, my intent wasn't. I stepped out of the car and hurried toward his front stoop.

Movement inside the house after I pressed the doorbell, and a few seconds later his door opened. Jeffrey stood there, paralyzed like a rabbit caught in headlights.

"Hey, Caroline. I can't talk now, I'm in the middle of something."

"I know you know about me," I said. "You're a reporter. Of course you know my story. That's why you ran from me that day at the food store. You were running from crazy."

"Look, I—"

"Annie Connolly was admitted to Mercy General's ER in late July," I blurted out. He met my gaze. "We can talk out here if you like."

He opened the door wide enough to see the yards and street beyond. Apparently satisfied by what he saw—or didn't—he opened it wider and ushered me in. I supposed having the neighbors witness him talking with the town loon was riskier than being alone with me inside his house.

I stepped into the sparse foyer and paused as he closed the door behind me. "I don't blame you for avoiding me, you know." I took a deep breath. "I wasn't doing well, but I'm better now. I spent more than a week at the hospital."

"I'm glad," he said, looking everywhere but at me.

"Annie was admitted to the ER exactly two months ago."

"I checked the hospitals." His eyes locked with mine. "They told me she wasn't there."

"That makes sense, you're not a relative. They don't just hand out information to anyone who waltzes in and asks."

"You're not her relative." Jeffrey tilted his head, looking skeptical. "So how did you find out?"

"I got my hands on a bill from Mercy General." I held his gaze. "And before you ask, yes, I rifled through her mailbox. Just last night. I called the hospital pretending to be her."

Jeffrey ran a hand through his hair. "Did you discover why Annie was at the ER?"

"Domestic abuse."

His eyes widened. "That prick! I knew it. Stupid professional body-builder. More like pro wife beater . . ." He looked at me, his face bright red.

"What's Ray Connolly like?" I thought again about the man I'd called Matt.

"I don't know." His voice notched up as his fury grew. "Like I told you, I never met him. Only saw him in the yard when I drove past their house."

"Could bodybuilding be a hobby?" I asked. "And maybe he had another job, like . . . um . . . an engineer?"

"An engineer?" Jeffrey's laugh echoed around me. "I doubt the guy even knows what an engineer is. When Annie met him, they were teens. According to her, the attraction was purely physical. But then she grew into an adult. And he didn't. He honestly thinks he's going to make a living off of endorsements, but the only deals he's been able to get are for free supplements and sports clothes. Meanwhile, she's been supporting him for years. She's sick of it."

"Oh, okay. I was just wondering." I didn't want to press my luck with Jeffrey's patience. I'd let him process the news I'd just shared. "I'll be going, but I thought you'd want to know about Annie. It might be useful."

He nodded. "Yeah, thanks."

I turned away and let myself out. Jeffrey had treated me as an oddity, like the barely tolerated neighbor living with seventeen cats and smelling of tuna. As I walked back to my car, I realized my story was far worse than that. To be relegated to the status of a cliché seemed almost mundane. An outcast others avoided rather than a monster everyone feared. I recalled the gossiping girls at the drugstore weeks earlier. Now I knew they were talking about me, the woman who killed her own baby.

*Mustn't think about that.*

I thought instead about what Tim had told me about Ray Connolly. I got into my car and pulled my cell phone from my pocket. I quickly called the main phone number for Kinney and McKean Engineering. When their long-time receptionist, Gloria, answered, I hoped she wouldn't recognize my voice.

"Ray Connolly, please," I asked, adopting a lower pitch.

"Excuse me?" Gloria asked. When I repeated the name, she didn't even pause before saying, "I'm afraid we don't have an employee by that name."

"Oh," I feigned surprise. "When did he leave the firm?"

"I . . . think you have the wrong number. I've been with this firm for eight years, and I've never heard of Ray Connolly."

"So sorry," I mumbled, clicking off. Why was I even surprised that Tim had lied to me? I'd suspected he hadn't been truthful about a lot of things during the course of our marriage, but why lie about Ray? Did Tim even know the guy? Uneasiness slid through my chest and churned my stomach. What else had Tim lied about?

# CHAPTER THIRTY-THREE

*Monday evening, September 18*

I HOVERED IN FRONT of Emmy's closed door. I'd noticed it was shut the first time I'd walked to my own bedroom after arriving home from the hospital, but up until this moment, I'd refused to even look toward the nursery. I couldn't ignore it forever. As difficult as it was going to be, I'd have to clean out the room. Now was a good time to tackle the task; with my mind focused on Tim's lie, I'd mull over his motives while I packed up the tiny clothes, crib, and baby monitor. I'd already decided to bring everything to Goodwill. Blinking back the sting in my eyes, I placed my hand on the metal doorknob and twisted.

As the door swung open, I caught my breath. The room was nearly empty—only the two small dressers still in place, their tops cleared of the baby monitor, stuffed toys, and music box.

Gone were the crib, the bassinet, and the rocking horse in the corner. I crossed to the closet and flung it open. The gaping emptiness hit me with an invisible force.

As I looked around, I noticed something else: the room and closet had been repainted a cream color. A toned-down version of the sunny yellow Tim and I had painstakingly layered on just before Emmy's birth, recalling how we'd laughed each time my bulging belly got in the way of my efforts, sending the paint roller veering in different directions.

I stood in the center of the alien space, more alone than I'd ever felt in my life, my eyes searching for anything that would remind me of her, my Emmy. A dropped pacifier under a dresser, a tinge of yellow in the corner where the cream shade hadn't completely concealed it. Nothing. My knees buckled and I dropped to the floor, a strange keening coming out of me. A sound so primeval I wouldn't have thought myself capable of making it. It didn't sound human.

I howled, long and hard, my eyes seeing nothing but empty space, my body feeling under attack from the hard floorboards under my knees and elbows. My mind darted like a victim trying to elude an attacker.

The shadows deepened around me, twilight turning into night. My howls eventually dwindled to whimpers. What was the point of going on without my girl? Flashes of Emmy motionless in the tub invaded my mind, and guilt wrapped me in its vise-like grip. I shook my head, trying to physically dislodge the image from my mind. I'd never get past what had happened. It had seemed possible when the medical professionals had held my hands at the hospital and reassured me. Like angels whispering inspirational messages into my ears. But the reality was nothing like that. It was as lonely and bleak as the empty space around me.

I thought about how Dr. Ellison had advised me to write down everything in my journal. I stirred and began to get up, but the thought of revealing the wrenching story of my loss, self-recrimination, and grief overwhelmed me. I paused halfway between standing and sitting, feeling like a one-winged moth, unable to get where I wanted to be. Destined to flit endlessly in circles until all my energy drained.

I thought about Tim packing up and moving Emmy's belongings while I'd been hospitalized. Had kindness prompted him to remove every trace of the child we'd once shared? Perhaps he thought my fragile mind couldn't handle the process of removing Emmy permanently from our lives. I should be grateful, right? Then why did I feel so empty, thrust into a life as barren as the room I'd once rocked and soothed my daughter in?

"You should have warned me," I whispered, as if Tim were standing next to me. "A text to let me know . . ."

I didn't even know what he'd done with Emmy's things. Probably sold them. He never passed up an opportunity to make a buck. I felt my face getting red, but, standing and leaving the room, I sighed, realizing what was done was done.

I couldn't expect Tim to change when I seemed unable to. And, in truth, I knew very little about his childhood or family. Growing up in a lower-middle-class suburb of Seattle with three brothers whom he wasn't very close with—who all still lived on the other side of the country, near his parents—Tim had become independent at an early age. The only one in his family to go to college, Tim once told me mechanical engineers made a lot more money in New York, so he'd headed east upon graduation. And he'd seldom gone home.

His family had never visited us, not even when we married. Tim explained they couldn't afford the expenditures—airfare, hotel—to join us at city hall. He claimed he didn't have enough money to fund their trip, as he'd surrendered all his cash on my engagement and wedding rings.

Feeling guilty about Tim lavishing money on me rather than his family, I didn't protest when they stayed put. I'd dutifully spoken with them all on the eve of our wedding when Tim called them during a family gathering. I'd repeated the same lines, infused with the same cheer, with every family member whose voice boomed through the cell phone mouthpiece: both parents; his big brother, Ben; and two younger siblings, Jake and Todd. All congratulated us and expressed regret at not being able to attend our nuptials. I'd not spoken again with his parents until after Emmy was born, and I'd never again talked with his brothers. I walked into the bathroom, catching a glimpse of my mottled face. I turned on the faucet and cupped the cool water in my hands, then bent over and splashed my face and pressed my fingers against my cheeks to dislodge the sweat and tears.

I reached behind me to snag a hand towel draped over the rack beside the shower, but my hand connected with nothing but the smooth metal towel bar.

*Damn, out of towels.*

I couldn't remember the last time I'd done laundry. Water dripping in my eyes, I opened the linen closet door and slid my hands over the nearly empty towel shelf, my fingers connecting with a thin piece of terry cloth. I snatched it up and pressed the flimsy material to my face, freezing as my nose connected with Emmy's smell, a combination of soap, milk, and fresh bread.

I pulled it away from my face and stared, joy and sorrow engulfing me at the sight of the hooded baby bath towel balanced between my palms: white background and yellow ducklings with exaggerated, adorably cartoonish orange beaks.

Forgetting about my wet face, I hugged the towel close, as though it were Emmy herself, shoving away the pain lodged in my throat, thanking God for this gift. When Tim had cleared the house, he'd forgotten about the baby's items in the bathroom.

Folding the towel and placing it carefully back on the shelf, I scanned the closet floor, searching for anything else of Emmy's, but the tangled wad of used bath towels wedged between the lowest shelf and the floor obscured whatever else might have been residing there. I bent down, threw my arms around the stale-smelling bundle, and yanked, dislodging the compacted mass. Hefting it upward, I marched the overflowing pile to the washing machine in the basement. Not taking the precious minutes to run a cycle, I headed back to the bathroom and knelt in front of the narrow closet, looking for a tub toy or the oversized pink box of bubble bath. I reached into the dim corner and grasped a plastic bottle, pulling it out and holding it in front of my face.

Baby shampoo.

The lights in the room seemed to darken and my body swirled like I was on a Tilt-A-Whirl amusement park ride. I squeezed my eyes shut and dropped the bottle, hearing the hollow echo of its flat plastic bottom hitting the tile floor. The memory came rushing in: that last day with my baby. Giving Emmy her bath.

*Giving Emmy her bath?*

I snapped my eyes open as realization washed over me like an acid rinse. Painful and clarifying. *I never gave Emmy her bath.* Tim did. Sometimes I'd dab at her soft skin with a baby washcloth while he balanced her in the tub, but I never trusted myself around water. The legacy of my dad's drowning was such that I trembled violently near any amount larger than the contents of a teacup. The thought of submerging my precious infant into its unreliable depths would send me into convulsions. How could I have forgotten that, especially after Brandon's plunge? And why did I specifically remember reaching into the water and pulling my baby out?

The memory spurred my body into motion, but for once I ignored the trembling. I began pacing, walking out to the living room and around my coffee table. There was something—something at the edge of my mind. I had to access it. *Please, God*, I prayed. *Reveal it to me.* I forced myself to recall my hands reaching into the water. How had Emmy gotten submerged? And why were my hands the only ones I could recall? Where were Tim's?

I paused in the middle of the room, rubbing my temples like a swami tapping into a wellspring of spiritual insight. Slowly, the scene came to me. Tim ordering me to find the baby wash, the tear-free shampoo, as he leaned over the tub, Emmy balanced in his open palms.

I saw my hands rifling frantically through dozens of bottles and jars in the vanity compartment under the sink—moisturizers, petroleum jelly, shaving gel—unable to find the baby's products.

"They aren't here."

"Of course, they are," Tim snapped. "Look harder. And look over here, in the towel cabinet."

"Why would I put the shampoo in with the towels?"

*I saw the back of his head shake. "Why do you do anything?"*

*I stuck my upper body into the cabinet under the sink, my eyes searching the corners. I spied a bottle of mouthwash and a new tube of toothpaste, but nothing else.*

*"I'm telling you her wash and shampoo aren't here."*

*His answer was a soft splash like a fish breaking the water's surface and sliding back under. I leaned out of the vanity cabinet and looked at Tim, just turning back from the towel cabinet next to the tub, one hand still in the water. He looked alarmed.*

*Confused, I glanced into the tub, at the bubbles bobbing along the surface of the water. I leaned in and there she was, just beyond Tim's outstretched hand. An encapsulated angel in the water. So peaceful. So still.*

*"NO!" I plunged forward, my hands instinctively scooping her up, water splashing everywhere. Emmy not moving.*

*"Caroline!" His voice boomed into my ear as he careened into me, his arms reaching out, snatching Emmy away. "How could you?"*

The last thing I remembered was him running from me, our dripping baby limp in his arms.

I didn't even bother trying to stop the seizures that overtook my body as I relived the horror of that day. Let them come, just like the truth had. *Tim* had left Emmy in the tub. He'd killed Emmy. Our baby girl.

And he'd blamed me.

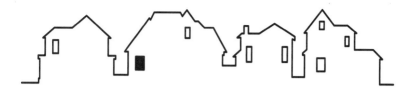

# CHAPTER THIRTY-FOUR

*Tuesday, September 19*

INSISTENT BUZZING JARRED me out of my zombie-like trance. It took a few seconds to understand what the noise was. As the realization of what Tim had done sank deeper into my mind, I'd spent hours on the couch. Had I even slept last night?

I reached for the phone.

"Caroline, it's Jeffrey. May I come over?"

"Yeah, sure." It amazed me how calm and collected my voice sounded, but as I hung up, I felt hollowed out, as I had when I'd stepped into Emmy's empty room. Tim had done that to me. He'd taken away what had mattered most. It was an accident. It had to be. He'd loved Emmy. I gnashed my teeth, wondering if he'd somehow convinced himself I really was to blame. Perhaps he couldn't live with himself if he faced what he'd done. Better to let me suffer.

I realized for the first time how weak he was. How self-involved and cowardly. It shifted the way I thought about our marriage, our family, and our daily lives. I sat for a long time, lost in thought. The doorbell intruded on my ruminations.

When I saw Jeffrey's unsmiling face, I hesitated before opening the door wider. But as he shouldered his way through my doorway, careful not to bump into me, he felt like a friend paying a visit. God, how I needed a friend.

We settled at the kitchen table, glasses of ice water for each of us. I had nothing else to offer him.

"I'm sorry I treated you so coldly, Caroline, but when I read the news article about the baby—"

"I understand." And I did. "Every time you were around me, I had Emmy. It must have freaked you out to discover she was never there."

"I was only thinking of myself." He looked down at our glasses. "But you aren't like that. You are obviously in so much pain over your loss, but you still dropped by to tell me about Annie in the ER." He finally glanced up at me, shaking his head slightly. "I'm such a shit."

The compassion in his voice nearly unhinged me. Blinking hard, I swallowed the urge to cry. "I think you reacted the way just about anyone would have, Jeffrey."

His expression softened. "Don't let me off that easy. I don't deserve it."

I smiled, savoring a rare kinship with another human. I'd had far too few of these moments in my life. But my smile wavered when I realized his expression might change once I told him that I remembered Tim letting Emmy go for that instant to find the shampoo bottle.

I imagined his lips tightening into a straight line and his eyes losing that spark of interest like Tim's had every time I mentioned topics he didn't want to discuss. For some reason, Jeffrey's reaction to what I was about to tell him mattered to me.

But then I thought of Emmy, of her little life cut short. Of all that she'd never know, learn, or experience. She'd been as alive as the woman I'd seen in the window. And now maybe neither of them were. It was a feeling as undeniable—as visceral—as my fingertips on the wooden tabletop. Impermeable to the whims and vagaries of the mind. I wasn't—could never be—able to simply accept and move on. Not until the truth was out there.

I started talking, my mouth moving, sharing our story of loss, Tim's, and mine. As I spoke, I felt the wetness on my cheeks, but I ignored it, so lost was I in the empathy in Jeffrey's gray eyes. For some reason, I thought of my father. His eyes were not the same color as Jeffrey's, but I envisioned the same expression as if he understood how impossible it was to say goodbye to those I'd loved most.

When I finished, I looked away, suddenly shy. I'd laid my life out before this man, like displaying my wares at a flea market. Would he look at the goods closely, searching for treasures, or simply smile politely and move on?

"I think you're very brave, Caroline."

"Brave?"

He leaned forward. "When I found you crawling out of the pond you couldn't even speak in coherent sentences. That's how traumatized you were. You could have said nothing about what you'd witnessed, just kept your mouth shut and let me drive you home. But as you recalled the events of that evening, you tried to do the right thing. You told me, and we alerted the police."

I snorted. "But they didn't believe me. Just like they won't believe that it was Tim's negligence, not mine, that . . ." I couldn't complete the sentence. Couldn't say *killed Emmy*.

Jeffrey rubbed the side of his face. "The truth has a way of coming out."

"Maybe not this time. I've been institutionalized for mental-health issues. Tim hasn't. If he tells the world I'm responsible for what happened, people will believe him—already *have* believed him." I sighed and ran a hand through my limp hair. "How do I change what people think?"

"You may not be able to . . . yet. But don't be a victim, Caroline. Don't give any old asshole permission to use you, cheat you, or hurt you. You have power too."

I laughed, sounding sad rather than happy. I was the most powerless person I knew. I hadn't figured out a way to hold on to my daughter, my husband, or even my dad. I didn't control my own destiny and never had. "I don't have power, Jeffrey, or anything of value. This crappy ranch is heavily mortgaged, and I can't hold down a job." My throat felt as dry as a bowl full of dust. I took a sip of water. "Hell, I don't even have a checking account."

"Why is that?" He tilted his head. "How do you pay your bills and buy necessities?"

"Tim handles all that."

Jeffrey's brow puckered. "But you mentioned you and Tim are separating. You need to know what your assets are."

I felt a tightness in my chest as I looked at him. "I'm sure we'll settle once the divorce . . ." I let my voice trail.

"That will be too late." Jeffrey rubbed his forehead, sat back in his chair. "Look, Caroline, you need to get a good lawyer. Someone who will help you divide your shared assets equitably."

"I don't need a lawyer. I don't own anything."

Jeffrey drummed his fingers on the table as he looked at his water glass, clearly in thought. Eventually, he said, "You mentioned your mother died recently. What about her estate?"

I blinked. "Tim and I went through the things in her apartment. I chose whatever trinkets I wanted, and we donated the rest."

"I'm sure you didn't donate her money."

"Tim told me she didn't have much. A few bonds and a couple thousand in her checking account. I must admit, I didn't pay much attention because by the time her will settled, I was in the institute." I blushed. "I guess I was so distraught over Emmy, I didn't see things too clearly."

Jeffrey nodded, the expression on his face indicating he saw things very clearly. "You have no family left, right?"

"My dad drowned when I was six."

"I recall you telling me that. Did your mother work?"

I nodded. "She worked for the same doctor for years," I paused, thinking. "Probably twenty-five years."

"She may have had a pension or 401-K. And as your father's widow, your mother would have gotten everything that had belonged to him. What did he do for a living?"

"He was a salesman. Pharmaceuticals, like his father before him."

"Pharmaceutical reps are often partially compensated in stock options. That could run into a lot of money." Jeffrey's eyes met mine. "Have you seen any recent financial statements?" When I shook my head no, he added, "I think you need to pay your husband a visit."

I nodded. A visit was the only thing I owed Tim. He'd apparently taken everything else from me.

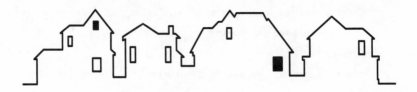

# CHAPTER THIRTY-FIVE

*Thursday, September 21*

I PLACED MY CELL phone, the running video camera facing out, in the mesh pocket along the outer edge of my handbag. Taking a deep breath, I knocked on Tim's apartment door.

He frowned as he opened it, realizing who'd disturbed him. "I told you to stay away from my place, Caroline."

"I know." I tried to keep my voice steady. "But I'm extending you a courtesy you never offered me."

His expression was halfway between annoyed and amused. "Oh yeah, what's that?"

"I'm letting you know in advance that you will be receiving a visit from the police."

He snorted. "What are you talking about?"

"I have excellent therapists, Tim. They're helping me remember things —things I'm sure you'd prefer I never recall." I made sure to project my voice so the residents of nearby apartments could hear me. "Like when you told me my mother had no money when she died. Or that you allowed everyone to believe it was my fault our daughter died when it was yours." I swallowed the choking tightness in my throat.

Tim's eyes sprang comically wide. He looked like a cartoon character. If the topic of my outburst hadn't been so devastating, I'd have laughed. Before I could even ask, Tim stepped aside and ushered me in. It was seven thirty, just after the dinner hour. I imagined he didn't want to risk any of his neighbors hearing my allegations.

I stepped into his vestibule, my jaw dropping as I peered into his living room. The rich leather sofa, cream linen chairs, and plush rug as thick as a mattress looked like something in a high-end showroom.

"This isn't what you think," said Tim, standing in front of me in what appeared to be a vain attempt to block my view. "This furniture belongs to my girlfriend."

"Is she a Kardashian?"

"No, just an attorney. Now, what did you need to tell me, Caroline? You think I *murdered* our child?"

"Not murdered. Neglected." I tried to keep my voice from shaking. "But the result was the same."

"Obviously your new meds need adjustment."

"Be sure to share your expert opinion with the police when they arrive, Tim. I'm sure they value the medical insights of mechanical engineers."

He stared at me, trying to gauge whether I was bluffing. "You keep going to counseling, but you never seem to get better. If anything, you're getting crazier. Accusing me of killing our daughter is a new twist. But maybe it's progress. At least you aren't still lugging around an empty baby carrier."

I pressed my lips together as my breath stalled in my throat. I couldn't let him goad me into submission. Taking a deep breath, I said, "I was looking for the baby bath items under the sink that day, remember? I searched and searched while you balanced Emmy in the tub, but when I turned back, you weren't holding her." I stared into his eyes, fighting the urge to circle my hands around his neck and squeeze as hard as I could.

He blinked and stepped away from me. "You're delusional, as usual."

"Am I?" I stared at him, wanting nothing more than to look away. I felt the sudden moisture pricking my eyes at the thought of Emmy in the tub. "You knew I didn't do well with water. I would never bathe her without you. I couldn't." I shuddered at the thought of it.

He rolled his eyes. "Just one more example of your everlasting neurosis."

"I've got problems, Tim. I admit it." My voice turned bitter. "Thanks for caring."

"Caring for you was exhausting, Caroline. It was like living with two infants rather than one."

"And now we have none." My voice broke and I had to look away. *Stay strong, Caroline.*

"It didn't have to be that way," he said, venom dripping from his words. "If you'd just put the shampoo where it belonged, I wouldn't have needed to look in the towel cabinet. I was only distracted for a second . . ."

"That's all it took."

Tim looked down, staring at the floor between us. Seconds ticked by, but he said nothing. Suddenly, his shoulders sagged. "I tried to revive her; I called for an ambulance."

"It didn't have to come to that." If he'd only been patient, Emmy would still be alive.

Now it was far too late.

He looked at me. "Caroline, please." His eyes looked moist. "We need to face this together, mourn together—"

"How dare you." My leg twitched with the need to knee him in the groan.

"I'm hurting too."

"Don't give me that! Your recovery was remarkably fast. By the time the authorities arrived, you had your story in place, didn't you? Said I'd been bathing Emmy and had let her slip into the bathwater." I shook my head, unbelieving even as I was figuring it out.

"Someone had to tell the police what happened. You wouldn't get off the bathroom floor. None of us could get you to speak. You simply stared into space like a zombie."

"You counted on my despair, pointed out my postpartum depression, I'm sure. You knew when it came right down to it, it would be my word against yours."

He stared at me, his jaw clenching and unclenching. The moisture breaching the lower rims of his eyes evaporated.

"Just tell me the truth," I whispered.

His eyes, as cold and hard as coal chips, held my gaze. A dangerous version of a staring contest. I didn't blink.

"I knew you wouldn't get blamed," he finally admitted, his voice low, measured. "If there was an inquiry, police would take your history into account."

"My history didn't matter," I ground out. "It was an accident."

"People have gone to prison for less." He looked away. "Once the cops discovered we weren't getting along, that you walked the streets at night, bringing Emmy out in winter weather—"

"No one has ever been imprisoned for pushing their properly dressed child in a stroller."

"In the middle of the night, Caroline? In below-freezing temperatures?" He paused, locking his gaze once again with mine. "If the police determined I was negligent too, who would keep us afloat? You had a hard time holding down a job, even before—"

"Only during the postpartum depression. I planned to go back to work—"

"You forget I was there, Caroline, watching you fall apart!"

"My hormones were raging. Anyone would have—"

"Accidentally drowned her baby." He swallowed hard but held my gaze. "Are you sure you're remembering things correctly?"

"Don't gaslight me, Tim." I shook my head violently. "I was institutionalized for two years. I'm never getting that time back." I threw my hands out in front of me. "And I'd gladly have given up my entire life if I could just have Emmy . . ." My voice broke. I covered my face with my hands, angry with myself. I'd vowed to rein in my emotions.

It was quiet in the apartment. As silent and empty as the atmosphere on the moon.

"Look, let's start over," came my husband's voice, contrite, tentative. "Maybe we could make it work this time."

I lowered my hands and looked at him.

"We could begin again. I'm sure of it."

I thought of all the times I'd yearned to hear those words from him. I studied his features, aware that his expression was more desperate than amorous. Did he honestly think there was a way to fix this?

"We've learned from our mistakes." His voice took on a pleading quality. "We'll know exactly what to avoid next time around."

He spoke as though we'd ruined a recipe or painted a wall in our house an unattractive color. How was I considered the crazy one in this relationship?

"Let's just give it a try."

There was more at stake here. Tim didn't long for a reunion. He was terrified I'd tell anyone who'd listen about what had really happened to Emmy. And I'd start asking questions about my mother's estate. The truth hit with the force of a sledgehammer. Fast on the heels of our shared tragedy, he saw an opportunity to be rid of me and he took it, feeding his carefully constructed narrative to anyone—and everyone—who would listen. Troubled woman with a tragic background—majorly depressed. Perhaps even suicidal. As time went on, he'd likely added to the story, concocting believable tidbits that would ensure my continued institutionalization.

And he'd never expected me to get out of the psych ward.

The desperation coming off him slammed into me just as forcefully. He had no choice but to keep me close, at least for a little while. I again recalled our early days, when he'd dramatically professed I was his oxygen, and it was true. Only my starry-eyed interpretation had been faulty. Oxygen, after all, is the one thing that feeds a fire. The more you have, the higher the flames leap. And Tim needed me to help him torch my life. He'd counted on me creating an inferno so intense and lasting, I'd not survive.

Infusing my voice with an encouraging note instead of what I really wanted to do—spit in his face—I said, "I've waited for months to hear you say that."

His smile looked hopeful. "The wait is over."

I forced an answering smile. I'd underestimated his arrogance. His certainty that I needed him so badly I'd be willing to accept him no matter what had happened between us. That I'd be able to overlook the fact that he'd allowed our baby to drown and blamed it on me. I had a weird impression of acting—as though we were in a play or, more appropriately, a soap opera. Tim was doing nothing more than spewing lines he was paid to recite. I suspected the payment was coming from my inheritance.

I stared at his smug expression, wanting to slap the self-satisfied grin off his face. My husband thought he'd won me over, again. He had no idea who I really was, and he never had. But that apparently hadn't mattered to him. He'd discovered my mother's financial status and realized I was vulnerable. The timing bore out this theory. After my mother died, he'd started pulling away.

Now that I viewed him without emotion, the picture was so clear. It hadn't occurred to me until this very moment I was bound to a narcissist. I thought about his lack of close friends, his physical and emotional distance from family members. Most of all, his strict judgment of others while allowing himself huge leeway for his own mistakes. Even foisting the deadly neglect of his child onto me. Why hadn't I noticed it before? Perhaps narcissism had seemed normal to my lithium-addled brain.

"What about your girlfriend?" I asked, trying to keep the sarcasm out of my voice.

He brushed his hand in the air. "That's not working out."

"Why is that?"

He looked away. "She's not really around anymore."

Perhaps she'd left him. Smart woman. But no, there had to be more to it than that. I looked back at the beautiful living room. "She left all this expensive furniture behind?"

Tim's eyes flickered with impatience for just a second, but he masked it quickly with an uneven grin, knowing the charming effect it always had on me. Again, I wanted to kick him in the groin. And kick myself while I was at it.

"I'm sure she'll pick it all up at some point, or I'll give her a few bucks for the stuff."

That was *literally* what he'd do. Pay her a pittance for the costly furnishings.

"Yes, well, I'm glad we talked." I slapped an earnest expression across my features as I turned and walked to his door, swinging it wide. Stepping out, I said, "Oh, by the way, I was bluffing about the police." I looked over my shoulder and smirked. "But you knew that, didn't you? You could always read me like a book."

His superior smile said more than words would ever convey. "I'll be in touch, Caroline."

I couldn't tell if that was a promise or a threat.

# CHAPTER THIRTY-SIX

*Friday, September 22*

"TAKE A LOOK at this." I passed my cell phone to Jeffrey across the greasy Formica tabletop. We'd set up Rex's Roadkill as our official meeting place.

He palmed the phone, angling its surface at eye level. I said nothing as he watched the shoddy video footage I'd recorded from the side pocket of my purse. It looked like something a child holding an iPhone for the first time might produce.

But the sound was perfect.

"Do you think I need to go to the police with this?"

"And tell them what? He accidentally killed your child?" Jeffrey handed the phone back. "It's incredibly sad, but not criminal."

"But he set me up." My back stiffened. "Lied to the police and let the world believe it was me—"

"Look, I'm not saying Tim isn't dangerous. I think he is, and there's no telling what he'll do now that you're questioning his handling of your mother's estate." He pushed his turkey club sandwich to the side and leaned his forearms on the table. "But you haven't exactly provided ironclad evidence of a crime."

I thought of the cops in my living room after I'd witnessed the bleeding woman at the Pine Hill house. If I handed over my odd cell phone recording, I could seem crazy, maybe even vindictive.

"You're probably right." I pressed my fingertips to my temples, feeling a tension headache developing.

"We'll use this, Caroline, but we need more evidence of wrongdoing. Do you recall the law firm who handled your mother's estate?"

"Yes." I rubbed my chin as it came to me. "Sloane and Sloane, a practice about forty minutes from here, in the town where I was raised. My mother set everything up through them. I remember it because I once told her it sounded more like a detective agency than a law firm."

Jeffrey stared at me. "You're kidding me."

I looked at him blankly. "About what? Sloane and Sloane? It *does* sound like a detective agency, right?"

His eyes darted to the sandwich he'd pushed aside moments earlier. He reached for it.

"Yeah, I guess it does."

I studied him. His demeanor had altered drastically in the last twenty seconds, but I couldn't make sense of the change.

"Do me a favor, Caroline," he said as he lifted the turkey club to his lips. "Record your conversation with them on your cell phone, just like you did at Tim's. We need to pile up as much evidence as we can."

"What's wrong?" I blurted out as I watched him bite into the sandwich. Something seemed odd about his behavior, but maybe it was just in my mind.

I wasn't adept at picking up on social cues.

"Could be nothing," Jeffrey said around a mouthful of meat and bread. "Just be sure to record your visit. And call me right after you leave the law firm."

FORTY-FIVE MINUTES later I turned the car into the parking lot next to Sloane and Sloane Law Associates. I stepped out of the car, stretching my legs and smoothing the wrinkles from the front of my slacks.

I made my way to the building, pausing to read the smaller bronze plaque under the firm name: "Brian Sloane, Esq. Stephanie Sloane, Esq." I'd phoned the law firm and made a hasty appointment as soon as I'd left Jeffrey to his sandwich, recalling the receptionist's reluctance to schedule anything new on a Friday afternoon. She'd tried to steer me to a time slot next week.

"I must talk with someone now. There is a lot of money at stake," I'd said. "And since your firm handled my mother's estate I'd hate to go elsewhere." Part truth, part lie. I'd hoped I got the balance right.

I had. I was told Brian Sloane had a few minutes to spare that afternoon.

As I stepped inside, I gave the studious-looking woman with tortoiserimmed glasses and a tidy dark bob behind the reception desk my name, and a few minutes later she ushered me into a richly appointed office with mahogany bookshelves and a tremendous antique desk in the center of the room. My gaze took in the heavy law tomes lining the shelves and the fastidiously neat desktop.

"Good afternoon," said a slim, dark-haired man with unremarkable features, standing up behind his desk and reaching out to clasp my hand. "I'm Brian Sloane." He gestured with his other hand for me to sit in one of two leatherbound chairs in front of his desk. "I'm afraid my receptionist didn't get your name."

"It's Caroline," I said, purposely not revealing my last name. Not yet. Jeffrey's odd behavior at the greasy spoon had made me wary.

"You said you have business with our firm?"

Glancing from his suit, which looked like it cost more than my monthly mortgage payment, to the cell phone camouflaged in the mesh side pocket of my purse, I was certain it was recording. As I sat, I angled the oversized handbag upward so that it rested against my chest, the mesh pocket facing the desk. "Actually, you handled my mother's finances while she was alive, and I believe you executed her estate upon her death." I gave him my mother's name: Lilith Messier.

"I see," said Sloane, turning to the laptop to his left. He typed quickly, his fingers flying over the keyboard. "Do you have identification?"

"Yes, I brought my original social security card with my maiden name as well as my license and the new social security card I received after I married."

He paused, his fingers hovering over the keyboard as he read the screen. I wished the laptop had been angled enough for me to read it as well. He looked up at me and placed his hands on the desk. "May I see the items?"

Keeping my handbag steady, I pulled my wallet out of the center pocket, dug my license and social security cards out, and held them out to him.

Instead of taking them he merely glanced at the cards spread across my palm and nodded. "I only have your husband listed as the contact, so what I can share is relatively little, Mrs. Case, but it hardly matters at this point. All the money has been transferred out of this account."

I felt a sickening twist in my stomach. "All the . . . Could you tell me where it's gone?"

Sloane pursed his lips. "I'm afraid I've told you all I know. My sister handled this account and she's not here. Now if you'll excuse me, I have another appointment in a few moments. I suggest you ask your husband about the account." He stood.

I stood as well. "My husband is presently indisposed. That's why I'm here." I tried to keep the annoyance out of my tone. This was *my* mother's account, not Tim's. "When will your sister be in the office?"

"I don't know." He looked toward the door. "Annie's on sabbatical."

A sudden pressure squeezed my chest. "Annie?"

Sloane looked as though he were suppressing a sigh as he glanced at me. "Yes, her nickname. It's short for Stephanie."

"Annie Connolly," I said. Jeffrey's strange reaction when I'd mentioned the name of the law firm suddenly made sense. "I've been looking for her."

Sloane's gaze turned sharp. "Why is that?"

"Because she's missing, isn't she?"

"Listen, Mrs. Case," he began, eyebrows lowering and voice steely, "I'll tell you what I told the others who came here searching for her: I don't know where she is, okay? She's an adult, free to go where she likes, do what she chooses. She's entitled to her privacy. And I am not my sister's keeper. Now, if you don't mind, I must insist you leave."

I stood up, my mind spinning. But one thought trumped the rest. "She's been gone for more than a month."

"I'm fully aware of that. She informed me before she left that she'd be gone indefinitely." He took a deep breath. "Now, if you don't mind, my patience with you is wearing thin."

"Fine." I backed away and turned toward the door, Brian Sloane hot on my heels. I stepped through the doorway and paused, looking back at the lawyer. "I find your lack of curiosity about your sister's whereabouts stunning. How do you know she's okay?"

"That is none of your concern," he said, closing the door in my face. I looked around the waiting room, which was empty except for the woman behind the desk. She gave me a nasty look, her face reddening.

As I walked toward my car, I could feel the receptionist's glare on the back of my head. I hurried around the front of the Honda, looking back at the building I'd just exited. Sure enough, a pair of heavily rimmed eyeglasses stared out at me from behind the window.

I sat for a moment in my car, readjusting my cell phone and turning over my conversation with Brian Sloane in my head. Stephanie Sloane was Annie Connolly. No wonder my searches for her always came up empty. And her brother mentioned others were looking for Annie. He was clearly angry with me for asking about her. How did all this tie together?

I rubbed a finger over my upper and lower lips to remove the hastily applied lipstick I'd slicked on before stepping into the law firm, thinking it would make me look more professional. There was something else at play, but I couldn't access what it was. Staring across the empty lot, I pictured

Brian Sloane's angry face as he told me to leave his office. There had been something in his eyes, something in addition to the anger. I glanced at my own eyes in my rearview mirror, seeing the same look harbored in their depths. Fear.

I remembered what Dr. Ellison had told me about anger. How it was an excellent cover-up for fear. Could Brian Sloane have been afraid that something might have happened to his sister? Or did he know exactly where she was? Maybe he was involved in her disappearance—if that's what it was—or perhaps he'd realized how much danger she could be in. Did my speculations even matter? The guy would never talk to me again.

I cursed my magical ability to alienate others in record time. But then I remembered that Jeffrey had circled back to me, even apologized. For the first time in my life, it occurred to me that maybe the people who'd pulled away from me did so because *they'd* been the flawed ones. Why did I always assume it was me? After all, my mother had turned away because of her own fragilities. And Tim was in the wrong. He'd lied about Emmy's accident and could very well be plotting against me. But now I was building a case against him.

Maybe I wasn't as unlovable as I'd assumed. Perhaps I'd just had the misfortune of having unloving people thrust upon me.

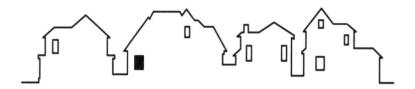

# CHAPTER THIRTY-SEVEN

*Saturday, September 23*

I THOUGHT ABOUT BRIAN Sloane incessantly, pacing endless laps around my coffee table. Did he truly have no knowledge of his sister's whereabouts? It seemed improbable. As unlikely as his supposed lack of familiarity with my mother's estate. How could siblings run a law practice together without knowing anything about each other's cases?

I must have legal options if Sloane couldn't—or wouldn't—share the details of my mother's financial holdings. I'd investigate that issue next week, but this evening my mind overflowed with thoughts of Annie Connolly. Where did she go? Or hadn't she gone anywhere? Perhaps she was still in town, residing in a shallow grave? I recalled the fear in Sloane's eyes, which quickly morphed into *another* pair of eyes squinting into my high-intensity light beam. If Matt was actually Ray Connolly, it made sense he was hiding out in another empty home nearby. He could be close to his lover and keep an eye on the Pine Hill house. Monitoring police activity or observing anyone else snooping around the property. My heart thudded heavily. He'd probably seen me trespassing. I pondered Sloane's reference to "the others" who'd inquired about his sister. If Matt was Ray Connolly, he'd be seeking the whereabouts of his wife—or pretend to be. I was pretty sure of who else had sought out the lawyer. I whipped my cell phone from a pocket and scrolled through the contact list, pressing Jeffrey's name.

When he answered, he didn't bother with a proper greeting. "What have you got?" he asked. I felt like a fellow reporter updating him on a lead.

"Did you go to the offices of Sloane and Sloane looking for Annie?" I asked.

"Yeah, more than a month ago. Turned up nothing. How did your meeting with the esteemed Brian Sloane go?"

I ignored the question, preferring to hit him with one of my own: "Why didn't you tell me you'd gone there? That you'd met Annie's brother?"

"I didn't want to bias you."

"Bias me? What does that mean?"

"I wanted you to go in fresh, with no preconceived notions about the man or their practice. Were you able to record the encounter on your phone?"

An unwelcome tightness radiated from throat to chest. "You're not sharing everything with me, Jeffrey, are you?"

Silence greeted me for a few beats. Eventually, he said, "I'm not sure what you mean."

"Not only did I walk into that law firm blind, you never even told me Annie's real name, or shared the fact that it was also her practice. Why would you withhold that information?"

"I just told you why."

"I know what you told me, I'm just not convinced it's the truth."

"Okay," he paused. "What can I say to convince you?"

"I'm not sure you can. I'll call you back later." I clicked off, anger roiling in my chest. Jeffrey was underestimating me, like Tim always had. If he'd already been rebuffed at the law office, was he hoping I'd have better luck? Probably. News reporters had to be flexible if they were going to get the story, right? If following all leads didn't get results, perhaps reexamining the situation from a different angle might be successful. He'd seen opportunity in my predicament. Maybe he'd even created an issue where there was none, to spur me into action. After all, Tim had always maintained my mother died with very little money. It could be true.

But what if it wasn't?

⌒⌒⌒⌒⌒⌒

IT WAS NEARLY midnight when the insistent pounding on my front door made me startle on the sofa, where I'd fallen asleep. Instantly awake, I stared at the built-in clock at the upper right corner of my television screen, above a high-speed car chase splayed across the TV's other 32 inches. Recalling Mary's mystery man who preferred unannounced visits after dark, I dropped to the floor, snatching the cell phone off my coffee table and pressing the telephone icon on the display screen.

"Caroline?" called a familiar voice, just as my pointer finger hovered over the nine, to be followed by two ones. "Are you there? We need to talk."

Jeffrey.

I clutched the phone as I stood and made my way to the front door but didn't open it. "What are you doing here at this time of night?" I demanded through the wooden barrier, my voice gruff.

"I tried calling you, ten times. Why didn't you answer me?"

I'd turned my phone silencer on after his fourth attempt. "I wasn't in the mood to talk."

"Are you going to leave me standing out here all night? That's what I'll do. I'm not leaving."

I almost smiled at his strategy. Hadn't I planned the same action when I'd stood on his doorstep?

"What is so urgent that you must talk to me in the middle of the night?" I asked, opening my door but keeping the chain in place so he could only see a thin slice of me.

253

"You're pissed at me, and you have every right to be."

"Go on," I said, not moving.

He tilted his head, looking exasperated. "It's getting kind of nippy out here, you know."

I kept my expression neutral but said, "You're not a very patient man, are you? You want *what* you want *when* you want it."

He blinked, clearly having no answer.

"Look, Jeffrey, I'm not a reporter at your paper. If you require my investigative services, you should pay me. At the very least I need to know what I'm getting myself into."

"You're right." He dug into his pocket and with a grin pulled out a five-dollar bill. "It's all I've got."

"A five-spot at midnight. What kind of girl do you think I am?" I grinned back, closed the door, unlatched the chain, and let him in.

He looked sheepish as he crossed the threshold. "I can't seem to get things right between us."

"Ain't that the truth," I agreed. "You want to tell me what we're apparently collaborating on?"

His features rearranged themselves into a serious expression. "I've looked everywhere for Annie, but I keep reaching dead ends." He ran a hand through his dark hair. "It's not that I'm digging up good news or bad news. I'm not unearthing *anything*."

I noted the worry in his eyes and the way his shoulders stooped.

"You really care about this woman," I said, my voice carrying a trace of envy.

How I'd love to be loved like that.

"I do," he said simply.

"Okay." I turned and walked into my living room. He followed and sat on the only chair. I flopped back onto the couch. "Fill me in on anything about your search that you didn't already tell me."

"I think you know just about everything now."

"Who else is looking for Annie?"

"I don't think anyone." His brows lowered in concentration. "Why do you ask?"

"Something Sloane said about others looking for her." I called up the video on my phone and handed it to Jeffrey.

His eyes focused on the screen with a single-minded intensity. "He's lying."

"How can you tell?"

Jeffrey pointed to the phone. "He's not making eye contact when he tells you he doesn't know where Annie is. And look how he abruptly stands, trying to get you away from him as quickly as he can? I interview scum like this nearly every day of my life." Jeffrey looked like he wanted to spit. "The store clerk who claims he never slipped his hand in the till, or the nice guy who declares he didn't batter his bloodied girlfriend."

I nodded. "What he *did* inadvertently confirm is that someone else is looking for her."

"Maybe a friend or her sister?"

I stared at him. "Annie has a sister?"

He nodded. "Her name is Cynthia Saunders. I don't know their family dynamic. I see no indication that Brian Sloane ever visits her. When I paid Cynthia a visit and explained I was a friend looking for Annie, she told me to go to hell and slammed the door in my face. Just like the brother did to you. I've been driving by her house each day for weeks now. I usually go in the early morning or on my way to my shift in the evening, looking for anything out of the ordinary. All I ever see is Cynthia and her husband leaving the place or coming home. Sometimes they're together, but usually they're alone. He leaves and returns at about the same time each day, which would indicate an off-site job, but her comings and goings are sporadic. Cynthia either works from home or doesn't have a job."

"Anyone else with her, like kids?"

"No." He yawned. "I've tried to get my buddy in the police department to check out her house, but without cause, he won't go near the place."

My eyes widened. "I'm glad to hear that. Officers aren't spies."

"I know." He shook his head. "But it's been weeks since Annie took off. I'm desperate. And I think the sister's on to me. I'm pretty sure she recognizes my Jeep. I've seen the curtains in her front window flutter a few times when I've driven by."

"Are Annie and Cynthia close?"

Jeffrey looked toward the kitchen, his eyes unfocused. "Annie and I didn't have that kind of relationship."

I scrunched my nose. "What do you mean?"

He looked back at me. "We seldom talked about anyone else. The two of us were caught in a maelstrom of our own making."

"Volatile?"

"Only in the sense that it was explosive. Like a confetti bomb detonating every time we were together." Jeffrey looked at me, his eyes shining in the dim light cast from my end-table lamp. "You know, new love and all that."

My face reddened. It had been such a long time since I'd felt that way about Tim. Maybe I'd never experienced such all-consuming enchantment. It was uncomfortable to think about.

I cleared my throat. "Where does Cynthia Saunders live?"

"Not far from here. Just on the other side of your neighborhood."

"Is that so?" I sat up, a plan instantly forming in my mind. Cynthia Saunders had better ensure her door-slamming hand was primed; she was about to get another visitor.

# CHAPTER THIRTY-EIGHT

*Sunday, September 24*

A S I DROVE along the maze of streets in my neighborhood, the recollection of Matt's eyes unexpectantly in my flashlight beam jolted me. I nearly jumped the curb. Breathing erratically, I stopped the car and put it in park. I had to get ahold of myself before I knocked on Cynthia Saunders's door. Setting my hands firmly on the steering wheel, I gave my body a few seconds to settle. I felt like I'd just guzzled ten cups of coffee.

One truth I knew for certain was that Annie was having an affair with Jeffrey. What I wasn't sure about was whether Annie had something going with Tim and Jeffrey at the same time. I didn't think so. Jeffrey hadn't lived in Deer Crossing three years ago when Tim met Annie and possibly hatched a plan to embezzle my inheritance. Tim may have begun cheating on me then too, but I had no proof that either of those things happened.

I had to admit to myself I had few facts but plenty of suppositions. Like the suspicion that my husband realized he could push me over the edge after

Emmy's death—get me committed and take over my mother's entire estate. After he tucked me away at the institute, he could pretend to hold the assets for me but instead keep them for himself. I let out a frustrated breath. All the more reason to align himself with a dodgy lawyer to navigate the paperwork. I considered the possibility of Tim keeping me committed for as long as possible, but insurance wasn't going to pay for an indefinite stay without reason. Maybe my doctors released me before Tim could finalize his plans. I sat back, pondering. Could my mother's estate be that significant? It could be—a good reason for Tim to stick around after he found someone else. Yet if Annie were double-crossing him by starting up with Jeffrey, I imagine Tim would have become very angry. Dr. Ellison told me angry people were unpredictable. They could do drastic, even violent things, like beat others up badly enough to send them to the ER. A chill washed over me.

I recalled Dr. Ellison's words during a recent session in my hospital room, when we were examining my mother's rage that day on the pond: "Anger turned inward becomes depression. Anger aimed outward is aggression."

Had Tim become enraged with Annie and beaten her? Did he have it in him to kill her? I had to discover whatever I could. I put the car in drive.

As I coasted along the streets, I realized if the bloodied woman I'd seen was, indeed, Annie Connolly, I had no business being alone with my husband ever again. Tim knew Annie, probably intimately. He had a motive to hurt her if she'd left him and absconded with his ill-gotten funds. Perhaps after the two colluded to gain control of my mother's estate she double-crossed him. She could use legalese to outmaneuver someone unfamiliar with the law. Of course she could.

Again, I wondered if Tim was capable of violence. I recalled him being so angry with me, his face had turned varying shades of red and purple. He'd often invaded my space during arguments, looming over me threateningly. He'd even shoved me a few times, but he'd never struck me.

Still, I'd always backed down when his temper flared. What would have happened if I hadn't? Would I have ended up in the ER?

"You're letting your imagination run away with you again," I chided myself as I turned onto the street where Cynthia and her husband lived. "You have no evidence that Tim is involved in Annie Connolly's disappearance. Get a handle on yourself, Caroline."

By the time I parked in front of the Saunderses' tidy sage-colored split-level, twilight was surrendering to night. I exited the Honda and marched up the concrete sidewalk as though I had a right to be on the property. I rapped on the fresh white paint coating the front door, startling like a newborn when a trim dark-haired woman opened it immediately, as though she'd been standing on the other side, anticipating my visit.

She looked at me warily. I noticed her rich, dark hair was ribboned with subtle gray strands.

"Hi, Mrs. Saunders?" I began. "My name is Caroline Case—"

"Case?" Her eyes connected with mine.

"Yes, I'm looking for your sister, Stephanie."

Her eyes narrowed. "Why?"

"It's a . . . business matter."

"How do you know her?" She leaned back, putting distance between us.

"She was the lawyer who worked on my mother's estate." I wondered if the woman picked up on the fact that I hadn't confirmed I knew Annie. "There have been some discrepancies and—"

"Why would you come to me? You need to talk to my brother, Brian. He and Annie practice—"

"I know, Mrs. Saunders," I cut in. "I've already spoken with Mr. Sloane. He couldn't tell me anything about my disappeared funds."

"Disappeared?"

"Yes, apparently he hadn't worked with your sister on my account. I've been trying to find her for a while, and I'm getting worried that she may also have vanished."

"Worried?" Her brows furrowed, creating stress lines in the center of her forehead. "Why are you worried about someone you know only professionally?"

"Nobody seems to know where she is." I schooled my features into an empathetic expression. "Not your brother or her friends."

"Look, Ms. Case, I'm afraid you've come to the wrong place. I don't keep tabs on my sister. Annie's a free spirit. She travels a lot. This is the first I've heard anything about her disappearing."

"But if I could just ask you a few questions, I'd really appreciate it."

"I'm afraid I can't help you." She stepped back. "Now I must ask you to leave."

"All right," I conceded. "Thank you for your time." As I spoke, she closed the door on me.

I retreated the way I'd come and got into my car, certain Cynthia Saunders was watching my every move from behind a window blind.

Two blocks later, I pulled up in front of a bi-level and quickly got out of the Honda, grabbing a black sweatshirt from my back seat before I exited. Pulling the sweatshirt over my pink top, I looked down at my attire: deep blue jeans and black sneakers. I was nearly indistinguishable from the dark.

I slunk through two yards, careful to make no noise. After my many forays into Deer Crossing, I was a pro at nighttime surveillance. Dodging between bushes and trees—and on the lookout for any of the dozen large dogs penned in their yards—I made my way to the Saunderses' side yard. I crept toward the house and hovered near a darkened window, hoping it was open. It wasn't.

Glancing around, I noticed a privacy fence extending from a back corner of the house. It comprised what looked like giant upside-down pencils with tapered tips pointed skyward. It was between five and six feet high. I pressed my body against the wood, stood on tiptoe, and glanced between two sharpened tips and into the backyard, seeing nothing at first. But as I scanned the shadows, a pinpoint of light in a back corner of the enclosed space moved up and down rhythmically. Too uniform to be a firefly. It took me a few seconds to realize it was the glowing tip of a cigarette. It sparked a tad brighter, then swerved upward to the left, suspended in the thick velvet of the night.

Brightness suddenly blazed through the dark, flooding the fenced yard in light, illuminating the woman sitting in the corner, one elbow leaning on a bistro table, her slender body settled in a small chair, legs crossed, hand with cigarette extended gracefully outward. She looked like the woman I'd just met, only younger. I squinted, taking in each feature.

"Turn that off," she hissed.

"There you are," Cynthia Saunders stepped out onto the patio just as the light went out. "We have the same problem as Brian. That woman—Caroline Case—showed up looking for you."

"Tim's wife came here?"

"Yeah, and we know what that means, don't we? Tim must know you're my sister." Cynthia's voice took on a desperate, high pitch. "You've got to leave now, or this time you may not escape with just a few cuts and bruises. This time he could kill you."

I slapped my hand over my mouth to cover my gasp. After all this time, I'd found Annie Connolly. She was hiding from Tim, but she was alive. My muscles released, the tension in my neck and between my shoulder blades dissipating—until a new, equally terrifying thought washed over me like a rogue wave poised to take out everything in its path.

Annie Connolly was not the woman I'd seen in the window at 21 Pine Hill Road.

# CHAPTER THIRTY-NINE

*Sunday evening, September 24*

I SAT IN MY car, fingers pressed into my temples, my mind spinning like a roulette wheel. I took a few deep breaths, telling myself to concentrate on getting air in and out of my lungs. Eventually, my adrenaline-spiked blood ceased skittering through my shaky limbs.

If Annie Connolly was hiding out in her sister's place, who was the doomed woman I'd seen at *her* house?

I stared into the night. Darkness was not the friend I'd so desperately relied upon these past months. Light was what I needed now. Illumination.

A streetlight flicked on overhead. I blinked. Divine Providence? I stared at the fluorescent globe, thinking again of Matt's eyes under my harsh cell phone light. Was he responsible for what I saw in the window that night? Melanie was not the same person as Annie Connolly, but I *had* seen her with Matt, hadn't I? Maybe Matt and Melanie had purchased the house from the Connollys. Perhaps they'd been fixing up the place before they moved in.

That made sense. Suddenly, I realized how off course I'd gotten, thinking the Connollys were the same couple I'd seen through their living-room window, dancing, that first night in August. Melanie and Annie both had dark hair and slight builds, but that may very well have been where the similarities ended. I remembered asking Jeffrey if Annie liked to dance and he'd been surprised by the question. I focused on Jeffrey. He'd been the man standing in the Connollys doorway, with Annie's arms wrapped around him. I'd noticed she'd cut her hair to a chin-length bob, but of course Melanie never had. I squeezed my eyes shut, picturing the ends of her dark tresses layered over her shoulders as she'd desperately clutched her neck and stared at me from the window. Oh God. I snapped my lids open. How could I have gotten things so wrong?

I blinked against the overly bright beam streaming from the streetlight, my mind sorting through the players in the macabre drama of my own making. I could account for Annie at her sister's house. Jeffrey was probably at his own place on a Sunday night. Matt was likely still squatting in an empty house on Woodmint, next to the Brocktons. But I had no idea where Melanie was, or if she was even alive. I took a ragged breath, suspecting I'd never see her again.

Her bloodied body loomed before me as I replayed the way I'd rushed into the foyer of 21 Pine Hill, stopping only when my head exploded, and I'd dropped into unconsciousness. I'd revived in the cold, watery depths of the nearby pond. The memory shot frost through my body, making me shiver uncontrollably. How had I gotten in the water? Had the killer dumped me there after what I'd seen? Preparing to pull me underwater, disposing of me too? No, that couldn't be right. I recalled Jeffrey's headlights cutting through the murky night as I was crawling *out* of the pond.

There was another possibility.

I rubbed my face as Emmy's sweet visage floated before me. For months I'd seen her, felt her—even reveled in her unique powder-and-milk scent— as I'd tended to a specter. A baby who had been dead for three years. Pain squeezed my throat, my chest. For a wild second I couldn't breathe.

I forced myself to swallow, focused on inhaling. As my lungs filled, I considered the horrifying possibility: Melanie was not real, and never had been. The anguished woman I'd seen that August night had been nothing more than a physical manifestation of my mounting stress. Once my issues with Tim resolved, would she fade into the recesses of my demented mind? I thought of the neon-orange fingernail fragment. Again I wondered if I'd conjured that as well. After all, I'd been the only one to see it. And now I no longer possessed the nail chip. Maybe never had.

I shook my head, praying for clarity, for a way to distinguish between reality and fantasy in my own mind. How to tackle such a formidable task? It seemed as impossible as singing the aria to an unfamiliar opera or conjugating verbs in Swahili.

How could I convey my conviction that a woman had been harmed in Deer Crossing one quiet summer evening when I couldn't even prove to *myself* it had happened? I pondered this for what seemed like hours but could have been mere minutes. Time lost meaning as my mind wound around the events of the past few weeks. I tried to isolate individual incidents and put them in chronological order, but they swirled together. One chaotic mass of confusion. I had to get out of there.

I put the car in drive, remembering that other night I'd driven through the darkened streets while the element of time eluded me. I'd been missing for hours after stalking Jeffrey. Had that been happening regularly? Was I losing pieces of my life without even knowing it? A trickle of sweat ran down my back at the possibility. I pulled into my dark driveway and walked to the front door, fishing for my key in my handbag and chiding myself, as usual, for not leaving even one light on.

I let myself in and flicked up the light switch, freezing when nothing happened. In the dark, I was unable to see anything.

I stumbled across the living room, approached the kitchenette, reaching toward the electrical switch to the right of the kitchen table as my eyes finally adjusted to the lack of light. I bucked like a startled mare when I saw Mary's shadowy form seated on one of the chairs at the table, her eyes starkly wide, noticeable even through the waxy darkness, a wad of material stuffed in her mouth.

I gasped.

A force hit me between the shoulder blades, shooting my upper body forward. I automatically reached out with both hands to break my fall, catching the table edge with my elbows, a howl of pain tumbling from my lips.

Something hard and unyielding was wedged into my lower back, pinning me against the table edge. I heard Mary moan and felt hot breath on the back of my neck. I tried to twist my head and catch a glimpse of my attacker.

Instant darkness filled my vision. I felt the sharp sting at the back of my head as the blindfold was knotted into place, painfully twisting my hair strands.

"Wait, what—"

Something was shoved into my mouth. I gagged. Terrified my air supply had been cut off, I breathed through my nose, relieved when I was able to get air into my lungs.

My arm was clamped in a vise-like grip. Using every ounce of energy I had, I twisted it, freeing my hand to claw the air. My fingertips connected with something solid. I dug my nails downward, but they only slid along material. Panicking, I kicked one foot harshly forward, my toes connecting with bone.

A grunt of pain followed by sudden excruciating pressure on my forearms. Strong fingers twisted my wrists together and pulled me forward. The sheer strength of my attacker revealed him to be a man.

Mind reeling, I battled for balance, my feet barely keeping up with the pace. Everything was happening so fast. Impressions of movement, pain, and speed bounced through me like dryer balls on the highest setting. This was all tied into what I'd seen. It had to be. I knew too much about the bleeding woman. She must be real—making my insistence that I'd seen her wounded and struggling a significant threat to the person who'd harmed her. The same man who was kidnapping me? Who was he?

It must be Matt. It was his bleeding wife I'd spied on and who was now missing, right? It couldn't be Tim. If he wanted to be rid of me, he could set up a meeting time or take me to dinner. In his arrogance, he was sure I'd drop everything to be in his presence. Of course, he could have hired someone to dispose of me. I immediately discounted that theory. Tim was too cheap to spend thousands on a hitman. But what about Jeffrey? What did I know about the guy other than what he'd told me? Maybe he'd made up everything . . .

I heard the front door's distinctive squeak and felt myself being dragged into the cool night air. The pervasive early-autumn smell of woodfire and the sound of crickets reminded me I was still in this world, even as I stumbled over the threshold, terrified the devil himself was leading me to the gates of hell.

He pulled me along my front yard, my toes catching on the edges of the stepping stones leading from my stoop to the driveway. I heard a door open and was shoved forward, headfirst.

My mind recoiled at the prospect of my face scraping the pavement, but I landed solidly on what could only be a car's back seat. I pushed myself upward just as a force at the back of my head shoved my face into the leather seat cushion, blocking my ability to breathe. I let my body go limp and became pliable enough for my attacker to release my head and lash my wrists together behind my back.

He left me sprawled on my side along the length of the back seat, pushing my legs toward my torso and slamming the car door with a resounding thud that seemed to seal my fate. A bubble of fear burst in my stomach, causing sharp stabs of pain in my abdomen.

I tried to figure out where we were going based on the number of times my body swerved in opposite directions, matching the swaying to my mental map of neighborhood streets. I also tried to calculate the length of time between each turn, but after swerving each way half a dozen times I became disoriented. I decided it would be better to dislodge the gag in my mouth so I could scream when—and if—my attacker pulled me out of the car. I pushed my tongue frantically against what felt like a terry washcloth solidly wedged between my upper and lower teeth, making my jaw ache.

The ride seemed endless, but when the car stopped, I had the impression we'd only driven a few miles. I couldn't get the gag out of my mouth, but I'd managed to move it forward, away from my throat. Still, my screams would be too muffled to be heard past a few feet. I heard a mechanical sound, like the automatic whir of a garage door lifting. The car nudged forward a few feet then died as the vibratory sound resumed behind me and settled with the finality of metal meeting concrete.

Pulling me from the car, the man half-dragged, half-carried me up a few short steps. My feet caught on the treads like a person who'd forgotten how to walk. Only the stranger's impersonal hands on my upper arms and consistent upward yanking kept me from plunging to the ground.

The sound of a tumbling latch accompanied the sensation of being dragged across floorboards. A click behind me revealed a door closing, punctuating the fact that I was now inside. The sudden, ominous quiet of an enclosed space was more terrifying than everything else I'd been through so far, but I suspected things were going to get worse. He dragged me along the interior of the building, neither of us bumping into anything, our footsteps bouncing off the walls and reverberating back. We were in an empty space.

I sensed rather than heard another door open, and the next thing I knew, I was stumbling behind him down another staircase. I screeched, feeling like I was tumbling headlong into a pit, but the material in my mouth absorbed the sound, allowing only a whimper to escape. Dank air assaulted my nostrils, and I guessed we were in a basement.

Hands pushed me back sharply. I cried out as my spine and wrist bones smashed into something unyielding—a stone wall?—but this squeal was also muffled by my gag. Pressure on the tops of my shoulders forced me to the ground, the sharp edges of the stones painfully scraping along my back through my T-shirt. My bladder released and I knew if it had been full, I'd have wet myself. As it was, a spot of moisture coated my underpants, but the discomfort was the least of my problems. I was truly screwed. Tied up and blindfolded in a smelly basement by God-knows-who, my fate not looking too promising.

A swooshing sounded above us—a door sliding open?—and the unmistakable tread of footsteps.

My assailant's feet shuffled, just inches in front of me, and immediately retreated. I heard him tiptoe up the basement steps. I tried to scream but it felt like I had a giant cork in my mouth, preventing any sound from escaping. Floorboards creaked directly above me; a door clicked softly shut. Must be the basement door. Suddenly, a cacophony of footfalls and raised voices joined the squeak on the level above, but I wasn't listening. This was my only chance to save myself. I'd try to sneak out before my attacker—or attackers—came back for me. Without my hands to push myself upward, I twisted to my right, hoping to flip onto my knees, making it easier to stand with my wrists still bound behind my back, but as I thrust my body to the side, I lost my balance and landed on top of something soft and utterly still.

My mind recoiled. Had something crawled into the basement and died? The cottony feel of material beneath my cheek revealed it was a clothed human body. A vision of the bleeding woman invaded my brain. I reared my head back and rolled sharply to the left. My face scraped the jagged wall, but the thick blindfold, ironically, protected my forehead and cheekbone from getting cut up. Brushing my head against the wall had also dislodged the cloth, turning it into a headband like the one Olivia Newton-John had worn in her *Let's Get Physical* video from the 1980s, my mom's favorite tape. My stomach heaved, the gag becoming a cork in my mouth. I thrust my tongue against the wad, forcing it, and the contents of my stomach, out. My mind whirled, trying to make sense of what was happening and separate real life from memories. My nose pressed against the musty basement floor, the stench churning my stomach and choking the air out of my lungs. I flopped on the cold concrete like a doomed trout at the bottom of a fishing boat, my only thought to get away from the dead body and my all-too-alive assailant. Pressing the toes of my right foot against the floor, I bent my left knee and shot that foot behind me, forcing my body onto my side, anchored by my right shoulder and hip bone. I bent my legs at the hips, took a big breath, and heaved my torso upward until I was again sitting on the floor. From there, I was able to bend my legs and make it onto my knees, my stomach dry-heaving as I stood.

There was no time to be sick or attempt to untie my hands. I raced forward until my right shoe encountered what looked like a flat riser, but it was so black in the basement it was hard to be certain. Staring down and tapping my foot along risers and treads, I let out a shaky breath of relief. I'd reached the basement staircase. I wanted to run, but I couldn't risk stumbling on the steps in the inky basement and falling backward onto the hard floor below. I gingerly climbed until I got to the basement door. Swiveling on the top step, turning my body away from the door, I stood on tiptoe and felt for the handle, nearly yelling out in triumph when my right palm connected with the chilly metal. I twisted gently and the latch gave way.

My heart pounded so hard my ears throbbed. I peered out, expecting a hand to lash out and strike me, but only shadows and shocking silence greeted me. A glow coming from outside a pair of French doors, thankfully open, revealed the way to freedom. I charged through them, pausing on an outdoor deck to get my bearings. A sound filtered to my ears—the trickle of water. My eyes scanned the trees stretched out before me, settling on a sliver of a lighted fountain beyond the scattered pines. It was a pond—*the* pond in Deer Crossing. The same one I'd recently crawled out of and had once watched my friend's toddler nearly drown in. I blinked and refocused on my immediate surroundings, concentrating on the rod of a street sign sticking into the curved mound of grass on the corner lot, reminding me of the plastic picks stuck into meat slabs at steak houses: *Rare. Medium. Well Done.*

I blinked again, panicked by the way my thoughts trailed away from me even as I strove to collect them. I forced my eyes to study the hulking shapes off in the distance, beyond the street sign. Squinting, I could just make out the silhouettes of a trampoline and swing set in a yard I'd spent so many hours in: Muzzy's. I got my bearings. I was standing across the street from my former friend's house and the hated pond. I was at 21 Pine Hill Road.

Where a dead woman resided in the basement. My brain screamed out even as my mouth clamped shut. Sweat broke out on my forehead and head-to-toe shaking rattled my body.

Motion in my peripheral vision made me hunch down. I watched two shadows running away, but in the pitch blackness of night my depth perception blurred. I couldn't tell if they were running together or if one was chasing the other. As the forms receded into deeper shadows, my eyes zeroed in on the one who appeared closer to the pond. Ambient light from the lit fountain drizzled a sheen along the right side of the runner. A swath of sandy blond hair, the outline of a man's solid shoulder, tapered waist. The loose swash of roomy shorts hovered over a powerful-looking calf. There was no doubt in my mind. I was looking at Matt. But why was he running away from the house? Was someone coming to Pine Hill Road? Someone threatening, like the police? Could I take the chance of waiting around to find out?

No, I couldn't. I had to get away. Fast.

The thought of the body in the basement propelled me forward. I couldn't allow the police to find me here to take the blame for a crime I didn't commit or, worse, risk Matt returning, looking for me. Oh God, Matt had killed his wife and left her to rot in their cellar. I ran in a different direction, along Primrose, past Muzzy's old house, going as fast as my legs could carry me with my hands tied behind my back. I rounded the bend onto Woodmint and headed straight for Jeffrey's place, halting only when I saw no lights on in his house and no car in the driveway. Breathing heavily, I wondered what to do next. I thought of the only other person I knew in Deer Crossing. I started down the street toward the Brocktons' house, but my steps faltered as I realized Jane Brockton was the one Matt was having the affair with. The likely reason he'd killed his wife. I recalled their whispered chatter on the street a few weeks earlier. She could be involved in the whole horrible mess. Maybe the other shadow running past the pond was Jane's. It would have to be, right? Matt was new to the neighborhood. Sure, he could have met other residents, but it was unlikely he'd known anyone well enough to involve in his treachery.

All the more reason to pound on the Brocktons' door—and alert Rod to what was happening. I started to run again, trying to decide exactly what I'd say to Rod to spur him into action. Telling him that as I'd spied on his family I'd discovered the liaison between Jane and their neighbor was probably not the best way to secure Rod's cooperation. But if I told him there was a body in the basement of 21 Pine Hill Road, he'd phone the cops first and ask questions later. Any innocent bystander would. I ran faster.

My mind whirled like a pinwheel in a windstorm as I made my way down Woodmint and turned up the Brocktons' driveway. I clamped my teeth together, forcing myself to focus. I had to sound reasonable when I spoke with Rod. If I came off like a raving maniac, Jane's husband would certainly call the police—on me. I couldn't risk his or the officers' doubt. If I wasn't credible, the officers could, indeed, blame me for the dead body.

I stopped at the top of the Brocktons' driveway. Their mudroom's interior door was open, only a screen providing a barrier between their home and the outdoors. Not surprising. Jane had obviously been in a hurry when she left. Balancing on one foot, I used the toe of my other shoe to bang on the door.

No answer.

Lifting my right knee, I pressed it against the lever, unlatching the aluminum screen door, but it closed before I could get anything wedged against the doorjamb. Should I go to the front door and ring the bell? Did I want to stand under the front porch light and risk Matt seeing me? Or alert the neighbors and expose Rod to potential embarrassment? He deserved better than that, didn't he? And now that I was free, I deserved to stay that way.

Peering through the screen door, my eyes met only shadows. Didn't anyone keep lights on anymore? I'd never again relish the dark. I lifted my knee to the latch again, and once more failed to open the door. About the only thing I was accomplishing was making a racket.

Something moved in the shadows beyond the screen. I squinted through the murk.

"Is that you, Rod?" I asked, my voice quivering.

"No, it's not." A light flicked on, and Jane Brockton stood before me, one hand clutching a steak knife, the other extended to the light switch on the wall. "What the hell are *you* doing here?"

# CHAPTER FORTY

*Sunday night, September 24*

I SHRANK BACK, LOOKING at her neat cloud of auburn hair, the ends kissing the straps of her skimpy fuchsia nightgown. She was equal parts frightened and angry, but she didn't seem guilty. I doubted she'd been jogging through the streets of Deer Crossing in her silky lingerie.

"I asked you a question," she charged through the door, ramming it into me. I had no choice but to back up and let her out. Standing too close, she lifted the knife until it was mere inches from my face. "Why are you here?"

I opened my mouth and shut it, unable to find my voice.

"I'm calling the police." The hand clutching the knife trembled.

I lowered my chin, losing eye contact. I may have been wrong about Jane's involvement with Matt's dead wife, but she was jittery. I didn't want to give her a reason to slash me. "I can explain everything but listen to me, please *do* call the police." I studied her through my lashes. "And stay away from that man."

She stilled. "What man?"

"The one you're seeing. He's dangerous, Jane."

"I don't know what you're talking about."

"Look, I'm not judging you." I inched back farther as her hand shook harder.

"I should hope not. My husband says anyone who would . . ."

I tuned her out, watching her lips move and her eyes narrow. Where *was* her husband? She wouldn't be standing in her nightwear with a weapon if Rod were here to defend her. I thought of the two shadows I'd seen running through the dark. Had Rod discovered Matt and Jane's clandestine relationship and taken it upon himself to confront the much younger man?

"Where's Rod?" I asked, hoping to cut off her self-righteous tirade. It worked. She stopped speaking, her eyes popping open.

"How do you know my husband's name?"

She got me there, but I didn't have time for a long explanation. "I heard you call to him once when I was in the neighborhood." I bit my lip, praying Rod was not where I thought he might be. I let my gaze wander suggestively to the dark house beside hers before glancing back at her.

"My husband is walking the dog." Jane had followed my gaze. "Not that it's any business of yours."

"Could you do me a favor and call the police to report a crime at 21 Pine Hill Road?"

"No, I could not!" But curiosity got the better of her. "What crime is supposed to have happened there?"

"Kidnapping," I said, turning around so she could see my bound hands. "And while you've so handily got a knife, could you please cut this rope?"

AFTER JANE GRUDGINGLY sliced the rope from my wrists and went back into her house to call the police, I realized Mary was still sitting, bound and gagged, at my kitchen table. Let the cops handle the issues at the Pine Hill house, I had an octogenarian to rescue. I ran home. It was much easier when I could pump with my arms, aiding the motion rather than having my bound hands behind my back acting as an anchor, slowing forward progress. Incredible that I had to learn that lesson the hard way.

When I got to my house, I scanned the immediate vicinity, my eyes searching for any car, person, or shadow that looked like it didn't belong in my neighborhood. I walked around my house and sat in the hedge for a while, listening for footsteps. When I was satisfied that nobody appeared to be monitoring my place, I slipped inside.

"Mary," I said on an expelled breath. She was right where I'd last seen her, her lumpy outline barely discernable in the dusky interior of the house. I didn't try to turn on a light, sure my attacker had turned off the breaker. Luckily, I knew my way around in the dark. I'd untie her and get us both the hell away from here. But as I crept forward, a thought struck me, something I'd been too desperate to think about before: when I'd first discovered my trussed neighbor and was attacked from behind, my home alarm hadn't gone off. Why was that? I remembered setting it when I left my house, and only a few people knew the code: me, Mary, and . . .

"Hello, Caroline," said Tim, stepping out of the galley kitchen. "You're a hard woman to hang on to."

"What the hell does that mean?" I snapped. "You never had any intention of holding on to me." But fear was rising from my clenched gut, quickly overtaking annoyance.

"Not until tonight." He chuckled, but it sounded mean rather than lighthearted. "That's changed. Now I'm taking both of you."

"Taking us?" I sneered. "Taking us where?"

"To a much better place."

# CHAPTER FORTY-ONE

I WAS BACK IN the basement with the dead body on one side of me and Mary on the other. It was well after midnight. The start of a new day whose dawn I feared I'd never see. Although Mary and I each had our wrists bound behind our backs, Tim hadn't gagged me this time. He'd even removed the cloth from my neighbor's mouth.

It was incredibly dark, and I didn't hear police sirens arriving. Damn Jane Brockton. I'd been a fool to think she'd help me. The police weren't on their way to us. Nobody was. My eyes darted around the dank enclosed space, seeing very little, yet something about the basement itself wasn't making sense to me. My mind was such a jumbled mess by now that I wasn't surprised. My whole body ached, and I was exhausted. I heard Mary breathing heavily beside me.

"I'm sorry," I whispered to her.

"Yes, she's sorry she's such a nutjob," sneered Tim, turning on his flashlight and pointing it from Mary's eyes to mine and back again. "And I'm sorry you're such an interfering old lush. You should have let me get the info I needed out of you the old-fashioned way. I'd have let you drink to your heart's content, and as soon as you returned the financial records you stole from me, I had even bigger plans for you, involving a handle of vodka."

"Those are Caroline's financial records I stole, not yours."

"Or yours," he snapped. "I need to know where that paperwork is, and you're going to tell me, or I promise to make things very painful for you."

"That's why you kept sneaking into Caroline's house? To get your hands on the documents from her mother's estate?"

"The ones with Lilith's authentic signatures, which couldn't be contested in a court of law," said Tim.

Mary cackled. "Took you long enough to figure out I had them. I thought you were smarter than that." In the flashlight's glow I could make out Mary grinning as she eyed my husband, whose brows had lowered menacingly over his eyes. He looked awful, as though he'd sweat buckets.

"So, you *did* steal my inheritance." I piped up to take Tim's rancor off Mary. My voice sounded weary. The man never missed an opportunity to disappoint me. "How predictable."

"The problem with you, Caroline, is that you're so damned unpredictable. I can never guess what you'll do next. The best place for you was at the institute. Since you had no money, you'd have become a ward of the state."

"Just stop talking, Tim. I don't care about what you have to say." Something was steadily creeping over me. Something like hopelessness. I glanced at the slight, still body slumped next to me. I'd finally found the woman I'd seen in the window. Staring at the dark cascade of hair covering her face, I recalled how graceful she'd looked dancing with Matt. "This poor woman. How could you just kill her?"

"I haven't done that, but I should." Tim kicked out, the toe of his shoe connecting with the woman's shin. She was jolted awake, a muffled moan escaping through the gag still in her mouth.

I flinched, gasping as I jerked toward Mary and inched sideways until I was nearly in my neighbor's lap. What the hell was going on? Unable to take my eyes off the woman, it suddenly occurred to me what hadn't seemed right about the basement: there was no stench of death surrounding what I'd assumed was a corpse stashed down there for weeks.

Tim reached out and removed the cloth from her mouth. She flinched and jerked her chin toward the shadowy wall when Tim angled his light on her torso, revealing a dark fleece pullover with the splashy Patagonia insignia plastered onto the front. His light trailed to shiny black leggings and black Balenciaga running shoes, which had to have set her back a couple grand. I'd seen the *Housewives* wearing those. My initial relief that she'd not been fatally wounded morphed into confusion when she whipped her face in my direction and looked at me; features I'd seen for the first time just hours before. *Annie Connolly.*

"You're not her," I said, hearing the wonder in my own voice. "Not the woman I saw in the window. You're the lawyer dating Tim . . . and Jeffrey Trembly?"

"I don't know what you mean." We locked eyes in the flashlight's ambient light, a mixture of defiance and fear in hers.

"Yes, you do, Annie," snarled Tim. "We had it all set up until you ruined everything—and with some moron who barely supports himself by reporting on the things *everyone else* in the world is doing." He spotlighted Annie's face in his light beam. "Caroline, meet the bitch who embezzled our funds." He angled the light into my eyes. "Annie, meet crazy."

She didn't acknowledge the introduction. To Tim, she said, "How did you find me?"

"Just followed my nutty wife. I didn't know what she was up to, but I was pleasantly surprised to discover she now fancies herself a private detective. She led me right to the house you were hiding in."

"I owe you nothing, Tim. I simply investigated ways for you to get your hands on your wife's money. I acted in good faith when Caroline here"— she angled her head my way—"entered the cuckoo factory."

"I saw the swanky furniture in Tim's apartment," I said, unable to stop myself.

What was I doing? The last thing I wanted to do was to support Tim in any way, shape, or form.

"I'd sold my house when Ray and I decided to separate. I needed somewhere to put my belongings. That was my only mistake. When I returned to Tim's for my stuff, he showed up, beat the crap out of me, and called the movers, telling them not to come over."

"I was at work," Tim pointed out. "You were being sneaky, collecting your furniture, and changing your phone number—not to mention taking my money."

*My money*, I thought angrily.

"Reach into my pocket," Mary whispered in my ear. I leaned slightly forward, giving myself room for my bound hands to reach behind me, the pads of my fingers connecting with the soft weave of her ever-present oatmeal sweater. I felt along the seam of a pocket and plunged my fingers inside it, the pointer and middle finger of my right hand curling around a cool, hard object.

As I pulled it out of her pocket, the tip of the object pierced the fleshy pad of my thumb. Sinking my teeth into my lower lip to keep from gasping in pain, I knew exactly what I was holding: a travel-sized bottle opener and corkscrew combo. The kind liquor stores give loyal patrons during the holiday season. Of course Mary would have one on her person at all times. She'd carry one as faithfully as an asthmatic toted an inhaler.

"I ended up in the ER, thanks to your fists," complained Annie.

"Consider yourself lucky," said Tim. "You could have ended up dead."

I grimaced in concentration, carefully wedging the tip of the corkscrew into the center of the knot binding my hands. The "Bickersons" were too distracted with each other to pay much attention to me. I rocked the metal implement back and forth, loosening the knotted rope until it slid off my wrists. Mary's shoulder bumped up against me encouragingly. I had to keep them talking while I devised a way to overpower Tim.

"There was another woman in your house, Annie. I thought she was you," I said.

"Caroline likes to spy on people," provided Tim. "Just another of her endearing qualities."

I wanted to kick him in the teeth. Wipe the smug smile right off his lips.

"Ava Hansen," said Annie, clearly ignoring Tim. "She and her husband, Tyler, are working with the realtors. Their company does small repairs, maintenance, and house staging. My ex-husband is a bodybuilder. He did some structural damage to the floors and walls with his weights."

"Ava Hansen," I repeated. Melanie's real name was Ava. And Matt was called Tyler. Why did the name Ava Hansen sound familiar? I knew I'd heard it before. I squeezed my eyes shut, concentrating, vaguely aware of Mary saying something to Annie. Ava Hansen. *Such a pretty name.* It came to me: the newspaper article—the blurb about the missing woman with a name far too lovely to be mixed up in the ugliness of a disappearance. Her family was looking for her.

Was that the first time I'd heard her beautiful name? It was, right? Then why was I picturing a newspaper clipping of a woman with stunningly gorgeous features?

"This isn't happy hour at the bar down the street," barked Tim. "Keep your traps shut before I gag you all again."

"What *are* you gonna do with us?" asked Mary, sounding more curious than afraid.

I glanced sideways at her, hoping she'd stop talking. She wouldn't hold up to a beating the way Annie had. And time was running out. Tim was going to get rid of us.

As if to confirm my thoughts, Tim reached out and pulled Annie upward. "On your feet," he commanded, placing the flashlight on a nearby shelf next to what appeared to be paint cans. The light beam shot into the corner of the basement, casting deep shadows around us. The feeble light stream didn't give off enough illumination to draw attention to our activity in the basement.

Nobody standing outside would notice anything amiss (not that anyone would be out walking in the wee hours of the morning—I seemed to have cornered the market on that action), but it appeared to be bright enough for whatever Tim had planned. He reached behind his back and pulled something out of his waistband. The small revolver that rested in his palm appeared like a trick of the light. A sleight of hand a magician uses to produce a floral bouquet from a pocket or pull the proverbial rabbit out of a hat. Annie straightened. Sheer willpower must have been the only thing keeping her standing.

"Whatcha gonna do with that, kill us?" asked Mary conversationally. I looked at her again. Was she *trying* to get herself shot? I jabbed her with my left elbow, hoping to nudge her into silence just as I realized why she wasn't afraid: not only was I untied but I also had a weapon in my hand.

"I don't kill people, Mary," said Tim, sounding calm and unaffected by the fact that he was holding the three of us against our will. "But I won't stop you from killing each other." He crossed the basement and stood in front of Mary and me. I flinched at his nearness. Still clutching the gun in his right hand, he reached down and clawed at Mary, catching her by one arm and yanking her up. "Stand right there," he ordered, pressing her back against the stone wall.

I stared at him, trying to read his expression in the dim light. He looked determined. My stomach cartwheeled, landing somewhere near my bowels. The only thing I could do was distract him—jump up and race toward him as he took aim, using the element of surprise—and my makeshift weapon— to my advantage. It was a half-assed plan, but I couldn't formulate a better one amid my panic.

"What happened to Matt?" A shout into the quiet basement. With shock, I realized it had come out of me.

Tim paused, looked at me. "Who?"

"Umm, Tyler Hansen?" That's what Annie had called him, right? "I saw him running by the lake with . . . someone else. Was it you?"

"Don't worry about Tyler Hansen, he's with his wife now."

"What?" My heart crashed painfully into my breastbone. Tyler reunited with a possibly dead Ava couldn't be good. "What are you saying?"

Tim crossed back over to Annie and took up a spot directly behind her. "The guy fell into the pond, and, as luck would have it, he couldn't swim." He quickly untied Annie's wrists.

I thought about how sweaty Tim looked. He wasn't coated in perspiration, but pond water.

"Of course, I tried to help him. I'm not a killer like you, Caroline." He sighed dramatically. He was enjoying his own performance. "Sadly, I couldn't save him."

I gasped, but as Tim raised the gun, my breath caught in my throat.

He reached his arms around Annie from behind, as if going in for a bear hug. He placed the gun in her right hand. "Grip this as tight as you can," he ordered as he slid both hands onto Annie's forearm and positioned it like a mannequin's. The gun barrel was pointed at Mary. Raising his voice, presumably so it would be heard by the octogenarian, he yelled, "Are you going to tell me where you hid those documents, Mary?"

For once, Mary remained silent. I didn't know which expression she'd plastered on her face because my gaze was glued to Tim and Annie, and the gun in the latter's trembling hand.

"Nothing to tell me?" Tim sighed again, keeping his hands on Annie's arm. "Okay, have it your way, old lady." He pressed his lips to Annie's ear. "Shoot her in the shoulder."

"I can't," Annie warbled, as though speaking around a mouthful of marbles. Her hand shook so violently that I feared she was having a seizure.

Now was the moment. I had to spring on them and grab the gun, using my corkscrew if I had to. Heart hammering so hard I could barely breathe and panic clouding my vision, I launched my body up and out into the darkness, arms stretched toward the shaking gun. I smashed into the pair, our forearms clashing against each other like swords. I plunged my makeshift weapon into what I hoped was Tim's limb as a blast of noise and flash of light lit up the basement, sending everything into slow motion. For a split second, I was floating in complete silence. Until the noises erupted full-force all around me: Tim yelping, Annie screaming, and a heartrending cry from across the room. Smoke filled the air and something hot and heavy pressed against my palm.

The gun, handed off by Annie.

I curled my fingers around it, yanked my hand up as I stood, and stumbled backward, not stopping until my shoulder blades and back hit the stone wall. My hand was now shaking as hard as Annie's had been. Tim was on the ground, Annie on top of him. Shoving her off, he got to his feet just as I stepped forward, widened my stance, making sure the revolver—secured with both hands—was aimed at him.

"Don't come any closer," I ordered.

"Shit, Caroline, did you stab me with something?" Tim looked down at his arm.

"Raise your hands," I yelled to hear my voice above the pounding in my brain. I cocked the gun.

Tim halted and raised his hands above his head. "I was never going to hurt you. You know that, right?" He took a step closer. "It was these two. They have no right to be in our business."

"So you were going to do what, just kill them?"

"No, I keep telling you I'm not a killer. Annie shot Mary, not me." He inched closer. I wanted to look at my neighbor, my *friend,* to ensure she was okay, but I didn't dare take my eyes off Tim, who was lowering his hands. "You saw that yourself, Carrie."

*Carrie.* Tim hadn't called me by that nickname in years. I gritted my teeth. "Don't gaslight me, Tim. It won't work this time. You ordered Mary shot because she's in the way, isn't she? She's keeping you from what you want: my mother's money. And Annie turned on you. Even worse, she tricked you, making you believe she cared when all she wanted was the cash."

Tim's eyes narrowed. Exaggerated by the shadows cast by the flashlight to his side, his face looked like the embodiment of evil. Why had it taken me so long to realize how dangerous he was? He'd stop at nothing to get his hands on my mother's estate.

What I didn't understand was what he had against Ava and Tyler Hansen, but I suddenly needed to know how deep his depravity went. "Why would you let Tyler Hansen die in the pond? What did the guy ever do to you?"

"That was out of my hands. I jumped in after him and tried to save him. More than you did for Muzzy's child, I might add."

Shame washed over me. The gun wavered in my hands. *Don't listen to him, he's trying to trip you up. Again.*

"You can see how wet I am, Caroline." He held his hands out and rocked back and forth as if modeling for my inspection.

"What about Tyler's wife, Ava? The poor woman had her throat slit open."

"I was too late to save her too." He inched closer.

"So you admit to being there when she was all . . . bloody?" I remembered Tim's car parked just yards away from the Pine Hill house that night.

"Yeah, I was there. I was looking for Annie when I came across both you and Ava."

"But why?" I asked, feeling the beginning of tears stinging the back of my eyes. "Why did you have to kill Ava?"

"I didn't kill her, Caroline." His eyes held mine. "I was only there to clean up."

"Clean up? What does that mean?" I shook my head. "Clean up after what?"

"Not what, but who." He spoke very clearly. "I had to clean up your mess."

"My mess? What did I do?"

"You killed Ava, Caroline."

# CHAPTER FORTY-TWO

*Monday, dawn, September 25*

"IT WAS THE thing that would get you committed for the rest of your life, but I covered for you," said Tim. "I saw you run into Annie's house, and I followed you. Unfortunately, by the time I got there you were already upstairs, stabbing that woman, Ava. She managed to get out one good scream before you got that crazy blade into her—"

"I wouldn't have done that! I was outside, seeing her fall against the window . . ."

"You ran out of the house and looked back up at her, Caroline. I know because you passed me on your way out, appearing to be in some sort of trance. I followed you, but you didn't even see me."

"That makes no sense."

Something squeezed my ribs, tightening them around my lungs. "You wouldn't have covered for me. You wanted me out of the way—back at the institute."

"I had no choice." Tim's voice was unnervingly calm.

"If the police discovered what you'd done, they'd have investigated my activities as well. I would have lost the money I'd worked so hard to get."

I stared at him. "Is there no end to your treachery?" The gun in my hand loosened and wavered.

Tim lunged, knocking me back against the wall, but his revelation already had me seeing stars. I reflexively forced my knee upward, missing his crotch but hitting the center of his stomach. As he doubled over, my survival instinct shot into overdrive, allowing me to scoot around him. I started forward but his fingers clamped around my ankle. Down I went, the gun flying out of my hand and skittering across the concrete floor.

Tim was right behind me as I got to my feet. Together we scrambled through the shadows, both of us searching for the revolver. Spotting it, I pounced, groping for the gun and clutching it, but Tim was stronger. Landing on my outstretched arm, he grabbed the hand gripping the firearm, and in one swift motion wrenched it from my grasp.

"See what I mean about you?" he gasped, his breath coming to him in pants as he clambered off me. "You're scary unpredictable."

"Look who's talking," I heaved, fury battling—and winning against—my fear. "Shooting off that thing, slicing knives across throats, and blaming me for the destruction. Again!"

"I had no choice. I told you, you wouldn't be the only one the police looked at closely."

My mouth dropped open as I realized what my crumb of a husband was telling me. "You're saying you covered for me only to save your own ass. Now *that* I believe! The rest is fanciful, to say the least. If you recall, I reported what I saw to the police."

"Luckily, I brained you in the foyer and cleaned up everything while you were out cold. By the time you summoned the authorities, there was nothing to see."

"You've got to be kidding," I snorted.

"How do you think you got in the pond, Caroline?" Tim raised both brows and puckered his lips in that superior way I hated. "You had so much blood on you that only an extended dunking could get it all off. Sadly, the cold water revived you too."

My brain swirled in my head. *This is not happening, Caroline. Tim is looking for a way to blame you for something you never did—never would do.* "I have been looking for Mel . . . Ava's killer for weeks, Tim."

"You thwart me even when you're not trying." He sighed. "I was so careful to clean everything, get all the blood off you—I even rolled the empty baby carriage from the house to the pond. All I had to do was sit back and wait for you to realize what you'd done. If you'd recalled it, I'd have been able to hold it over you. Control you. But what did you do? You went out looking for the *killer.* You even went back to the house and found evidence of the crime. I know because I saw you discover Ava's fake nail. I was at this house, double-checking I'd not missed anything the day you and that reporter broke in. I had to hide in the master bedroom closet. From there I saw you make your little discovery."

"The louvered slats," I whispered. "You saw me through them."

"You don't make things easy on me, Caroline. When I snuck into our house looking for your mother's missing papers, I also had to find that nail fragment of Ava's." He shook his head, a look resembling admiration crossing over his features. "For a second there, I thought you might be a genius rather than a pyscho, but then I remembered all the other crazy shit you've pulled."

I looked at Annie. She was strangely silent.

"Tell me you don't believe this liar," I pleaded. "He beat you up, Annie, and got you to shoot Mary!"

"I only wanted to scare Annie and Mary," he said as we both looked toward the still form stretched across the floor. "That's why I told Annie to hit her in the shoulder. A nonfatal shot to show I meant business."

To my right, I heard Annie moan softly, clearly anguished by her role in harming the old woman.

"Mary's eighty years old, asshole!" Hoping Tim felt properly rebuked, I ignored the gun for a second, and raced over to my neighbor. I knelt and placed my fingertips against her neck, searching for a pulse. My shaky digits made the task impossible. As I leaned forward to listen for breathing, her head popped up with surprising vigor. I jumped. "Mary, you're okay?" I eyed her chest and shoulders in the dim light and tapped her upper body for wounds. I found none. Annie had clearly missed the mark.

"I wouldn't say that." Mary struggled to sit. "Feels like a truck ran me over."

I released a breath I didn't even know I was holding. "Thank God you aren't shot." My face flushed with anger as I started to stand.

"Sit down," said Tim.

I sat but spun around to face him. The dawn was just creeping in through the basement window, glazing our dismal gathering in a deceptively cheery yellow light. Tim's arms stretched out in front of him, the revolver trained on me. His wide-legged stance would make pivoting to Annie easy. I risked a glance her way. She seemed to be receding into the dark corner, getting smaller.

"What's the plan now, Tim?" I taunted him, even as a voice in my head cautioned me to be quiet. Rage clouded my vision and crowded out the sensible warning. I shot off my mouth again. "Are you going to kill us *all*? How are you going to pull that one off?"

"Don't tempt me, Caroline. I got rid of the evidence once. I can do it again."

"Oh yeah, right." I rolled my eyes. "After *I* murdered a complete stranger in cold blood. Nice try, liar."

"She didn't seem a stranger to you. You called her Melanie," he said in a low, measured voice. "Asked her how she could cheat on Matt?"

My blood froze in my veins. How could he know that? I'd never mentioned Matt and Melanie to anyone, had I? It had to be a trick. Tim was sneakier than anyone I'd ever met. Hadn't he managed to take my family money right from under my nose? "You're doing it again—making things up to get me committed. Figuring out how to make your theft legal. It's been your goal for years."

"Longer than you know."

"What does that mean?"

"When your mother struck her bargain, I figured I got a pretty good deal. You didn't look half bad in those days, and your snarky attitude was kind of appealing."

My heart stilled.

"What bargain?"

"She told me where I could find you. Said if I convinced you to accept me, she'd leave us both a substantial sum of money in her will."

"She did *what*?" My body began to tremble. "No, that's not true. Nothing you say is true."

"Nothing *she* said was true, that's for sure," he yelled. "She promised to leave her estate to both of us, but when Annie read me the will, you were the sole beneficiary of . . . of everything!" His face turned crimson.

"But that would mean . . . we didn't meet by chance?" I pictured Tim standing by my cart in the supermarket—sent there by my mother? He'd never loved me? That wasn't true; it was a story he'd made up to hurt me because he wasn't getting what he wanted.

*What he wanted.*

He wanted the money. That was all he'd ever wanted. The money. Not me. A sob escaped from my throat.

My vision blurred as I studied the concrete floor in front of me. I couldn't understand, couldn't breathe. Nothing between Tim and me had been real?

"Don't listen to him, dolly." Mary's voice floated through the dusty air as if on the wings of a specter. Why was she so far away?

"Stop right there, Caroline," warned Tim. "I don't want to kill you, but I will if I have to."

"Kill me!" I challenged. "You want to be rid of me, just kill me!" I dropped to the floor as if fainting in grief, but I'd spied the corkscrew mere inches away. I made sure I fell on top of it.

"I wouldn't do that, I'm not like that—"

"You're such a liar!" I struggled back to my feet, the implement once more secreted in my hand. "Because of you, Emmy is dead. You lie about everything, everything!"

"No, Caroline, no," yelled Mary, but I had no time to look for her in the suddenly dark basement. Clouds must have been obscuring the dawn. I reached out with the corkscrew, my only intent to hurt Tim. I could hurt him as badly as he hurt me. An explosion rocked my body, sending flashes of bright light in a halo around me.

And then I was running, chasing nothing more than a shadow. Down the hall and into the kitchen. Following closely, almost reaching my target. Spotting the blender on the empty counter, reaching out, clasping the lid wildly and flinging it. Shoving my hand inside it and clutching the blade. The sting of it slicing my fingers, infuriating me, pushing me faster. Running, chasing the shadow up the stairs and through the hallway until there was no place left for either of us to go.

I pushed myself forward, feeling the resistance of him. Another deafening noise split the air around us as I thrust the object at him, slashing left and right, feeling a splatter of something warm and sticky coat my arm. He made an odd noise, like air whooshing from a bellows. I squinted through the dark, trying to see his face, and I could, I could! A cheekbone, and dark hair, a set of lips, and deep brown eyes. Eyes that apologized and pleaded with me to stop.

*Her eyes*, terrified, as I plunged the weapon into her again.

"I'm sorry," she pleaded, her blood spurting into my eyes, blurring everything. "So sorry."

# CHAPTER FORTY-THREE

*Monday, early morning, September 25*

T HE FAMILIAR SWOOSH of the back slider gave way to the shuffling steps that radiated through the floorboards above us. Someone had arrived. Was it the police? Had Jane finally alerted them? They'd come for a kidnapper, but what they'd get was a killer. The realization sent blood surging through me. I couldn't stop shaking.

"Down here," Mary yelled, her voice surprisingly strong for a woman in her eighties who'd been through everything she had in the past few hours.

Something about the ragged pounding of feet on the staircase made me doubt the presence of police officers.

When the hazy early morning light revealed the fit outline and sandy blond hair of the man I'd thought of as Matt, my eyes widened, and my jaw dropped.

"Tyler?" asked Annie, incredulous. "We thought you were dead."

"Tim told us you drowned," I added, my voice shaky. I took in his stringy, uncombed hair and soggy, torn sweatshirt.

"Is that the man who attacked me when I got here earlier—the same guy who chased me around the pond and shoved me into a tree? His name is Tim?" He squinted against the sunbeam just edging through the basement window. "I was so dazed, I fell into the pond and nearly drowned. I'm gonna kill him!"

"Too late," said Mary, looking at the center of the basement floor.

He swiveled his head toward her voice and followed her gaze to where Tim lay motionless, blood pooling around his torso like gravy. "What happened?"

"I was meeting with my client, Caroline, and her neighbor, Mary, when this man, Caroline's estranged husband, arrived," said Annie, sitting forward so Tyler could get a clear view of her. "Tim held a gun on us, forced us into Caroline's car, and drove here, to my old house," she lied.

"My God," said Tyler. "Why would he come here?"

"He was angry with me," I began.

"Yes, he'd discovered he hadn't been included in Caroline's dead mother's will. He thought it unfair," explained the lawyer.

"Unfair is putting it mildly," mumbled Mary as though talking to herself.

"Anyway, he lost his mind," continued Annie, as vocal now as she was silent before. "He threatened to kill us if we didn't work with him to change the will." Her face was a mask of professionalism and her voice held none of the whimpering of mere moments ago. I stared at her.

"But here? In the basement?" asked Tyler, shaking his head as if trying to clear his mind to make room for the new information.

"The house is empty, quiet. An easy place to commit a crime," said Annie smoothly, shooting me a conspiratorial look. "Tim would know. He'd already done something horrendous here, just weeks ago." She looked back at Tyler. "Maybe I should share this information in front of the police."

"The police?" Tyler's face went blank. "But why—"

"It's a criminal act that won't be easy to listen to."

"Is it about Ava?" Tyler's voice was barely a whisper.

"Yes," Annie stood and walked stiffly over to him, trying to stretch her cramped legs as she moved. Reaching out her hands to clasp his, she said, "You need to call 911."

"Why?" He pulled back. When Annie remained silent, he said, "Just tell me."

Annie looked at me again, deciding something. My fate. She took a deep breath. "Tim murdered your wife in this house."

"No!" He collapsed onto the basement steps.

"I'm so sorry to be the one to tell you." She wedged herself beside him on the lowest step and placed a hand awkwardly on his shoulder. "Based on what Tim said tonight, we think he may have dumped Ava's . . . ummm . . . body in the pond."

"Oh my God! Not there! I was in that pond, I could have been in there with her, with her corpse," he rambled, running his hands through his hair. Suddenly he stopped. "You don't know this is true. You haven't seen her . . .?"

I stepped back, let myself slide down the wall as I stared at nothing. My mouth was as dry as dust. I swallowed. I had to speak up, had to admit what I'd done. I was the one who'd killed an innocent woman. I was the very thing Tim had always accused me of being: a monster. And now I'd silenced him too. Why couldn't I get my mouth to work, or my voice to confess?

"We *do* have to call the police," prodded Mary from her dark corner. "Do you have a cell phone, young man?"

Tyler looked at her, his expression dazed in the tentative glow of a new day. He didn't seem to understand what Mary was asking him.

*Is this happening or am I imagining the whole scene?*

"Tyler," prompted Annie, rubbing his arm. "Could I borrow your cell phone?"

He reached into the pocket of his slouchy shorts and produced the phone, his actions mechanical and jerky as an automaton.

Annie spoke into the phone, but her words were too soft to hear. I tried again to speak but my jaw tightened around my silence.

"Tyler?" A woman's voice at the top of the basement staircase, accompanied by light footsteps. "Did you get my text to meet me here?"

A strangled cry issued from the man's lips as he leaned his head forward, dropping it into his hands.

"Is that you down there?" came the voice I now knew so well: Jane Brockton. "I've been looking everywhere for you. You weren't next door. And that crazy bitch who stalks the neighborhood tried to get in my house. Can you believe it? She said she'd been kidnapped and brought here. And then she ran off." Jane had been talking so fast she had to pause to catch her breath. "I came right over and found the house empty, but I didn't look down there. It was so dark." She paused. "Can you come up here?"

"Just come down," called Mary, her tone tinged with irritation. Jane clearly annoyed everyone.

"I don't . . . Who are you?" Jane faltered.

"Come down and find out," said Mary. "Or better still, wait up there and direct the police to us."

"But I didn't call the—"

"I can't talk, Jane," interrupted Tyler. "Not now, not . . ."

I couldn't stop looking at him, at the way he hung his head. I'd done this to him. I loathed myself with an intensity that made my stomach knot and churn.

"Could you untie my hands?" asked Mary from a few feet away. I looked at her—at the awkward position she was forced to sit in with her hands bound behind her. Guilt added to the toxic brew bubbling in my gut. Why hadn't I untied her?

I got up and stumbled over to her. *This is a dream. Only a dream.* A nightmare I'd awaken from and chastise myself for my hideous imagination. After all, how could I kill a woman I'd never met—and not even remember I'd done it? But I had recalled parts of it. I knelt beside the old lady and began tugging at the knotted rope binding her wrists.

"When the police come, don't say a word," Mary whispered. "Let Annie and me do all the talking."

"But I can't, I—"

"Just stay quiet," she warned.

Noise above us cut off our discussion. Jane's high pitch echoed down the basement steps, followed by deeper male voices. The police had arrived.

The footsteps on the basement staircase were measured, precise. Tyler scrambled off the lowest one and stood, spotlighted in an officer's flashlight beam, even though sunshine had fully engulfed the dismal interior of our makeshift dungeon. Two officers stood looking around as Jane hovered on the staircase behind them like a moth trying to get closer to a lit lantern. I stared at the men in their blue uniforms: Skinny and Chubby from the fateful day I'd encountered Ava Hansen. I opened my mouth to confess the truth, but stiffness engulfed my neck and jaw, freezing the bones in place. Taking each of us in, Skinny introduced himself and his partner, but, as before, I couldn't get my mind to focus on their names. He then crossed to Tim and placed a finger against the pulpy mass that was once my husband's neck. His eyes met Chubby's and he shook his head.

"What happened here?" asked Chubby, angling his light beam on Tim's pathetic corpse, weighed down by massive amounts of blood. I looked away from the man I'd vowed to honor until "death us do part" as Annie launched into her altered tale of events, adding embellishments this time around.

The officers listened quietly as the lawyer produced testimony worthy of a court defense: the abduction, Tim's confession, and the life-and-death struggle between my estranged husband and myself.

Chubby looked at me, a quizzical expression on his face.

"Is this true, Mrs. Case?"

I stared back, unable to say a word.

"She's in shock," piped up Mary from her corner. "She doesn't even realize she's been shot. You really need to call for an ambulance."

I was afraid to look at my neighbor. Mary's tall tale was bound to unravel Annie's carefully plotted storyline. I looked down at my arms. Blood coated my hands, forearms, and chest. *Tim's blood.*

The police would discover the truth. I wanted them to.

Skinny removed a cell phone from his pocket and pressed the surface. A dispatcher's voice blared out of the phone speaker. He paused, listening, then started speaking into it.

I caught very little of what he said other than, "We have two victims, one deceased and one shot in the left shoulder."

As soon as he said it, intense pain radiated down my left arm. I looked at my shoulder where the dark hoodie was ripped and torn, blood and tatters of the pink T-shirt beneath spilling through the gouge.

The room began to spin. I let my head drop against the wall and closed my eyes. With any luck, I'd die of blood loss before the ambulance arrived.

"Why are you here?" asked Chubby. I didn't know whom he was addressing until Tyler's tenor answered the question, relaying his role in our drama.

"But why would you show up in the middle of the night?" pressed Chubby.

"Ava's family is wealthy and powerful. They own the house we live in," said Tyler. "They kicked me out after Ava went missing and threatened my life. Her brothers have people looking for me. They think I did something to her."

"Did you?" asked Skinny, point-blank.

"No, of course not! I've stayed away because this is the first place they'd look for me. I thought this Tim, who I met earlier tonight, was one of those hunting me. I ran when he approached me in the dark kitchen upstairs."

"Why?" asked Skinny.

"Wouldn't you run if a man came out of the shadows and started yelling at you?"

I raised my forehead and opened my eyes, which were level with Tyler's droopy shorts. The baggy drawers began to quiver. The officers said nothing more.

"I'm staying over on Woodmint at a client's house." Tyler's voice notched up and he began talking faster. "He got transferred across the country for a year and he asked me to keep an eye on the place. But he doesn't know I've been living there, camped out in the back bedroom, where I disabled his monitoring camera. Only that room and the garage are free from surveillance."

"What does that have to do with your visit to *this* house tonight?" Chubby interjected.

"Ava's brothers found me at the other house. Blasted me with a flashlight when I was sleeping. I'm lucky they didn't shoot me, but I wasn't going to wait around until they changed their minds. This is the only other empty house in the neighborhood that I know of. I figured I'd wait until well after midnight when all was quiet before letting myself in. My plan was to crash for a few hours and leave before dawn."

My arm throbbed, and my gut twisted in remorse. Not only had I killed Ava, but I'd devastated her family and terrorized her husband.

"But this other man—Tim Case—harmed Ava?" asked Chubby.

Tyler nodded. "And dumped her body in the pond across the street."

"How do you know that?" asked Skinny.

"Tim told us." Annie's voice.

"You don't know that's true," cut in Jane. "You can't rely on what these women tell you."

"And you are . . . who?" Chubby asked.

"Jane Brockton," she announced, straightening her spine, and stepping onto the concrete floor. "I live in the neighborhood, and I can tell you that woman is crazy." She pointed at me. "She could have attacked Tyler's wife. She walks the streets pushing an empty baby carriage and spies on the residents."

My eyes connected with Jane's. I was speechless in the face of her narrowed eyes, pursed lips, and bunched eyebrows. Jane Brockton hated me. She was also more astute than I'd realized.

"That's not exactly true," Annie chimed in. "Caroline went undercover, so to speak, monitoring her estranged husband's activities. She knew Tim was creeping around the neighborhood and inserting himself into the lives of the residents."

"What better way to investigate than by pretending to soothe a colicky child with a nightly stroll?" Mary added.

"We're familiar with Mrs. Case," said Skinny. "Ava Hansen's disappearance correlates with the night and time she reported seeing Mrs. Hansen, clearly hurt, fall into an upstairs window of her home."

"Why didn't you take me seriously?" I asked, my voice husky from disuse. "You might have caught . . ." *me.*

Skinny sighed. "We had no evidence other than—"

"An eyewitness account," finished Annie.

"You mean she—this woman has been working with you?" Jane flushed. "All this time, she's been working with the police?"

"She's been trying to," said Mary. "But nobody would believe her."

# CHAPTER FORTY-FOUR

*Two months later*

THE CEMETERY WAS frigid this time of year, just days before Thanksgiving, the grass around Emmy's grave stiff with frost. I reached down and placed the tender pink carnations against the tombstone, assuring my baby that once I was settled in the South Carolina town Mary had chosen for us, I'd have her moved near me. It was surprisingly inexpensive to exhume a casket and relocate it.

Not that money was a problem anymore. Annie had settled the details of my mother's estate for me, once she returned what she'd stolen. Saving her life, and disposing of Tim's, which had freed her to be with Jeffrey, had prompted the change of heart and established our circle of trust. She knew I'd keep her secret, and she'd keep mine—for a price. Murder, after all, carries a much harsher penalty than embezzlement. And Annie was a businesswoman through and through. Like it or not, the lawyer and her exorbitant fees would be with me *in perpetuity*.

The other professionals in my life would have to go.

Dr. Ellison and Tasha Turner knew me too well to remain my head doctors. Mary explained it was just a matter of time until they figured out what had actually happened to the woman I'd seen in the window, and my role in it. Even keeping connected through Zoom was out of the question. But my mental health advocates both wished me well and recommended colleagues in the area where we were relocating. All Mary and I had to do was call the movers and head out of town. We'd already packed our belongings. I'd reluctantly agreed to my neighbor's plan, still amazed she'd want anything to do with me. I murdered a complete stranger, I'd reminded her. What was to stop me from killing a friend? But Mary wasn't worried. She'd explained she believed it was the rage against Tim deep inside me that had taken over. She wasn't going to do anything to incite such deep-seated fury.

I looked around the barren cemetery. Not a living soul in sight. The trees breaking up the endless rows of marble markers appeared as nothing more than massive sticks, adding to, instead of relieving, the starkness. The wind whipped my hair wildly around my head and sent a chill into me that my wool coat couldn't protect me from.

Could I do it? Walk away from the chaos I'd created and start a new life elsewhere? It was so selfish of me. So wrong. I'd taken a life. Two lives, really, if you counted Tim, but I didn't. Mary helped me realize how much toxicity my husband had injected into our sham of a marriage. His bargain with my mother had perpetuated the myth she'd created and carefully maintained over the years: that I was unable to make good enough choices to have a successful life on my own terms. Knowing all I did about my mother now, I realized *her* choices had screwed me. Her decision to take away my loving father—and even my memory of the event—and to one day replace him with a self-involved narcissist.

I stood and, wiping frozen grass from my knees, looked up the hill. There was one more grave I needed to visit. I trudged up the asphalt path, head down, careful to avoid random ice patches. When I strolled around the bend and looked up, I saw him. I paused, toyed with the idea of turning around. But he saw me too. He lifted his hand in a tentative wave.

As I plopped to my knees beside Tyler in front of Ava's gravestone, I tried to think of something to say, but nothing came to me. I fought the urge to prostrate myself and beg her forgiveness.

"It's her birthday," he said simply, explaining his presence among the stoic slabs. "It's the least I can do for her."

"More than I've done for Tim," I said, recalling how I'd let his parents handle the burial arrangements. I secured a funeral home to contact them and made sure I wasn't around when they flew in from Seattle to claim their son's body.

"How does life get so off course?" he asked, still looking at the marker with Ava's name and statistics spread across its surface. "She'd been suffering, and I'd only made things worse, hooking up with Jane. I'd let my loneliness replace common sense. Jane Brockton is a rather horrible person."

I couldn't disagree with him, but my opinion hardly mattered. I was the worst person I knew. Yet something he'd just uttered struck me.

"Suffering?" I repeated. "How so?" I looked at him. The woman dancing with him in Annie's empty house seemed happy, even carefree.

"Ava was the only daughter of people with immense wealth," Tyler said, shrugging. "She was coddled, catered to, spoiled, even after her parents died. When she started our decor and renovating business, her brothers funded it. Even our success couldn't temper her restlessness. The result of always getting what she wanted, I guess. She tired of me, the business, and our life together." He ran a hand through his hair. "She began drinking. Heavily. One night she blacked out behind the wheel and hit a driver head-on, killing her."

My hand went to my mouth. Ava had killed someone too.

"The older woman, a retired nurse I think, died instantly, but Ava received little more than a bump and scratch on her forehead." Tyler looked at me for the first time, his eyes mirroring the agony I tried to blink out of mine. "For the past four years, she couldn't live with herself. She stopped drinking and threw everything she had into work, but human interaction was tougher. She'd let me touch her when we danced together, but that was it. Ballroom dancing was her passion and the only time I'd seen her happy these past few years. The dizzying speed and rotation of a Viennese waltz or the intricate footwork of a foxtrot took all her concentration. Let her forget everything else."

"That's so sad." I blinked the stinging moisture from my eyes away.

"She tried to kill herself—twice."

My entire body stilled.

"She didn't think she deserved to live?" I asked, already knowing the answer. I had, after all, spent endless hours trying to justify my own life after my child's ended.

"No, not after she took that woman's life. Lilith, I think, her name was."

"Lilith?" My heart twisted. The only woman I'd ever known by that name had been my mother. I couldn't breathe.

"Yes, a local woman named Lilith Messier." Tyler sighed, got to his feet, oblivious to my shock at hearing my maiden name cross his lips. "Ava's family connections got her out of jail time, but I often thought she'd have fared better if she'd had to pay for what she'd done, with her freedom. She was chained by guilt—a prison she locked herself into each and every day." He looked down at me. "Are you ready to go?"

I stared at him for so long as I processed the ramifications of Ava's actions that he looked away, uncomfortable. Spots of frozen cold pecked at my cheeks, nose, and the backs of my ungloved hands. It was snowing. Eventually, it would cover everything in a layer of clean, pure white, hiding all that had been before, turning the landscape into something foreign and fresh. My mother hadn't escaped the consequences of her actions after all. Fate had waited patiently to exact retribution.

Things were suddenly clear. I didn't have to go to South Carolina or eschew my mental health professionals. My place was here. I stood and began walking next to Tyler, halting after a few steps. He paused and looked at me.

"I have to go somewhere," I said, horror mingling with certainty in my chest. "Would you come with me?"

His face screwed into confusion. "Where to?"

"The police station."

Tyler stared at me, saying nothing, but another voice came to me.

*It's going to be all right, Caroline.*

My father's voice, as clear as if he were standing next to me. As if I'd been hearing it daily for the past twenty years. He'd been with me all along.

I looked into the swirling flakes billowing between Tyler and me and thought about Ava's apology as I'd watched the life bleed out of her. She'd known who I was and why I was there. We'd both known. But now I'd do what she could not: confess to the life I'd stolen and pay the price with my freedom. I couldn't live with the same atrocious lie my mother had. Emmy's memory deserved more than that. It was time to break the cycle.

# ABOUT THE AUTHOR

J ENNIFER SADERA BEGAN her writing career just out of college as a junior copywriter at book publisher NAL before transitioning to the editorial departments of national women's magazines *Woman's World, Redbook,* and *Beauty Digest.* She'd already established herself as a freelance writer and blogger when she decided to follow her true passion: creating novels. She is an active member of International Thriller Writers, Mystery Writers of America, and Sisters in Crime; her writing has earned her multiple awards at Atlanta Writers Conferences and a fellowship at the Martha's Vineyard Institute of Creative Writing. *I Know She Was There* is Jennifer's debut psychological suspense novel. When not writing, Jennifer can be found gardening, traveling throughout her beloved New York State and beyond, or reading anything she can get her hands on. She is blessed with CJ, her husband of many years, two adult children, Amanda and Ryan, and two adorable rescue granddogs named Sunny and Moonie.

# ACKNOWLEDGMENTS

WHILE IT IS true that writing is a solitary endeavor, producing a book that others *want* to read is not. So many people devoted their time, interest, and talents to this novel that mere words will not truly convey how thankful I am. My publisher, CamCat Books, has the most incredible team: Publisher Sue Arroyo, the enterprising force behind this dynamic company, leading it with imagination and wisdom; Acquisitions Editor Elana Gibson, whom I felt an instant connection with at ITW's Pitch Fest; Editor-in-Chief extraordinaire, Helga Schier, whose inspiring edits have a way of bringing out the very best in my writing, which, honestly, feels magical; Business Manager Bill Lehto, who managed the vital details of my contract with aplomb, generosity, and kindness; Art Director Maryann Appel, who created a striking cover that reflects in exquisite detail what I most want readers to know about the storyline; and copyeditor Ellen Leach, whose expert editing makes me appear smarter than I really am. Heartfelt thanks to every single member of the CamCat staff, including

Laura Wooffitt, Meredith Lyons, Abigail Miles, Gabe Schier, Nicole DeLise, Jessica Homami, Kayla Webb, and Maxwell Smitherman. And to my fellow CamCat authors whose support and advice have been nothing short of inspiring. All of you contributed to making my lifelong publishing dream come true. I will do my best to make everyone in the CamCat family as grateful for me as I am for you.

From childhood, my dad and writing mentor, James McGill, and mom and reading role model, Lynne McGill, nurtured my love of the written word. Along the way, others tapped into my enthusiasm and contributed invaluably to my fledgling writing attempts. Peter SanGiovanni and fellow writer Doris Eder, my first beta readers who have struggled through just about every word I've ever written: your insightful observations and everlasting friendship mean more to me than you will ever know. Fellow writers and readers Beth Lahaie and Jessica DeHart: where would I be without your knowledge, friendship, devotion to craft, and kindness? To the many, many friends and family members who became my readers and offered unfailing support, especially Lou Tubolino, Winnie Yu, Barb Rimoshytus, Mark Maron, Kathy Falcone, Debbie Martin, Jaycee Welsh, Cheri Stevens, Burt Lesnick, Neil Turner, Sandy Zelka, Drew Ross, Sue Russell, Sherrie Cole, and Gabrielle Story. Thanks also to the devoted readers in book clubs, and the amazing friendships I've made through in-person and online writing classes. I truly value my affiliation with professional organizations: Mystery Writers of America, Sisters in Crime, International Thriller Writers, Atlanta Writers Club, and Martha's Vineyard Institute of Creative Writing. Inspiring authors Erica Orloff, Bonnar Spring, Lane Stone, Elena Hartwell Taylor, Jen Delozier, and Lisa Malice, I'm thankful for your advice and friendship. Immense thanks to Sandra Herner, who took the first editorial pass on this manuscript. To the experts across the pond, Louise Dean and Tash Barsby from the writing organization The Novelry, and literary agent Liza DeBlock: your advice was invaluable, helping me dig deeper to unearth the best possible story. My writing advanced to a new level when I was accepted into ITW's Thriller-tique writing critique group, pulled together by devoted

ITW members under the leadership of Joel Burcat. Heartfelt thanks go out to Nan Cappo to whom I will be forever grateful for choosing me, Leigh Turner, Leslie Karen Lutz, Brenda Neil McQueen, J. Morgyn White, and Harriet Garfinkle. It's a pleasure and honor to read your writing and receive your feedback on mine. Fellow author Holly Stevens Howley, there is little I enjoy more than sitting with you on the porch discussing books and writing. Thank you for your insightful advice.

To my girls: Chrisann Senerchia, Lyn Vite, Bridget Seitz, Debi Tschinkle, Kerry Rooney, Martha Donovan, and June Ellen Notaro. You all put the *S* in support, whether it be reading my stories, listening to me, or offering advice. I am so thankful to have such amazing lasting friendships. And to my family, my mom; my in-laws, Joan and Joe Gelardi; my brothers and sisters-in-law; nieces and nephews; my children, Amanda and Ryan, and their significant others, Andy and Sophie: thank you. You are the family I would have chosen had I not been blessed with you.

To the memory of my father, who first saw the spark in my scribbling and nurtured it into a flame that has never been extinguished.

To the higher power that guides me, whom I call God, but others recognize as the Universe. All things are possible for those who have faith.

Last but never least, to my CJ. Living with a writer is not always easy. There can be a lot more drama in the day-to-day than even an ardent suspense reader might desire. Your shoulders sopped up the thousands of tears dripped amid the hundreds of rejections I've endured. And your strong arms have pulled me back from countless metaphorical cliffs. Through it all, you've shown me by your own work ethic how important it is to keep striving—and to appreciate success. Of the countless things you've bestowed upon me over the years, I value most the way you've always encouraged me to do what I love no matter the outcome.

If you enjoyed
Jennifer Sadera's *I Know She Was There*,
consider leaving a review
to help our authors.

And take a look at
Stephen Holgate's *A Promise to Die For*.

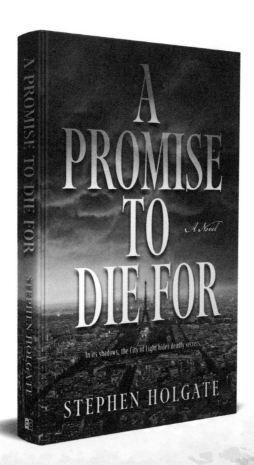

# A SUMMONS

I HADN'T REALIZED I'D fallen asleep until the cab driver said, "We've arrived, sir."

Struggling with the cobwebs clouding my mind after the all night flight from Portland, I blinked vacantly at the quiet residential street, bleak and drained of color in the early morning light, trying to recall where I was and what I was doing here, feeling that I had come so far so fast that I'd left some important part of myself behind and needed to wait for it to catch up.

Yes, Arlington, Virginia. Curt Hansen was dying. And he said he needed to see me.

His call had caught me raking leaves at the back end of my property outside Eugene, Oregon. At first I didn't recognize the thin and weary voice that had always rung with strength and good humor.

Cancer, he told me, leaving him no more than a few weeks.

"Curt, I'm so sorry."

He grunted to deflect the inadequacy of my words.

"Look, Sam, I need to ask a favor."

"Of course, Curt, anything."

"It's not something I can explain over the phone. I know it's asking a lot, but could you come out and see me?"

There are some requests you can't turn down.

"I can catch a flight to D.C. out of Portland. When do you need me?"

"How soon can you come?"

Taken aback by his urgency, I said, "What's today, Friday . . .?"

Curt chuckled faintly. "It's funny how we lose track of the days when we retire."

"I can catch a red-eye tomorrow night, be there Sunday morning."

"I wouldn't ask, Sam, but there's something I've left too late. Something important."

"I'll book the flight today and can—"

He cut me off. "Sam, you don't understand what I'm asking of you. You'll need to bring your passport. You may be gone for a while."

Despite all my years in the Foreign Service, with its eight-, ten-, twelve-hour flights, I've never learned to sleep on a plane. I'm too tall for the seats and at fifty-three I don't curl up as well as I used to. So, while my fellow passengers dozed in the darkened cabin I had a lot of time to think of my friendship with Curt Hansen, and to wonder what it was he had left too late—and why it might require me to travel overseas.

We had served together for three years in Pakistan, not a long time in the course of a normal life, but life in an embassy doesn't follow a normal course. Deep friendships are forged with a speed and intensity unknown to those who don't live and work within a small, close community far from home.

I'd served in Islamabad as the embassy's public affairs officer, in charge of press relations and cultural programs. Curt headed up the admin section. With the many small grants my office awarded to universities, and the needed repairs to our aging library, we had worked together often, adapting to each other's contrasting natures.

Within the service I had a reputation as a straight arrow, something I found both flattering and a little embarrassing, as if it spoke less to virtue than to a failure of imagination, a certain naiveté. Curt was what a scientist might call a free radical, doing whatever he thought needed doing and however he wanted to do it.

The truth was I envied guys like Curt, who treated the rules as mere suggestions drafted by a bunch of constipated desk jockeys back in Washington. While the rest of us toed lines as straight as those on our pin-striped suits, Curt approached his work like a pirate approaching a wallowing merchant ship. He would cut a corner here, ignore a reg there, bend rules that hindered his intent. The rest of us gasped. We tsked. We loved it.

In fact we were all complicit in his buccaneering ways. If we agreed not to look too closely, Curt would get us larger budgets, better housing, and cheaper contracts than we deserved. "All for the greater good," he'd say with a wolfish smile.

Still, while I took a guilty pleasure in watching Curt's unorthodox ways, and happily benefitted from his rules-be-damned style, his practices made me uneasy and I kept him at a little bit of a distance.

We served in Islamabad at a dangerous time. The war next door in Afghanistan stirred fierce psychic winds among the Pakistanis, engendering deep but conflicting emotions of horror, religious pride, and a fear of—or yearning for—instability.

With security tight and knowing that Washington might any day issue orders to evacuate family members, I received a call from a man representing, he said, a small delegation visiting from Peshawar that wanted to open an American library and study center in their city.

Peshawar lies on Pakistan's border with Afghanistan at the edge of the Hindu Kush, which means Killer of Hindus. It's a tough neighborhood. The region had for centuries defied whatever central government might lay claim to it. I'd visited the city a couple of times, briefly and nervously. An air of the Wild West hung over the place. Soldiers and tribesmen walked its dusty streets, assault rifles slung over their shoulders as casually as an

American might carry a laptop to work—and more necessary to their profession. An office worker isn't going to die for lack of a laptop.

Wanting to establish an American center in the middle of this scene was an odd notion, but if it worked out I'd earn professional favor for establishing an outpost of American influence in a sensitive region. If these visitors thought it worth trying, I didn't want to say no. So I told my caller to stop by my office on Monday morning.

He told me that, unfortunately, his group would only be in Islamabad for two days. Their schedule already crowded, he asked if I could meet them at our library on Sunday afternoon.

The American Library in Islamabad was located nearly a mile from my office in the main part of the embassy. To encourage walk-ins, the library kept security loose, posting only two unarmed local guards, a near mockery of the main embassy's Fort Knox-style security with Marines, soaring concrete walls, and armed checkpoints. The embassy security officer hated our light hand, but with the ambassador on our side he could only mutter and acquiesce. On a Sunday afternoon the place would be deserted, even our rudimentary security reduced to a single guard.

Thinking we'd be discussing budget, staffing, and rental of a building in Peshawar, I asked Curt to join me.

"On a Sunday afternoon? This is too weird, Sam. You're sure you want to do this?"

When I told him it was important he laughed and said, "Okay, I'll be there."

Curt and I met at the library a few minutes early. I unlocked the door, turned on some lights, and waited for our visitors to arrive. We didn't have to wait long.

We heard the chanting first. I couldn't make out the words, but it didn't sound friendly. Moments later they appeared on the street in front of the building, not four men, as promised, but a couple of hundred, young and angry, their rage leavened only by their delight in suckering two American diplomats into a trap.

This didn't seem like the moment to remind Curt that you're more likely to die in the Foreign Service than in the military.

For a moment we felt more abashed at our foolishness than actually frightened, though the balance would quickly shift.

Our security guard had already made like a shooting star and disappeared over the horizon. I didn't blame him. The few dollars we paid him wasn't enough to get killed protecting a couple of infidels from an angry mob.

I rushed to the front door just in time to bolt it shut and keep the mob from simply walking in and killing us. By the time we thought to run out the back door, they had curled around the building, blocking any attempt to flee.

Momentarily checked by the locked doors, some of them began to throw rocks at the reinforced windows. A few of the biggest men put their shoulders to the heavy security door, trying to bash it in. Someone threw a Molotov cocktail at Curt's car and it quickly went up in flames. A moment later mine joined it, the two cars putting out billows of black smoke. Another of the homemade bombs shattered against a window in a starburst of yellow and blue.

I grabbed a phone and tried to call the Marine at Post One, the main entrance to the embassy, to tell him we were under attack, but the line had gone dead. Curt and I both tried our cell phones, but reception at the center, always iffy, failed.

With no way to get the embassy's attention we could do little but watch our attackers through the spiderweb cracks appearing in the windows and wonder how long it would take them to break in.

Curt said, "I'll bet they're not even from Peshawar," a remark that doesn't sound so funny now, but actually got a laugh out of me at the time.

The young men who made up the mob had probably thought they would get in easily. A few rocks at the windows and presto. Frustrated that their assault might take some unexpected effort, they tossed a couple of homemade fire bombs onto the roof. We soon heard the crackle of a spreading fire over our heads. A few wisps of smoke seeped downward, carrying the smell of gasoline and burning tar.

As we began to cough from the smoke I recalled that the building had been issued one of the embassy's two-way radios, kept in the head librarian's office.

Working hard to control my panic, I turned it on and tried again to tell the Marine at Post One that we had an angry mob breaking in, the place was on fire, and we needed help, fast. But the fire on the roof must have taken down the antenna and I got nothing but static.

Over the shouting of the mob we heard more stones crash against the windows, saw the cracks growing deeper. The men attacking the front door had scavenged a wooden beam from a construction site across the street and were using it as a battering ram, the front door shaking in its frame with every blow. Behind us, we could hear others trying to bash in the back door.

Though he might have justifiably lit into me for dragging him into this ambush, Curt took it in with as little complaint as Captain Kidd resigning himself to a final downturn in the play of odds. His remarkable calm helped steady my own nerves. I don't think I could have held myself together without him.

Perhaps twenty minutes had gone by since the mob appeared. We could feel the heat from the fire on the roof, and the smoke curling through the room burned in our lungs. Our phone calls and radio message had failed to get through. We could expect no rescue.

Without a word, we solemnly shook hands, a gesture that would raise a cynical hoot if you put it in a movie, but affirmed a solidarity and, yes, a sense of honor we could not have put into words. It calmed us both as we prepared to die. I thought of my wife, Janet, and our son, Tom, and how hard this would be on them.

We took the first spatter of gunfire as an escalation of the attack, the mob resorting to Kalashnikovs to finish breaking through the windows. Instinctively, we dropped to the floor.

The gunshots continued. The cries of the mob rose to a climactic pitch. I pressed my face against the carpet, tried to control my ragged breath and racing heart.

The unexpected tramping of many feet brought our heads up, both of us thinking the door had given in and we had only moments to live.

As we raised our eyes, though, the howling voices outside were descending into knots of confused shouting and cries of alarm. The popping of gunfire grew closer.

Through the cracks in the windows, the forms of our attackers fractured into rapidly shifting shards of color and then vanished, replaced seconds later by slowly moving blocks of khaki.

It was the Molotov cocktails that had saved us. The Marine at Post One saw the black smoke rising into the sky, put that together with the puzzling attempts to contact him, and called for help. His intuition saved our lives. And from that day on I've never said a bad word about the Pakistani army, which quickly responded to the Marine's call and drove the mob away, saving our unworthy behinds.

As the burning roof began to cave in, Curt and I scrambled to our feet, unlocked the door, and tumbled outside, hardly able to grasp the fact that we were still alive.

Over the next few days Curt and I received an outpouring of affection and thankfulness from the embassy community at our escape. People were kind enough to ignore the fact that my folly in agreeing to walk into a trap was the only reason we'd needed to escape.

Everyone wanted to hear our description of the attack and of our rescue, and we both developed narratives rich with hair-raising detail and self-deprecating humor. Yet, when we were around each other—and, with so many administrative matters to take care of in the wake of the library's destruction, we spent a lot of time together after the attack—we never spoke of it. Perhaps we had no need. More likely, we knew that, despite the tales we shared with others, there was no way to put into words what had happened to us. Only we knew.

A few weeks later, we both got medals for valor from the Department. Though awarded with no apparent irony, I felt embarrassed, as the whole mess had been due to my poor judgement.

On the other hand, I thought Curt's medal well-deserved. He had sensed the risk and agreed to come anyway. Naturally, Curt leveraged his new status as a Department-certified hero to score serious money for a new library.

Just as naturally, there was a downside. For library employees, all of them locals, our days of being open to the world had ended. An American engineering firm made sure the new center had high walls, concertina wire, security checkpoints, and armed guards. The head of embassy security would occasionally stop by and watch the construction with a smile on his face. Whatever the trauma of our shared experience, its terrors didn't so much change us as make us more deeply who we had been before. Curt, feeling indestructible now, became even less bound by regulations clearly meant for lesser beings, while I turned perhaps more cautious and rule-bound—in short, an even bigger bore.

Even as Curt and I were thrown together more frequently at work, he and his wife, Taylor, started spending almost every weekend with Janet and me, sometimes at their house, sometimes at ours. Our wives understood we were still working through what had happened that day. Our son, Tom, came to call them Uncle Curt and Aunt Taylor.

Though a good sport about all of it, Janet didn't much care for Curt. "He's a charming man," she said. "Women know not to trust charming men."

In fact, Curt already had one divorce behind him and we hoped, a little forlornly, that our own stability might help keep him and Taylor together, or at least reduce their constant bickering.

By contrast, ours was an extraordinarily happy marriage. Though Janet never loved Foreign Service life, we loved each other, and that love grew deeper every year. We dreamed often of retirement, of going home to Oregon and leading a quiet life, free of the stresses, dangers, and constant uprootings of the Foreign Service.

Diplomatic careers often work out as a long exercise in irony. The fallout from our misadventure at the library in Islamabad propelled me to quick advancement within the service, while Curt did little but tread water. Fairness would have demanded the opposite. After a tour as head of public affairs in Cairo, I landed the plum post of deputy chief of mission in Tunis, the number two position in the embassy.

Despite the imbalance of our professional rewards, the bond we'd forged with Curt and Taylor remained strong even after we'd moved on to new posts, with frequent emails and occasional phone calls.

Other, more treasured bonds proved far too fragile. Four years after we'd left Islamabad, while we were posted to Tunis, my Janet was killed in a traffic accident. To lose her was like losing my own life.

Our son, Tom, was riding with her. He escaped serious injury but fell into a deep depression that took months to overcome—if one can ever overcome something like that.

An embassy community is an extraordinarily close one, and my colleagues, American and Tunisian, shared our grief. Curt heard about Janet's death and called from Riyadh, offering to come out on the next flight if he could be of any help. I was deeply touched but told him I was heading out the next day, back to Oregon and a cemetery outside Salem, Janet's hometown. After the funeral, Tom and I returned to Tunis. While Tom finished high school, I went through the motions of work, but living in the place we'd shared with Janet made me feel like the last ghost in a haunted house.

I was only fifty, but my twenty-five years of service allowed me to take retirement. I bought a couple of acres outside a small town less than thirty minutes from Eugene and put Tom into the University of Oregon.

My three years back home had healed the worst of the wounds. I'd made some friends, got recruited for the local library board, and become active in environmental issues. The Foreign Service gradually became a memory, something I used to do.

Then Curt's call came, and I was once again on a plane heading toward Washington.

While the taxi idled outside Curt's place, I paid the cabbie, giving him, in my muddled state, a huge tip.

"Shall I wait?" he asked hopefully, no doubt thinking he might get the chance to drive me somewhere else before I came to my senses.

"Yeah. But I may be a while."

He beamed with pleasure. "That's not a problem, sir."

Leaving my suitcase in the car, I made my way up the walk and rang the bell. A young woman in blue nurse's scrubs answered the door.

"Sam Hough," I told her. "I'm here to see Curt."

"Come in," she said. "He's been awake for hours, waiting for you."

# "AN ADDRESS IS ALL I NEED."

T HE CURTAINS WERE still drawn, lending Curt's sickroom a gloom only slightly eased by a lamp that shared a nightstand with pill bottles, a glass of water, and other odds and ends, its disorder somehow a measure of his illness.

Curt lay in a hospital bed, the head cranked so he could sit up. His sandy hair had thinned, and his face, always heavily lined, looked older than his years. He smiled as I came in.

"Sam, it's good of you to come."

Given the long flight and my lack of sleep, I felt pretty wan. Curt joked that I looked worse than he did. In fact, the glow from the light gave his features a deceptive rosiness.

He waved me into a chair at his bedside.

We spoke awkwardly at first, neither of us wishing to discuss the obvious truth of his illness. We skipped over the present, avoided the future, and spoke only of the past, of our days in Islamabad and people we'd known there, rehashing stories of life overseas. I reminded him of how he had once managed to hide from visiting inspectors a small slush fund used for irregular purchases.

Curt smiled. "You disapproved of that particular shenanigan as I recall."

I had to chuckle at the vision of my button-down self. "The truth is I always envied your ability to ignore the rules. You were like one of those great chefs who don't bother with recipes anymore."

"Maybe the envy went both ways. You played it straight and excelled. I couldn't have done that. The Department favors guys like you. You'd have made ambassador in a few years."

I shrugged off the compliment. "I couldn't stay after Janet . . ."

"Yeah."

He winced as he shifted position, waving me back into my seat when I rose to help him. When he'd settled back into his pillows he took a deep breath and said, "I've been a rogue, Sam. Bigger than you realize. I've got a lot of regrets."

Knowing I had to be thinking of his failed marriages, he shook his head. "No. It's not what you suppose—not directly, anyway." He paused and gazed at the ceiling for a moment, putting his thoughts together. "I have to admit I grew bitter after Islamabad. Despite everything I did, I wasn't moving up the ladder. The front office always loved the way I got things done. But after I'd delivered what they wanted, the ambassadors felt they had to spread a bunch of 'tsk-tsks' across my yearly review, sniffing at my 'unorthodox practices,' as one of them put it."

I tried to make light of it. "I guess I was always pretty orthodox. Some people just called me naive. Or worse."

"No. You were always wiser than me. I wasn't wise. Maybe that's why my career didn't go as well. And maybe that's why I couldn't stay married. I mean, Taylor put up with Islamabad mainly because of you and Janet. I can't thank you enough for that. But she hated Riyadh and the Saudis. When we got to Morocco a couple of years later, she hated that too. Pretty soon she decided she didn't much care for me either. She went back to the States and filed for divorce." He tried to make like it was no big deal, but the pain in his face didn't come entirely from the cancer. "Rabat was a bad time for me. My career was going nowhere, and after Taylor left I went home to an empty house every night. I'm not much good at staying married, but I'm no good at living alone either. Those first couple of years in Rabat were hard."

His expression softened and he said, "I met a young woman." He cast a tentative smile, looking for my reaction. "My section held a reception to thank some of the local contractors we worked with. One of the Moroccans, Miloud Benaboud, owned a transport company we used now and then. He brought his daughter with him. Chantal."

It seemed to comfort him simply to speak her name.

"There was quite a crowd of us that evening, but Chantal and I kept bumping into each other. After the third or fourth time, we both laughed and started talking. It felt like I hadn't laughed in months. Finally, we gave up mingling with the others and spent most of the evening together. She'd just finished university in France, and her time overseas had made her very liberated, by Moroccan standards. She was smart, charming, attractive. I fell in love." Curt made a wry smile. "I never learn, do I? I still can't imagine what she saw in me, but we began to spend a lot of time together. I'm sure she didn't tell her father she was seeing an American more than twice her age. Our relationship became . . . intimate. I asked her to marry me. She told me no, said I didn't really mean it. Maybe she was right. Or maybe I should have insisted, and I failed some test when I didn't. Our relationship cooled after that. At some point you have to commit to each other or there's no point going on. Or maybe she just came to her senses and realized she had no business marrying a guy like me. Life's full of maybes. Anyway . . . By that time, my posting to Morocco was nearly over. I was heading for Paris as the number three in the admin section. Before I left, Chantal asked to see me one more time. A way of closing out the books, I figured. We met at a favorite café in the old medina, overlooking the river.

"It was strange. Though she was the one who asked to get together, she seemed a long way off, had this look in her eyes, like she wanted me to understand something. We had a short, awkward conversation about nothing in particular. The whole time I felt we were circling around something I couldn't figure out. That was the last time I saw her. I can't remember if she even said goodbye.

"After I got to Paris I tried once or twice to reach her through her father, but got nothing but silence. A couple of years go by. Then a guy named Rick Ziglinski, who'd succeeded me in Rabat, came through Paris on his way to Washington and asked me out to lunch. A courtesy call, nothing more. He'd gotten to know all my old contacts, of course, and I asked him about Miloud Benaboud, thinking maybe Ziglinski might say something about Chantal, let me know how she was doing. At the mention of Miloud, Rick went quiet. I asked what was wrong. He told me Miloud was furious with me, lashing his tail around, threatening to cancel his contract with the embassy. I asked Ziglinski why. He says, 'Jesus, Curt, I thought you knew.' 'Knew what?' I asked him. He told me the whole story. Chantal had gotten pregnant. I was the father. You can imagine, I was floored. Her behavior that last time suddenly made sense. She'd needed me to ask her what was wrong, let her know I cared. And I'd have done it, if I'd only known. When I didn't ask, she was through with me. I can't blame her?

"Of course, when Miloud found out about the baby, he was enraged, humiliated. He threatened to kill me, kill her, sue the embassy. Out of shame, he disowned her and packed her off to France to have the baby. It was a boy, Ziglinksi told me. They were living in Paris with a cousin, who's apparently part of a really bad crowd. But her father had told her he'd never take her back. Ever. And it's my fault."

He had gotten more wound up as he spoke, but now closed his eyes, exhausted by the effort to tell his story. I started to say something sympathetic, but he waved me down and continued.

"At the time Ziglinski told me all this, I still had a few months left in Paris. I should have spent them looking for Chantal. For the boy. My son. But I was too ashamed. And afraid. Afraid to face her. Yeah, pretty cowardly. I left Paris and took up my assignment here in Washington. All the time,

I kept telling myself I needed to go back and find them. But then this hit me, hard and fast." Curt looked at his form under the thin blanket as if it belonged to someone else. "I got too sick to work and had to retire. Now I can't do any of the things I meant to do."

However much this mess was Curt's own fault, I still felt awful for him.

"What is it you want me to do, Curt?"

"I need you to find the boy."

Only sleep deprivation can explain my surprise. He hadn't called me all the way to Virginia, passport in hand, simply to tell me this tale.

"Find the boy for me, Sam. You know I never had any kids with Taylor or Ann. He's the only thing I'm leaving behind in this world. And I have to take some responsibility for him. He must be about five by now. Find out where he lives. Give me an address." He lay back, looking at the ceiling. I noticed that he kept patting himself, as if to make sure he was still there, still alive.

"My exes get alimonies from me. They'll get my pension and the life insurance. That doesn't leave much. This house, some savings. I want the boy to have them. I brought it up with my lawyer. He tried to talk me out of giving it all to someone I've never seen and can't locate. But I'm insisting. Like I say, Ziglinski told me he thought this cousin of Chantal's is part of a bad crowd in Paris. I want something better for the boy."

"Curt, I'm not sure I'm the one to—"

He cut me off. "Go to Paris. Find the boy. My lawyer says all I need is an address. He can arrange the rest from here."

"That's it? His address?"

"My lawyer has contacts in France. He'll work with them and get it done."

"Can't I just get a phone number?"

"No, I don't think that's going to work. If you find Chantal and she knows it's about me she probably wouldn't give you her number."

Curt had made a life of playing things fast and loose. It had cost him two marriages and professional success. But, whatever Janet might have thought of him, I'd always felt he was at heart a decent guy.

And this, about his son, was eating him worse than the cancer.

"I know it's a lot to ask," he said.

"I'd be nuts to take this on, wouldn't I?"

He gave a flash of his old charming smile. "You'd have to be."

But I'd already made up my mind. "I'll do whatever you need me to do."

The enormity of the promise hit me only after I'd made it. Once said, though, there was no taking it back.

He reached up and gripped my hand. "Thanks, Sam. I'd ask someone at the embassy to do this, but all the Americans I knew there are gone. And I don't want to tell any of the local employees about this. They looked up to me, and . . . Well, I don't want them to think so poorly of me now. Bad for the raj," he said, trying to make a joke of it.

"Don't worry, I won't tell anyone what I'm doing."

"You don't know what this means to me." He must have seen something in my face as I tried to take all this in. "I know it's really too much to ask. But I haven't got anyone else to turn to. This means the world to me."

"I'm glad I came. But how do I do this? Where do I start?"

Gritting his teeth against a spasm of pain, Curt leaned over and drew a couple of pieces of paper from the mess on the nightstand and handed one of them to me.

"I've got two addresses here. One is a shipping company out by Charles de Gaulle airport. When we had the occasional truck shipment from Rabat to Paris this is where Miloud would send it. Maybe someone there will know something about Chantal. The other address is a garage near Montmartre. When Miloud's drivers needed to spend the night in Paris, he would have them leave their trucks there. There might be someone at the garage who can tell you something."

I looked blankly at the piece of paper. Two addresses, nothing more.

"I'm sorry I don't have anything else, Sam. Not even phone numbers for them. Maybe you can find the numbers online. But I think you might have better luck just stopping by and asking."

"And if they don't know anything?"

"This might help," he said and handed me the second piece of paper. It was a photo of a young woman seated at a table in what appeared to be a crowded restaurant. She looked to be in her early twenties, round-faced, with lively intelligent eyes full of good humor. At the edge of the photograph was Curt's hand resting on hers, wearing the sort of fancy signet ring a guy like Curt would wear.

"This is Chantal a few years ago. Maybe she hasn't changed all that much. If those other two places can't give you anything to work on, maybe you could ask around the Montmartre area—in shops, restaurants. A lot of North Africans live around there, especially at the bottom of the hill, an area they call la Goutte d'Or."

"'A drop of gold.'"

"Yeah. Funny name for a neighborhood. Someone may recognize her, give you some idea of where she lives. But you have to be discreet. She's probably there illegally."

"I'll be careful. And what's the boy's name?"

Curt dropped his gaze. "I don't know."

His words hung in the air. To get past them, he reached toward the table again and gave me a third piece of paper. It was a check for five thousand dollars.

"What? No, Curt. I can't."

"You have to. Booking a flight this late and getting a hotel, you'll run through this pretty fast." He tried to smile. "We both know a Foreign Service pension doesn't go very far. I can't ask you to spend your own money. Take it."

Reluctantly, I took the check, setting the seal on my offer to help.

A few moments later the nurse poked her head in the door and asked Curt if he needed anything.

I knew she was telling me it was time to go.

Curt thanked me again, and I repeated my promise to do everything I could. Neither of us had to say I didn't have much time.

There was another thing that didn't get said. Curt's request opened up a different possibility for me, something entirely apart from finding the boy, a possibility I hadn't allowed myself to consider for many years. No, Curt couldn't have known that I had my own, very personal reasons for going to Paris.

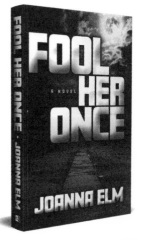

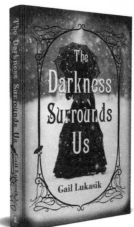

# CamCat Books

VISIT US ONLINE FOR MORE BOOKS TO LIVE IN:
CAMCATBOOKS.COM

SIGN UP FOR CAMCAT'S FICTION NEWSLETTER FOR
COVER REVEALS, EBOOK DEALS, AND MORE EXCLUSIVE CONTENT.

CamCatBooks

@CamCatBooks

@CamCat_Books

@CamCatBooks